4/26/91

To Ed
a grand and great guy.

Fred.

OUR DOUBTS
ARE TRAITORS

FREDERICK M. HANSON

VANTAGE PRESS
New York • Los Angeles

FIRST EDITION

Copyright © 1991 by Frederick M. Hanson

Published by Vantage Press, Inc.
516 West 34th Street, New York, New York 10001

Manufactured in the United States of America
ISBN: 0-533-09137-3

Library of Congress Catalog Card No.: 90-90160

1 2 3 4 5 6 7 8 9 0

Dedicated, with love, to my wife
Diane
for her love and affection
— Fred

Our doubts are traitors,
And make us lose the good we oft might win,
By fearing to attempt.

— William Shakespeare, *Measure for Measure*

Foreword

In this book I have tried to create a new medium in writing. The book is written in the first person in an attempt to write emotion into the composition. At times the writing may seem frantic and frenetic, with the long paragraphs of thoughts the main character indulges in, such as one might display while under great stress, portraying anxiety and free association. At other times, when external pressures are decreased the writing will be more placid, at times joyous, at times depressed, at times paranoic, just as one's emotions will vary with different levels of stress. Through the book, a subtle and progressive lessening of his anxiety will occur as his successes allow him to gain confidence, and his personality will seem to change, and the writing will become more easily readable.

As in all anxiety-ridden persons, inaction is a major problem of the personality; yet the book title portrays what all such persons must accomplish to find peace, security, and equanimity. All persons must make an attempt to overcome fears and doubts, lest they lose the chance for happiness. Trial and error, and, through them, eventual success, is the method we all must use. If we choose not to try, then we remain forever with a sense of inferiority and insecurity. Our doubts really are traitors, for they work against us and are capable of preventing action that is the key to success and happiness. Our pride, which is our eventual happiness, is based on our achievements, big and small.

Displayed herein is a young, still immature personality, trying through various means to falsely disguise his true self and to overcome an overwhelming and near crippling guilt complex. I hope you enjoy the character and will feel the emotion written into the story, and that it will give you understanding of what, in lesser or greater degree, we must all experience in "growing up."

OUR DOUBTS
ARE TRAITORS

Chapter 1

It was a hot day in North Carolina—July 8, 1940, if anyone cared. All July days were hot. Hot, dry, dusty days, every year. I arose from my swivel chair and looked out the large window at the front of my consultation room. Since my office was on the second floor, I had a good view of the road running through the town of Bennettsboro. It stretched out just below me. In a southerly direction the road led to the County Seat and in a northerly direction it led to Eldorado, if one were brave enough to follow it. I wasn't brave enough.

At the **Y** the main road veered obliquely to the left and disappeared beyond the large elm trees bordering each side. Just below me a porch roof obscured my view of the grocery store entrance. I fantasized a dozen Negroes or more resting in the shade avoiding the noonday sun, since an equal number stood or squatted similarly across the street beneath the counterpart of our building. Nothing stirred as time inexorably passed. Occasionally a car droned by, disturbing little, yet bringing momentary activity to this listless scene.

I sat down in my chair, looked once more out the window into the distance and felt a sense of loneliness. I turned back to the desk, felt the silent cooling breeze of my oscillating fan, and decided to take a nap. Lunch seemed unattractive on hot days. A glass of iced tea was more than sufficient, but my glass had lost its attraction. Only tiny floats of ice were left, suggesting loss of coolness. A fly which alternately landed and crawled around the rim only added to the repugnance. I angrily waved my hand at the fly, hitting the glass and spilling a small amount of tea. I leaned back and put my feet on the desk hoping to sleep soon. I rarely had trouble sleeping short periods of time since I'd learned to do that when an intern. As an intern, I was frequently exhausted from little or no sleep and needed

1

snatches of refreshing rest. While loosening my tie I had a fleeting recall of my medical school dean lecturing on professional demeanor. Ties and white shirts were required at all times, no matter how hot the day; *we must look like doctors at all times.* I wondered if he'd be proud of me following his dictum even in this small town. Whether or not he had lectured me, though, I would have worn the tie. No one around here ever wore a tie. Doing so satisfied my need to be different from the others. The tie was a symbol. Arrogance or anxiety—I wondered which.

That miserably annoying fly was now methodically attacking my forehead, preferring salty sweat to bitter tea and then conveniently escaping to safety beyond my reach just as I was going to swat it.

But gradually I dozed off, only to be awakened by a strange sound not readily recognizable, like metal clanking. Shortly thereafter it was apparent that someone of considerable weight, and with haste, was running up my office steps. The ascending stair was along another wall of the office, and no window opened to that side, preventing me from seeing the runner. The running footsteps startled, then frightened me. Of late the sound of running footsteps had this effect on me. I wondered why. My pulse began to pound and a cold chill coursed through me. The portent was unmistakable. Someone, in a hurry, was about to present me with an emergency. I hated the thought. But no one would run that way on a hot day unless something was very troubling. I heard the waiting room door open and slam, and then the call bell ringing frantically. I could have met my lunch-hour intruder at the door, but waiting to be summoned delayed facing the problem, if only for a moment. I hoped the problem presented would turn out to be less frightening than anticipated.

I went to the door of the waiting room and opened it slowly. There confronting me was a very large, muscular Negro, face and clothes bathed in sweat, and before I could say hello, he blurted out: "Doctuh, yu gotta come right now. Mah wife's got terrible troubles." I did not recognize him and tried to retain a calm demeanor, though I felt my heart pounding. I feared hearing the problem.

2

Proceeding slowly, hoping to appear calm, I asked him for his wife's name, as if it made any difference in the emergency.

He seemed to relax slightly and said, "She be Mary Belle Lincoln. She having a baby." He said it with authority, but no pride.

"Well," I said, considerably relieved, "that's nothing to get so excited about. Lots of people have babies." I further started to admonish him for running on a hot day, explaining the danger to his heart, only to be interrupted.

"But Doctuh, she bleedin' somethin' fierce. The midwife's scared."

I felt then the panic I had feared. My knees weakened and I was certain I wavered, about to collapse. My heart pounded wildly, and I rubbed my temples while sighing audibly, taking deep breaths to regain my composure.

I said, "Wait there, I'll be right with you."

I closed the door in his face and turned in my panic to collect my thoughts. "Bleedin' somethin' fierce." That had to be *placenta abruptio* or *placenta previa*, both dire emergencies that frequently lead to the death of both mother and baby. I looked at my hands which by now were icy cold. I wondered how they could be so cold on such a hot day. I grabbed my black bag, the symbol of my profession, and rapidly went over a mental list of things to take to help: Rubber gloves, clamp to rupture the membranes, syringe, tourniquet, morphine, oxytocics. All items were thrown in the bag with great haste. I looked around then, with nothing in mind, hoping some item would command my attention. Then back to Mr. Lincoln. He was still there pacing and biting his lip.

"Let's go quickly," I said. "You drive ahead. I'll follow." As we raced out the door I found myself ahead of him on the stairs and hoped he wouldn't recognize this as evidence of my anxiety but rather would think of it as concern for his wife's welfare.

His truck was old and when I heard the motor start I wondered how I'd not heard it arrive, and if he would ever successfully return to his house. We took the alternate road at the **Y** away from Eldorado, and headed down the dusty route.

My heart still pounded, occasionally causing me to breathe deeply. I wondered if he'd sensed my panic; I was certain he

3

had. It galled me to think he might recognize it. It was to be a well-kept secret when I came here to Bennettsboro. It was a stupid assumption to believe that somehow I could hide out in a small town, manage minor problems, deceive and dupe the local citizens and never face the gibes and sneers or knowing looks of colleagues. How could I have believed that I would not be faced with a terrible emergency such as this. And how could I ever have believed that people would not sense my anxiety and panic. At least driving my own car allowed time to think without conversation, and time to compose myself as well. Occasionally the truck motor groaned and creaked and back-fired, reminding me of my task.

I tried mentally to recreate that part of the textbooks dealing with "bleedin' somethin' fierce."

> *Abruptio Placenta—Sudden violent separation of the placenta from the uterus leading to excessive bleeding, usually with pain and tender uterus. Cause unknown. Often accompanied by previous hypertension or toxemia; more common the greater number of children. Treatment: rupture membranes. Institute labor. Rupturing membranes leads to tamponade of the placenta by the collapse of the sac, the baby pressuring the placenta. Hemorrhage diminished. This way labor is also helped to proceed faster, or start, if none. Therefore, rupture membranes, start labor.*

> *Placenta Previa—Sudden bleeding, painless usually, due to implantation of the placenta low in the uterus and partially or completely covering the cervical os. As the lower part of the uterus begins to stretch in late pregnancy the placenta pulls loose and starts bleeding. Cause unknown. More common with increasing numbers of children. Often accompanied by abnormal position of baby, breech or transverse lie (crosswise). Treatment: rupture membranes, tamponade placenta with some part of baby. If head presenting, grab scalp with willett's clamp and attach to a weight over the end of the bed. The head compresses the placenta, stops bleeding, helps start labor. If a breech, pull down a foot, attach weight and use buttocks as a pressure tamponade.*

"Sounds so easy—Ha!" I said aloud.

4

Rupture of Uterus—Tearing open of uterus, accompanying prolonged labors. Can be abnormal position of baby, too large an infant, infection of uterus weakening it, previous tears from improper deliveries with trauma. In all instances chances are the baby will die, and most likely the mother too.

I bit my lip and shook my head disbelievingly. Panic was now mixed with depression. I felt the sweat rolling down my back and wondered again how my hands could be so cold on such a hot day. I held my hand out to see if it trembled. It did, somewhat!

A horn honking frantically recalled reality. I had failed to follow the truck. It had turned and I hadn't. I was chagrined to have made such an error—only more proof of my anxiety. I wondered why he proceeded so slowly, but decided his truck would go no faster, and that my anxiety made the trip seem slow. Waiting to face a problem only heightened anxiety. Meeting and conquering it was much preferable. I assumed that others would not feel the same anxiety, a galling thought.

"Everyone can master a grief but he that has it." Wasn't that Shakespeare? I believed so.

More thoughts raced through my head.

Rupture membranes, start labor. Not a lot of alternatives. If ruptured uterus exists, sit back and watch her die. When is anxiety reasonable, and when is it not? Can't some doctors display reasonable anxiety? Surely the patient wants to believe the doctor has none at all—he must be a smooth, efficient, emotionless, operating machine. But how can one such as me with only textbook knowledge and little experience be that efficient? I knew why my confidence was gone, but was my guilt reasonable?

Poor Mary Belle. I really knew nothing about her but decided she must be fat, hypertensive, in her thirties, toxemic, probably with several children, poor diet, and no rest. Her diet probably consisted of fatback and beans, hominy, and some greens—whatever could be grown where they lived. Far from a nutritious diet more than likely, and most of the food went to the children in any event. A strange thought crossed my mind. She isn't even my patient—though in truth almost everyone in this area was potentially mine, since there were no other doctors for a radius of fifty or more miles.

Here I was in a race between life and death, carried on in poor surroundings, with poor equipment, few treatment alternatives, no blood transfusion capability, no surgery capability, no one to consult, frightened and nervous, near panic.

The day grew hotter, I was sure, and the dust from the truck's tracks was choking. I knew a doctor couldn't save every case, but I longed not to have the panic I felt, just reasonable concern and little or no guilt.

The truck backfired again and my attention was refocused to the trip. I wondered if I'd thought of everything possible to do for her. I wondered if my haste at the office had revealed my panic and had led to wasteful motions equally blatant.

"Haste maketh waste." Wasn't that Shakespeare? No, that was another poet—couldn't remember who.

There was no haste in the truck's progress. If Sarah had been in the office she would have thought of other things to help, I was certain. I longed to talk to her.

But we had finally arrived at the farm. No time for thoughts of Sarah.

Mr. Lincoln turned through an open gate into two deep, muddy ruts that stopped at a small creek. The truck forded it easily and took up the path opposite. I followed, but with dismay. Should my car sink in the stream, I would seem awfully ridiculous with wet shoes and pants. Yet the car mastered the stream without difficulty and I went on across on the final leg to the homestead. The house was in marked disrepair, a two-story clapboard building with a high roof, dormer window, and a front porch with railing. A better home than those expected to belong to Negroes. The house was gray with age, lacking paint totally. It sat on foundation blocks—occasionally showing daylight beneath and giving it an eerie, suspended appearance of being unattached to earth. A picket fence, lacking many pickets, surrounded a small front lawn, if indeed it could be called a lawn. It was more a feeding patch for chickens and pigs. The absence of a gate and pickets provided easy access for all such feeders. A huge elm tree and small lilac bush were the only other foliage. The tree's branches seemed to droop, lifeless. Nearby sagged a swaybacked barn, also gray and unpainted, which bulged at the sides as if some unknown force had dealt it a mighty blow from above. A chickenhouse, or roost, where only a chicken would choose to live, adjoined the barn. Judging from the number of chickens on the lawn, I doubted that any did, indeed, choose to live there.

I approached the porch and steps. The tilt of the porch railing gave the house an uneasy look of sudden impending disaster. The entire farm seemed to portray my fear of sudden collapse. I mounted the stairs, avoiding a broken step. The front door was open. The screen door was weathered and broken with numerous rents in the screening; no protection from flies at all. I wondered why they had not removed it completely. Probably because it kept out other, larger, unwanted guests. An aged gray-haired, obese Negro woman in the doorway entreated me,

"Oh, Doctuh, please hurree, please hurree."

In the living room my suspicion about the number of children was confirmed. Here were five children, the oldest about eight, all looking frightened, all stony quiet. None spoke to me or smiled though I glanced in their direction. I followed my guide into a short hall while Mr. Lincoln stayed behind. The short, dark hall led to the bedrooms. Directly ahead was the door to Mary Belle's room. As we approached it and it was identified, I turned to my guide and said, "Why don't you let me go in alone and when I need your help, I'll call."

I didn't want the old woman hovering over me, making suggestions, entreating me to quicker action and showing her nervousness. She seemed to welcome this release from responsibility and quickly returned to the living room. With a deep breath and sigh, my heart pounding in my chest and hand trembling, I took hold of the door knob. I then realized how sweaty my palm was and how tightly I gripped my bag with the other hand. The door creaked slightly as I slowly opened it. I forced a smile as I made ready to greet the patient with all my sham calm and charm, hoping to inspire in her the confidence I didn't feel. The room was darkened by half-closed shutters and was hot. The air reeked, a malodorous smell of mixed content. The ammonia-like odor of amniotic fluid was obvious and the fleeting thought crossed my mind: *Dammit, the membranes are already ruptured and that blows half of my proposed treatment.*

The room was deathly quiet except for flies buzzing. The window screen had been as ineffective as the front door screen in keeping out the flies. They buzzed in generous number; only their noise was audible. My heart quickened at this ominous note. As I entered, I noticed to the left an unoccupied double bed and to the right, obscured at first by the door, an old iron bedstead in which the patient lay. Mary Belle was propped up in bed in a half-sitting position, and it was readily evident she was probably dead. More flies, on the bed, undisturbed until my presence, now flew up in a small swarm and I summarily waved them away. Their interest was, of course, a large pool of semi-clotted blood, serum and amniotic fluid—a tasty, sweet-scented ambrosia to them. It surrounded the patient's buttocks and legs, soaked into the bedding and mattress. I gently and carefully raised Mary Belle's head which lay to one side, her mouth gaping, to a more normal position. The coldness of her skin against my hand surprised me. I realized all of a sudden that my anxiety had disappeared. I now knew this case would be no test of my ability or skill. Nothing could be done to help. The signs were unmistakable. She had died some time ago, and probably quickly, from blood loss. I confirmed the diagnosis of death, which was part of my role, by determining the lack of pulse, respiration, and heart sounds. Suddenly, I remembered the fetus and listened for fetal heartbeats with my stethoscope, but heard none. The death of the fetus relieved me of the responsibility of postmortem Cesarean section, an abhorrent procedure. I was convinced that both patients were beyond my help.

Suddenly I realized I was exhausted. Without thinking, I sat down on the bed aside her legs totally oblivious of the soiled bedsheets, only to soil my own trousers with blood. I stared at Mary Belle for a few moments. Her face had a look of incredulity, of disbelief that death could have come to her. She was a large woman, bloated, puffy, in late pregnancy, and much older in appearance than I would have bet she was in years. I looked around at the squalor of the room, the dirty wallpaper, the pattern almost obscured. The window was small, the screen worn and rusted. The room was depressing, oppressively hot, and I desired to leave but knew I still had to face and console the family. What could one say to ease their anguish: that better diet, better care would have helped; that such conditions are more common with increasing numbers of children; to have known sooner she was bleeding or was in labor would have helped. All I could say and yet be compassionate would be untruthfully that nothing could have helped, that she'd had a rare disease, not of her or their fault—or mine—I added to myself. Rebuke wouldn't help. The overwhelming futility of it all saddened me.

I stood to leave and felt compelled to place her in a more comfortable position, though comfort would help her none. Pulling the body down in bed demonstrated again the enormous pool of clotted blood and serum through which her life had been quickly drained away. I wondered whether the baby would have been a boy or a girl. Last of all I bent over and closed Mary Belle's eyelids and mouth and then pulled up the sheet thereby covering her lifeless body; the act of finality traditional with death. I braced myself to meet the family, then gently and quietly closed the door of the bedroom as I left: a futile, unnecessary, yet automatic gesture, one of respect.

Reentering the living room, I noticed the children were gone, as if the message I carried had been sensed already. I asked Mr. Lincoln to sit down. He must have read my gloom as he said:

"She dead, Doctuh, ain't she?" a question and statement combined. I could only nod assent with tight lips.

"There was nothing I could do," I offered in explanation, as trite a phrase as ever there was available. "You see, she probably had this rare condition where her afterbirth had come loose starting profuse bleeding. She bled to death quickly. She didn't suffer long." The words trailed off into nowhere and I was aware that only I was listening to them. Mr. Lincoln was deep in thought and the old woman was turned away and was sobbing.

I asked him his name and he replied, "James."

9

"James," I said, "I wish there was something I could have done, some way I could have helped," meaningless words, but seemingly necessary. "Can I help you?"

"No, no," he replied, "it's all right. I know, Doctuh, yu did all yu could. We'll work things out. We'll be all right. Don't yu worry 'bout us."

His courage surprised me. I couldn't help but wonder how this simple man with so little in life could be so strong. Under similar circumstances I doubted I'd feel as confident. I said my goodbyes and left as hurriedly as possible, assuming I would no longer be needed. Returning to the car I was grateful to have been spared having to see the children and their expressions.

Driving out of the yard, I glanced again at the house and felt that it looked more dead than ever now, more in danger of sudden collapse. I was glad to turn back on the road and start back toward life, even though returning meant more office work. I wasn't in the mood for meeting patients. After a short drive, I realized I didn't really know the way back, as I hadn't really been aware of the road or directions while driving out, having been too engulfed by my anxiety. Yet I was determined to drive in the direction that seemed most appropriate. Small roads seemed to lead to larger ones, and once in a while I noticed a familiar landmark that I must have seen and remembered, though unaware at the time. Farther and farther from the house, the oppressiveness of death diminished and life asserted itself. The cotton fields on both sides of the road showed bolls of ripe cotton bursting forth their white blooms. Yet, I couldn't help but wonder how many bolls would never ripen and would die before they had a chance for life.

Returning to town I thought again of Sarah and the office. I'd forgotten to leave a note for her explaining my absence. She'd returned, no doubt, at 1:30 to start afternoon office hours and I wasn't there. It was now about 2:30. I wondered if failure to leave a note would reveal, somehow, the anxiety I'd felt when leaving the office, or if it would just be accepted as an oversight. I wondered how she had explained my absence to the waiting patients and if she had sent some home rather than keep them much longer.

Though I'd been here in Bennettsboro but a short time, my

practice at times was quite active. Sarah's reaction to me had always seemed respectful and admiring and she had filled the role of office nurse perfectly, but I wondered if she sensed my feelings of inadequacy. I'd been in the habit of referring many cases to Duke University Medical School, especially those in whom a diagnosis was difficult to make, to avoid the chance I was missing serious illnesses. I sent them, supposedly, for consultation. This, of course, freed me of responsibility and anxiety. But, if too many patients went and came back with only minor diagnoses, in time my ability to diagnose anything would be questioned in town. A fine line between a facade of thoroughness and concern, and a revelation of my anxiety and ability existed. Enormous emotional energy was required to maintain the balance. Rigid organization and control was needed in every situation. Sarah, above all, must not sense my anxiety. I needed her admiration. Yet I longed so to tell her, or someone, of my feelings and get help. She could betray and embarrass me, though. I wasn't sure I knew her well enough to take her into my confidence.

As to my ability, I'd had the usual medical school training, an internship in surgery, and one year of neurosurgical training before coming here to practice—or should I say, coming here to hide, running away like a fugitive. I had had great confidence in all those previous years. Yet during all those years I'd had little chance to handle emergencies, since the very nature of the problems required someone with more experience. I had merely observed others at work. So why should anyone expect me to handle a dire emergency with skill.

Truthfully, it was I who demanded it of myself, yet I found it difficult most of the time to make any decisions about a patient, questioning constantly my diagnosis, always expecting I'd overlooked some detail. I wanted to succeed here. It meant so much to regain my confidence. I couldn't live like this. Burying myself here, far away from colleagues who might recognize my fears, sending away all worrisome problems, working with people who might not see my frailties seemed best when I did it. Now, however, recognizing the panic generated by Mary Belle's problem I wondered if I'd made the right choice. I wanted to leave. I knew I couldn't face another crisis.

I didn't think I could even try. To succeed through a process of steps, all involving correct decisions, was the real quest for me. Instinctively I realized how important it was. Once I had had that ability but had lost it when Carolyn died. I needed renewal of faith in myself, desperately.

Reentering Bennettsboro I passed the triangular park which was the town's pride. My office was at the base of the park. With bag in hand I ascended the steps slowly and remembered the haste of my earlier steps. I reflected about how short a period of time can change life so completely. And yet, nothing had changed. The heat was unchanged, and the stillness seemed omnipresent again. I was greeted by the faces in the waiting room I had expected, and faced an afternoon of unfinished work, though it would have been most desirable to have no more challenges. This afternoon I would have to force myself to be charming and alert, even though feeling exhausted.

Sarah was her usual calm self. I nodded to the waiting room in general and entered the inner office. Everyone stared at my trousers. It was then I realized they were stained with blood, and I felt somehow proud. It was my *Red Badge of Courage* and relieved me of the necessity of explaining my tardiness. The nurse's station was just inside the door on the right facing the waiting room with sliding glass doors closing out the view. Though there was no center divider in the waiting room, the colored people sat on one side and the white patients on the other. I don't know how the division had been determined, as there was no sign on the wall, but every day the sides were similarly divided, whites near the nurse's window, colored opposite. And Sarah just maintained a similar division in the examining rooms—white on the right and colored on the left. There was no favoritism in my consultation room though, since the desk was right in the middle and all patients sat in the same two chairs, facing the desk.

A coatrack, filing cabinet, and a small table with an electric fan and a phonograph were the only other items of furniture. The floors were bare because as yet I couldn't afford a carpet. I had been in practice too short a time. The large consultation room was perhaps a bit ostentatious, though the space was available and I had no other use for it. On the colored examining room side of the wall, there was also a small laboratory with a refrigerator, not a new refrigerator, but an old G.E. with the round coil on top. I always hated that thing on top. Though not too beautiful, the refrigerator was inexpensive when I bought it. Certainly the cost had made it attractive. It made ice and kept things reasonably cold—what more could one ask. We stored blood and urine samples there prior to my examination or to sending them to Duke University Laboratory for analysis. We also kept some food in it, next to the urine and blood. It might have bothered others that I did this, but not Sarah or me.

I hung up my suit coat, but couldn't bear to put on a white coat as it was still too hot. Crossing to my desk I glanced out of the window. There at the **Y** at the end of the park was Bennettsboro's source of pride, the statue of their namesake, William Augustus Bennett, in his Southern colonel's Confederate gray, including face; saber at his side, sheathed, of course. His right hand was on the saber's hilt and his left at his side. His eyes stared directly down the road. I'm sure he was to appear to survey a battlefield with determination, planning maneuvers while courageously disregarding whirring minié balls. To his left was a fieldpiece and a neat pyramid of cannonballs, fused together to prevent pilfering. A concrete pad on the other side was similarly shaped, probably designed originally to hold another cannon. I suspected the town's coffers were exhausted before the second cannon could be financed and in the ensuing years no one particularly had wanted to spend more money to complete the memorial. A plaque proclaimed his name and rank, "Colonel William Augustus Bennett." I wondered, derisively, if there had been any captains or lieutenants in *that* Army. His position and vast plantation holdings probably had dictated his rank, and it had little or nothing to do with ability or military experience. "Born March 10, 1813. Killed in action September 17, 1862, at Antietam Creek in the courageous performance of his duty." Rumor had it that he had died of smallpox, but that scurrilous rumor was, no doubt, proffered by Yankees. Each town, I guess, had to have its heritage and proud lineage. Yet to spend that much money on a statue in an area of such poverty, for the sake of pride alone, seemed stupid and unwarranted. I wondered what Colonel Bennett had done for this town to deserve such honor. At least the birds were not aware of his importance, having desecrated the figure repeatedly. I wondered if they were mockingbirds, and smiled. Anyone in town could tell you proudly of the colonel's glorious exploits, though I doubted such information had ever come from a valid historical source. Was he really worthy of this accolade, and, if the truth were known, would they be so proud of him? Would he be a hero? Why couldn't one's hero be himself with his pride based solely on his own accomplishments? Was it necessary to choose others as recipients of our pride? I was depressed, though, and my thoughts were consistent with that state of mind.

Sarah entered the room and announced my first patient was ready. She asked no questions about where I'd been or what had detained me. I felt compelled to tell her, though, and longed to do so. I asked if she remembered Mary Belle, not really expecting her to know her. She seemed honestly shocked to hear of the sad ending. I wondered, as she listened to my story, if she had worked for me long enough to perceive what my reaction to an emergency had been, or if the lack of a note explaining my absence had given away my anxiety. I wanted to tell her of my nervousness and seek her solace and understanding, but protocol dictated a different relationship. God, who was I to talk to! Carolyn would have understood and been helpful. Yet while we had dated, no such problems had ever arisen, and I didn't exactly know why I felt Carolyn would have understood.

I tried Sarah's reaction. "Boy, Mary Belle's problem really made me nervous," I said.

"I'll bet," she said.

Johnny Buell, white, and ten years old was the first afternoon patient. As I opened the door to the examining room I was very aware that Johnny, my old friend, did not regard me with trust today. His eyes were acutely aware of my every move anticipating the worst.

"What's the trouble, Johnny?" I asked.

In the usual fashion, his mother answered, though I had hoped to encourage his faith by assuming he was man enough to tell me.

"It's his ear, Doctor," she answered. "Ever since he had that cold his ear's been bothering him a fright. It's the same ear as last year."

I certainly remembered "last year's ear" well, though it hadn't really been a year ago when it had had to be lanced. I had doubted Johnny would ever return to my office again, unless dragged. The battle to lance his ear had been one of such magnitude it would have rivaled Colonel Bennett's Antietam, I was sure.

Johnny demanded anxiously, "What are you gonna do?" and his mother admonished him to call me doctor when speaking to me. But he was in no frame of mind to observe such amenities.

I said, "Well, I don't suppose you want me to look into that ear, do you?"

His quick agreement was apparent. So we delayed the inevitable by asking that he demonstrate what ability he had to breathe through his nose, thereby spreading droplets of water and virus about the room, as he wasn't aware that under such circumstances one breathes in, rather than blows out. The battle to see his throat was accompanied by gags and coughs and many attempts to turn away. But Johnny had been here for enough previous visits to know the routine, and that very soon now it would be time to test his courage and have the sore ear examined. I reached for my otoscope, the appearance of which was all too familiar to him, as he watched my every move. I tried to subvert his interest and asked,

"How's your old alligator doing, Johnny?"

He didn't answer since his thoughts were elsewhere. The sight of the otoscope in my hand entirely changed his not-so-hidden anxiety into open and vocal terror, and he began to yell.

"Don't, no."

A glance at Sarah was all that was required to effect the examination. Johnny was hopelessly overpowered and then subjected to the worst of ordeals for him. Soon we released his bonds, though, and made the pronouncement that his ear was only minimally affected and that no special treatment was needed. But Johnny was not reassured. To make certain his escape he had already climbed off the table and was on his way to the door. I prescribed the usual treatment, steam, rest, aspirin, and nose drops, and once again turned to Johnny.

As much to myself as to him, I said, "You see, now that wasn't too bad after all, was it? You didn't have to be afraid. Being afraid is silly. It's all over and you did the right thing. You knew you could do it, didn't you?"

Mrs. Buell thanked me and opened the door to leave. Johnny turned, shot me a smile and said, "My 'gator is big enough to eat you now, and he'll do it someday."

"Stop that," Mrs. Buell said, and cuffed at him angrily. They left.

Sarah looked at me, as if to learn what was on my mind and said, "Like you say, our doubts really are traitors." Then she laughed and added,

"That's Shakespeare, isn't it?" as she walked out of the room. Sassy and impertinent, but cute, and observant. She knew me well.

I wondered where she had learned that line from Shakespeare, but her observation implied that she'd understand my problem, and that she might already know what it was.

Chapter 2

The train rolled on through a new and strange terrain. I was fascinated and thrilled by the new landscape and how it differed from the flat Illinois plains I had been used to. Leaving Ohio on the Norfolk and Western, we had crossed the Ohio River into the South. I'd never been in the South before. I felt different somehow, as if entering into a new nation. The South had always been of special interest to me. Stories of the "War Between the States"—never the Civil War—had seemed exciting and fascinating. The names Manassas, Fredericksburg, Vicksburg, Antietam, and many others had long entranced me and conjured up exotic, romantic daydreams of glory. Now they were to be visited and consumed. As a child I had studied battlefield maps over and over. All of the well-known characters of this war were like old friends. My excitement was great. This was a new adventure and I was to experience it alone, without parental supervision. In college, I'd been so close to home that I hadn't had a chance to know the enjoyment of being responsible on one's own without parental direction. I was amazed at my confidence in meeting new experiences. We crossed into West Virginia and then into Virginia, where at Lynchburg I changed trains for Durham, North Carolina, and my ultimate destination of Duke University Medical School. Lynchburg was built on a hill or mountain, depending on one's interpretation, and reminded me of scenes of European cities in encyclopedias. The station was covered with soot, since the valley in which we waited collected the smoke and eventually deposited its debris on all surroundings. I wondered if this was why they called the mountains the Smokies.

As a matter of fact, after leaving the train, I realized the city was also dirty with soot and not as attractive as my first impression. I wondered who lived here and what they were like, if they were different from me or other Northerners. The train from which I had just disembarked pulled out of the station shortly and left me and my baggage alone on the platform except for another couple of people, who then soon left the station for their nearby destinations. On a siding sat another older and less powerful engine than the one that had just departed, connected to a tender and two antiquated wooden cars as if left here mistakenly from a prior era. It was a lonely scene. The day was hot and sticky and the dirty air was unpleasant to breathe. I stood for a short time watching my previous train disappear around a bend with a lonely whistle and then felt quite alone. Standing behind me, a station attendant startled me by asking my destination. It must have been obvious to him that I wasn't staying in Lynchburg.

"Duke University Medical School," I announced proudly, and then wished I hadn't, since it sounded ostentatious and was not the destination that a station attendant would be seeking. Laconically, and I thought somewhat patronizingly, he answered, "The train to Durham is there," pointing to the previously noted apparition, "departing in ten minutes." He turned away. After the encounter I wondered, somehow, if I would like Southerners.

This local train was a castoff, an abortion, I thought, and flinched slightly over this idea. Mother wouldn't have approved of the use of that word, abortion. I crossed the tracks and boarded the train. Once aboard, I had to open the window. The interior heat was overwhelming. The window could barely be opened, which demonstrated to an extent the train's age. Once in a while, the window fell shut when the car lurched, discouraging any attempt to put an arm or head outside. The heat was little changed by opening the windows and the smoke was only increased, along with the grime and soot. But it seemed that unless the window was open we would all surely perish of anoxia—a word I had learned in college. I knew that my knowledge of medical terms would surely be impressive to my superiors at "med school."

There were only three other people in my car, one of the two cars on this train, and we all sat far apart. I didn't want to seem too excited to them, but I surveyed all the countryside with abiding interest. The hills looked arid and devoid of vegetation except for pines and scrubby bushes. There were many small hills, and here and there a cotton field, and then a tobacco field, with a colored man walking behind a mule and plow. The train went on, whistling at every crossing, on its single track, and finally stopped in a small station—a boro—every place seemed to be a -boro or -ville. The first time we stopped to take on passengers, I fully understood why there were two cars when one had seemed sufficient. The second and end car was for colored people alone. It probably received more smoke from the stack, being the rear car, and would be dirtier than this one. I was suddenly aware of an inner uneasy feeling and felt a little conspicuous and apologetic to no one in particular. The separation of peoples was blatant and invidious. My high spirits were dimmed and the rest of the trip was less exciting and seemed only hot and oppressive.

We arrived at Durham near dusk, and in the semi-dark and dusty station I waited for the rest of my luggage. I stepped outside but nothing within view of the train station looked very inviting. The air was muggy, as if a storm was approaching. It was nine P.M. and it was getting dark rapidly. I was anxious to get to the campus, since from the pictures I'd seen I knew it would be a more inviting place than this. I went back inside, received my extra luggage from a slow, dull man who was bored, and then went out again for fresh air and to find a cab.

"How much to the Duke campus?" I asked.

The cab driver, a fat, sloppy man, chewing tobacco, surveyed me sourly and drawled, "Two-fifty, about."

"Two-fifty!" I echoed, "that's a lot of money!"

"It's a helluva long way," he replied. I couldn't dispute that. Since I really had little alternative, I accepted. As we rode through the city, somewhat nervously, I asked repeated questions of him, expecting my enthusiasm would somehow arouse his interest and felicity. Yet, it became apparent that a person must not always expect cab drivers to be warm, friendly people. His bile was running thick that night, his answers acerb and unfriendly. But it was my first trip there, and it was so painfully obvious, he reluctantly pointed out some landmarks.

"To the right is the Washington Duke Hotel, the tallest

building in town." Later, the Duke Mansion on the left—an imposing, old two-story house, run-down, unimaginative looking, with clapboard siding and screened-in balcony porches, standing amidst a group of trees—the only oasis left downtown. Everything else was dusty, dirty, dry, and devoid of vegetation it seemed. And then we approached two large buildings, several stories high, connected by a covered walkway high above the street on which we traveled.

"This here's the Chesterfield Cigarette Company," he announced in bored tones. I was thrilled to see my first cigarette company. "And over there the American Tobacco Company," more bored than ever.

These were enormous businesses and thrilling to me. "Lucky Strike Green" and "They Satisfy." How could he be so bored I wondered.

Then in the short distance we turned right and he slowed, to allow me a better view, as we passed between two large brick pillars. "Duke University," he announced stentoriously.

Before he could finish his statement I challenged him with "But it doesn't look like the pictures I've seen."

"This is the Women's Campus, dammit," he said. My pictures were of the men's campus. His voice revealed his disgust over my ignorance. Directly ahead at the far end of the quadrangle was a building resembling closely a Greek edifice with imposing colonnades and rounded roof illuminated by floodlights. I wondered if Jefferson had designed it but knew better than to ask this driver. He was beginning to dislike his tour already. But I couldn't resist asking who the statue was; a large statue of a man sitting in an overstuffed chair, or was it a Roman chair? It was dark. He was "Washington Duke," I was informed.

We turned left then and started slightly downhill on a long winding road which seemed to be in a small valley, under an overpass and on into the night which now was becoming misty. At a distance on both sides of the road there were dimly visible masses of darker color which I decided were forests. Soon we passed a few nicely landscaped homes, English Tudor in appearance, then to a circular drive and on the right again passed through two stone pillars. Once again the cab paused as if awestruck by this sight. There in the distance was the Duke Chapel rising into the night and illuminated by floodlights. The sight was imposing, breathtaking, and exhilarating, and was the confirmation I had sought. Here at last was the photograph I knew so well! The driver seemed to have been impressed enough also to have found his voice again and drawled, "Well now, that's pretty, don't ya think?" I agreed hastily. Once again we were friends with a common ground.

On either side of the long entrance drive were sunken areas with tall pines, one side a garden setting. Pines seemed to be everywhere. At the end of the long entrance drive, when we entered the quadrangle, other buildings came into view. All were effectively illuminated. The sight was truly beautiful, as he had said. Stone buildings were built around quadrangles, with towers and spires and high peaked roofs, English Gothic. Long wide stone steps led up to the door of the chapel, which was on a higher plateau than the other buildings. The tall cathedral face was overpowering in its magnificence. And there, in the center of the entrance quadrangle, was another statue of a standing man.

"Washington Duke, I suppose," I said.

My guide found his acerbity again and corrected me. "No, for God's sake. That's James B. Duke."

This was no time to explore the lineage of the Duke family, I decided, and opened the door to get out.

Two-forty was the tariff. I was too thrilled to notice the dime savings. After depositing my luggage with me, the driver said, "You can see the ghost chapels in the sky tonight." He departed then.

There in the sky above and on either side of the chapel bell tower were two ghost chapels, shadow reflections on a fog-mist layer. It was only about 9:30, but I had an uneasy feeling of being very alone amid these imposing buildings, perhaps because of them. I wondered why I could feel uneasy with all the surrounding beauty. I was lonely, with no one to talk to, no one to guide me. I knew then I would probably be homesick soon.

There seemed to be more lights on in a building to my left and some activity and voices in that direction, so I went there. It proved to be a wise decision as it was the student

21

union, and there I found live people again.

Together, the student clerk and I walked across a quadrangle to an adjoining building. I longed to have a room in one of the towers, but had been assigned a ground-floor room in the back, not facing the quadrangle. My guide observed the usual social amenities and welcomed me, while praising Duke's many features with enthusiasm. When we arrived at the room he knocked and introduced me to my roommate, John Little. John Little was from Wyoming, a small, partially balding peacock, obsequiously friendly in a hostile way. It was quickly determined that he had observed first-come, first-served rights and selected the more desirable bed location, the handier closet and the more accessible desk.

I merely observed, "I guess this bed is mine." He agreed that my observation was correct. I should have asked him if he wanted to fight now rather than later, but decided to bide my time. I hoped he might even have a good point of character somewhere. As I unpacked he observed how few medical texts I owned, demonstrated his vast superiority in books already acquired in the medical line, told me that *Gray's Anatomy* was the text to get, and that he had had vast experience in medicine already as an aide in the Student Health Clinic at dear old Wyoming U. But he did know more medical terms than I, I had to admit to myself grudgingly. He was eager to demonstrate how many such words, without prompting. I was then forced to admit that I had only completed the usual premed courses without any special medical training. Certainly I'd had nothing comparable to his vast experience. I did inform him of my invaluable experience in playing the saxophone. He wasn't impressed. We were truly off to a happy year's companionship. Sleep was to be my salvation, but in the darkened room, before I slept, I was forced to admit to myself that I had known happier days than this one that had just closed.

Morning came, and unfortunately I was somewhat forced to rely on John's superior knowledge of the campus to get breakfast. During breakfast, I was further regaled with his knowledge and experience. I looked across at my breakfast partner and absolutely knew that in addition to not liking Southerners, I would probably not like Westerners. We then left for the medi-

22

cal school, something I anticipated with wild, yet unexpressed enthusiasm. To me the medical school building was the most impressive of all buildings though it appeared similar in architecture to all the others. It was a sanctuary of learning and skill, a parthenon of medical gods. It, too, like the chapel, was at the end of a quadrangle on a rise in the ground and required a few steps up to enter. But before I did enter, I turned to look down the quadrangle past James Duke's statue to the counterpart of the medical school at the far end, all on a lower level. Yes, I thought, this is where I deserve to be. This is a most beautiful campus, and now I am about to enter this temple and be a part of it. A mimosa tree in full bloom decorated the garden on the left and cast its fragrance all about. I thought I had never seen a tree so delicate and silken. All around the campus were tall, slender Southern pines, sugar pines. We were isolated in a pine forest. It was truly beautiful.

I turned to the entrance door. This was to be *my moment.* I felt strong and noble, yet goose-pimply, omniscient and omnipotent, yet rapacious and omnivorous—truly I would devour this place. Here was my Colossus. Were they prepared to receive me? I walked in the entrance, expecting a trumpet fanfare. Yet no one noticed me. Horatio was at the bridge and no one cared. How dare they inflict this affront. Those lousy miscreants!

"Doctor! Doctor! Doctor Jenson." Sarah had had trouble awakening me from my nap this time. She had returned to reopen the office and found me asleep.

"I'm sorry, Sarah, I was dreaming about the past as I seem prone to do of late. You'll have to excuse my reveries. They aren't all pleasant, unfortunately."

"I'm sorry, too, Doctor," Sarah said, "I wish I could let you sleep some more, but patients are waiting and I've kept them quite a while already."

She was right, always so, but always pleasant, always quiet and soft-spoken, a perfect aide, efficient, never seeming to hurry, calm, respectful, thoughtful. I looked at her appreciatively; five foot five, soft blue eyes, smooth fair skin, blond hair that hung with a soft wave to her shoulders, beautiful figure, white knee-length dress. Why were nurses so alluring, I wondered. Angels of mercy? Kind, helpful? I wondered. I felt fortunate to be able to find her in a town this size.

Actually, when first I met her she had come home to bury her father, her last remaining relative. She had only recently finished her nurses' training in Baltimore. Since I had treated her father prior to his death from cancer, she had come to discuss his illness and death with me. I hadn't as yet felt the need of a nurse in the office prior to having met her, but somehow when she had come to talk to me the need had uncontrollably asserted itself. I never had quite decided why I asked her so suddenly to work for me, and it was odd, too, how suddenly she had accepted my job offer. There was no haggling. I remembered laughing about her salary, $100 per month, unless the only payment I might receive in a given month was potatoes and corn, in which case she would share them. I even had said, "As a matter of fact I'll let you cook them for me," and then had been embarrassed. Here we had just met and already I had in effect suggested a closer relationship. She, too, had been embarrassed, but not annoyed, apparently. We both were in need of companionship and reluctant to admit it. It was decided that very day that she would be my girl Friday and start to work immediately.

As she had left I wondered if my sudden decision was wise. What was that Latin expression? *Caveat emptor.* Impulsive behavior was not like me, especially now that I didn't seem to make any decisions easily. This was the first decision I had made since Carolyn's death that I hadn't weighed and balanced for hours, days, or even longer. Something about Sarah's quiet confidence and friendly manner had helped me to forget my indecision. Or was it her fragile, pristine beauty and feminine manner. She was what I needed in this office, and I had known it immediately. Somehow the need for her presence was by far the most important aspect of my decision.

The first afternoon patient was Amanda James, a large, sixtyish, obese, colored female breathing heavily; a new patient to me. She reeked of inexpensive perfume and had on her best dress, black lace bodice and satin skirt. The thought crossed my mind, "I'll bet they didn't name Jamesboro after her family."

I liked colored people and I never could bring myself to think of them as "niggers," as they were referred to repeatedly by others in town. I had been raised in a small Illinois town where no colored families had lived. The one colored man who worked for my dad and came from a nearby town was very pleasant and jolly and fun to talk to. My mother and dad indoctrinated me with the religious attitude of "all people are equal in the eyes of the Lord" and therefore worthy of respect. "Niggers" was not a term of respect and I knew it. "One of the Wise Men had been colored," Mother had said, "and if he could call on the Christ child, that is good enough for us."

"Charity for all, firmness in the right." Illinois had claimed Abraham Lincoln, also. Next to Christ, I think Lincoln commanded the greatest respect in our home.

I was comfortable around colored people. They were almost kindred folk. I sort of knew what prejudice was, since our family was Danish and most of the families in our area were Swedish. The Swedes didn't even like the fact that my grandfather had misspelled his name. Jenson with an "o" was Swedish. It should have been Jensen because that's Danish. The name Jenson had been given to us by my grandfather though, and my dad was not about to change it, even if incorrectly spelled. Anyhow, I felt ostracized in a predominantly Swedish community. I detested people who practiced prejudice. It was incongruous that I should be here in the South, of all places. Something had changed with Carolyn's death.

"Amanda," I said, "weren't you at Mary Belle Lincoln's the other day?"

She nodded and said, "Yussir, a sad day."

I agreed. "Well it's nice to see you again," I said. "What's the trouble anyhow?"

"Doctuh, Suh," she said, "Ah's been wheezing awful bad lately with the asthma, and there be times when Ah's laying down that Ah can't get my breath at all."

Her voice made me realize where the word wheeze had originated. The word, itself, had a hollow twang which sounded just like her voice. Amanda's legs were badly swollen, and the lungs echoed the classic wheezes and rales. Her heart was enlarged. I wished then that all cases I would have to see could be as easy to diagnose as this: cardiac failure with cardiac asthma, edema, and enlarged heart. I knew she must have hypertension also, which she did. And Amanda had never been to a doctor before. All of her own children had been delivered with the help of a neighbor's wife.

I wanted to apologize for my office's second floor location. It must have been a fantastic ordeal for her to climb those stairs when she hardly had enough lung capacity to move around a one-story house. My respect and pity went out to her. Any minute I expected her to collapse, gasp once or twice, and die. All of a sudden I began to feel that ever-pernicious anxiety creeping through my body. She mustn't die, I thought, and especially not as a result of my office location on a second floor.

While choosing an office, I had looked for a place in which I also might live. After I chose the office, though, and realized it was lonely, I then found it preferable to rent a room in a local residence, if only for a place to sleep. It had offered companionship, in a vague way, at night. Being alone in this office at night was in a sense too frightening for comfortable rest. Still, I knew it wasn't the office, but rather a dislike for being alone that made it seem malevolent. And even that knowledge was of no help in preventing my uneasiness. It wasn't like me. I had never felt this way before, before Carolyn had died. Somehow it reminded me of how I used to feel in church when I was a boy feeling guilty for my misdeeds of the previous week.

"Amanda," I said, "I'm going to give you a drug for your heart, and a shot to get rid of those swollen legs."

Amanda "allowed as how" she didn't like to take drugs and "'specially shots," but I reassured her this was not the sort she feared and was also very necessary to save her life.

"And I bet you'll lose fifteen pounds soon," I said.

"Land sakes, Doctuh," she laughed, "I'se always been heavy like this. You do that and ma best dress won't fit me no more." Every breath was an effort.

"No, just your shoes won't fit," I said. I noticed they were thickly covered with what looked like black paint. The leather was cracked in just about every conceivable wrinkle and peeling here and there.

I gave her enough digitalis from the office supply to last a month and a shot of ammoniated mercury to relieve her edema. I decided she probably didn't have enough money to buy her prescription at the local drug store. I kept some medications on supply here at the office. The local druggist didn't complain about my intrusion into his business as he knew equally as well as I, that I probably wouldn't be paid for medicines I dispensed.

Amanda left then with many thanks, and expressing concern about how soon she would pay.

"Amanda," I said, "will you let me know tomorrow how you are?" Somehow, I thought I was asking the impossible. She seemed flattered that I wanted to know and was more prepared to follow my instructions than I had hoped. "I have a nephew, Andrew," she said, "he works at the grocery store as a helper. Ah'll have him come and tell you how Ah is. Thank you, thank you," she nodded as she was leaving.

Andrew was waiting for her and supported one shoulder as she walked. Amanda looked as if any minute she might collapse in one big final sigh of life. I was anxious that she leave before the inevitable happened.

I asked Sarah to help get her down the stairs. I think I would have helped myself if my anxiety had permitted. I was too afraid she'd die on the way. When Sarah returned, I knew Amanda had made it to the car. What would happen after that at home was anyone's guess.

Sarah said, "I feel so sorry for people like her. She has so little and yet is not complaining."

I liked Sarah. She was like me. I remembered now that day in Lynchburg when I wondered if I'd ever like Southerners. My original judgment had proved too hasty.

"Well, Sarah, who's next?"

"Mr. Jason Robertson, who runs the furniture store, is here," she said, "and he's mighty put out that he'd been made to wait."

"What's his trouble?" I asked.

"He wouldn't tell me. Something personal, I guess."

I'd met Mr. Robertson only briefly in the past, not having much need of furniture in my few months in town. He was a paunchy, tense man, in a white palm beach suit and no tie. His neck and forehead were wet with sweat and he mopped them alternately and frequently. He sat there on the examining table, his legs swinging, his pot belly resting on the table between his legs, and fanned his face with his hat. He was polite but didn't wait for me to greet him.

"Doc, Ah got trouble and Ah need help right away."

"You look like you're very worried," I said. "Is something wrong with you?"

"Yes, damn it, that's why Ah'm here." His impatience was showing. He added, "And Ah don't like to have to be kept waiting while you take care of a nigger." I stared at him in disbelief, saying nothing. He went on. "Who was that, anyhow? That old midwife, Amanda James? Didn't know she was still alive. Doesn't deserve to be, what with the poor way she helped my Margaret when our first was born. My son's head was all out of shape, thanks to her mishandlin' and he's never been any good since."

I began to feel angry. Yet I couldn't express my displeasure at anyone's attitude. I was to treat all alike, at least that was how I was taught. Moreover, I'd just started practicing here in Bennettsboro, and no doubt Mr. Robertson was head of one of the prominent families as owner of the furniture store. I decided it was best to ignore his vitriol. No need to anger him.

He continued, "And Margaret's not the only one she's messed up around here. After I seen our baby, she didn't get a penny out of me. Didn't deserve anything. Should have been run out of town." He fanned himself again. "Anyhow, what about me, what are you gonna do about my trouble?"

I managed to say, "But you haven't even told me what your trouble is yet," none too politely.

He glanced furtively about as if looking for someone listening and then said, nervously, "Damn it, Ah think Ah got the clap. The strain. You know. Just noticed it today. Ain't seen it before now. Ah felt this wet discharge and then I looked and it was drippin'."

"Where would you get gonorrhea?" I asked, or perhaps, demanded.

"Well where else but at the furniture convention in Atlanta, of course. Ah suppose from one of those damn daughters of joy. Damned whores. Pay 'em well and this is what Ah get. Niggers are all filthy."

I choked on that statement. I suddenly realized I detested

this unregenerate slob. My anger had now reached the blazing stage, but I controlled it. The treatment he must endure as a result of his nefarious tryst was not too pleasant and would repay him, perhaps.

"Well," I said, "Y'all ain't gonna like the treatment." Then I wished I hadn't lowered myself to his level.

"What is it, Doc?" he asked.

"Silver nitrate solution washings," I answered.

I didn't like being called "Doc" by this repugnant man. A slide exam of the discharge confirmed the diagnosis. As I suspected, he didn't like the idea of having his "privates" washed out with silver nitrate even once, let alone several times and was annoyed that I wanted to do a blood test in the future to see if he had contracted syphilis as well. Obviously he wasn't prepared to suffer the consequences of his activities, as he yelled and cursed during treatment. I knew the treatment was painful, but cared little. I even threatened to have Sarah hold his penis while I irrigated if he didn't cease complaining. That would have completed his embarrassment. He warned me to keep this secret, an unmitigated slur to a doctor, yet consistent with his character.

I charged him twenty dollars and made a mental note that I'd credit Amanda James's account as paid in full, part of what he had owed her for years. He left, muttering all the way down the stairs. Sarah was quick to observe his disgruntlement, but she was her usual charming self. Her smile and knowing remark, "My! He certainly was burned up," dissolved my anger and I could see some of the humor in this outrageous scene. I was certain, though, that Jason Robertson would burn all day, literally and figuratively. I'd left my mark. That little black staining from the silver nitrate on the penis would be hard to explain at home. I wondered also how he would explain the trips to the doctor. It must have been even more depressing to him to know he might have contracted syphilis and require many more treatments. He and I were in no danger of becoming fast friends.

The rest of the afternoon was a smattering of the usual minor problems, a cut finger in need of washing and dressing, a cold in need of cough syrup, a headache in need of aspirin, a foreign body in the eye in need of removal, and others. One patient, however, pleased me greatly, a routine prenatal patient who was coming to all of her visits just as requested. Surely her pregnancy would be more rewarding than that of Mary Belle. At least I liked to believe it would. She was young and healthy, first baby, and for four out of her six months had visited the office for checkups. Still, I couldn't dispel the haunting afterthoughts of that previous day's harrowing experience at Mary Belle's. But this girl's quiet confidence in my judgment was most reassuring to me. I looked forward to seeing her again.

Sarah came into the consultation room after the day's work was ended to give me the messages I needed to know about, and to ask if there were any further requests before leaving. Her demeanor seemed unusually warm, I thought, and I hadn't noticed it before. As she said goodnight and turned to leave, I said impulsively, "Sarah, stay a minute and talk to me."

She seemed hesitant, but agreed and accepted a seat. What was I to say then? Why had I asked her to stay? I guess my impulse had been one of a desire for company. Perhaps I really wanted to talk about my anxiety and doubts about Mary Belle. But I knew of no way to begin. She must have wondered what my motive was.

I fumbled and asked, pointlessly, "How are you getting along lately, Sarah?"

Her polite and expected reply was, "Just fine."

"Things are okay at home?"

"Yes, of course."

"You like the office work very much?" I asked.

"Oh yes, very much," she replied.

"But it's certainly a far cry from hospital nursing," I added.

"Yes, that's true," she said, "but I like it. It brings me nearer to people and somehow I feel more involved than I did in the hospital. I sort of feel like, well, if you'll excuse my saying it, like we're treating the patients. I know that sounds presumptuous."

"No, not at all," I replied. "I'm glad you feel that close to the work. Work certainly helps to occupy my time enough so I don't get lonely." That was an outright lie, but at least it broached the subject of loneliness.

"That's nice," she said, offering no further conversational help.

I could have asked her if she was lonely, knowing her father had died and she was alone most of the time. I wondered if she came to work for me for that reason when first we met. Instead I asked, "But what do you do with yourself evenings?" I hadn't meant to ask it quite that way, having intended it more as a topic of conversation than as an invitation to call on her. She seemed to regard it differently, however.

"Well, I stay home and clean and read and—you know, house sorts of things." Her slow reply had trailed off into nowhere.

I decided to change the subject.

"Mr. Robertson sure was funny, wasn't he?" Actually, the situation wasn't funny at all and neither was he. She looked perplexed at my reversal of topic of conversation. Now I wished I hadn't begun this conversation at all. She was a kind, warm, and calm person, and I couldn't even converse with her easily.

"Where did you get your nursing training?" I asked.

"In Baltimore, at Johns Hopkins," she replied, but I already knew that fact.

"How did you like Baltimore?" I asked.

"Very well."

"I was in Baltimore myself, you know, as a resident in neurosurgery."

She didn't know.

"I left after two years, though, and came here." I wished I hadn't told her that. I was sure she'd ask why and I didn't really want to discuss it with her, even though I wanted to talk to somebody about it sometime. But she seemed as eager to end the trend of conversation as I did and asked no further questions but said, "Well you certainly are needed here."

"You know, Sarah," I said without thinking, "I always wanted to be a neurosurgeon and don't really know why I came here. I never imagined myself as a dedicated person of the type to go into a rural area to be a general practitioner. Most of my classmates aspired to specialty work, so I chose neurosurgery." I paused, and my expression must have saddened. Sarah, very understanding, did not ask the obvious question again, but

31

seemed anxious to help. She sensed my loneliness and asked if I'd like sometime to meet some of her family's old friends.

I lied when I said, "Maybe sometime in the future, but I have a number of things to do meanwhile." I really had nothing to do. I added, "You'd better go now. I've kept you too long, anyhow. Thanks for staying. I'll see you in the morning."

"Good night, Doctor," she said. "I'll lock the front door on my way out."

A minute or two later I heard the door shut and her footsteps descend the stairs. I rose to look out the window. She crossed the road and turned back, looked up and smiled, and waved a small gesture of farewell, which I appreciated. I felt ridiculous standing there and looking, but waved back and watched her disappear up the street. As she disappeared from view, a deep sadness seemed to engulf me. I realized how lonely I really was. It was only six o'clock but the office was quiet and still. I could hear dull sounds of life through the floor from the grocery store below as I sat there and then the distant, muffled "good night" of a departing customer. A short time later the familiar locking up sounds of the door to the grocery store came to my ears and again I arose to look out of the window. Following his daily routine, the grocer, my landlord, looked up and called, "Good night, Doc, hope you'll have a pleasant evenin'."

A pleasant evening consisted of my usual activity—a book and music. I felt I'd read everything, except medicine, ten times. Medical texts didn't dispel gloom very well, but Shakespeare was one of my favorites, and with some records of symphonic music to play, I did manage to accept my every night's boredom. Colonel Bennett now had shadows highlighting him and the warm glow of the setting sun softened his steel-gray face and made his military demeanor less apparent. The square took on a less arid appearance also, as night descended and lights of homes were illuminated, and the hot dryness of the day gave way to a balmier, cooler evening. A gentle soft wind wafted sweet fragrant scents of mimosa and magnolia blossoms through my window. Instinctively, I rose and looked out in the direction of Sarah's route homeward and wondered what she was doing at this minute. It was curious how calm and self-assured I felt right now.

Chapter 3

A sudden noise startled me. It was only my foot which had fallen off the desk. I sprang out of my chair. Then I realized I had fallen asleep so readily with my legs propped up on the desk that I had slept in the same place all night. The phonograph was still grinding out the center of the last record. It was seven A.M. and I was sticky and hot. The night hadn't cooled as I'd hoped it would. My legs were rubbery, both asleep, from the absurd position in which they were all night. I beat them furiously to awaken them. Then, I went down the stairs to the car to go home, shave, shower, and get fresh clothes. The dawn light was already high and I hurried so no one would see my disheveled appearance, though I always had a convenient excuse to be away from home all night. I entered my rooming house and went immediately to my bath. The landlady knocked a short time later and announced breakfast was served. When I came to the table later her husband and two children were present.

"Good mornin', Doctuh," they all greeted me one by one, except Mr. Apperson, who nodded hello.

"Good morning," I answered and sat down.

Mrs. Apperson, my landlady, was busy cooking eggs. The grits were on the table, steaming hot. I added butter and salt which always annoyed her since she added sugar and milk. I always kidded the children that hominy should be eaten with butter and salt, "Just because you grind corn, why change how you eat it?" They all considered me the usual Northern oddball, in a good-natured way, as they seemed to have little rancor for Yankees and had long since forgotten the War. Mrs. Apperson turned to the table then and spied Susannah, her "youngin," aged nine, with her middle finger dipped deep in grits and about to scoop a fingerful into her mouth.

"Susannah, you get that finger out o' yo grits, lessen yu' want a spankin'."

Susannah hastily retracted it and adopted a more customary utensil.

Then Mrs. Apperson turned to me and said, "Doctuh, Ah see yu' didn't come in all night."

I didn't want to admit I'd fallen asleep in my office. My image, you know. Must keep up the facade of responsibility. I lied, "I had a bad case which kept me up most of the night and I finished off my sleep in the office so as not to disturb you."

"Oh who was that?" she asked.

"Can't tell you," I said.

"Well, now, that's too bad workin' all the time," she said. "Yu should have some relaxin' once in awhile, take out a girl or somethin'. Why don't yu go a-courtin' that Miss Sarah who works for you? She's a nice girl. She'd help keep your evenings easy."

With that I dropped my spoonful of grits, and Susannah and Billy-Boy tittered and hid their faces. I couldn't help but wonder if the family had accepted my story about a case that kept me up. In a small town such a lie was probably not wise. Everyone knew when somebody was sick enough to keep me up all night. Much worse, Sarah lived alone. But maybe the truth, no matter how foolish, would have sounded better. Too late now.

Mr. Apperson, probably accustomed to his wife's chatter, didn't show any surprise, and I wondered if they had talked about this prior, and if they had seen her leave the office late when she stayed to talk. I knew how vicious people could be if they wanted to be. What better place than in a small town where nothing of interest happens for months at a time. But to worry was stupid. She hadn't alluded to anything suspicious and was probably sincere in wanting me to be less lonely. She was probably only friendly. I wondered if I was more interested in Sarah than I admitted to myself. Had Mrs. Apperson's foolish question only stimulated guilt feelings about my interest? I mustn't let them see how I feel, I decided. A short answer would be best.

"Perhaps some day I will date her, if she agrees."

34

I changed the subject. "Susie," I said, "how about trying some of my grits with butter?"

Susie grimaced and Billy-Boy, her brother, parroted her. Mr. Apperson went on eating in deadpan silence. He was a foreman for a road construction gang and his facial skin was hard as leather from prolonged sun exposure. Though he had never asked for my diagnosis, the several small excrescences on his face, I was sure, were skin cancers. And though they were probably not malignant, I wanted to tell him what they were and to have them removed. Yet if he wanted me to be his doctor he'd tell me at the appropriate time. Each day at breakfast I wondered if he'd ever ask! Since he rarely talked, I didn't really know his personality. Mrs. Apperson kept the conversation rolling. She was a bit on the obese side, in her mid-thirties, jolly, motherly, and solicitous, maybe a bit too concerned with my needs. I'd been told she was proud to say I lived in her house.

I decided not to prolong the conversation this morning since Sarah was the topic of discussion. So I pled "not hungry" and missed the eggs and country sausage which were a daily routine and far too greasy for my everyday pleasure. I'd eat dinner downtown tonight.

Leaving the house I walked to the office, a distance of three city blocks up north, but not so well delineated here. On the way the sheriff slowly pulled his Dodge alongside the curb to pass the time of day. I liked Sheriff Carstairs. He was a large, blunt man, with a heavy drawl, a hearty laugh, and a seemingly non-suspicious mind. Yet, I had an uneasy feeling about him, as if he might have a vicious streak beneath that bluff, extroverted exterior.

"Mornin', Doc," he drawled. Even a short phrase was long in saying. Funny how so many of the white folks called me Doc, whereas the colored people all called me "Doctuh."

"Mornin', Sheriff," I echoed.

"Sorry to hear 'bout Mary Belle Lincoln. Shame. Too bad she couldn'ta gone to Duke like so many of your other cases. Wasn't time, huh?"

The insult had been said.

"No," I said, feeling needled, "wasn't time."

"Nuthin' yu could do, I spose."

"No, nothing I could do. She was already dead and I haven't figured out a way of correcting that yet." I was angry.

He laughed heartily, "Hmm; well; it's just too bad. Well, better luck next time, Doc. Come'n see me sometime."

As he pulled away I gritted my teeth in anger and waved halfheartedly. I wondered how much the townsfolk were talking about my cases sent to Duke. One would think difficult cases that needed specialist care would be better off there, and I'd be praised for sending them. Yet, I wondered if maybe they felt I should make a greater effort toward diagnosis and treatment here at home. Perhaps they regarded me as a lousy doctor, or was that my own conscience talking. None of them actually had expressed such a view. Doubts—too many doubts.

Someone yelled at me and I was suddenly aware I was walking across the road without looking. A car honked and came to an abrupt, skidding halt.

"What's the matter with you, Doc?" someone cursed from the car.

"Damn it!" I said. That was a lousy impression to create for all the townsfolk. I was so preoccupied, however, that the near-accident didn't alarm me. I was presently obsessed with the possibility that I might not recognize the importance of symptoms in patients until too late. Better, I thought, to send the case away than risk that chance. Some of my patients had returned from Duke with clean bills of health and without major problems. Though those patients had never told me they were disappointed that I had sent them all that way for nothing, I wondered if they had been. I wanted to tell them it wasn't my fault that I was this way.

I ascended the stairs to the office ever so slowly, almost exhausted. Sheriff Carstairs's remark about Mary Belle had been very irritating. I couldn't understand why I liked him. The office seemed chilly and musty even though the temperature must have been 75 degrees at this early hour. North Carolina never cooled off well in July at night. I snapped on the fan, by habit, looked over the office and wished I had rugs. The room would look so much more cheery and warm. That was an amusing idea, since at noon I'd be roasting again. Warmth was the least of my needs just now. The office was quiet. Every examining room door was open. Sarah never forgot what she was told. I had instructed her to be sure to leave all doors open because when I came into the office at night for charts, or medicines for house calls, each closed door was foreboding. With doors open no one could hide from me as I walked by.

I never had worried about such things before Carolyn died, but then I'd never had an office before and maybe it would have been the same regardless. At least I liked to think so. Carolyn's death had changed me in many ways. I doubted I'd ever quite get over the effects of it, and further, that I could ever fall in love again. I hung up my coat and heard the door close in the waiting room. Then the inner door opened and Sarah came in. The day brightened, it seemed, immediately. The room was warmer and less forbidding. Curious how her presence could change things so totally. I was glad to see her.

"Good morning, Sarah! How nice you look today."

She returned the compliment, though I wondered if she really had meant it the way I did. It would be nice to know. I doubted she did. After all hadn't she told me she had a boy-friend at Johns Hopkins? Suddenly, I wondered if he was study-ing neurosurgery.

"What's on the roster for today?" I asked.

"Not much as yet," she replied. I wondered what had hap-pened to her Southern accent. I'd never thought about it before. She was raised here and didn't get very far away from home, yet she rarely had any trace of accent.

We didn't see all our patients by appointment in the office, of course. Most were drop-ins, and a seemingly slow day could sometimes become very busy as it wore on. Sarah began to busy herself with the many duties of an office nurse—accounts, tidy-ing up rooms, putting out instruments for examinations to be done. I didn't have a janitor so she filled in on duties of that kind—cleaning sinks, dusting, sweeping, and all the other un-interesting janitorial jobs. But always willingly, without com-plaint. I hadn't told her to do these things, nor even discussed it with her. She just did it. What a jewel, I thought. But more feeling was involved on my part than just appreciation of her work. It troubled me.

On slow days I couldn't help but wonder if people had lost confidence in me with the many referrals and were just not coming in to see me. Where would they go, though? Slow days did, however, have some good points. At least they were free of panic. At times, however, I longed for a trying case to prove myself and yet—that ever-present ambivalence was my curse. But my first patient did arrive soon, an accident case, and I was glad to see my practice was not gradually disappearing.

Joe Downey was from the grocery store and had a severely cut finger. *This could be a problem*, I thought, *a real problem*, and my breath drew in, my palms became sweaty. I immediately wanted to ship him away to Duke. Think of all the problems that could occur—tetanus, severed tendons, severed nerves, muscles, even bone injury. And surgery required careful repair. Ridiculous, stupid, I told myself. I hadn't even as yet looked at the injury and all these fears had rushed to the forefront. Surely, it was normal to assess all the possibilities, but not before I'd seen the extent of the injury. It would seem ridiculous to send a cut finger such a distance for repair. I was still annoyed by the implied insult of Sheriff Carstairs. Somehow I worked better when angry. It seemed to help relieve my anxiety. I remembered I hadn't felt at all anxious about treating Mr. Robertson's gonorrhea. I'd try to repair the finger.

Joe worked for Mr. Brownley, my landlord; did his meatcutting. He was a small, thin man with intelligence to match, but well suited to his work. I always marveled while watching butchers at work, that with the speed they wielded the cleaver they didn't consistently cut off fingers. I was sure every butcher had been asked in time "how come?" and was tired of the question, but it was standard to ask, so I said, "How come this has never happened to you before, Joe?"

I got the answer I expected.

"Jes' lucky, Ah guess."

It was an opener. I asked, "What happened?"

Often questions in a doctor's day seemed so meaningless. What happened was obvious, the man had cut his finger. Would it make any difference if the instrument was a knife or a cleaver, or if he'd been slicing tripe or tongue? He, of course, answered in the way I expected.

"Ah cut it with a knife. The boss insisted I have it looked at. Ah just wanted to bandage it up and keep workin' but the blood kept drippin' out and gettin' on the meat."

And this is our only meat market, I thought. I'd probably order that steak well done tonight.

"Is it numb, Joe?" I asked. A seemingly stupid question, but I wanted to know if he had severed his main nerve.

"Hurts, but not bad," he added. "Feels numb, sort of, in places."

Ambiguous answer. The type so often given. And so useless. But then most people can't clearly describe the symptoms they have.

I unwound a long piece of dirty, blood-soaked rag. No other description fit this bandage. I assumed his bandage must have been the rag with which he wiped the chopping block, as it had other stains consistent with meat cutting, and bits of grease and fat as well. The laceration was a nasty long slice, though straight. The skin edges were retracted and slightly bluish. The laceration extended from the base of the nail of the thumb medially to the lateral edge of the finger, sort of diagonally across the knuckle, and looked deep. The bone was exposed on the knuckle. The tendon must be cut, I thought. The edges of the skin were bleeding, but underneath somewhere an artery was pumping unchecked as the intermittent jets of blood were easily evident. He could not be sent to Duke. It must be fixed here. I hoped I could do it right.

First, I must control the bleeding, I thought. I had to grab that artery and clamp it. Once bleeding was stopped I'd have time to collect my thoughts. I turned to Sarah and realized that as I talked, she had, in proper fashion, laid out all the instruments I would need. Without asking or being told, she handed me a mosquito clamp, as if reading my thoughts. I told Joe it would hurt and proceeded to probe back the skin until I saw the artery. He confirmed my assessment of pain by hollering a bit. Once the artery was located and clamped, the major portion of the bleeding stopped. Then I asked Sarah to wash the finger thoroughly with soap and water.

This would give me time to read the anatomy book and see what I had to put back together. The book, which was dusty in the rack, revealed the following interesting facts: In the area of the laceration were present these structures: the artery (digitalis dorsalis pollicis), the tendon (extensor pollicis longus), the nerve (digitalis dorsalis), skin, and fat. That didn't sound too complicated. The artery would be tied off, the nerve could not be repaired, but would repair itself in time, the tendon would need repair, if cut, and I didn't as yet know. Then the closure of the fat and skin would be easy. I went back reassured.

I looked at the scrubbed wound which was draped for surgery. Sarah was a marvel.

"Joe," I said, "straighten out your thumb."

He tried and seemed very surprised to find he couldn't. He had been so intent on work and the fact he could grasp the meat as yet, that he wasn't worried about the bleeding and had never thought about whether or not he could move his finger as before.

"You see," I said proudly, "the tendon is cut."

He was impressed. Joe knew about tendons as a meat cutter. I don't think he'd ever thought about humans having such things, though.

I picked up the sterile gloves and donned them, then a syringe of novocaine, and realized I had forgotten it would not be sterile externally as Sarah had filled it. I would have to change my gloves again before surgery. Nevertheless, I injected the novocaine at the base of the finger on both sides to deaden it. Joe's eyes flinched and his pupils retracted as I placed the needle.

"Now we'll wait a minute," I said and took off my gloves.

Sarah noticed immediately that I had put on the gloves before injecting the finger and had a new pair ready. Joe was impressed with all this ceremony.

"How many stitches, Doc?" he asked.

"About six or so," elicited a "Whew" from Joe.

He soon "allowed as how his finger was gettin' awful dead."

I put on the new gloves, picked up a catgut ligature and tied the bleeding artery, removing the mosquito clamp. I then probed for the tendon ends, and with some difficulty found them, as they had retracted under the tissue. These were sutured together and then with the bleeding controlled, I closed the skin and fat with seven sutures. Surprisingly, when I removed my gloves my hands weren't even moist. Sarah helped me put on a dressing. I splinted it and wrapped it with gauze. Joe was stunned when I told him how long it would be before he could bend his finger, but accepted his new fame gladly. I knew he could hardly wait to tell his friends of the size of the wound and the number of stitches it took to close it. He was to return in a week to have them checked. Sarah gave him a tetanus shot in the arm since he wasn't about to bare his buttocks for her.

"Hey, Doc," he called back, "what'd ya say the name of that tendon was?"

"Extensor pollicis longus," I answered.

"Whew," he said, shook his head, and left.

My reputation would be heightened by this. If the tendon healed, and if it was sutured correctly, he'd move his finger again. It would be my therapeutic triumph.

Sarah was cleaning up. "That was very nicely done, Doctor," she said.

It had only been a minor skirmish, yet I had won, and it would help my image when Sheriff Carstairs heard. At least this patient hadn't died or made a long trip.

The remainder of the morning went easily and the day seemed less hot and much brighter. Even Sarah seemed more lighthearted, if that could be true. I wondered if she felt my anxiety over problems along with me and if she reacted like I did when a difficult case was mastered. Even my appetite was better. I offered to take her to lunch. She declined. I wondered if she was thinking of her friend in Baltimore. I imagined him as probably handsome, and tall, *all the rest of the damned baloney*. I wondered how I could imagine she might like an anxiety-plagued neurotic like me. She must know how I am. I'm sure a cloud passed over the sun just then. Yet, all she had done was decline my invitation. *What is wrong with me*, I wondered. I must be running away from something to be doubting myself so constantly. Well, I decided, I'd not ask her again. And then the morning dragged on unhappily.

Here I was again, feet on the desk, listening to Sarah's steps going down the stairs, as she left for lunch. Her attitude annoyed me. Carolyn had been more receptive when I first met her. I remembered that time so well. I was a third-year medical student when I met her, fresh white coat, entering that sanctuary called a ward on which there were honest-to-God live patients. Some were not so alive, but at least they were actual beings with actual diseases and not pictures in a textbook or slides in a laboratory. With all this background knowledge, I assumed I must be a sure-fire good doctor and accepted no alternative conclusion. I was to examine a heart, a case of mitral stenosis, and report back my findings. This was my charge. The patient was a good-natured man whose heartbeat sounds must have filled more stethoscopes daily than imaginable. It was all too unbelievable, me with a stethoscope and sphygmomanometer listening to a heart and taking a blood pressure.

A lyrical voice behind me questioned, "Can I help you in any way, Doctor?"

She was a most perceptive person, doubtless, to have recognized my worth, a woman with unusual attributes, beauty, and a voice of angels. With hauteur I turned to greet my addresser. That had done it. This must be Florence Nightingale, I thought. The deification of femininity. It was Carolyn. And this goddess, so prim in her starched uniform, even though a student nurse, had golden blond hair that shone and shimmered and dazzled my befuddled eyes. Her blue eyes sparkled and her lips were moist and soft-appearing. A white starched apron hid almost completely, yet allowed, a curved edge of her breasts to show to the side beneath a blue gown. I couldn't look further. Impulsively I said, in answer to her question, "Yes, have a date with me tonight." What a stupid thing to say—and in front of a patient. He laughed. She smiled, blushed, and walked away.

Never had a mitral stenosis danced and sung as did that patient's that day. He had a blood pressure, but I didn't recall whether or not I'd even taken it. Upon going to the desk to look at the patient's chart I encountered her again. She sprang to her feet from the chair, the mark of respect of a nurse for the doctor when he entered. If there was ever to be a grander day than this, I couldn't imagine it.

"Please," I pleaded, "tell me your name. I'm Doctor Jenson. I apologize for being so forward in there and for the embarrassment it must have caused you. I hope you'll overlook it. But I truly meant every word." For gosh sakes, shut up, I thought. "But what is your name?"

"Carolyn, Carolyn Owens," she answered.

What a beautiful name, I thought.

It was the laugh in my smile that "did it," she told me many months later, but she accepted my invitation and one date led to another. The perfume was sweet and the Duke Campus never looked prettier. She was from Virginia. In my and her spare time we wandered the gardens and fell in love, deeply, hopelessly. How marvelous it was to plan for our future. The Duke woods were never oppressive then, never frightening, even at night, as we wandered around, loved, and made plans, always laughing, always happy. Once we found a cannonball, rusty and flattened on one side in the creek—Civil War, no doubt. It was to always be one of our most prized possessions. Even the ghost chapel held beauty that was never previously appreciated. I wanted to write music or poetry, as have all who have been in love. The nurses' home was next to the hospital, so I could see her frequently. As the two years passed we solidified our plans. I would get an internship in Baltimore and she would come there to nurse. After I completed my first year of residency in neurosurgery (we both wanted me to become a brain surgeon) we would be married. Nothing could have sounded more exhilarating, more promising. I had never had such confidence and courage, such vitality, such awareness of the world, such love, such love. "Carolyn," I said, "I adore you."

She said so softly, "I adore you too, darling, with all my heart."

It took a real shaking to awaken me this time. Sarah was almost pale from trying. Lunch was over and she was back. "I hope you were dreaming something wonderful because you had the most blissful look on your face. I'd like to hear about it some time."

I smiled sheepishly. "I doubt you would. Back to work, eh, Sarah?"

It was a dismal thought, but a real one. Sarah had a lot of Carolyn's qualities, I thought, but no time for that now. Work, always work, and yet if there wasn't work, what would I do?

"Mrs. Trumbull's here and her boy has the measles."

"No diagnosing, Sarah," I chided. "You'll leave me nothing to do."

She smiled with those laughing eyes I'd seen so many times and said, "I thought you'd be proud of my perceptiveness."

I stepped into the room and laughed aloud. He was covered with spots. He said the light hurt his eyes and his mouth was sore. Mrs. Trumbull didn't appreciate my laugh but I apologized and told her the joke was on me, not about him. Actually, it was the thought of Sarah's expertise in this difficult diagnosis that had amused me. Though I desired it, this case was surely no challenge. And yet how stupid, to wish for a hard case when I knew that diagnosing problems was so difficult for me—particularly a case where the symptoms were mild. All such cases have serious possibilities. The symptoms can be the same sometimes for both mild and more serious diseases and who's to know which is which. I detested the anxiety aroused by such fears. Having overlooked a serious illness once before had been my fatal mistake. *Oh, Carolyn*, I thought, *if only you were here.*

The afternoon was very busy with minor problems. Mrs. Buell called to say Johnny's ear was much improved. I smiled in thanksgiving that now that "ol 'gator wouldn't have to eat me up." Joe called to say his finger was okay but that "bulky bandage sure gets in my way when I slice meat." Not too much, I hoped. And Sarah informed me that Amanda was feeling much better according to her nephew in the store. My practice was doing well. My diagnoses were holding up, as were my treatments. Mr. Robertson hadn't informed me of his state of health and I wondered if he was still "burned up."

Sarah came into the consultation room then. If looks could reveal one's thoughts, hers certainly expressed an air of excitement far greater than I would have expected to be possible in Bennettsboro. Her eyes were wide with disbelief as well.

"You'd better sit down, Sarah," I chided. "You look like you are going to explode. I wouldn't want anything to happen to you. You've grown too important to me."

"Doctor, you've arrived," she said and then apologized for her seeming but unintended effrontery. "I didn't mean it to sound as if—" she continued, but I interrupted her.

"I know, Sarah. I'm not offended. You're just wound up. Now what's there to be so excited about?"

"You can't imagine who has just come in to see you as a new patient."

I half-expected, or should I say hoped, it was Scarlett O'Hara. Anything to brighten up a dull day.

"You'd better tell me, I guess," I said, "before you or I burst." She still seemed too overwhelmed to speak.

"Melanie Bennett," she announced breathlessly and probably proudly I thought.

"Is that so?" I queried. "Now who is Melanie Bennett, and why should she cause such excitement?"

"She is the granddaughter of Colonel Bennett."

"Oh. The statue," I said, surprised. She obviously was an important person in this area. "I wasn't even aware any of his kinfolk still lived," I said.

It's strange that a statue, so inanimate, so ornamental, so heroic, would seem to portray a person who was more of an ideal than a real person. The old boy apparently at least had sired a few kin before his untimely death in Antietam, and now I was to be one of the chosen few and have this celebrity as a patient. I wondered how my image could have been lofty enough to secure this great honor. I asked Sarah how, and she scoffed at my idiocy.

Sarah reminded me of a kid watching a parade while describing her feelings. I'd forgotten that she probably had seen Confederate-type parades, having lived here as a child, and the name of Bennett had a special significance to her, exciting, thrilling: emotional feelings. To be actually talking to and helping care for a Bennett was a new and thrilling experience for her. I daresay I began to feel a little excited also about my new charge, seeing Sarah's reaction, and thinking here was a member of the family for which this town I'd chosen to live in was named. If she was on my side! If I could cure her without sending her to Duke! If somehow I could gain her confidence and goodwill, I'd be a definite success.

Sarah couldn't resist telling me how important, exciting, and unusual an occasion this truly was.

"I haven't seen her for years. Nobody has. She's a spinster."

"Is that right?" A question not requiring or allowing an answer as she went on.

"Yes, that's right. She's Colonel Bennett's granddaughter, and she used to ride in the main car in the parade on Confederate Day, and would lay a wreath at the base of her grandfather's statue. She always wore a long, white, lacy dress and a big floppy white hat. She was so tiny and graceful and pretty. All of us kids used to wait at the statue rather than watch the parade so we'd be sure to see her. She was like a goddess, a fairy queen in white, and surely the most illustrious celebrity we ever hoped to see. Once she winked at me and I knew instantly she was kind and sweet, though most of the kids said she was mean and snarly and a witch, living way down there in the woods. We only saw her on Confederate Day, she never came out at any other time. And she had the nicest auto, driven by a chauffeur with black suit and hat."

I wondered if Sarah would find time to let me see the patient.

"She was a woman of mystery."

I took advantage of a slight pause in her biographical sketch to interrupt. "Sarah, maybe I should see her now and we can stay after work and have you tell me the rest of the story."

Sarah was not quite recovered when she answered "yes" in a faraway tone, as if she was still standing there admiringly at the foot of Colonel Bennett's statue. I prompted her once more by suggesting she go get Miss Bennett and bring her in. She departed down the hall toward the waiting room, closing the door behind her. I knew I felt a bit anxious and tense about my coming trial. I hoped Miss Bennett's disease would be easy to diagnose. I could use a Bennett as a satisfied patient. What could a woman be like, who was both a fairy and a witch? My anticipation grew until I too was about to burst. I could hear her footsteps approaching the door. At the last second I reminded myself that my image was all important, drew in a big breath and assumed my forced calm, though I knew my heart was pounding and my throat was tense.

The door opened and Sarah very courteously, almost ceremoniously, ushered in my new patient. It was interesting that even Sarah's calm had a forced look about it. She was too stilted in her introduction.

"Doctor Jenson, may I introduce you to Miss Melanie Bennett."

Sarah looked as if any moment she might detonate. Miss Bennett entered. She was a small, frail woman in her late sixties, probably. Her carriage was that of a·well-bred, proud person but with quick, floating, gliding step. She was dressed in a plain, long, pale blue, silk dress with long sleeves, cuffed and collared with lace, and carried a sweater, purse, and parasol. Her hat looked somewhat antique, I thought, as did the dress, once I looked more carefully. I couldn't see her shoes on the other side of the desk but wondered if they were the button type.

She extended her frail hand with the palm down as if expecting an old-world-type formal bow and kiss on the back of the hand. I took her hand lightly and nodded courteously. She smiled and her lips formed a straight line, not an ellipse. It was surprising to me that her confident manner had a calming effect on me. Her demeanor was one of intense respect for my position and title, curiously a new experience for me. I couldn't help but feel more assured and less tense. That so important a person in this community, who must have heard about me and my Duke cases, would come for my advice was very warming and reassuring. She could have gone anywhere for care, and was obviously accustomed to the best of everything.

"How do you do, Doctor," she said in the finest finishing school English—not a trace of Southern accent. "Doctor" had never quite sounded that respectful before.

I responded just as respectfully, "How do you do, Miss Bennett. It's a pleasure to meet you. Won't you please sit down?"

I was surprised at how formal and correct I was. Let's see, I thought, what do I say now—can't just say, "What's wrong?" What did they teach us in med school—don't dive into the case history. Yet the patient didn't come in to pass the time of day with small, inconsequential talk. I decided the weather was a good topic and opened, "I hope your trip into town was not too uncomfortable on this very hot day."

"No, of course not," she said, "I like the heat, you know. I'm so thin the cold weather chills my bones quickly."

That certainly took care of the weather. I decided to plunge into the problem without further delay.

"Yes, you are very correct. Heat isn't nearly as uncomfortable to thin people as to others more padded." That sounded dumb, I thought. I went on. "Have you some problem that's brought you all this way to see me?"

"Doctor," she said, "I have a cold."

"A cold?" I asked in disbelief. In truth, I was stunned. Miss Melanie Bennett couldn't have come into town to see me just for a cold.

I must have shown the incredulity on my face because before I could say more she continued.

"I'm sure that sounds ridiculous to you, but this is a very peculiar cold. You see, Doctor, about two months ago I developed these very mild symptoms of a cold with nasal discharge and watering of the eyes, occasional sneezing, and a very mild sore throat. Of course I've had symptoms such as this on many occasions, have never paid them much mind, and have always treated myself with aspirin and quinine and, occasionally, camphor steam inhalations. Yet, though these remedies have always succeeded in the past, this time they have failed me. I'm perplexed and a little frightened."

She truly was beautiful in her regal way and I understood Sarah's excitement. I asked if she had ever seemed to improve or if it seemed to steadily increase in severity.

She replied, "It increases very gradually. I'm even embarrassed to say I have a good deal more saliva than previously."

Could she have trench mouth, I wondered. A fine lady like this wouldn't have that, yet I asked, "Has the saliva been stringy?"

"Oh, my no," she said. "Had it been that way, I would have been in to see you weeks ago. Lately also I have lost my appetite somewhat and on occasion am slightly but just barely nauseated. Yet, warm milk usually helps that."

I could see she didn't eat well. Her lack of appetite was no surprise.

"I've never had much appetite, though. You know, we girls have to keep our figures; wouldn't want to lose my slim waist." Her eyes twinkled. Her twinkle was infectious and I smiled. I could easily imagine her being strapped into a fancy corset to narrow her waist before donning petticoats, bustle, and ball gown. She even appeared to have the iron deficiency anemia women got from strapping their abdomens so tight. She must have been beautiful as a young girl, so petite, so sweet and so proper; a real charmer. I wondered why she had never married.

"Has your nausea ever led to vomiting?" I asked.

"No never!" It was almost an insult to suggest this fine person vomited. "But, you know, last week when I was working in my garden I felt faint for a minute. Ben, he's my overseer, had to help me into the house. I'm really worried, Doctor. I've hardly known a sick day in my whole life."

She was so nice and appeared so distraught that I felt constrained to reassure her. "Oh, I doubt sincerely it's anything serious," I said, without conviction. I was beginning to worry myself. This didn't sound like the run-of-the-mill cold, but if not that, what then! "Have you any other symptoms besides those you told me about?" I asked.

"No. That's all, but that's enough. I'm worried and of course," she smiled, "I don't want to blow my nose forever."

"No, of course not," I said, returning her smile. "Let me ask you some questions about your past life." I then proceeded to take a full case history, which I did on few of my patients even though this was my training. Up to now, none of them had held the fascination for me this patient did. Something about this lady made me uneasy. Yet she calmed me sufficiently to allay temporarily my anxiety.

She told me she had been born here in Bennettsboro, that her father and mother were both dead of old age—type illnesses, a stroke and heart failure, and that her grandfather had died in the Civil War. I found it interesting that she said he had "died" instead of "killed in action" but I was wise enough not to pursue it. I did say jokingly, however, that he and I were, in a way, fast friends, to which she replied, "I never knew him, so I envy you your friendship."

Otherwise, a review of all of her systems was generally negative as she had always enjoyed good health. She said she lived alone except for her overseer and housekeeper who also lived on the old plantation. Her avocation was gardening, mainly a vegetable garden, and her diet consisted largely of what she grew, with occasional meat from the market. She had a grandnephew, Ambrose, and he was her only living relative. She had never married. I wanted to ask why, but declined, realizing it wasn't within my rights to ask personal questions not connected with the case. All of the time she talked, she sat on the edge of the chair, her knees together, her legs tilted to one side, back erect and head high. She reminded me of an excited, yet contained young maiden at her first party awaiting a suitor's invitation to dance. Every mannerism was flawless.

"Well," I said, "I'd better examine you now to see why this cold hangs on," to which she agreed politely. This office had never been so formal. I buzzed Sarah who must have been at the door, since it sprang open. She could well have been at the keyhole, eavesdropping. At my request she showed Miss Bennett to an examining room. Sarah was agog. Her excitement hadn't abated yet. I knew she was eager to ask many details of the case, but if I had told her Miss Bennett had a cold she would have been let down. The patient was soon ready for examination and I entered the room. In her white gown, with her white hair, and general pallor she looked a little like a ghost, with sunken cheeks and hollow eyes. She did not look well. It didn't seem logical that she would have a minor illness and look this sick. Yet I realized she was aging, which would add to her frailty.

I said, "I never asked that one improper question a gentleman never asks a lady."

"I knew I couldn't avoid it forever and I won't make you guess," she replied. "I'm seventy-four."

Well, I thought, that partially explains her appearance. Old age certainly is a ravager of beauty and vitality. Yet, her personality sparkled a lot and her blue eyes were bright. I couldn't dispel the nagging notion that some more serious illness existed. But such concern was consistent with me, suspecting a serious illness in every symptom. "Common diseases are common," Sir William Osler had said, and aphorisms of his had been drummed into me through medical school. Why couldn't I believe this dictum and cease looking for hidden problems? It was stupid not to accept the obvious.

The exam revealed little: a clear chest, clear eyes, nose, and throat, except for a little redness, and even that might merely be the contrast of mucous membranes against chalk-white skin. We chatted while I examined her, mainly about herself. I asked her where she lived.

"In a beautiful, fine, old home. Bennett Plantation House. It's about five miles from here, deep in the pines. Have you ever been down Highway 89 and seen the two large old gates opening onto a bridge? It's hard to tell you exactly where, but it's near a long row of poplar trees that my grandfather planted, on the north side of the highway."

I was drawing a mental picture of the highway. Actually I had ventured forth from town very little since my arrival and was essentially unfamiliar with the area. I did sort of recall the large gates and pillars, though, and had wondered where they led. She want on.

"It's a beautiful mansion, vast lawns, a huge magnolia in front with a circular drive around, a long row of tall trees leading up to the circle, and all set deep in the pines. The plantation spreads out for several miles in all directions and you enter across one of our largest cotton fields."

It was obvious she was immensely proud of it. I wondered why she mentioned only one overseer to run such a large place. Probably neglected to tell me of the rest of the plantation hands. I suspected an old woman such as this would, without doubt, have an overseer and many hands to pick cotton and cut tobacco.

"It sounds very pretty," I said. "I've actually never seen a large plantation except from a distance so I'm unfamiliar with them."

"Well," she offered, "it may quiver or shake a little if a Yankee gentleman comes on the premises, but if you'd like to see it sometime, I'd be much obliged to have you come to call." She was teasingly coquettish in her manner.

I was embarrassed. I had almost asked for that invitation. I wondered how she knew I was a Yankee.

"It's very kind of you," I answered, "but my practice keeps me busy much of the time and it might be difficult. Someday, perhaps."

51

She saw through that flimsy excuse quickly. She laughed.

"Oh, now, a young man like you certainly can't be that busy, but, if you find the time, the invitation is open. And don't be afraid. Once a long time ago when I was at Sweet Briar College, I invited a Yankee gentleman from Washington and Lee University to visit and Papa Bennett was very annoyed to have a Yankee in the house. But he's dead now, so there's little to fear."

I couldn't help but wonder if that Yankee ever went back north or just disappeared in the woods.

I returned to her case. "In my examination I haven't found any signs of serious illness, and don't feel you should be frightened," though the very words made me uneasy again. "I will give you some medications you haven't had, however, to see if they help."

I wrote her out several prescriptions and said, "It was very nice to have met you. Your grandfather's statue has been such a companion, it's nice to meet one of the family. I do hope you'll let me know if this doesn't help you."

"I'll have my nephew stop and tell you in a week or so when he's in town, thank you, Doctor. It was a pleasure meeting you, too. I've heard so many nice things about you," she said. "I do hope you'll come to call."

"Thank you and good-bye," I said.

"Good afternoon," she answered, more correctly.

I was troubled. What could she have heard? She must know about my Duke cases. In fact, I wished she were one of them. She had heard, she said, so many nice things about me. Yet nothing had happened to make me wonder if she distrusted me. Once again it was my fear of misdiagnosis that tormented me. Something seemed wrong about this case. I returned to my office and in a few minutes heard her say good-bye to Sarah, who was once again extra courteous as if paying court to a celebrity. Her quick footstep descending the stairs was accompanied by a heavier pounding pair belonging to someone who weighed a lot more than she. They must be her nephew's, I thought. Strange, I thought, how footsteps can sound ominous. These were heavy and dragging and sort of overshadowed and drowned out the delicate sounds of hers. I resisted the urge to look out the front window to see him, half expecting to see a demoniacal pair of eyes returning the look. What was it about these Bennetts that was so disquieting?

The remainder of the afternoon was boring and uninteresting, and I was unable to concentrate. Mrs. Gentry called to say she thought her labor was starting and I hoped it wasn't, even though I expected no problems. If only she could wait until I'd recovered from Mary Belle's death. I wanted no more problems like Mary Belle's. No more moments of terror, please, no more. A prayer to anyone or to all. A prayer to Fate.

Curiously, Sarah had little to say when she left the office. I expected more discussion about Melanie Bennett, but she didn't broach the subject and neither did I. Maybe she had recovered her composure and was no longer as overwhelmed as she'd been at first. Or maybe she wouldn't ask out of medical propriety, as all case histories are supposed to be kept confidential. Office nurses can't help but know something about the illnesses patients have, of course.

I watched her go across the street from the window in the usual way, the sun casting shadows on and beyond Colonel Bennett. This time she didn't turn to wave and a gloom settled on me. I'd hoped she would wave. The room seemed colder and I felt lonely and deserted. Now there were no sounds and soon I'd be hearing the door lock below. I had no appetite and wished the coming evening would hold more promise than a book or music. What a contrast from the evenings Carolyn and I had spent together before that awful day she died. If only I hadn't been so stupid, so blind, she might be here with me tonight or, even more, I probably wouldn't be here at all worrying about diagnoses.

Chapter 4

Dinner was over and I returned to the office. I couldn't go to my room at the Appersons', as it was too uninviting. Their home was a place to sleep and to eat breakfast but nothing more. Mrs. Apperson had allowed me to sit in the living room and listen to the radio whenever I wished but this always meant small talk and she was not one to carry on an enlightening or stimulating conversation. Mr. Apperson never said a word, just read his newspaper and worked on reports and actually slept a good deal of the time.

Time weighed heavy on my hands. Interesting companionship was never more needed. I was desperately lonely. I much preferred the office where at least I didn't feel compelled to offer inane comments on uninteresting topics. I ascended the steps to the office. Each step was a staccato sound in the night unmistakable as such. The door squeaked as it opened, and I was overwhelmed with how malevolent the waiting room seemed. I switched on the lights. Lights certainly helped. The switch to my consultation room, though, was far away and to get there I had to pass each examining room. It was senseless to turn on every light merely to alleviate my disquietude, but my heart pounded every time I passed one of those doors. Had I switched on the light and seen someone standing there, I would certainly have died of coronary occlusion. They say animals die of fear when about to be devoured, so why not humans? Being alone was a terrible ordeal for me, particularly at night.

I had never minded the dark when I was with Carolyn. There had been nothing ominous about it when we were dating. We had walked in the Duke forests, picnicked there, and stayed into the night and never felt afraid or alone or watched by eyes in the night. Why was it so different now? I ran past the examining room. I was angered by that stupid, childish act. The lights in the consultation room, though, did help and closing the door seemed to close out the potential malevolence. Soon after I sat down, the refrigerator motor popped on. The sound startled me momentarily but then rang a familiar note and the fear was gone. I looked out the window, in the direction of Sarah's and wondered if she too felt the same uneasiness alone in that big house. I wished I could go to her, any excuse to talk to her, any excuse just to be with her and not alone. But I mustn't kid myself into thinking company was the only reason. I knew it that first day she walked in, but was unable to believe it. Something about her had stimulated me much more than I was ordinarily stimulated by women. Particularly since Carolyn died.

I grew restive while thinking first of Sarah, then of Carolyn, so I chose a book to change my trend of thought. Shakespeare, my favorite, was the choice. *Hamlet*, particularly, held a fascination for me. I'd read it many times. Perhaps Hamlet's weakness of character intrigued me in some way. I wanted to understand his doubts and his character flaws. Maybe then I'd understand mine better. I began reading but couldn't concentrate on it. Sarah kept popping into mind, and also the quiet night bothered me. I decided to play a record and picked up *Romeo and Juliet* by Tchaikovsky. That's ridiculous, I thought, and slammed it down and paced around a little, glancing out the window. When I went back for another record, I chose *Death and Transfiguration* without thinking. Richard Strauss had always been one of my favorite composers. The strains of the music diverted my mind from thoughts of Sarah, and I settled down to my reading. Time passed. My restlessness eased. Once again, I was on the parapet with Hamlet eagerly and uneasily awaiting the ghost who walks in the night.

> I am thy father's spirit,
> Doom'd for a certain term to walk the night,
> And for the day confin'd to fast in fires,
> Till the foul crimes done in my days of nature
> Are burnt and purg'd away. But that I am forbid
> To tell the secrets of my prison-house,
> I could a tale unfold whose lightest word

Would harrow up thy soul, freeze thy young blood,
Make thy two eyes, like stars, start from their spheres,
Thy knotted and combined locks to part,
And each particular hair to stand on end,
Like quills upon the fretful porpentine.
But this eternal blazon must not be
To ears of flesh and blood. List, list, oh list!

I was listening and I felt I was even hearing the ghost's footsteps coming toward me. My God, I thought, I am hearing footsteps on the stairs outside. A man's steps, unmistakable. Heavy steps. An icy chill crept up my back. Who was coming for me? The steps were at the door now. I hoped I had locked it behind me. I hadn't. The door was opening. My heart was pounding. Any minute I'd hear those steps in the hall and then my office door would open. Instead, the bell, that ever-familiar bell, rang. "It must be a patient," I said to no one. It has to be. I waited. A voice called "Doc, Doc, are you there? It's Mr. Gentry. My wife's getting ready." My anxiety was gone. What a relief. I could have kissed him, inappropriate as it would seem. I opened the door and suddenly I was no longer alone or fearful. He was a mild-mannered, small man, hardly the type to be considered fearsome.

"How's she doing?" I asked.

"Oh, she's having pains about every five minutes or so, but she says yu'all better be thinkin' 'bout comin' soon, since she goes fast near the end."

"I'll hurry," I promised. Even the prospect of a delivery and possible complications was better than sitting alone at night.

"I'll be out as soon as I get my things. You tell them to boil some water." People expected me to say that, so I did.

He went on ahead, running down the steps, but this time the sound was more musical and the office no longer had a gloomy look.

My gosh, I thought, I don't know where he lives. I ran to the window only to see him driving off in a southerly direction. Somebody'd have to show me the way. I called the phone operator, but she didn't know where he lived. It was nine o'clock and all stores were closed. The sheriff's office was over at the county seat and he wouldn't be able to get here fast enough. Sarah, I thought, she'd be the one to know, having grown up here. It was only nine and I was sure she wouldn't mind an evening's drive. I raced over to her house, this time with a reasonable and valid excuse for being there. None of the neighbors could question our behavior, even if they observed it.

The house was lighted in the living room and one upstairs room. It was a neat, white, two-story home with porches below and above across the front of the house. I knocked. A light lit up inside the door and Sarah peeked out through the curtain. She opened the door.

"Good evening, Sarah," I said. "I'm sorry to disturb you but I need your assistance. I'm glad you haven't gone to bed."

"Come in," she offered, somewhat perplexed.

"Really no time for that, Sarah. I'm on my way to a delivery—Mrs. Gentry. But I realized I don't know where she lives and hoped you could help."

"I'll be glad to tell you the way," she answered.

Could it actually be she didn't realize I wanted her to come along or was she just going to make me ask.

"If you're not busy, I'd appreciate your help on the delivery, too."

I knew Sarah wouldn't let me down. She agreed immediately. Her agreement was enthusiastic and her activity almost frenzied. In no time at all, her lights were out and she had closed the door and was ready. I let her into the car and we started out, past the **Y** and the colonel, south through town on Highway 89. Sarah was gay and her mood was infectious. I felt happily excited also though I couldn't understand why. One would have thought we were off to a party or dance instead of another test of my therapeutic ability. And in truth we said very little to each other except for small talk about Mrs. Gentry's pregnancy. I hadn't even thought of Mrs. Gentry's condition or the possible complications. After a while I asked, "Is it much farther?"

"No, just a short ways now. Turn at the next road to the left."

Shortly, we pulled up at the house. Harry Gentry was at the door and ready to greet us, as was his dog, who barked loudly.

Every expectant husband wants the doctor to hurry and he was no exception. It was a modest farm, but the house was immaculate inside and out. They were obviously very proud of their place. We went into Mrs. Gentry's bedroom. The contrast here with the Lincoln household was striking. She was in clean sheets, one bed in the room, a rug on the floor and curtains on the windows. Mr. Gentry was very nervous, sat down on a chair and held her hand and looked quite pale. His wife reassured him that he mustn't worry, that all would go well.

"The doctuh's here, honey, he'll know what's best and he'll do everything he can," she said.

Her calm trust I hoped would be fulfilled. It was a strange sight seeing the patient reassure the relative, but I prevailed upon Mr. Gentry that, in spite of his anxiety, he leave the room. I even had eventually to plead with him and even then he paused to say, "You'll take good care of her won't you, Doc?"

I said I would, then wondered fleetingly if it were true. Sarah's presence suddenly made me anxious. If I were to become nervous she would surely see it immediately as she must know me well by now. Yet she seemed to display confidence. I began to get cold feet again; maybe I shouldn't be here, maybe I shouldn't have brought Sarah. She meant too much to me to let her down with a display of anxiety. Fortunately, Mrs. Gentry was not ready to deliver so there was time to curb my anxiety before the awful moment arrived. With each pain she bit hard on a rolled piece of cloth to prevent herself from screaming and grabbed the headboard for something to hang onto. I gave her a shot of morphine to help ease the pain, though I knew it might depress the baby, but I couldn't let her suffer. I went out to see Mr. Gentry. He was sitting in an overstuffed chair in the living room. The chair had been designed for comfort but he looked anything but comfortable—on the edge, worried, supplying his need to be active by scratching his hound dog's ears and back. The dog was panting comfortably and looked not at all disturbed and acknowledged my entry with a friendly whimper and glance at me.

"Your wife will be a while longer, Mr. Gentry," I said and he nodded three or four times in acknowledgement, unable to speak. I asked him where Miss Hughes, my nurse, was, and again, without speaking, he waved his index finger up and down three or four times toward a door. Just then Sarah appeared at the door, and as she opened it a large volume of steamy air billowed through the door like smoke. She beckoned for me to come and as I entered the kitchen we both smiled at each other jovially to see the steam bath into which the kitchen had been converted. Four separate large kettles were steaming on the old iron stove and a roaring wood fire was adding to the heat in the room. I suggested we eliminate all but one of those kettles in the interest of lowering the humidity and Sarah laughed. The other kettle I'd use so his effort would not have gone for naught.

It was then about ten o'clock and it seemed the visit would be interminable. There was no phone and once again I wished I'd taken time to notify the operator where I'd gone or left a note on the door.

I returned to Mrs. Gentry's side and talked quietly to her about her condition. She had had one previous baby and knew much of what I said, and seemed unafraid. She said she had been terribly afraid with the first but knew her second couldn't be as hard. Only a midwife had been in attendance then so she felt much more privileged and reassured to have me there at this birth. I wished I felt as secure about my work. She was becoming sedated from the morphine, and on occasion drowsed off and trailed her words into nowhere. Intermittently she uttered a stentorian snore and aroused slightly with contractions only to moan somewhat. The baby's heart was steady and strong. There was no unusual bleeding, her blood pressure was normal. She was a bit on the plump side but not fat. I sat on the straight-back chair at her side and waited. An hour passed, then another. I wondered what Sarah was doing. I remembered someone's description of the practice of obstetrics, "hours of inescapable boredom, interspersed with moments of sheer terror." An apt description. I dozed. I felt a hand gently pressing my shoulder and awakened. Sarah was standing by me smiling, appreciative of my efforts, sharing in camaraderie and respectful of my quest. I could see her admiration without question.

"Why don't you lie down and rest, Doctor?" she said. "I'll watch awhile in your place."

I accepted her offer. In the living room Mr. Gentry had fallen back into the chair using its comfort to good advantage. His mouth hung open and his head lay back at an angle, his arm hung loose over the chair arms. He, too, snored loudly. The dog lay dutifully at his feet and seemed uninterested in my entrance except to raise his eyelids for an identifying look only to droop them again along with his ears. I tiptoed by him and he gave me another glance. I lay down on the couch being certain to keep my feet over the edge so as not to dirty it. In spite of nocturnal grinding snores, I was soon fast asleep.

The operating corridor was bleak and white and the beautiful girl lay on the gurney with a cap over her head. Once that scalp had had a beautiful, soft, lovely covering of hair, so silky, so blond, so radiant, so desirable. Now it was gone, shaved off for brain surgery. She was calm and trusting and sweet. I wanted to pour my heart out, say all the things I hadn't had time to say, ask her forebearance for all my mistakes, all the little hurts I might have caused. I stood there feeling conspicuous, wanting to hug her every last minute before surgery. Some invisible force held me back. We couldn't reach each other. I struggled and fought. Her lips parted to say something and I couldn't hear her. An invisible barrier kept her words from reaching me. I beat on the barrier wildly. Soon the men in green came, with baleful looks. They looked in my direction and slowly shook their heads to and fro with reproachful, quarrelsome movements. I cowered and refused to meet their eyes. I flailed out and tried to strike them from her side, to prevent them from taking her. A large man with a prognathous jaw and sardonic grin came forward. He was satanic and carried a large knife and a saw. I fought harder. The wall was there. I was powerless to help. He ignored my entreaty. He was implacable. With slow measured steps he pushed her gurney away into a narrowing, darkening channel until she was no longer visible. All the while her arm extended back to me beseeching my aid. I cried out, no, no, no, no, help, someone help, help!

Sarah was there at my side. The dog was no longer asleep. He was cowering behind the chair and Mr. Gentry was erect and wide-eyed, terrified.

"Oh, Sarah," I said. "I'm so embarrassed. I was dreaming

something, something awful. I apologize. I hope I didn't disturb Mrs. Gentry or arouse her daughter."

"No, no," she said, "but I must admit you gave me a bit of a start."

Mr. Gentry just look terrified.

"How's the patient?" I asked Sarah.

"Well, she's fairly close, I think. I was going to wake y'all anyhow."

"Y'all?" I questioned and she smiled sweetly.

"I meant all of you."

"I guess I took care of waking y'all anyhow," I said. "Let's go see the patient."

Mrs. Gentry had certainly aroused from her morphine as her labor was at the end of the first stage and her contractions were hard. With each contraction she was straining and writhing, saying over and over, "Oh, Lord, help me Lord." How many times I'd heard that.

I said, "I'm here Mrs. Gentry." A rather presumptuous statement but someone had to answer and I doubted the Lord would.

"Now's the time for hot water, Sarah—not too hot, though. I'll wash up."

When I returned the head was crowning. The caput of the baby could easily be seen at the vaginal opening. How I would have liked to cut an episiotomy and help it out, but without the chance of suturing it later, I was unable to. "Sarah," I said, "let's put those clean towels I brought under her and over her legs and lay one on the abdomen so this is a little more clean, if not sterile."

She complied readily as I donned my rubber gloves. They had been boiled at the office and placed between freshly laundered towels so were perhaps moderately sterile. I sat on the edge of the bed. Her legs were pulled up in a jackknife position and Sarah was there to help keep them in that position, and to administer some ether on a gauze.

"Now, Mrs. Gentry," I said, "when you get a pain take several quick short breaths of the ether and then a long breath and hold it and push hard, as hard and as long as you can. When you tire take another breath or two of ether and then push again."

She followed instructions as best as possible but disliked the ether smell and pulled away from the gauze repeatedly. With each contraction the head crowned higher. Soon she delivered, with little difficulty. I was glad when the baby cried readily—a boy—which would certainly please Mr. Gentry. I tied the cord and cut it. Sarah took the baby and handed it to Mrs. Gentry who smiled maternally and cuddled it. The baby was unmoved and just cried. She cradled it in her arms lovingly. I handed the pan with the placenta to Sarah, who took it out of the room. We tidied up and called Mr. Gentry. He was so excited and happy he could hardly contain himself, shook my hand vigorously and even Sarah's hand. I told him we'd go now as everything was fine and we must get back. He was so grateful it was difficult to free ourselves. As we were about to depart I remembered the placenta. I told Sarah we should wrap it in paper and ask him to bury it so she returned to the kitchen to get it. She came out with a startled look.

"It's gone," she cried. "I left it on the floor in that pan."

A stream of blood on the floor indicated its passage to the front door where a look confirmed our suspicions. The dog had made off with it. "No case is perfectly managed I guess." We looked at each other and laughed almost to the point of tears.

Returning home we both were tired but satisfied. My thoughts were almost totally occupied with the success I'd just had in spite of all my doubts and anxiety.

In a while Sarah leaned back and then turned to me and said, "That was such fun, so wonderful. I hope you'll take me along on more of your deliveries. It gave me such a feeling of accomplishment. I used to like deliveries in training, but it's been so long since I've seen one I'd forgotten how thrilling a birth is."

"There's nothing finer in medicine when it goes well," I said, satisfied.

"Do you miss Baltimore?" I asked.

"I did for a while, but not so much anymore. I have to make a trip there again, though, have some unfinished business."

I wanted to ask what, but didn't want to ask as well. I knew what she meant, yet feared what I would hear.

"I'll miss you when you go," I said, feeling strangely lonely.

She laughed, "It sounds so final that way. Of course, without your permission for time off I won't be going anywhere."

"What fabulous power I have over you," I said. "I might never let you go." That sounded like an admission of something. I suddenly realized I was grateful it was night because I was sure I was blushing. Yet I wondered if it really implied something more. It was nice to be next to her and I had to admit I enjoyed it. Yet, more than anything I just wanted to talk, to unburden my soul to someone whom I could trust. I knew she was going to see the man she'd left behind in Baltimore. A doctor, I'd bet—no doubt, a specialist. The thought annoyed me. I even felt a little jealous, probably only of a close relationship since I'd known one so intimately. How I missed Carolyn. Whatever feelings I had for Sarah must be a product of loneliness or an attempt to recreate the relationship I'd once known. Or could it be purely a sexual attraction? God knows she is pretty enough, and having her always near me does have its effect. I felt that certain restlessness spreading over me.

Sarah interrupted my thoughts. "Doctor, we're coming up to the entrance to Bennett House Plantation; you know, where Miss Bennett lives."

I slowed the car. Just as Miss Bennett had described it, there were two iron gates and the bridge. In the dark it was hard to make out anything but the outlines of trees and gates against a less dark sky, but the lights of the car illuminated the gates enough to reveal a large "B" centered on each gate.

I wondered why I slowed down. What was the fascination that Miss Bennett held for me? Now that the subject had been raised, Sarah couldn't resist asking about Miss Bennett's illness.

"What was wrong with her?" she asked.

"Of course, I'm not supposed to tell you," I said, smiling, "but I am worried about her. She has all the symptoms of a cold but I can't help but worry that I'm overlooking something more serious. If she doesn't get better soon I may refer her to Duke."

Sarah said nothing for a minute, then replied, "Oh, I don't imagine that will be necessary. You'll find the cause. You know I was so excited to see her after all these years. She rarely comes out and no one ever seems to visit her. You're quite privileged to have been extended an invitation. You must have made quite an impression on her."

"I don't know how," I said. "All I did was discuss her illness, but she seemed lonely to me. Maybe she needs company. Did you get the impression her hat and dress were sort of, antique, let's say?"

"No, I don't think so, but then my eyes were sort of starstruck. Maybe I was too stunned to notice." That was an admission I hadn't expected.

"Yes," I said, "I did notice a bit of that, but then it was a new side of you and I can't say I didn't enjoy it."

I hoped she had smiled at that statement but I didn't look.

"Do you know her nephew?" I asked.

"No, he brought her but I didn't see him," she said. "The last time I saw him was many years ago. He is her only living relative, I guess, her brother's son." I confirmed this and she continued.

"I don't really know what happened to his mother and father, an accident, I think. The family has always been sort of mysterious, aloof from everyone else, and there are lots of rumors, but no real fact. I didn't like the nephew when I knew him years ago. Something about him gave me chills. But maybe I was jealous," she added as an afterthought. Sarah was not one to judge people harshly and if he gave her chills he must have been repugnant.

"Is he married?" I asked.

"I think so," she answered. "I don't know if I've ever seen his wife. They may have been married when I was in Baltimore."

Sarah's mood was much friendlier tonight, I thought. She was much more talkative than usual, but perhaps it was just the delivery and the Bennetts that made her so. She was the type of person I felt I could confide in, but actually she had worked for me only five or six months and I could be wrong. I doubted I'd ever manage to tell her of my fears and doubts. She'd probably never respect me after that. What woman could respect a man without the courage to act with conviction—specifically, could a nurse respect a frightened doctor? If only she could have known me years ago, there'd be no worry of that. I hoped she'd understand why I was changed, and even hoped that her kindliness would help me solve the riddle. Here I was, in the back woods of North Carolina under the guise of helping a needy people while in fact hiding from the reality of my fears of diagnosing incorrectly. I could have stayed nearer Duke and leaned on their assistance but that had its drawbacks, too. I wouldn't like their recognition of my queasiness any better. Even the cases I'd sent there already must, to a certain degree, have labeled me as timid, a galling thought. The important thing, I kept telling myself, however, was only that the patient get the best possible diagnosis and care. Yet, on the other hand, such action was certainly an escape from doubt and attendant anxiety and one I probably overused.

Sarah had been very patient while I sat there deep in thought, but did finally interrupt me to say, "Doctor, you're going the wrong way to take me home."

I had automatically turned right in the **Y** heading for my room, oblivious of her presence. She must have wondered what was on my mind.

"Good grief, Sarah, I must have been asleep. I'll just swing across the top of the **Y** here and get you home soon. I guess I was enjoying our drive so much I hadn't recognized we were home. I wanted to take the long way anyhow. That's supposed to be the sweetest."

"You're awfully nice," she said, "and this has been a very enjoyable evening. It's strange how work can sometimes be more fun than leisure, even though requiring more concentration and worry."

"It's the successful result that makes it pleasurable. Our toils bear many fruits," I said.

"That sounds like another Shakespearean quotation," she said.

"You're too flattering. That's a Dr. Jensonism, the net result of too many quiet evenings reading books alone."

It seemed I always got back to the same subject—loneliness. It was a picture I wasn't anxious to portray for any desired result, but was one that popped up regularly from almost unconscious thought.

"Here we are," she said. "And again let me thank you for including me in the night's fun. I haven't had as enjoyable an evening in months."

"Nor have I," I answered, "and thanks for your help."

I let her out of the car and walked her to the door. For a moment she fumbled to get the key in the lock in the dark and then succeeded. She turned and said, "Good night, Doctor."

She smiled sweetly and I thought I had never seen her look more attractive. It bothered me to the extent that I barely managed to answer good night. I had an almost insatiable desire to take her in my arms. The feeling was so overwhelming that I was glad to have her shut the door, thereby making pursuance of that desire impossible.

I returned to the car and sat awhile thinking of my reaction. Sarah's every feature was now vivid in my mind. I wondered as I drove away what tomorrow would bring.

Chapter 5

The next few weeks passed rapidly. The office seemed much happier than before. Probably I was happier and this made the difference. Even my nights were somewhat less lonely. Fortunately, there were no new large problems to plague me. Mr. Robertson was in for treatment, the next-to-final indignity he had to accept. He was his usual sour self. I guess he and I were never to be friends or even congenial. But one shouldn't expect to be friendly with everyone. I had tried to establish some relationship with him other than doctor-patient as I didn't enjoy his aggrieved attitude each time he received treatment. We discussed my office needs, a rug, and the possibility of buying it at his store. He hadn't wanted my trade apparently and expressed doubt that I'd like anything he had—"too fancy" for my office.

His illness was onerous to me and I wished he didn't have need of any further therapy. His personality was just as execrable to Sarah, too, as I could tell from her reaction. I was beginning to understand Sarah more and more as the days went by, and had an abiding interest in her which I hadn't allowed myself to enjoy heretofore. She seemed more friendly, too, or perhaps I just wished it were true. She'd even taken to occasionally bringing her lunch and eating in the office rather than walking home at noon. I had taken to keeping cold cuts in the refrigerator and occasionally fixing my own also, though most of the time I skipped lunch to make whatever house calls were necessary.

On the way back to the office today I stopped in my landlord's store to buy a candy bar, a substitute lunch, and the only lunch for which there was time. Business was slow for Mr. Brownley, and he was in a talkative mood.

"Hey, Doc," he addressed me, "haven't seen you for a long

time. "How's the Hippocratic practice goin' these days?" He was trying to be clever and friendly, but had trouble with the word.

"Same old sixes and sevens," I said.

"Say, I hear'd you did a right fine job bringin' the Gentry young'un into this old world a while back. He's sure proud of that son."

"Yes," I said, "it was a nice boy. Good healthy lad—we didn't weigh it but I'd guess it was around eight pounds or so."

"Well, he's sure pleased. His missus is a right fine lady, too."

I had to agree.

"Say, how's things workin' out upstairs, there?" he inquired. "Got enough heat? A landlord oughta know, yu know." His idea of a joke.

"Yes, plenty of that. You might turn the furnace off." I edged toward the door, but he seemed to want to say more as he edged along with me. We walked outside and he commented on the weather which needed none as the day was hot and muggy as usual.

"There's a few clouds getherin' o'er there. Suppose we're goin' to have some rain?"

"Could be," I said.

"Well, guess you want to get back to work, Doc, so I'd better let you go. Oh, by the way, hear tell yu'all had Miss Bennett in as a patient the other day. How's she? Hope she ain't ailin'." Now I knew why he wanted to talk.

News travels, I see, and her visit apparently was news. I didn't tell anyone and I'm sure Sarah wouldn't have. I supposed he had seen her get out of the car from his grocery. It wasn't too surprising at that.

"No, she's all right," I said.

"I didn't get to see her myself, just heard she'd been in. Heard she had a cold, huh?"

I was truly amazed. He couldn't have seen that.

"Amazing how word gets around, isn't it?" I said in wonderment. Now I was really getting interested in his informant.

"Yeah, ain't it though. Well, better let you go, Doc. Nice to see you." He left. He wasn't volunteering anything either. I unwrapped my candy bar and ascended the steps to the office wondering again how everyone finds things out so fast.

I walked in, candy bar in hand, chewing a bite, deep in thought. Sarah chided, "From the expression on your face you don't seem to be enjoying your lunch, Doctor."

"No," I smiled, "something amazing just happened to confuse me and I guess I was deep in thought when I came in. Candy isn't much of a lunch to be ecstatic about, anyway."

"Let me make you a sandwich, then," she offered. "There're cold cuts in the refrigerator and I have some bread in there I use for sandwiches, even some butter and mayonnaise."

"Fine," I answered, "if we have time."

"Your afternoon hasn't begun yet. Mrs. Jacobs had an appointment at two, but she's not here yet." It was about 1:30, so there was plenty of time. "Salami all right?" she asked from the refrigerator door.

I watched her standing there, back to me, and once again had that urge to put my arms around her. Her legs were beautiful. The rounded curve of her buttocks, so evenly proportioned, exquisitely formed, quickened my pulse.

She laughed and said, "You know, if anyone saw us making you a sandwich out of here where all these urine and blood samples are, they'd think we were crazy." That statement brought me back to earth.

"That's the value of being medically trained, I guess. All doctors and nurses seem to be unafraid of such things. I remember how squeamish my mother was about keeping food isolated from all would-be contaminants, but when I was in medical school I couldn't worry about germs and contamination or I'd never have made it through. People really don't know how sterile blood and urine are."

"It's really more the thought," she said, "than the fact."

"Yep, maybe Pasteur was wrong after all," I added, "and there's no such thing as bacteria."

We laughed, ending the subject. Then, I became serious. "Something troubles me, you know, Sarah. Let me ask you about it. You haven't talked to anyone about Miss Bennett's visit, have you?"

"I don't think so. I may have inadvertently told someone I had seen her again recently, but I don't remember discussing it with anyone. Why?"

"Well, I met Mr. Brownley at noon downstairs—that's what I was thinking about when I came upstairs, and he asked me about her. He knew that she had been here. I figured he could have seen her come in but he said, also, he'd heard she had a cold. Where would he get that information?"

Sarah looked genuinely perplexed. "Well," she said, "I certainly didn't tell anybody that, I'm sure."

I hastened to assure her I wasn't accusing her but was just puzzled. "She must have told someone herself and it got back to him. Oh, I know, I'll bet the druggist told him. He probably figured it out from the prescriptions you wrote." Good old Sarah. So much for that mystery.

"You're right, Sarah, I'm sure. That's what's wrong with doubting everything. I guess Melanie Bennett is such a popular figure around here that anything new about her would be the choice piece of news about town."

"Not 'popular,' Doctor, mysterious and prominent. The whole family's been that way. I wonder if she likes all the talk, or even knows about it."

"Probably not," I said in answer to both questions. The sandwich tasted good and I washed it down with a Coke.

"Thanks, Sarah," I said, "you're a fine cook."

"A born flatterer," she replied, accepting the compliment with a curtsy.

The bell rang and she left to answer it, closing my office door. I swallowed the last bite and walked to the window. In the sky, small clouds were present in large numbers like tufts of cotton, arranged in rows. There were large cumulus clouds in the far distance with dark, flat bases. A mackerel sky, I said to myself, probably rain tonight. We could surely use it. It would cool us off for a short while even though tomorrow would be humid. It would also settle this red clay dust for a few days. Every night when I took off my white shirt the collar was filthy with a reddish sweat stain from this dust. Thank gosh Mrs. Apperson agreed to do my shirts and other laundry for a fee. I'd hate to do them myself.

Sarah knocked on the door and I called to "come in." She entered with a new chart for Mrs. Malvina Jacobs. Mrs. Jacobs was thin, of moderate height, with dark hair, dark eyes, sallow complexion and a frown on her face. She greeted me pleasantly but curtly and seated herself without being asked. Her eyes were dull, her brow wrinkled and her breath came in short gasps. I bet myself she'd have headaches and my original reaction proved correct. I asked her how she was today. She answered quickly, "Doctor, I have such awful headaches lately."

"Just lately? Are they something new?" I asked.

"No, I've always had some headaches. Even as a young girl I had them. With my periods mostly. For awhile after my youngest was born I was free of them but then they came back. Never like this though."

"How long have they been worse?" I inquired.

"For several months now I've almost never been free of them." Her whole body reflected her agony. She seemed to droop, her forehead tense, her neck stiff, and she constantly wrung her hands when she wasn't rubbing the back of her neck.

"My mother had awful migraines—do you think I could have inherited it from her?"

"I don't know," I answered, "are they one-sided headaches, and are there any visual changes with them?"

"I don't know what you mean, doctor—they are sort of all over and mainly in the back of my neck."

This was sort of a general answer. A specific answer might help a lot in diagnosis. I'd try again. "Do they cause any changes in your vision?"

"Well, I don't know. They are what I'd call blinding headaches."

"You mean you actually can't see?"

"Not exactly. You see I feel them across here," indicating the forehead, having just told me they were mainly in the back of the neck, "and when they are bad I sometimes feel as though I can't open my eyes well."

I persisted. "Are you ever actually blind, actually unable to see?"

"Well, I don't know. When the kids holler I think I'll go out of my mind. It pounds and pounds."

"Do you ever see double?"

She laughed, "When they holler I see triple."

I decided I'd leave that particular subject and come back to it later. I wasn't going to get a straight answer. Headache patients often won't give straightforward answers, almost to the point of annoyance. There's often a vast amount of hostility related to headaches whether the primary cause or secondary to the constant annoying pain. Patients are often angered by the persistence of the examiner in asking questions. ("Just treat me and stop all those damnable questions.") To her, it's probably like being home, feeling sick, and having her children fire seemingly endless and nonsensical questions at her. Yet from my standpoint certain specific questions might help in delineating the cause. Unfortunately, the patient often can't describe his or her symptoms, since the most prominent and remembered feature is the pain, making diagnosis more difficult. Other symptoms are secondary and often overlooked. All the questions, though, are vitally important to the differential diagnosis. "Well, let's see," I said, "do you ever get sick to your stomach with them?"

"Sometimes when they hurt so bad I feel sick." Another general answer.

"I mean actively sick, sick to the point of vomiting?"

"Well, once in a while I vomit."

"How often would you say?" I continued

"Well, I don't know. I don't count them."

"Would you say once a week?" I persisted.

"Maybe. I don't know, sometimes more, sometimes less."

Where now? I wondered. Again, I lacked a straight answer. Let's see. "How about dizziness? Do you ever get dizzy?" What I wanted to know was if she ever had true vertigo. I could have asked it directly but felt it was better to start with general questions even though I'd get general answers. It's nice to hear all of a patient's symptoms without prompting. That way I wouldn't chance suggesting symptoms which the patient might incorporate in her illness. Some patients will agree to everything you ask, have every symptom, or soon adopt them after you've suggested them.

"Yes, I feel dizzy, but then I always have at times."

"Is this dizziness that you have now different than others you've had in the past?"

"I'm not dizzy now," she answered, somewhat annoyed.

"I don't mean right this minute, but what you've had recently."

"Well, I haven't had any recently."

"When was the last time?"

"Well, I don't remember, maybe a week ago."

That would be recently to me. "When you were dizzy, Mrs. Jacobs, did the room spin in circles?"

"Sort of," was her answer.

"Did it spin bad enough that you couldn't stand up?"

"I don't know, I always lie down when I get dizzy." From her tone of voice I could tell she was becoming more annoyed. I predicted she'd think my questions a bunch of tiresome idiotic nonsense when she was suffering so badly. This was the only point on which Carolyn and I had argued when she had had headaches. In her instance I had felt so guilty about persisting with questions I finally had given up. I just had loved her too much. This time, though, I'd be persistent. It would be difficult. Yet I didn't want Mrs. Jacobs to be sent off with aspirin if there was something more serious going on.

"When you have these headaches do you have trouble walking?" I asked.

"I just feel like lying down." An evasive answer.

"Well, do you have any other symptoms you haven't told me about?"

"Such as?" she answered.

"Oh, things like changes in your sense of smell." Now she had me making the suggestions.

"Well, smells bother me when I have a headache, just like noise. I seem to hear better, or maybe it just seems everything is louder." Her appearance showed she was tiring badly.

"Do you see double?" I repeated, hoping this time she'd just answer straightforwardly.

"Honestly, Doctor," she said, "can't we stop all these questions? I'm so hot and my head hurts something awful. Can't you just give me a shot to relieve it and let me go home to rest and lie down?"

"Of course I can," I said with compassion, "but you should be examined before I give you anything. I don't really know what's wrong with you."

"It's just one of my usual sick headaches," she said, "I'm so tired. It's hot and I feel sick. Can't we let the examination go?"

This kind of entreaty is hard to turn down. It's hard not to be empathetic since everyone has had a headache and felt similarly. For her comfort I decided it was better to give in and I gave her the shot she requested but only with the understanding she'd return another day when she felt better for a complete exam. She left then without making another appointment, but that wasn't unusual since most patients came in without appointments, and she couldn't hope to know in advance when she would be free of a headache.

I was frustrated. I couldn't dispel the feeling that she had something serious. I had no real assurance she'd come back as agreed, none that she'd ever come back, and if in truth she had a serious illness that she'd come to the office in time. And if she did have something serious maybe I wouldn't recognize it.

Dammit, I said, *I should have made her stay.* I thought about her symptoms and how little I knew about her. My mind wandered terribly—thoughts directed to diagnosis, thoughts of self-doubt, self-incrimination, angry thoughts, hateful thoughts, frightened thoughts. I really knew nothing of importance. She had headaches, blinding in type, which made her dizzy occasionally, how dizzy I didn't know; sick occasionally, how sick I also didn't know; maybe her sense of smell was different. Not much to go on. If she had a brain tumor! No, no, no! Every headache isn't a brain tumor. Maybe I ought to send her to Duke. They had the facilities there for diagnosis, much better than I. If she did have a brain tumor I couldn't operate on her here. I'd just have to send her there anyhow. I wish I'd insisted she take another appointment. The more I thought about the case, the more I worried I'd miss the real diagnosis and the more convinced I became she should be referred. Headache cases are hard cases to diagnose and worse to treat. Usually they need lots of attention, and I really don't have time to give all of that. Such patients are hard to deal with sometimes, too. I was talking myself out of the case. Damn those doubts. If I could just find a bona fide reason for referral. God, headache cases are real headaches to me, and I had been in training as a neurosurgeon!

Sarah came in then to tell me about my next case. I was grateful for the distraction from my previous thoughts. This day, however, had been ruined by another problem which tested my courage. All those doubts were loose again. I'd hoped they were gone after Mrs. Gentry's delivery. They weren't. What would it take!

The rest of the day was fogged by continued thought about the headache patient. Thank heaven all of the other patients for the day were minor problems which required but little attention and concentration. At the end of the day I was grateful for the close of the office activities. Maybe now I could think less about the headache case. I wondered how many children Mrs. Jacobs had. I hadn't asked. She could easily have tension headaches, I thought. All of her symptoms were of that nature. Only my fears kept me brooding about the possibility of a more serious disease.

Sarah got ready to leave and seemed to be hurrying. "What's the hurry?" I asked.

"Guess you haven't noticed there's a storm coming up fast," she answered. "I didn't bring my raincoat, so I wanted to hurry."

The lightning flashed brightly and a few seconds later the thunder clapped. I said to Sarah, "Three miles away."

She looked puzzled and asked, "What did you say, Doctor?"

"Three miles away. You know that old superstition that if you count the seconds from the flash to the thunder, that's how far the lightning is away. I counted about ten seconds."

"I know but it may rain any minute," she said. And then the first drops of rain, as if on cue, began to patter on the roof. Sarah said she was going to leave immediately and ran to the door calling good night. I called to her that I'd be glad to drive her but she said, "It's only two blocks and I'll be all right if I hurry. Good night." And she was gone.

I heard her steps race down the stairs, went to the window, and watched her race across the street with a newspaper over her head and on toward home. The lightning flashed and I felt frightened briefly that Sarah would be struck down. My pulse raced slightly and then I realized she was still all right and dashing on down the street. I could just make out a distant triangle of white newspaper gradually disappearing from view. It was beginning to rain hard now. As Sarah had said, I hadn't noticed that the storm was coming. It was dark from the storm clouds and lights were on here and there around town. Even my consultation room light was on and I hadn't noticed it. Sarah, always aware, must have wondered how I missed the approaching storm. How could I tell her I was so worried about Mrs. Jacobs that I hadn't even been aware the sky was dark.

Another flash of lightning dimmed the lights momentarily and recalled my attention to the storm. I turned out the light then, turned the swivel chair around, leaned back, and put my feet up on the windowsill to watch the storm. I'd always liked storms. Something about rain seemed to soothe my nerves. The storm was reaching its height with one flash after another for an almost continuous clamor. I wondered which tall tree in which forest acted as a lightning-rod for each bolt. I hoped no one would be foolish enough to be out in this storm and be the recipient of one of those bolts. Such a catastrophe would really ruin the evening, since I'd then be called to help. Inside, in the dryness of my office, there seemed to be no danger. It was always amazing to me how the inside of an office or home or building could seem so fair under certain circumstances, yet so foreboding under others. If the storm or danger is without, the inside is secure; whereas, if the suspected danger is within, the same outside can seem so protective. I wondered if Sarah felt secure alone in that big house amidst the storm. A flash lit the silhouettes of surrounding buildings, trees, and distant houses. Automatically I turned in the direction of Sarah's house. I imagined I could see her busying herself with tidying up the house and preparing dinner. She had a frilly apron over her white uniform and it hid her breasts except for the edges. They seemed so alluring behind that apron. Amazing how many times I'd seen them in a dress, yet in my imagination they were even more alluring when only an edge was visible. I longed to hold her in my arms.

A particularly loud thunderclap diverted my attention from the illusion to the reality. I realized I shouldn't continue these thoughts, as they were too unsettling and I had yet another evening to spend alone. Also, I had to go out for dinner, although the restaurant was only a few doors away. But, there was no hurry. My thoughts strayed once again to Sarah and I saw her eyes, sparkling for sure, her laugh, her smile, her white teeth, her sensuous lips, her curved breasts. My fantasy followed the curves down across her hips, down her beautiful legs. I took her in my arms. My lips were close to hers. *Goddammit, why can't I stop this stupid daydreaming. I am not in love with her.* I knew that I couldn't be in love with anyone like I had been with Carolyn. It was almost sacrilegious to forget her memory to the point that I could allow Sarah to affect me this way. I remembered Carolyn's beautiful smile, her lovely eyes, her sweet voice, her complete feminity. So many of my med school colleagues wanted to date her and once one had when she was angry with me, but in the end he had been cast aside and once again we had realized how much we meant to each other.

She was so willing to do what I liked. Being a history nut, whenever we could go anywhere on a trip, I would choose to visit some historic site. And boring as it was for her, she always went along, willingly, always interested in what we saw. I'd always regale her with inconsequential facts, and she'd find them interesting. She'd listen attentively and then marvel at my wealth of information, usually obtained from reading about it before we went. Many times I apologized for dragging her along but to her it was only important she be with me. No two people could have been so sincerely and completely in love. When in Baltimore we had climbed to a parapet of Fort McHenry and I stood there amid the cannon, transfixed, with the Stars and Stripes flying nearby. As I saw it that day, it was tattered and torn, waving as it had in song so many times. I turned to Carolyn and said, "Honey, do you know that this flag had fifteen stripes and fifteen stars at the time the song was written?" She hadn't. Big deal. It was one of those inconsequential facts of which I had so many.

A few moments later, as I stood there entranced, she shook my arm and said, mockingly, "Francis, darling, do you see the rockets' red glare and hear the bombs bursting in air?"

I turned to her with a smile, having been well analyzed by

her psychiatric acumen. She ran and I chased her around the parapet until I caught her. Laughing gaily, we embraced and kissed and laughed again. Suddenly, Carolyn put her hand to her head over one eye, bent her head slightly, and grimaced. I was alarmed. "Honey," I said, "what happened? Are you all right?"

"I guess so," she answered, "it's nothing."

I wouldn't accept her evasion. I demanded a fuller explanation.

"It's nothing, really. I just have a headache."

"Have you had it long, honey?" I asked. "Did it just start?" Always playing doctor. My role.

"Sort of all day but I was awfully tired when I got off the late shift last night. It sort of started then. I took an aspirin, though, and that seemed to take care of it."

I must have looked terribly worried as she reassured me. "Oh, please, don't look so worried. I'll be all right. Everyone's entitled to a headache once in a while. You don't think it means anything serious, do you?" She now sounded worried.

Now I was on the spot to reassure her. I wondered if the fact that I was a neurosurgical resident and had shown considerable concern had frightened her a little. "No, no, no," I said, "one swallow doesn't make a summer, you know. There's nothing to worry about. You're probably tired. That's all. And here I am dragging you off on another history lesson. I don't blame you for having a headache."

"What with all the noise of bombs bursting?" she chided.

We smiled and laughed again and the incident was over. But as we left to return home, we didn't laugh and chatter as we usually did. Both of us were concerned, I was sure. I turned to her as we walked, silent and serious, and said, "I love you very much."

She thanked me as she always did when I told her I loved her, as if she was complimented and then returned my love.

I couldn't dispel the thought that something was wrong. I entreated her to go to bed early when we arrived home and told her to call me immediately if her headache got worse. As I left her at the nurses' home I rubbed the back of my neck over and over again, moving my head to and fro, and realized that I, too, had a headache.

Once again, the lightning flashed and automatically and silently I counted out the seconds. The thunder sounded distantly. Four miles away, I thought. The storm must be passing. I realized that an hour had passed, the rain was still falling gently as it probably would for a while. The room had a deep silence except for the raindrops, a deadly silence, in fact. Once again, now that the storm was passing, the room in its silence took on a loneliness that brought back the sense of foreboding I'd forgotten for a while. Obviously, I didn't like being alone.

The phone rang. In a way, I disliked the phone. Too often its ring meant an emergency that hadn't arisen during the day. Most people managed to come in for non-emergencies during office hours, so late calls often meant problems. It had to be answered, though.

"Hello! Doctor Jenson," I said, picking it up with some trepidation. It was Sarah.

"How do you do, Doctor?" she said. "I have a serious problem. In my worried frenzy I made a serious mistake. Unforgivable. I cooked too much for dinner. Must have been the storm upsetting me. I need someone to help me eat it. Can you think of anyone that I might call to help me out of this dilemma?"

"That is indeed a serious problem. Let me think," I answered. "Only one. Myself. But how did you know I liked home cooking?"

"Mrs. Apperson told me," she kidded.

"Yeah, I'll just bet that's true. You know I'd love to come over. How about letting me go home and clean up first?"

"It's almost ready and fried chicken is much better when eaten as soon as done, so I'll accept you as you are, if that's all right."

"It is, it is," I said, "never keep a lady waiting. I'll be right over. By the way, I'll bring some champagne that's in the refrigerator if you don't mind."

"A most gallant offer and one a lady would never refuse," she said. "See you soon. Bye-bye."

I was very pleased. It felt good to realize Sarah was interested enough to invite me to dinner. No one cooks too much chicken by accident. I welcomed the chance to have her companionship, yet wondered why Sarah had decided to invite me. I suspected she felt sorry for me being alone, yet I hoped she didn't because I didn't want to go there as a result of her pity but rather because she desired my company. I quickly threw off my shirt and tie, washed my face and combed my hair, then shaved, cutting my face in several places. I donned the clean shirt I kept in the office, but up to now had never used, and my tie, and coat, and looked around to see if I'd forgotten anything. Nothing but my head, I thought. I started for the door. Halfway down the stairs I remembered the champagne and went back. I wasn't excited. Not much. I was amazed at my reaction. Sarah mustn't know I was this way. *Calm down*, I thought, *calm down*.

It was still raining slightly, for which I felt grateful. Rain calmed me. I remembered how often Carolyn and I used to walk in the rain. On such occasions I would turn up my collar, turn my pipe bowl down and we'd walk for hours. She had always worn a scarf which only partially covered her beautiful blond hair. The ends would always be wet when we returned. She never worried about it, though. We never worried about anything in those days. I had loved that blond hair so. I had loved everything about her. It had been hard to accept her death.

I arrived at Sarah's house. As I shut off the ignition and lights I reminded myself that reminiscing about Carolyn wasn't a good prelude to a dinner with Sarah. She'd hope for gaiety and light conversation and I shouldn't be morose or arrive with Carolyn on my mind. For a minute I really couldn't understand what I was doing here at all. In the past, I had tried to date a couple of times but canceled at the last minute. The longing I still had for Carolyn had been too overwhelming.

I got out of the car and walked slowly to the door, hiding the champagne beneath my coat, lest the neighbors see it. I was sure they were already talking about the other night and here I was again. I knocked and Sarah was at the door quickly. She turned on the porch light, and I felt even more conspicuous. I'm sure no one expected me not to date or not to go out to dinner, yet somehow I felt terribly out of place and unprofessional, like a 1920s suitor with a straw hat and a big bunch of flowers in my hand hiding candy behind my back.

Sarah opened the door. I was overwhelmed. She looked marvelous. I almost dropped the champagne. "Hi," she said, "come on in."

As I struggled to gain control again of the champagne bottle, I managed an answer, "Sarah, it was so nice of you to invite me to dinner. I can't tell you how much."

"Come in, please, come in," she laughed. There I stood on the mat talking. I was embarrassed I hadn't gone in immediately. But I recovered and handed her the bottle.

"I brought this to help brighten the evening."

That was a dumb thing to say. It was as if I was implying the evening might otherwise be dull and needed brightening. But Sarah eyed the champagne appreciatively and said, "Yes, it will cause a lot of sparkle, I'll bet. Come in."

"Oh yes," I said. I wiped my feet on the mat as Mother had always taught me was the polite thing to do. But that teaching was more to impress young ladies' mothers than the young ladies, I was sure. Still it was a good lesson and applied well on this rainy night.

She led me into the living room. It was very tastefully decorated with modest furnishings, one antique highboy desk which was solid cherry and an occasional side table with marble top on which there was a very mature and large fern.

"Please sit down," she said, indicating the sofa, "and if you'll excuse me, I'll get a tray and glasses for the champagne." She disappeared through the dining room into the kitchen and the swinging door shut behind her. She soon returned with a small silver tray and two cut crystal glasses which, I suspected, were dessert glasses.

She put the bottle and glasses on a mahogany coffee table and then sat at the other end of the sofa. I looked at her in silence for a minute overwhelmed with how beautiful she was. She said, "I hope those glasses will do."

I then realized I was staring at her beauty and ignoring the job of opening and pouring, "Oh, yes, very nicely," I said. "I was staring, I mean, yes, I'll open it right away."

As I unwound the metal foil covering the cap I realized I'd never opened one of these before, though I'd seen it done in the movies—where, it occurred to me, they had never shown anyone take the wire off, just the popping of the cork. Finally I solved the dilemma of the wire, removed it, and turned to put it down somewhere. The jostling the bottle received at the front door had apparently freed enough carbon dioxide to increase the inner pressure greatly, since almost as soon as I turned away I heard Sarah say, "Oh," and turned back just in time to see the cork clear the top of the bottle. This was followed by a loud pop and the disappearance of the cork across the room in a sky-bound arc, returning to earth somewhere in the dining room. And that was followed by a sudden fountain of champagne which ran down the bottle. I quickly poured it into the glasses, though, losing only a little on the floor. Sarah laughed heartily and I, too. "As you can readily see," I said, "I'm an old pro at this." We laughed again. I wouldn't tell her it was my first.

"Well," I said, raising the glass, "let's see. Here's to the finest office nurse I've ever had."

She laughed and said, "And to the only one you've ever had, but I accept the compliment, thank you."

We sipped the champagne then and oohed about how cold it was, how bubbly and how good it tasted. "It's fine vintage champagne," I said, indicating my vast knowledge of the subject of wines. "At least that's what the clerk told me who sold it to me."

"It certainly must be," she said, "I'm no authority on it, but I like the taste of it."

I continued my bluff. "It has a smooth flavor, very dry (whatever that means) goes down with so little effort. I like your glasses."

"They're only dessert glasses," she said, "though I guess they'll have to do."

"Oh, they are just fine," I said, "and so pretty."

"They were Mother's," she answered. "Mother had a few very nice things and one was her set of crystal. She was very proud of it."

"I should think so," I said. "Your mother isn't living, I assume."

"She died, many years ago, giving birth to my brother. He died soon after. I was little then."

I wished now I hadn't asked. This was not the sort of topic

one discusses while drinking champagne.

"But you've certainly grown up now," I said. She brightened. "What have you done to yourself. You're so—so different somehow." I couldn't say so beautiful, even though that's what I meant.

"You've never seen me like this before," she said.

You are so right, I thought, *I never have seen you this way, so stunning with that gorgeous blond hair falling to your shoulders, those deep blue eyes and sensuous lips, the breasts I've noticed for such a long time. Behind that apron they are so marvelous, not large or small, just medium as we learned in med school.* A poor description for such fine anatomy, and undoubtedly devised by Victorian doctors. There must be a more perceptively descriptive classification possible. I continued my examination mentally. She was thin in a way, maybe 105 and 5 feet 5. Her legs were very shapely with narrow ankles and tapered calves. I could easily imagine how beautiful they were where they joined the pelvis. The pelvis! God, have some more champagne. Sarah must have been aware of my staring at her torso since she said, "Oh, I forgot to take off my apron. I'm sorry."

"No, no," I said. "It's beautiful." *What an asinine statement.* "I mean, you're, well, you know. You're beautiful and I guess I never noticed it before. That's strictly a medical comment, though," I chided. I poured more champagne in our glasses.

"Well, I'll have to admit I let my hair down on purpose tonight. I always wear it up in the office. It makes me look more professional and I like the way the cap sits on the top of my hair when it's up."

"Come to think of it," I said with mock seriousness, stroking my chin, "so do I." *That's a silly thing to say*, I thought, *what's the matter with me. I'd better get hold of myself.*

"It was a lovely rain, don't you think?" I asked. Without letting her answer, I went on. "I like rain, and storms, don't you? Storms have always fascinated me. My mother used to get us up out of bed every time there was a storm and take us into the basement. She was afraid of tornadoes and to her every storm was an impending tornado. I used to find it quite exciting. Sometimes she used to keep us home from school for the same reason. If the sky was orange and the air still, that always meant a tornado to her. We weren't at all unhappy about staying home, though. The rain has always been soothing to me." Suddenly, I realized I was talking too much. "I'm sorry, Sarah, I really am talking too much."

"Oh, I like it," she said, "I so rarely have anyone to talk to, particularly at night. All I seem to do is read and write letters, and occasionally listen to the radio."

I had stopped hearing her when she said letters. I guessed I knew to whom she wrote.

"I'm sort of the same," I said. "I listen to records and read a lot, too. Shakespeare's my favorite. You remember 'This above all, to thine own self be true'?"

"I don't know much Shakespeare," she said, "but I do know that if we don't eat soon the chicken will be overdone."

We both laughed and I said with flourish, "Well then, lead on and this poor mortal will follow, forsooth."

"Pray now, aren't you the gentleman," she said, and led me into the dining room. We carried the champagne with us. The oval mahogany table was covered with an Irish linen embroidered tablecloth and had two place settings with china and two crystal goblets from her mother's set. Over the table hung a Victorian Tiffany-style lamp, but Sarah had preferred candlelight. She asked me to be seated, but I waited until she came in with the plates. My plate was obvious as it had two extra pieces of chicken and a generous helping of mashed potatoes and peas. I helped her into her chair and then took mine at the other end. It was only about four feet away but seemed so terribly far from her.

"Would you like to say grace?" she asked.

"No, thank you, you'd better say it, Sarah. I'm sort of rusty."

"We thank thee, O Lord, for all your blessings. Guide us and protect us, and give us the courage to face each day's problems with calm and assurance. We ask it in the Lord's name. Amen."

I wondered if she knew my problems, but rather than meet her glance, I looked down and picked up a chicken leg. "It smells and looks divine," I said.

"Not divine," she corrected, "not even mortal. Just chicken."

"It's a marvelous change from my usual evening fare," I hastened to add.

She was gay again now after the solemnity of grace.

"I agree," she said, "and it's even better since you're here for dinner. I couldn't bear the thought of being alone tonight. You see, it's my birthday."

"Your birthday?" I hollered. At least it seemed I was hollering. "Why didn't you tell me? For sooth, fair maiden, I never knew. May I ask how old you are?"

"A gentleman never asks a lady, you know, but I'll tell you, since doctors know all, it seems. I'm twenty-two. How old are you?"

"I'm twenty-six, I hate to say. Just awhile ago, though." I didn't want to seem too old for her.

"I like older men," she smiled, reading my thoughts.

"Sarah," I said, "you're incorrigible, but in a nice way. I wish you'd told me. I would have bought you a present."

"Just you and your champagne is enough," she said and raised her glass in another toast. I raised mine, also.

"It *is* good," I said.

She agreed and admitted to feeling a little giddy, to which I also agreed. We ate then for a minute and she asked if I liked it. "It's delicious," I said. "When I came south to Duke, you know, I was really looking forward to Shuthern fried chicken. I almost said that wrong. I think this champagne is affecting me. But everything I got, that is, all the chicken I ate, was so greasy, I was terribly disappointed. But yours is de-lishus. Wow! This champagne is good too."

"Yes," Sarah laughed and agreed. "How is it that you had a bottle in the refrigerator?"

"Well, that's a really long story," I said. "But, if you have time." I had wanted for so long to talk about anything, she should never have asked me to start. I told her everything from the day I was born, up to and through college and into medical school while we ate. She interrupted then to ask if I wanted more to eat.

"Sarah," I said, "I am sated." I had already eaten three extra pieces of chicken.

"I just have apple pie for dessert," she said.

"My very favorite," I answered.

"I don't like to interrupt you," she said, "but I'll get the dessert and put on the coffee. I think I need it."

When she cleared the table and left for the kitchen, I shook my head to clear away the cobwebs. She returned and placed dessert in front of me.

"Tell me," she said, "from what you've said I get the impression you are very interested in Civil War history since you've visited so many historic places in the South." I hadn't told her I'd visited them with Carolyn though.

"Yes," I said, "very much."

"Well, how did you get so interested in the Civil War?" she said.

"Well, maybe because I've heard so much about Abraham Lincoln at home," I said. "My mother and dad talked about him all the time. He was a household god of sorts and I came to revere him just as much. But I guess Lincoln is a bad word to a southern girl."

"Yes," she laughed, "Robert E. Lee might be better." We laughed together.

"I'll tell you, anyhow," I said, "my great-grandmother worked as Lincoln's housekeeper when he lived in Illinois."

"You're kidding," she said.

"No," I said, "it's true. Mary Todd Lincoln bit her in the arm in one of her rages and Grandfather told me his mother wore those teeth marks to her grave."

"That's fabulous," Sarah said. "I can't believe I know personally the great-grandson of a celebrity." We laughed again.

"What was her name?" Sarah asked.

"Sarah Jenson," I said.

There was a long silence. I'd never thought of the coincidence before. Sarah looked stunned and I seemed unable to offer any diverting conversation.

"It's a pretty name, though," I offered.

"Yes," she said, "I think so, too." It had sobered us somewhat. "I'll get the coffee," she said.

We went back into the living room. We sat again on the sofa and she said, "You never told me how you got that delicious champagne."

"I did tell you it was a long story, didn't I? Maybe too long for one evening." I was balking at continuing the explanation.

"Oh, please don't leave," she pleaded. "I think I hear thunder again. You couldn't go out in this storm."

"Why not?" I chided. "You did, to prepare this wonderful surprise party on your birthday. It isn't fair that you should have to do it."

I realized then that Sarah was lonely, too. I wanted to hold her in my arms close to me. My heart beat wildly. The urge was so great I decided I'd better start a conversation again.

"You asked about the champagne," was all I could think to say. It was a topic I didn't really want to discuss fully, not with Sarah, anyhow.

"Well, I bought it in Baltimore, just before I came in to practice." That was a lie. Actually, Carolyn and I had bought it on a lark one night when we were feeling giddy. We intended using it when I opened my first office as a neurosurgeon.

"I was going to drink it when I opened my office in sort of an opening celebration, but when the day finally arrived I somehow didn't feel in a celebrating mood, so I never needed it." My somber mood needed change. "But I'm glad now I saved it for this special occasion."

"Me, too. I can't thank you enough for bringing it with you. It was my very first and I really liked it. I've never had much to drink. Have you?"

"Obviously not, as you can see," I admitted honestly.

Sarah wanted me to stay awhile longer I could see, so I told her of the parties we used to have at the medical school and how we used to steal the lab alcohol as it was 180 proof, so to speak, and used it to mix with grape juice. "We called the drinks Purple Jesus." I also told her with great flair of how my roommate, a Virginia boy, had gone out into the country with me to buy some corn liquor one day. The Lincolns' house sort of reminded me of the place we had bought it.

"Later that night we went back to the hospital in a hilarious state, mildly staggering, and ran into our chief who was a nice guy really, though we didn't know it. We gave him the silliest greeting. His name was Kelly and of course I had to ask him if he was of French or German descent. We were put to bed by someone and the next morning awakened rudely by our chief who wanted to make rounds immediately on Sunday morning. You never refuse the chief anything, of course. We staggered to attention, but had a monumental hangover. Our chief put us down on a gurney, said 'stay there' and then came back soon with two IV's of dextrose and water loaded with vitamins, put them in our arm veins and tied the bottle around our necks, then made us get up and make rounds with him while receiving an IV for the hangover. If you could have seen the looks on the faces of patients receiving IVs when their doctors came in carrying one around their neck, you'd have died laughing."

Sarah was laughing and so was I. We laughed and laughed. Suddenly, I remembered how Carolyn and I had laughed so much and then I felt guilty that I was repeating the same with Sarah. My sudden guilt was overwhelming and very sobering. Sarah noticed the change immediately, too, and asked if I was all right.

"Oh, yes, I'm fine," I lied. "I remembered something just now that somehow I'd forgotten about."

She waited for me to continue, but when I didn't, asked, "What?" She persisted. "Can you tell me? I'd be very happy to listen." I said nothing.

"I really have enjoyed having you here tonight and would love to help in any way I can, if you'll let me." She could see I was troubled.

"It's just that—" I paused. I was trying to think of a diverting conversation and it was significant that Mrs. Jacobs came to mind.

"It's that I suddenly remembered Mrs. Jacobs who was in today. Probably the association of the terrible headache with the hangover I had that morning reminded me of her."

"Oh," she said, not convinced that was the trouble.

"Before you called I was thinking about her and her headache. I sort of feel I didn't diagnose her properly. I can't get it out of my mind that she has something serious."

"Such as what?" Sarah inquired.

"Well, a brain tumor, I guess. I really think I should send her down to Duke for a checkup."

"Couldn't you do the checkup?" she asked. "You have had some training in neurosurgery, haven't you?"

"Yes, but a limited amount. They really have the full equipment there, X-ray, EEG, the whole thing. She needs air encephalograms and skull films, tracings, even maybe burr holes."

Sarah persisted, "But you don't even know if she has a tumor yet or even that you suspect she does. There could be lots of reasons for headaches. She should have some other physical signs that would help you decide whether or not she might have a tumor before you refer her. Maybe you'd decide she didn't after you studied her awhile." Sarah was trying to encourage me.

"Yes, I guess you're right," I said. "I haven't done a physical on her yet and I wish I had, but you know, she had such a terrible headache when she was there—I couldn't refuse her a shot, and so I let her go home to bed without further ado."

"But that's because you're so compassionate. I've noticed this about you since I've worked for you." I wondered what else she'd noticed. "She'll come back," she reassured me, "and a couple of days or so won't make any difference really."

"No, you're right," I said, and she was. "But if even then I can't decide, I could let it go too long and she might have lost valuable time toward surgery and eventual recovery."

"Oh, I'm sure you're right, Doctor," she said. Now we were almost formal again. "I just thought, though, that since tumors aren't too common maybe there's be no harm in waiting a while longer and seeing what you could find out. It would be unlikely you'd overlook a symptom of major importance and lasting harm."

"I wish that were true, Sarah," I said, almost wistfully.

She tried to reassure me, seeing my disconsolate manner. "Perhaps you're too compassionate and worry too much about your patients."

Sarah was great, as if I hadn't already known it. She had my best interests in mind. There was no doubt of that. I hoped she liked me as much. I tried to lighten the conversation. "Sarah, I think you should have been a psychiatrist."

She laughed and said, "No, I'm just interested in you and I hate to see you troubled. I've enjoyed working with you so much the short time I've been there. And I do think you're a fine doctor."

"Wow," I said, "that's a nice compliment coming from you."

I decided I'd better leave. Soon I'd have that urge again to take her in my arms and kiss her. "I'd better go, Sarah," I said after considerable misgiving. "It's late and what will the neighbors think? You know."

She understood but I was sure she wasn't worried about the neighbors. We went to the door. I turned to her. "Thank you very much for the delicious dinner. I haven't enjoyed myself so much in years. I hope to see you again soon." We laughed.

"No sooner than in the morning," she said. "I haven't enjoyed myself so much in years, either."

"Let's see," I said, "August twentieth, I'll remember that, and next year I'll be prepared. I'll see that I take you to dinner somewhere."

"And I'll bring the champagne," she added.

We both laughed again and our eyes met. Hers were so blue, so lovely, so inviting. I felt a wonderful tension spreading through me, every nerve-ending tingling. I took her hand as if to shake it goodbye. "Sarah," I said, and hesitated. "I—"

"What was it you said," she reminded me, "'to thine own self be true.'"

She was irresistible. I gently pulled her to me, engulfed her in an embrace and kissed her rapturously. She met my kiss as willingly, and we held each other fast. Then I put my cheek to hers and said, "Oh Sarah." I felt her firm breasts against me and knew I'd never experienced such happiness. Truly, nothing could be like this. Somehow at this point I also knew instinctively I must leave before my rapturous mood led to deeper involvement. I released her and turned almost abruptly to the door, opened it, and walked out. She appeared puzzled.

"Good night and happy birthday, Sarah," I said, and after a short pause, "my darling." As I backed away from the door and as she closed it she threw me a kiss. I slipped and skidded down the stairs in excitement but landed on my feet.

I glowed from toe to ear, and it was definitely not due to champagne. The few raindrops still falling felt marvelous on my face. I lifted it and cupped my lips to catch them as they fell. I'll bet I looked a rare sight to the neighbors, who no doubt were watching. I got into the car and looked back toward the house. Throwing her a silent kiss I remembered Juliet's words, "This bud of love by summer's ripening breath may prove a beauteous flower when next we meet." For a minute I considered returning to the house under the pretense of helping with the dishes. But professionalism prevailed and I drove away. I hadn't felt as happy in years and years. I went directly home to bed without even looking to see what time it was. I hummed and whistled and lay in the dark looking at the ceiling with my hands behind my head, too excited to sleep. A gentle rain began to fall and the sounds of the drops on the roof soothed and mellowed me and soon I dozed off into a half-sleep state. What fun, what wonderful fun, I thought, just like Carolyn and me. Carolyn! A twinge of intense guilt spread through me and ruined my new-formed joy. "Carolyn," I said to the ceiling, "I'm sorry."

I lay back listening to the rain which had a different sound now, not nearly as comforting as previously. A lightning flash briefly lit the room casting the shadow of the cross-barred window frame on the wall. I looked at it and realized that truly I was in prison, hopelessly, irremediably, endlessly. "Sarah, dear Sarah, it isn't fair to you," I said. "Eyes, look your last. Arms, take your last embrace." Wasn't that what Shakespeare had said. Damn it, damn it, I repeated again and again turning in discomfiture until too tired to think.

The operating room doors swung back and forth in ever-decreasing arcs, one past the other until I knew they were closed forever. From a distance I could hear strange noises, at first the measured beat of an anesthesia machine discharging its used gases, then the sound of running water. Scrubbing, that's what they're doing. In a few minutes they would cut open that beloved head, the blood would be sticky and red in that beautiful blond hair. Oh God, I've got to break out of this barrier and run to her aid. The door, the door, I must get to the door—it's gone! A chair, that's it, hurry, hurry. The climb over the wall was difficult, almost impossible. I'd never reach the top in time. I'm slipping. I'm falling, down, down, down. A bright light shone in my face. I shielded my eyes. A grotesque face looked down at me in dismay. I'm there, I think, in the room. "You mustn't," I pleaded, "you mustn't do it." Snarling, accusing faces condemned my action, condemned my inaction. "You can't, you can't," I cried, "leave her alone. You mustn't. I didn't mean to ignore her symptoms. It's only because I loved her so deeply. Please don't kill her. It's not her fault. She trusted me. She shouldn't be punished. Punish *me*." I ran to her side to protect her, their circle of faces closed in on me; I turned to take her in my arms—*her head was bald!* Help, help, somebody help. Her hair was gone. That beautiful blond hair, all gone. "You butcher," I screamed. A large prognathic man walked slowly forward with heavy measured footsteps, raised a giant, gleaming cleaver and brought it down violently, severing the top of her head. The blood raced down her forehead and face in rivulets, in all directions. The man raised the cleaver again. "Oh no, no, no," I screamed. "God. Strike him dead. Strike him dead."

I sat up in bed, sweat pouring down my forehead. A loud thunder roll was subsiding. The pace of the rain quickened and my pulse raced frantically. I looked out through my prison bars, thinking, *Guilt is a cruel disciplinarian.*

Chapter 6

The dawning of the morning was almost a relief, the night having been restless because of disturbing, twisted dreams. I tried to remember my dream as soon as I awoke in hopes it could be analyzed, but memory of dreams is usually so short-lived that in a fleeting instant they are gone. Such thoughts are too painful to keep in one's mind. The mind has convenient pockets for disturbing memories, those too painful for consciousness, and as a result the painful conflicts are never really solved. Only in sleep can the mind risk the release of these thoughts, and even then the blunt truth is so unpleasant that the events are distorted and disguised—hardly recognizable as the original conflict. Nevertheless, the retreat of the disturbing thoughts, though unsolved, was welcomed. Being awake, even though not rested, was in this way therapeutic.

I was glad to be awake. It was much earlier than I usually awoke for the day's routine. The sky was a dull gray. A few raindrops still fell, but the main force of the storm had passed. I knew I wouldn't sleep any longer and that there was little point in remaining in bed. Activity would tend to bury those painful dreams deeper and dispel the unhappiness that attended them. I thought of Sarah, dear Sarah, and for a brief moment my thoughts were lightened, my leaden unhappiness gone. But those pleasant thoughts were brief, and gradually the disquietude returned. I had expected to be wild with excitement about seeing Sarah today when I had left her last night. Now I realized I almost dreaded the encounter which once held such promise. What had happened? I wondered if some of the exuberance and ebullience of last night which led to that wonderful embrace hadn't been based more on champagne than on real feeling for someone as lovely as she. If I were to go to the office and find I wasn't as attracted as I had been last night I would be terribly deflated. Yet in the cold, gray light of dawn and the slight chilliness of a wet morning, I couldn't help but feel that this might be the case. If only the sun could shine a little. Or if only I could doubt less. That might help.

I busied myself getting dressed and cleaned up as quietly as possible. I didn't want to awaken Mrs. Apperson who was probably going to sleep at least another hour. And I decided I'd leave her a note and go on down to the office for awhile, then to breakfast at the cafe. Cafe breakfast was usually greasy and unpleasant, but my appetite was poor this morning anyhow. Somehow, strangely, in my sour mood I could face the dirty cafe.

After dressing I left Mrs. Apperson a brief note saying only I would not be there for breakfast, offering no explanation. Strange how my doubts about myself led me to feel guilty even about that. She demanded no explanation and none was needed, yet my departure from normal routine was seemingly foolish and therefore I felt my behavior somewhat absurd and in need of explanation. It was really worthless to go to the office since there was nothing to do there that could occupy or divert me. But the walk to the office and cafe, along with the time consumed, would afford some needed activity. A walk on a wet morning at six A.M. would certainly cause comment though. Since I had never before gone walking at such an early hour, I decided to drive, hoping not to evoke gossip. Perhaps no prying eyes would as yet be awake. The office held little promise of better refuge from my thoughts than where I was, but it was more spacious than my bedroom and there was some solace in that. Maybe my presence there would even remind me of something needing attention. Activity is good diversion from unpleasant thoughts; if only I could find some! Doubts, doubts, indecision. Stupidity.

I left the house, closing the door behind me very quietly. It was only 6:20 A.M. Mrs. Apperson always arose about 6:45. I hurried to avoid an early arising on her part and the resultant confrontation. Even though the air was moist, it had a certain clamminess about it that assured that the coming day, with its inevitable heat, would be most unpleasant. The car had a musty smell inside and I half expected to find moss growing and hanging from the fenders. During the short trip to the office I couldn't get Sarah out of my mind—so sweet, so inviting, so warm. I wondered if she was up yet, and wanted to turn around immediately and go to her house to say hello. What would I say after hello? Darling? I love you? Last night was so marvelous, yet so unfinished somehow. I wished I'd held her longer in that embrace. It might be a long time before I had another opportunity. Her lips were so soft, so moist, so alluring and the tip of her tongue had just met mine so lightly. Her breasts—good God! I realized then I had to quit thinking that way. Maybe the office would help. I'd get a paper and read it. I was so pent-up—so troubled—so unfulfilled, in a way.

I started up the steps but stopped halfway. What could there possibly be up there to divert me! Besides I had been on my way to breakfast. The office would only remind me more of Sarah. Maybe I should take the day off and take a walk in the woods. Alone!

I walked back down the steps and turned towards the cafe. A short walk down the street brought me to my destination. Entering, I realized how few people got up to eat at this hour— at this cafe in any event. Only one customer was there besides myself. He was unknown to me. The proprietor, Hank George, threw me an acknowledging nod. I sat at the counter to avoid the necessity of Hank waiting table. It was a small place with only a few tables and hadn't been painted in years. Behind the counter was another counter holding silver, dishes, and glassware. All the glasses were stacked upside down to help them stay clean. Most of the lower glasses in the stack were covered with a greasy, dulling film whereas the higher perched ones showed signs of more recent usage and were cleaner, yet checked and scratched from wear and age. I wondered how long the lower glasses had stayed in their state of desuetude. They were a mute testimonial to the paucity of business. I reflected that Hank must be a poor man, with a business no more than marginally successful, dependent to large degree on the casual drop-in trade of passing motorists. He was open early to encourage passing truck trade.

Most of the local residents reacted much as I did to the thought of eating there, with a mild abhorrence. He was purported to cook a fairly good meal if one could stomach the idea of eating it there. Since, in the absence of another cafe, there was no other choice, I ate there frequently and was a practiced critic. Sometimes when I couldn't face it, I would open canned soup and warm it on the burner at the office. A bigger problem was Hank himself. He was a small, waspish sort of man, married, I guess, with cold eyes and leathery skin, an avowed member of the Ku Klux Klan. The Klan wasn't very active in North Carolina, and he had to travel to other areas occasionally to spew out his venom. But he was proud of the Klan affiliation, enough so that he bragged about it to his customers frequently, and loyally tried to convert them to his brand of irrationalism. I disliked eating there even more because of his bigotry. Being one of the few regular customers and one of the few he knew well, I was all too often the unhappy recipient of his vitriol. I honestly believed he lived almost solely for his hatred, feeding and nurturing on it. His Klan robes were of the finest cloth, he said, and gaudily decorated. When he was wearing them he looked to me like Beelzebub with a pointed head and but one horn, centrally placed. Yet I allowed him his irrationality and assumed probably his miniature size forced him to be terrified of people in general. Then his terror was transposed into a fierce front for the purpose of scaring off the frightening enemy. But I never openly offered my analysis of his personality to him; rather avoided conflict when possible.

He handed me the menu, a greasy, well-used piece of type-written paper, a carbon copy to be exact. I always asked what he recommended first, knowing full well what the answer would be.

"Hominy grits is good today, Doc. An' how 'bout some po'k chops, couple or four?"

He spit out his words, in keeping with his bogus fierce demeanor. I would have dropped dead had he ever offered anything like a sweet roll or doughnuts.

"Let's see," I said, "got any juice?"

"Some of that canned stuff, yu know the kind?" His voice spewed nastiness.

"Okay, tomato. And how about bacon and eggs?"

"Po'k chops are awful good today," he reminded me in a sharp tone.

I figured they were left over from last night. The thought of eating that greasy fried mess was almost too much. It sounded more nauseating than usual. Maybe it was the champagne.

"All right. Hominy grits and eggs. Is that all right with you?"

"And coffee," he added to my menu. "Look like yu could use it. Been tipplin', Doc?" he snickered.

An impertinent question, and if he hadn't accidentally hit on the truth, I might have resented the accusation. As it was, I was caught off guard and passed the inference and impertinence with mere silence.

He disappeared into the kitchen then, a welcome respite from what I knew would come—the usual harangue about "niggers" and the Klan. I was certain my northern lineage led to many of his harangues, though perhaps I was only his most regular customer and therefore statistically his most constant listener. Somehow I always managed to keep my patience and not get embroiled in a racist argument, though it was difficult. I was sure his intent was to provoke and inflame me into an argument. His barbs were often severe enough to make me want to tell him my great-grandfather was General Sherman.

He returned then with a glass of juice. It was obvious from its color that it wasn't tomato, unless an anemic version of the same. He noted my recognition of the change and without giving me the chance to correct his mistake, said "Ain't got any of that tomato kind today. But this here's good. Apricot. Better for you than tomato."

I choked back an angry *Thank you, Mother*, and nodded. I wondered briefly why I had come in here when I knew how the morning would go, especially today when my thoughts of Sarah were so befuddled and disquieting. I needed a change of thought, a dramatic change. Here at least I could vent hatred to a certain extent and one powerful emotion will sometimes expend the energy of another which by itself is too upsetting for catharsis.

"I'll bring the grits and eggs soon," he said, "though yu all really oughta have one uh them po'k chops." As he disappeared again behind the kitchen door I detected the odor of grease blown out into the room by the swinging of the door. *Old grease*, probably pork fat, used over and over for frying all kinds of things, including my present morning eggs. It was almost too much, and I think I would have left if Sheriff Carstairs hadn't come into the cafe at just that time.

He was his usual boisterous, good-natured self. I never could quite decide whether he was sincere in his joviality and friendliness or whether it was part of a grand characterization of the large, jolly, friend-of-everyone sheriff, dedicated to the defense of one and all as equals, a false image, but one that he wanted to portray. He was very large, maybe six feet four, 275 pounds, with a fairly large pot. His trousers clung to his hips while his belt rode helplessly below his potbelly. A large silver buckle glittered occasionally when the sun struck it just the right way, alternately calling attention away from the rotund belly above. The trousers bagged at the knees and laid on his shoes at the cuff in general folds. The shirt was always stretched open just below the crest of his belly, giving a glimpse of the undershirt beneath. The gunbelt clung to his hips, a symbol of authority, along with his large, shiny badge and Texas ranger–style hat. His teeth were pearly white though, sort of a paradox with his otherwise seamy appearance.

But his ebullience and affability were hard to resist. He drawled out "Mornin' Doc, didn't expect the pleasure of your company so early now."

I thought to myself that he must arise awfully early to be this far away from the county seat in the morning.

"Hi, Sheriff, awfully nice to see you. Sit down and have breakfast with me," I said.

"Well, now that's might friendly of yu, but I've had mine an hour ago," he answered.

"A cup of coffee, maybe then," I insisted. I didn't want him to leave, as I figured his presence would probably prevent the racist harangue. The prospect of a pleasant breakfast now seemed much more promising than it had a few minutes ago.

"Well, now that sounds to be a good idea," he agreed.

Hank appeared with my grits and eggs and set them down in front of me. He said hello to the sheriff, "How are yu, Bill?"

"How goes it, Hank?" he answered.

"Same as always," was the reply. "Have somethin' to eat?"

"Well, I've already eaten, but those grits look so delectable, I guess I'd better have a few." Now I knew why he had a pot.

Hank added, "And po'k chops, maybe?" He was really pushing those chops.

"No, don't think so, might get fat."

Everyone laughed including the stranger, but Hank's laugh was tight and stifled. He never relaxed, even while laughing; always on guard. As Hank started to the kitchen, Sheriff Carstairs called, "And fry 'em."

Hank nodded.

"And in *new* lard." I wished I had had the guts to be that bold.

"Sheriff," I said, between bites, "what brings you to Bennettsboro so early in the morning?"

"Oh, business. Not here, over in Chaunceyville."

"Serious business?" I asked.

"Never can tell 'til it's been investigated," he dodged laughingly.

Nothing more was said about it. Hank had returned soon with his fried grits. "Smell good," the sheriff said, complimenting him. As a matter of fact, they did, better than mine.

"What business?" I asked. The subject intrigued me.

"Well now, don't know as how I should tell yu, but I guess it wouldn't hurt. A burglary. Breaking and entering," he added in his best legal phraseology.

"A burglary?" I parroted. "Important enough to bring you? Why didn't you send the deputy?"

"He's busy testifying at the trial of a colored boy who pulled a knife on a white man." Naturally, I thought. I wondered about the provocation.

"I'll bet that one'll be a speedy trial," Hank snickered. "Damned niggers, always causin' trouble."

Sheriff Carstairs ignored him. I did, too. "What was robbed?" I asked.

"A grocery store," he answered. "Took a lot of things: food, shotgun shells, just general stuff."

"Shotgun shells," I said, amazed. "That's an odd one."

"Yeh, sounds like someone's gonna shoot somebody. We think we know who it is, though."

"A nigger, I'll bet," Hank said in diabolic anticipation.

"Can't say," the sheriff went on. "Only strange thing is the same sort of robbery occurred two months ago or so over at the county seat."

"The same person, you think?" I asked.

"Well, don't really see how, seein' the suspect hasn't got a car and couldn't go that far. Just coincidence I guess that they were the same."

"Interesting," I said. "Hope it isn't one of my disgruntled patients." We all laughed, except Hank who looked like maybe I'd just given him an idea. Hank didn't seem to like anybody—the Jews, the Catholics, the niggers, the northerners, the rich. But then, little men have to have some claim to strength, and his strong point was a fierce hatred.

The sheriff changed the subject. "Say, Doc, hear you delivered a mighty nice young 'un for the Gentrys, a boy, just what they wanted. They sure are mighty proud of him. Made you feel good, I'll bet, to have such a successful case. Always knew you could do it."

There was that barb again, intended or not. He was a master at the disguised barb—by no means a bumbling, jolly fool though he wanted everyone to think it. There was more to him than a lot of people realized. Yet somehow, curiously, he made me feel safe. I respected him as a capable law officer. Hank couldn't contain himself, though, and had to ask more about the knifing trial over at the county seat. The sheriff was more voluble about this, as undoubtedly the case had already been tried several times by the local people and newspapers and would be common knowledge. I rarely read the local news so I wouldn't have been up on it, anyhow. As the sheriff talked, it was obvious that Hank was enjoying the case, his face twisted with sadistic glee. He uttered a small, tight, gleeful giggle every now and then when anticipation of the sentence became too overwhelming to stifle. Once he said almost with enthusiasm of anticipation, "They'll hang the nigger, won't they?"

I could see from his satanic look that if they did he'd attend the ceremony. One of the greatest temptations to join the Klan must have been his sadistic desire to injure someone. Yet his fears couldn't allow this and he sublimated his desire by watch-

100

ing injury done by someone else. He probably attended all hangings.

Hank's statement was too upsetting for the stranger in the cafe who broke the silence by asking for his check. Hank was visibly annoyed at the interruption and only turned his head to spit out in his Southern twang, "One dollah, twenty cents—leave it on the countuh," and then turned back to the sheriff and said, "Go on, Bill, tell me how they'll do it to 'im."

I turned to watch the stranger beat a hasty retreat to the door leaving one dollar and a quarter, obviously not wanting to ask for change. He looked at me with incredulity, making my skin tingle, as if to say to me, "How could you, a professional man, even listen to this repugnant diatribe, or even more abominable, participate in it without either challenging it or vomiting?" Or were those my thoughts surging forth. He's a northerner, I thought. I wanted to follow him out and explain that I didn't condone it, but it would have been useless since the voice within me expressing the stranger's views was merely my own conscience or rather guilt at being unable to speak out in protest, pusillanimous as always, content to stew within, taciturn to the end. I credited this attitude to my professional demeanor and stoicism when the credit really belonged to cowardice and lack of self-assurance. In a way I was no better than Hank, except that I expressed my cowardice in a different way. Doubts, doubts, doubts, so strong there was no chance to arouse any reckless behavior. I detested myself for the fears that filled me with such helplessness. It was even more detestable to hide behind a facade of professionalism, wisdom, and prudence through silence, and lend a certain credence to the discussion.

The sheriff seemed to also have had enough of the discussion. The stranger had had an effect on him as well. I wondered if his conscience had been stirred, and if he was degraded by feeling less a defender of "charity for all and firmness in the right with malice toward none," though I suppose it was probably ridiculous to ascribe such grandiloquent feelings to him.

I arose to leave. "Well, back to work," I said. "How much, Hank?"

Eighty-five cents was all. I was glad to be leaving. The sheriff seemed equally glad to leave and walked out with me.

After we left, he slapped me on the back in buoyant enthusiasm and said, "Be seein' ya, Doc. Keep up the good work."

"You too, Sheriff," I said. "Drive carefully. I don't want to set any broken bones."

He laughed and got in the car. As I walked up the sidewalk toward the office, he drove by and waved one final good-bye. I watched his car pass the colonel on its trip down the highway. The colonel remained motionless, imperturbed, unaware of the hatred and violence that persisted despite the eighty-one years since his war was over.

The sight of the grocery store brought back with suddenness the memory of Sarah, her warmth, her patience, her understanding, all in all a welcome change from the atmosphere of the cafe. I climbed the stairs and entered the office knowing that soon Sarah would come to work and I would be faced with a decision as to how I felt. "To thine own self be true," she reminded me, not to the image of the past. The phone rang. It sounded strange somehow, incongruous with my thoughts. I was suddenly returned to the realization I was a doctor. I seemed to have forgotten it in the past twelve hours.

It was a male voice on the phone. He identified himself as Ambrose Bennett, the grandnephew of Miss Melanie Bennett, my patient. He was very concerned with his aunt's health he said, and asked me to come to the house immediately, if possible, and see her. I asked what had happened, hoping to have some piece of information to think about before I got there, a chance to go over differential diagnoses in my mind ahead of time. He couldn't say anything that had happened. All he could say was she looked poorly. I tried to question him about symptoms but got no response of value other than she was very weak and unable to get up this morning. His voice was quietly frantic and most concerned, and he seemed a little annoyed at my refusal to come without asking questions first. In truth, I had no valid reason for the delay nor for these questions, but tried to excuse it on the basis of needing some information to enable me to bring the correct medications. It was a feeble excuse and I knew it. I told him I'd leave very soon. He asked if I knew the way and I said I did. He said he'd see that the front gate was unlocked and that I should drive on in, the house would be about two miles back from the road and I couldn't miss it when I got there. I was impressed with his concern but couldn't help but wonder how he happened to be there since I hadn't remembered that she had said anyone lived there except her overseer. Just a concerned and dutiful nephew, I decided.

Let's see, I said to myself, she had a cold when she was here before—that was almost a month ago. She couldn't still have that. I felt that old familiar anxiety creeping back through me, the worry about making the correct diagnosis. I wished I had something, even a tidbit of information, to use to help me search out the problem in advance of my arrival there. A few symptoms would have given me a chance at exploring the illnesses which could fit them. Weakness, he had said. That was no help. Weakness could accompany dozens of illnesses or none at all: just old age and heat could be enough. Everyone gets tired enough to feel weak occasionally.

I picked up my bag and looked around aimlessly as if perhaps my eyes would settle on something that would help in some indescribable way. It was more a gesture of delaying action to keep me from meeting the crisis at hand. I went to the door, then to the bottom of the stairs before I remembered Sarah. A note, I said, I've got to leave a note. If only I could be more calm and collected at times of stress. I raced back up the stairs, two at a time, scribbled a note saying "Sarah, I've gone to the Bennett house for a call. Doubt I'll be back before ten," and signed it "Dr. J." Very formal, very brief. I ran back down the steps hoping to get away before she came to work.

While driving away from town my worrying gradually subsided. At least one problem was put aside for awhile, that of meeting Sarah at the office.

The day was becoming beautiful, damp, and somewhat muggy perhaps, but the sun was shining and there were patches of billowing clouds left over from the storm in the sky, pristine and white against the bright blue. I couldn't help but marvel at the beauty of the landscape after the rains. The air was so clear, the trees so distinct against the blue sky. The road had a patch of water here and there, reminders of last night's downpour. I couldn't help but notice the layer of red dirt over the hood as I drove, laid down by the rain as it cleansed the air. A dirty car was a small price to pay for a cleansing rain. I even felt the air was cleaner.

My thoughts wandered back to Miss Bennett, a small, frail woman at best, who probably shouldn't feel strong in keeping with her size. Yet she certainly had looked strong enough when she had been in the office. She had marched in regally and seated herself without help, sat erect through my entire history and physical examination. Certainly these were not signs of weakness. If she was weak from age and frailty at this time, certainly she should have been similar a few short weeks ago. The more I thought about her problem the more confusing it became and soon the confusion led to greater and greater anxiety. A few more miles, and I reached the Bennett gate. It looked different in the daytime, but the large iron gates with the "B" in each gate were as I remembered. I stopped, got out, and opened the gates to allow the car inside, drove by and onto the bridge which spanned a small stream just beyond. I closed the gates behind me and wondered briefly how they locked them. Getting into the car again I noticed the stream and thought how like a bastion this was, with gates and even a moat. The house was nowhere in sight, but in the distance was a large group of trees, far across the fields. Cotton plants were everywhere around me as I drove. Most of the blooms had been picked, but a few still clung and were visible. It seemed to be an extensive plantation. After a while the road, which was full of ruts, split into three parts—a new situation of which I hadn't been informed. I stopped briefly to ponder and chose the middle one, which turned out correctly. Soon I found myself closed in by neat rows of large trees that bordered both sides of the road and intertwined in the center overhead providing a canopy of greenery. The day darkened suddenly as I entered under the trees and a cool gust of air seemed to invade the car and my spine slightly. I felt closed in, chilled, and automatically slowed the car. The surroundings forebode misfortune. Their ominous character chilled me, much like walking suddenly from the light and warmth of life into the dark chill of a morgue. I drove on slowly unable to keep from looking up frequently at the branches overhead through the windshield. It was almost as if I expected to see bats or some indescribably diabolical creatures peering down at me. I couldn't understand why something that was obviously done to lend beauty and elegance to the approach to a mansion should affect me in this way. Spanish moss hung from some of the branches in silent disarray without pattern and without root, nurturing on other life for sustenance. Diabolically it seemed to reach down as if to grasp the car, though actually it hung far above. Farther ahead I could make out the mansion nestled within a large grove of trees.

I entered the main courtyard between two tall Italian cypress trees and there before me was a large neo-Grecian style home with tall, white, fluted Doric columns in the portico centered in the front of the house, which was one story on the sides and two stories in the center, with a high peaked pediment continuing onto the roof. A balcony over the front entrance was surrounded by a small railing. Several steps led up to the porch of the portico and to a huge front door. A large, no, a huge magnolia tree, probably the largest I'd even seen, was centered in a lawn around which the circular driveway ran to and from the house. I entered clockwise and wondered for a moment why I hadn't gone the other way deciding it was probably a habit of turning to the left, the sinister side. As I neared the house I became aware of its rundown appearance. The first thing to catch my eye was a shutter hanging at an angle to the line of the window, obviously broken free at the upper hinge. The paint showed similar neglect, peeling in many areas and leaving some boards almost bare and gray due to weathering without protection. A large hole in the road jolted the car and water splashed to both sides as the tire passed through. There was no sign of life anywhere as I came to a stop near the porch.

I got out of the car and slammed the door behind me, hoping the noise would arouse someone. The noise died quickly in the shrouded canopy of trees. I felt too much alone. I wondered where the nephew had called from: it seemed anachronistic that this old house should have a phone. The appearance of the mansion and surroundings was obviously antebellum and the quietness of the atmosphere gave it a dreadful dead look. I felt as if I had accidentally stepped into a time machine and been transported back a hundred years except for the lack of life. I could easily imagine that a hundred years ago

105

this plantation teemed with activity, many people, horses, slaves. I nervously turned around and looked at my car for reassurance, half expecting to not see it, that through some peculiar transposition I was no longer in the twentieth century.

I walked up the steps, which creaked slightly, and crossed the porch to the door. A large brass knocker was the only evidence of a way to summon the household. As I raised it and brought it down, I was startled at the clamor created by the brass plate it struck. A couple of crows, equally startled from their rest in the magnolia, took wing with loud squawks protesting my intrusion into their solitude. I wondered what or whom another rap would startle and was reluctant to reapply the knocker to its plate even though the first rap had apparently not achieved its purpose. After several more raps, the sound was less and less startling and my primary feeling of apprehension changed—first to concern and then gradually, as fear pervaded me, to anger. At last I became almost openly hostile and pounded the knocker against the door.

The squeak of footsteps on the stairs behind me startled me almost to the point of fainting. My heart raced with palpitations beating my chest. I'm sure I expected on turning around to see the Devil himself, a ghost, or some other hideous creature about to devour me. Yet it was merely an aged colored man with a balding head. White fringes of hair on the sides continued in front of the ears into a beard which was equally white and well cropped. He had a kindly, quiet face, and obviously found walking painful, moving every arthritic limb with care, his back bent with age.

I said the obvious, trite statement, "You startled me," which must have been blatantly obvious because I'm sure I uttered a cry when I heard his footsteps on the stairs. "I thought no one was at home, it took so long."

"I'se sorry, Suh," he answered. "Yu see I couldn't git here any soonuh wit my artritis."

I felt an utter fool. I had let my imagination and fantasy change all this beauty into something hideous much as in a grade-B movie. I was acting as if it were a hundred years ago and I was truly a stranger in a hostile land. I was annoyed that footsteps had been enough to startle me so badly. Yet something

106

about the creakiness and sound of those steps had really set me off.

He said, "Can I help yu, Suh?"

"I'm the doctor," I announced. It must have been obvious with my black bag in hand.

"Oh," he replied. "I'se the overseeuh."

Well, we were introduced, at least our respective roles were.

After a pause, he ventured, "Didja'all want somethin'?"

"Want something? Why, I was called here to see Miss Bennett who I was told was very weak," I said, perplexed at this strange twist.

"Das all true," he said, "but who was da one who called?"

"Well," I said, "he told me he was Ambrose Bennett."

"Oh, Mr. Ambrose," he said, "Ah didn't know he done called. Miz Bennett don't have no phone."

I was not amazed at that since, as earlier noted, the home hadn't seemed to be up-to-date enough for a phone.

"May I see Miss Bennett?" I asked.

"Oh yassuh, Doctor, yassuh. Yu'all jes go right on in. De door's open and Miz Bennett's room's at de top of de stairs in de back." I hated to drop in on her as perhaps she didn't know of my visit either.

"Thank you," I said and turned to the door. I felt like I hadn't repaid him for his courtesy or for the scolding about taking so much time to answer the door.

I turned to him again and he was walking slowly away, bent and pained. I didn't know his name so I called out, "Sir." I'll bet no white ever addressed a colored man in that manner before. "Mr. Overseer."

He turned back and addressed me, "Yassuh, Doctor."

"What's your name?" I asked.

"Ben, Suh," he answered.

Colored people were so used to servitude they usually never gave a last name, as if never allowed the distinction of a family name—not allowed to be an entity in themselves, but existing only as appendages to other entities. Since colored people took presidents' names often, I guessed it was probably Monroe or Jefferson.

"Well, Ben," I said, "when I'm through with Miss Bennett maybe I can give you something for your arthritis."

He was obviously pleased. "Oh, thankya, Suh, dat's awful nice. Thankya." He bowed and bobbed two or three times, painful as it must have been, while standing there. I acknowledged his acceptance with a smile and wave and once again turned to the door and entered.

I expected the door to creak as I opened it but it didn't. I closed it behind me and turned to the inside. The entry hall was paneled with knotty pine boards with a beautiful and soft appearance, the patina of aging. To the right, off the hall, a door opened into a room which appeared, at quick glance, to be the library, since a wall of books was partly visible through the open door. To the left was another room whose tall paneled doors were open revealing a fireplace on the opposite wall, framed in by panels and pillars and capped near the ceiling by a capitol pediment, ornately carved. Each door, including the entry, was framed by rectangular pilasters of Corinthian type capped by a pediment of a lesser size than that over the fireplace. The ceiling in the entry hall was two stories high and, winding up to a second floor on the left, was a graceful carpeted stairway. The carpet, however, was worn through to the wood in most areas and frayed elsewhere. An oriental rug graced the center of the entry hall and its innate quality had allowed it to survive in fairly good condition over these many years of use. The floor beneath was of plank wood secured by pegs at the ends and, probably due to the thickness of the planks and quality of the workmanship, the boards had remained flat and secure. The wall paneling was equally well preserved even though I doubted that it had had adequate maintenance over the many years. On either side of the front door was a window draped with heavy velvet maroon drapes which were yet another sign of decay, since they looked grimy, dusty, motheaten, and in such a tenuous state that I felt they would shatter into a thousand tiny pieces if so much as touched.

I walked toward the stairs, passing beneath a large brass chandelier that hung overhead on a sturdy chain. As I put my foot on the bottom stair, a grandfather clock on a wall to the right sounded its chimes, surprising me, but bringing me back to the reality of my visit, Miss Bennett's illness. As I wound up the curving stairs my steps were accompanied by the measured beat of the clock chimes sounding out the hour as they had done for who knows how many years. I turned to the clock briefly as I walked, and watched the pendulum slowly pass through its arc and then back again as if in perpetual motion, slowly counting out the minutes, hours, days, years, and decades from time immemorial. I had never known anything this grand in Illinois, though I had always aspired someday to own or live in a home such as this. To me, its architectural beauty was unparalleled. The stair rail was a smooth, ascending, rounded flow of walnut held up by a continuous line of spindles, three to a stair. At the top of the stairs was the landing which soon turned right and passed on into a hallway with paneled doors. I assumed they led to bedrooms on either side of the hall. At the end of the hall directly ahead was Miss Bennett's room. I walked with quiet steps to the door and knocked gently. A weak voice which was barely audible through the door asked me to enter. Opening the door I entered a large room which seemed to cross the back of the house in its extent. As I closed the door I saw Miss Bennett's large four-poster bed with canopy and tester just to my left, with the head of the bed against the door wall and the foot facing a group of French doors which opened out onto a balcony. The doors were opened allowing the warm, moist air to fill the room. A fireplace was present in the wall at the far end of the room. The firebox was faced with slate and surrounded by a wood paneled wall. A portrait hung on the wall above the mantle, a military figure in dress uniform. There was a small bedside table on her right. A water jar and glass adorned the small table. A Governor Winthrop desk was on another wall with a small chair.

Miss Bennett lay in bed beneath a large comforter on a silk-cased pillow. She seemed very surprised to see me and pulled the comforter higher.

"Good morning, Miss Bennett," I said. "How are you today?"

"Why, just fine," she answered. "I see you accepted my invitation to visit sooner than I expected." She was definitely surprised to have me there. When I reflected on it, I agreed it must have seemed ridiculous not to have known I was coming. Then to suddenly have me standing in her bedroom at nine o'clock in the morning paying a courtesy call was ridiculous. I hastened to explain.

"I am sorry about the intrusion. But, you see, I received a phone call from your grandnephew this morning. He asked me to come over to see you immediately because you were very weak. I thought he had called from here and was with you, and that you knew."

"Oh my, no," she said. "We don't have a phone. But the dear boy was over here early this morning. He just worries too much about me. He asked how I was feeling and I told him I was weak, so he must have gone right home and called you. Now that was thoughtful of him, wasn't it?"

Though I was annoyed at being brought out here on the pretext of a semi-emergency, disrupting my office hours—all because of an overprotective, anxious relative—I could say nothing else but "Yes, very thoughtful." She sensed my annoyance, and with true breeding hastened to placate me.

"Of course, it was wrong to bring you so far away from town and your office expecting an emergency, only to find a well patient. I'll be glad to pay you for the time," she said.

"I wasn't worried about that," I said, revealing that in truth something had annoyed me, confirming her suspicion. "What I mean is that I was worried about your health and am surprised to find you so well."

"I understand," she said, and I'm sure she did. I didn't have a poker face and showed my emotions easily. It always annoyed me that since Carolyn died I seemed almost unable to control any emotion in a way, particularly that of fear. I already knew that my deep-seated guilt feelings more than likely caused this, but such knowledge was not sufficient to correct it. There had to be some other key to unlock the door and reveal what I needed to know within my mind. If only I could find the key and relieve my guilt. I had felt that in going to the South to practice, serving the people Carolyn had loved so much, would help. Yet here I was doing just that and had not improved in any way. Even giving up my residency in neurosurgery had been in a sense a sacrifice, though I had thought the main reason for quitting was my lack of confidence in handling of patients' problems. Neurosurgery presented problems of surgery far too frightening for my trembling hands and weak resolve.

Miss Bennett interrupted my reverie by asking, "Are you all right, Doctor?"

I had been lost in thought. I smiled and answered yes, but once again I had revealed that something troubled me, and to one of my patients, an ignominious act. She went on. "Perhaps your visit is not altogether a loss. I do have some things to ask you about but why don't I get dressed and then we can talk? I never arise in the morning early if I can avoid it. You've caught me being lazy."

"I'll just wait down in the library," I said wishing to get a chance to see that room.

"That's fine," she said. "I'll only be a minute."

I left then, closing the door behind me. When I reached the landing, I paused momentarily to look out a window. I could just see the edge of a very formal garden behind the house with its paths and boxwood hedges and small flower plots. Sadly, though, the garden was terribly overgrown with weeds. The hedges in their geometrical patterns must have once been very beautiful but now grew irregularly, unclipped, and presented a mass of vegetation which all but occluded the usual pathways between. Large boxwood bushes showed signs of having once been rounded into shapes but now were irregular, grotesque, and ugly, looking like ghouls reaching out to grasp and engulf a neighbor bush. What a peaceful picture orderliness can present and how disturbing disorderliness and neglect can appear. In Heaven, I mused, everything must surely be in place whereas in Hell there must be frightening frenzy.

As I looked, suddenly a horse with a rider galloped out and away between a hedgerow. I could just make out a man riding very well and in a hurry. At a distance he looked a little too fat to be riding in such a professional manner. At the end of the garden his horse vaulted, dragging its hind legs through the hedge, and then raced on across the field into the distance and finally out of sight. Rather shaken, I went downstairs and into the library on the left.

The door creaked slightly on its very heavy decorative

brass hinges, hand-hewn, sturdily made to last forever, antiqued from time and air. Entering the library I realized this was the type of room I'd always dreamed of having someday as my study. The room was moderately large with the fireplace at one end, paneled with knotty pine everywhere. Bookcases on both sides of the door framed the entrance in such a way as to create an alcove for the door. Above the door was a three-masted ship model, the rat lines of the ship interlaced with cobwebs, nature's lines. The mantle over the fireplace held a steeple clock which was ticking lightly and unobtrusively. Directly in front of the fireplace were two love seats facing each other. A large desk was at the other end facing the fireplace and a captain's chair backed up to a many-paned window. There was another door on the opposite wall which led to somewhere, no telling where. I chose not to open it to look. Bookcases framed it as well, so that on both side walls were large collections of books which were beautifully appointed in leather bindings with gold printing. Another oriental rug covered most of the hardwood flooring. Once again, everything was covered thickly with dust. I stood in front of the desk which was large, paneled, sturdy, a kneehole-type with leather inserts on top showing signs of aging, darkened and obscuring the gold filigree that outlined each leather panel. A small model of a Confederate field piece sat on one end of the desk and a student-type lamp with double globes on the other. I pulled my forefinger along in the dust to verify its thickness leaving a long groove of cleaned area. I looked at my finger confirming the thickness of the layer and then wiped it on my trouser leg. I crossed to one of the bookshelves and idly began reading titles. *The Republic* by Plato, Sir Francis Bacon's *Eassy*, the *Aeneid*, the *Iliad*, the complete works of Shakespeare—numerous fine sets and individual volumes. Truly, I could almost lose my mind if allowed to use this library.

Miss Bennett entered. Once again, she had on a dress that looked antique, hung almost to the floor, probably originated in the early 1900s when she was in her thirties.

"Won't you sit down?" she asked indicating the love seats.

"Thank you," I said, and sat. She sat across from me. I had never noticed before, and maybe it was the half-light of the room, but she had a classic face, and I realized she must have been a beautiful girl when younger. I wondered again why she had never married. We looked at each other in silence for an embarrassing moment. I felt a little like a salesman who should be making a pitch for my product. I chose the room as an opener.

"It's a beautiful room," I said, "just the type I've always dreamed of having someday."

"Yes, isn't it?" she answered. "This was, of course, my granddaddy's study years ago, then my father's and now mine." She had said "and now mine" a little wistfully, I thought.

"Daddy loved this room. I never knew my granddaddy for he was killed in the war before I was born. My daddy. That's him," she said, pointing.

I hadn't noticed the portrait before now, hanging there over the mantle, but it was of a handsome gentleman with a dark velvet jacket and ruffled shirt. I wondered where Grandpa's portrait was.

"Grandpa's is in the living room," she said as if reading my mind. "Daddy was such a wonderful man. We had such fun. We used to ride and hunt together, play chess, and read. He was an avid hunter—rabbits, fox, bobcat, wild hog, coons. He was a fine man, a wonderful daddy." Her face saddened. "My brother was just the opposite. He hated guns and hunting. Daddy used to be so angry at him, angry enough often to beat him with a horse crop because he was such a sissy. Mama used to plead with him to stop but Daddy would get very upset and come in here and close himself in."

Yes, I thought, a wonderful man. She went on, "I'd sneak in and sit by his feet and he'd stroke my hair and tell me how he wished Bill could be like me. After a while he'd mellow and we'd sit and talk for hours. I sat on his lap until I was thirteen or fourteen. Daddy was so sad when I went away to finishing school. He said he didn't know what he'd do without me."

She seemed to love to talk all of a sudden. She was curiously different than when she had been in the office, no longer austere and proper, almost child-like, wistfully telling a wonderful odyssey, skipping from one place to another. I wondered if it might be the room that was doing it.

She seemed lost in thought for a while. Suddenly her expression changed completely and she was once again the austere woman I'd known in the office. Once again patient and doctor, and not old friends.

"But then," she said, "you didn't come here for a tea party and lesson in family history. We had better get back to what I was going to tell you. I have been feeling poorly lately. This past few months have been very unpleasant. I seem to have had all kinds of problems. All my life I've had such good health and now sort of all at once I seem to be falling to pieces. It sort of scares me."

I listened and made no comment. A good doctor knows how to listen. If you listen carefully enough and long enough, the patient will tell you what is wrong. She was voluble enough that I needed only occasionally to nod assent and understanding or to comment yes, no, or oh.

"You remember when I saw you I had this cold?" I nodded.

"Well, the medicine you gave me did help me a lot, but I still have those symptoms. And now I seem to get nauseated, occasionally to the point of vomiting."

I nodded again, a professional gesture, showing concern, understanding, and wise interpretation.

"I've tried to attribute this to what I eat but it doesn't seem to have any relationship."

I wondered what she ate and, somewhat hostilely, if it, too, was covered with a layer of dust. As a matter of fact, I wondered who cooked it. She didn't seem the type to be in the kitchen cooking. She couldn't be bothered with such routine, mundane duties. She must have a cook and housekeeper. No, I thought, looking around, not a housekeeper. That would be unlikely. Just a cook.

"I eat a good variety of things," she said, "the same type I've always eaten except perhaps less of each." That was confirmed by her frail stature.

"I don't cook my own meals. Bessie, who works for my grandnephew, comes over and cooks for me every day. She's not his cook, of course, they have another one. But it's awfully nice of him to send her over to help."

Very nice, I thought. The Dean was right, if you listen long enough the patient will answer your questions without your having asked them.

"My grandnephew, Ambrose, comes over almost every night to see how I am, and if I want anything. Usually he waits until I go to bed, then locks up the house, puts out the lights, and rides back to his house."

"Rides?" I uttered incredulously remembering the horseman earlier.

"Yes, a horse, he's an excellent equestrian."

It had to have been him. But we were off the subject of the illness and I wanted to get back.

"He takes after my Daddy who was such an excellent horseman." I knew then from the look she had on her face we were back to the subject of her Daddy.

"You should have seen him hurdle the hedgerows on the hunt. His favorite horse was a spirited chestnut gelding named Prometheus. When he ran you could almost see fire coming from his nostrils." She said it with obvious pride.

I wondered if she knew what had happened to the real Prometheus for his disobedience.

"Daddy would never let me ride Prometheus. He was afraid I'd get hurt. He used to ride in at night, vault the hedge into the garden, come down the path to the back of the house riding fast and suddenly rein in quickly rearing the horse up in the air, then down. The horse would snort and Daddy would jump off and pat his neck calming him down. He was so handsome in his britches and boots. He loved that horse so dearly. He was such a man."

Hm, I thought, making my own analysis, a driven hostile man, almost possessed with the devil. I wondered if he had been beaten by his father, the colonel, or if he was only trying to emulate the image of a father who must have been a handsome figure in his Confederate grays, saber in hand, yelling "Charge!" as he drove his troop across the bridge against the Blue line and sudden death, or was it the other way around at the bridge? Maybe in truth the Colonel had been "killed in action" after all. Certainly if his son took after him, I could believe it.

She went on. "Daddy was a lieutenant in Granddaddy's cavalry. He was so proud of Granddaddy that when he died, at his request, Daddy named my brother after their general at Antietam, Ambrose P. Hill."

I noted she had said "died." I wondered if she knew the Northern general's name at Antietam was also Ambrose—Ambrose Burnside, the enemy. Then I remembered something else strange.

"But you said," I interrupted, "that your brother's name was Bill."

"That was my older brother," she corrected me, "he was named after Daddy. Ambrose was my brother who died. He had the spotted fever." I nodded.

Damn ticks, I thought, remembering my tropical medicine course in school and the rickettsial diseases they carry.

"Daddy was so upset when Ambrose died he closed himself off in this room and wouldn't let anyone in for a week. Wouldn't eat. Ambrose was the youngest. I was in between."

And Bill was the oldest, I thought. And Daddy was very disappointed in Bill. Probably he intended to fashion Ambrose in his image but was cut off from his venture when Ambrose died, leaving him a very bitter man.

"When did your father die?" I asked.

Once again she stiffened, her face became austere and it was obvious my question had been too painful to discuss.

"I should let you return to your office," she said. "I've kept you so long." She stood up. I stood also.

The question must really have been painful. I was being politely asked to leave. I had become so engrossed with the family background history I had ignored the illness, if there was one. So many other facets of her life were now coming forward, I wondered if her illness might be a bid for attention after these many years of loneliness and boredom without the dynamic man to whom she had become so attached. Any poor fool wanting to marry her and who tried to measure up to that ideal would certainly be doomed to ignominious defeat. Maybe that explained why she had never married. She could never find a Prince Charming with the dash of Daddy. An old story.

"I should have asked you more about your nausea," I said.

"Oh, it's all right," she replied. "I will let you know if it gets worse." She went to the front door.

"And your weakness," I persisted, trying to delay leaving.

"No," she said, "that, too, I'll let you know about."

It was no use. I was being rejected and ejected, but politely so. "Well, then," I said, "I'll expect to see you in the office; soon, I hope, if it persists."

She extended her hand as she had done in the office and again I shook it feeling that she expected me to kiss it instead.

She closed the door behind me and once again all surroundings took on an air of loneliness and quiet. Nothing stirred. No noise was audible. Then suddenly a crow flew by, sounding out his "caw, caw," loudly. I looked up to see him fleeing the pursuit of a small bird who was probably protecting his nest from this big intruder. I got back into my car and was pleased to hear the motor start. Leaving here would be a welcome change. As I continued my circle around the drive and again came parallel with the house I paused briefly to look once more. The mansion had a certain serenity about it, but its decay, overgrowth of foliage, unkempt appearance, and particularly its quietness, gave it a certain element of gloom and of sinister bearing. I shuddered slightly and drove on to the lane of trees. Looking to the left I saw at a great distance from the car a rider on a fleet horse racing parallel to me, visible alternately as I passed by each tree, his image blotted out at regular intervals, giving the scene a stroboscopic appearance. He seemed to be following me. And I couldn't make out his face or any other features at that distance. When I reached the main gate it was open. I crossed through, stopped, and closed it and turned left toward town. Driving up the highway the rider and horse passed my car going the opposite direction again at a distance so I was unable to make out features. I pulled up to see his destination. He stopped at the gate, probably locking it, then flew off down the road in a gallop. I smiled and laughed slightly—was it Colonel Bennett or Lieutenant Bennett? It wouldn't have surprised me if either ghost, or both, were still around—though I knew it must be Ambrose, the grandnephew.

Chapter 7

The office was extremely busy that afternoon. All of the morning patients had been crammed into the schedule, and it was too busy for Sarah and me to do more than acknowledge each other's presence, having practically no time alone together. Most of my examinations were almost perfunctory since I was unable to dispel the image of the Bennett house and the characters involved in it. Nevertheless, the afternoon passed rapidly, and because of the workload, the office was open almost to seven o'clock before the last patient left. I went back to my consultation room to sort out charts. Soon Sarah, in her usual way, came back with the day's receipts and any messages she had not as yet given me. At last, I thought, we're alone, without diversions or annoyances, and can have time to talk. Whereas this morning I had been anxious to avoid her, now after my morning experiences I felt the need of her presence and longed for the serenity I knew her understanding would bring. I wanted to say something about last night but still was embarrassed and too flustered to broach a discussion of that immediately. The correct and proper words were not easy to come by and particularly since I really didn't know how she felt.

I started talking about the visit to Miss Bennett's house leaving out the parts about how eerie it all seemed. I told it in a brief narrative, colored to appear as though I was particularly interested in how the surroundings might be related to her illness. Sarah seemed genuinely interested but commented little. I found out, though, that she had no real knowledge of what had happened to Miss Bennett's father nor her brother, Bill, Jr., William Augustus Bennett III, at least. It was now almost eight o'clock and I was running out of things to say about the Bennetts. Sarah looked ill at ease and I noticed she often looked at her watch. Finally she interrupted and said, "I'm sorry, Dr.

Jenson, but I must leave. I'm expecting a phone call from Baltimore soon."

I don't believe she could have said anything at that moment that would have hurt me more deeply or filled me with more doubts.

"Of course, Sarah," I said, "go ahead."

Once again, she said, "I'm awfully sorry," and she did seem genuinely sorry, but now I thought it smacked of pity, which I abhorred from her. She left then. I crossed to the window and looked out to watch her leave. This time she didn't wave or look back. I was overwhelmed with a peculiar kind of grief as if something precious and dear was going out of my life. I smiled wryly. Here I had been worried how I was going to feel when I saw her this morning not knowing whether I would hurt her by coolness on my part. And then to have her be seemingly indifferent enough to last night's activity to not even mention it was a terrible blow. And worse than that to actually tell me she was expecting a phone call from Baltimore. She could have given me any old excuse. Any other would have been kinder.

I fancied she probably hadn't enjoyed last night. It had been only the champagne. The trouble with me, I decided, was that I was unable to put things in their proper perspective. Anybody under the influence of champagne and unused to it would tend to act giddy and silly, even romantic, and when the glow had worn off realize the whole mood was temporary and not necessarily serious. Only a fool would try to prolong the feeling as if it had been based on real emotions. Damn, damn, damn. I was in the depths of despair. Prometheus, having his liver eaten out for daring to capture a little fire and trying to hang on to it. That was me, a stupid horse, a dolt. Wear my heart on the sleeve will I! I deserved to have it trod upon. My self-reproach mounted until I resolved to be totally on guard again and never let down those defenses I'd so laboriously constructed.

I sat down at the desk, looked at the calendar, and realized it was now late August. I really don't think I'd thought about it before. Soon fall would be here with its splendorous beauty, and I'd have none of the love which was so vital to the enjoyment of all things beautiful. I knew then that all anyone gets out of life is love, or affection, call it what you like. The rest is just damn misery and work.

If only Carolyn hadn't died. How many times I had said that to myself. Well at least now I didn't have to worry about being unfaithful to her memory. No longer would I suffer from my guilt as I had done last night.

I arose and crossed over to the phonograph and selected the album of Strauss's *A Hero's Life*. I hoped the dynamism of the music would inspire a new quest in me like the knights of old: even if destined to be a sad and unfulfilled quest, it would give me purpose and rid me of my gloom. Its strains filled the room with irrepressible music that commanded sufficient attention to alter my mood. It had been one of Carolyn's favorites, too. Maybe that's why I chose it. "'Tis better to have loved and lost—" I wondered who said that, and what the circumstances were. Anyhow, I told myself, one great love, even if short and unfulfilled should be enough for any man. It's better to have a good memory than an unrequited love. Of that, I felt certain, there could be no doubt. I drifted off into reverie about the past, the music having its salubrious and soporific effect.

The Duke woods were quiet and still, just the romantic setting Carolyn and I always sought when we had time alone together. Lunch was always a hurried meeting, sometimes only a few minutes to grasp between us since our time off usually coincided but for a brief span. We usually spent those brief moments in the garden, which was close by and somewhat secluded, except that other lovers and anyone else seeking quiet and seclusion used the garden as well. Since the privacy we sought was not afforded here, we had no choice but to go into the surrounding forest.

Today was Saturday, ward rounds were over, and classes completed. The time was ours. Since she was a student nurse her hours required occasionally that she work on Saturdays, usually only until three o'clock, but today was ours, from noon or when my classes ceased. It was a beautiful, warm, balmy spring day and we hadn't been together a full afternoon for weeks. It seemed we'd only had a brief minute together for years, since I'd studied so hard recently for quarter-finals. But at long last finals were over, and now we had our full afternoon and evening.

I met her at the nurses' home. She was beautiful in a light-colored spring dress. Her shoulders and neck were bare. There were no straps to hide her natural beauty. Her skin was white and smooth and soft. I wanted to take her shoulders firmly in my grasp, but no display of affection was allowed in or around the nurses' home quarters. Student nurses were warned to maintain strict decorum at all times, particularly in or near the home. We weren't even allowed to kiss good night so the final kiss was always given out of sight of the home and the final walk to the door was very cold, no hand holding, no lazing along the way, a polite good night and departure—no dawdling or delaying. Other affection outside the immediate confines of the home was also verboten if seen, but most people managed to avoid being seen, and in truth this rule was not as strictly enforced. Failure to observe the rules, of course, led to dismissal from the program and everyone was anxious to avoid this eventuality.

I met her, greeted her politely at the door and walked down the long walk from the home as though I were a suitor meeting her for the first date—chatting amiably, but showing no other sign of affection. My almost irrepressible impulse was to take her in my arms in a mad embrace caressing the soft skin of her shoulders and feeling the warmth of her kiss, but it was taboo for the next few minutes. We walked around the sidewalk, then down along the road behind the nurses' home, still within sight of prying eyes, still exhibiting full control. A few feet from the stairs to the garden I looked at her, we smiled, and then ran to the stairs, down them towards the garden until our heads were beneath the road level, and we knew exactly on which step they were below. Then I held her in my grasp and kissed her passionately. We laughed and raced on down the stairs and out across the garden lawn past the many trees, hand in hand until we were out of breath. Then we threw ourselves on the ground and just lay back next to each other looking at the sky and holding hands. It was a beautiful day, and all ours. There wasn't another person anywhere. At least we felt alone. But, in truth, there were myriad couples walking around, all enjoying themselves just as we were. She lay on her back and I rolled over and partially sat up, leaning on one arm to look at her. She was so beautiful, her long silken blond hair, the white smoothness of her complexion against the green grass. I bent down and kissed her lightly and she turned to look admiringly at me and smiled slightly.

"Carolyn," I said, "I love you so very much." She reached over and took my hand and squeezed it ever so lightly.

"I love you, too," she said.

I looked at her gorgeous face, her blue eyes, the flowing lines of her neck into beautifully rounded shoulders and to the white dress with yellow and blue floral print. The dress seemed to cling perilously at the sides to her arms and straight across the top of her bosom revealing only the barest hint of cleavage. The rounded contour of her breasts below were partially obscured by occasional folds of her dress, until she, probably recognizing my admiring gaze, stretched her shoulders back to fully round out the contour of the dress. I was embarrassed to be caught in sexual admiration, but instead pulled her up in my arms and kissed and embraced her. She whispered in my ear, "Let's walk down to the woods, my darling, away from all these people."

I needed no additional prompting, arose immediately to my feet, and pulled her up with both hands. We put an arm around each other's waist and went off across the garden jumping the small brook and then up the other side to the road. After a short walk we came to the main gate. I turned briefly to look back down the long drive toward the quadrangle. The chapel rose majestically and serenely against the blue skies. The carillon bells were playing. It was a perfect day for lovers. We walked away, the bells fading in the distance, towards the woods area that was our favorite. For a long distance we followed the path between the tall trees across soft padding of growth nurtured by the leaves of countless past autumns, the fragrance of a vernal wood in the air, hand in hand. At times the path narrowed and she was forced to walk ahead of me, but we never released our grip on each other's hand. We came to our favorite area deep in the woods and usually not known to others. At least we had never seen anybody there before. A tree at the edge of the deep ravine had fallen conveniently across the chasm many years ago and formed a bridge over the brook below, though it was necessary to climb between the branched areas to cross. Near the center was an area on which we both could sit comfortably. We dangled our feet high above the shallow brook below and listened to the softly flowing and tumbling water and to the soft wind blowing through the trees. Luminous rays of sunlight filtered through the trees to brighten the area. It was so peaceful and serene. We talked about innumerable things, all inconsequential as we had done a million times. I was overwhelmed with her beauty and with desire for her today, yet I was nervous and a little fidgety and she commented on it. Her appeal was becoming too powerful to resist. As I leaned over to kiss her I noticed the delicate fragrance of a perfume which was so inviting. I stood up abruptly on the log, almost teetering and falling and said, "Let's go, Carolyn. Please. Let's walk some more."

"But why?" she asked, though I suspected she knew. "We have the whole day to ourselves."

"It's just that—well, I just want to walk some more." I offered this excuse. It must have sounded lame to her. Grudgingly she moved.

We threaded our way off the log to the ground and started up the path. We came to a small clearing and had not spoken until then. She stopped walking and turned around to me. "Is something wrong?" she asked.

I was so tense with her beautiful body close to mine I didn't seem to know how to act or what to say. "Of course nothing's wrong," I said to reassure her. "Can't you imagine what I'm trying to say. We should leave now—before—before it's too late."

"Darling," she answered, "let's sit down over here," indicating a secluded area of grassy soft terrain well sheltered from prying eyes. Then without my approval, she went over and seated herself. I seemed to be unable to resist any further. I followed and sat down next to her. We said nothing, just looked at each other briefly, knowing what was in our minds. Softly, I kissed her ear, her neck, her shoulders again and again until overwhelmed with passion. Placing one hand on either side of her shoulders, I slowly pulled the gown down exposing her beautiful, round, firm breasts. The sight of her breasts filled me with absolute joy. I lay her gently back onto the ground and smothered her with kisses. Soon our union was complete and our love reached a marvelous climax in unison, releasing our tension in a grand, final burst of ecstasy and feeling. We remained together until all the magnetism holding had quieted, and them we parted and lay side by side on the warm grass, breathing deeply and slowly, relaxed and calm, listening to the quiet sounds of the forest, reveling in our love, our satisfaction, and our union, not thinking of the future or the past, just of the wonderful present.

After a while we dressed and laughed in an embarrassed way about doing this act in front of each other. She again stood next to me and I kissed her gently. I looked again at her beautiful body and stroked her beautiful skin, pressing her against me. We said not a word. Anything we could have said would have been inadequate. Our communication had been different, but yet complete and fulfilling and nothing else needed to be added. This time I didn't want to leave. She felt we should, and I acquiesed.

We went back to the path, walking arm in arm, not speaking, moving as if in a trance of satisfaction and union, as if merged into one being with identical thought. Occasionally we turned to each other and smiled and gently laughed. Then she ran and I chased her. I caught her and kissed her and she broke loose and ran again, laughing and inviting me to chase without saying a word. Once I ran ahead of her then embraced her and we fell onto the ground together, kissing and laughing.

"Darling," she said, "I love you. I adore you."

"I adore you, too," I answered. "More than you'll ever know."

"And now you're mine, forever and ever," she said. "I know we'll always be together. I had only felt we would before but now I'm sure, more than I would have believed. You're mine, mine, mine, and I'll never let you go."

Her burst of possessiveness was pleasing and flattering, yet frightened me a little. But then, she knew how greatly I desired her. Why wasn't it natural for a young girl who has just allowed herself to be taken by the man she loves in her first union to be possessive and to glory in his attraction for her. Even so, the rest of the walk back to the university area was less ecstatic and we spoke little. We were troubled; at least, I was.

We walked the last distance to the nurses' home in the acceptable legal manner, apart from each other, showing no affection, and I left her at the front door with a handshake, expecting to meet again in two hours for dinner after we'd had a chance to clean up. As I walked away I wondered why I hadn't taken the opportunity to kiss her one final time as we ascended the stairs from the garden at our designated step. I was upset, and I knew it. What a short time ago was ecstasy was now becoming apprehension, mixed with many doubts. Suppose she was to get pregnant. What a stupid ass I'd been to get carried away with my passion and not protect her or myself from the possibility of pregnancy. Why in Heaven hadn't I thought of that aspect? On the one hand I was proud to be proved a man, and on the other hand I was angry and frightened of the future. I showered and changed and looked out the window of my room in silence, wondering what next would happen. The sun slowly set and the warm rays gradually disappeared, the streaks of light through the pines dimming slowly and leaving a sinister mass of greenish-black color against a rapidly darkening sky. How different, I thought, the forests are when it's light and warm and thoughts are similar, and yet how sinister and gloomy it can become when guilt and fear hang over one's head. The forest's mood is reflected in the mood of the beholder.

We met in the manner we always did at the nursing home door and walked away in cold distance from each other, except that this time when out of sight of prying eyes we didn't lock in warm embrace. We were both troubled, it seemed, though soon she broke the gloom by saying, "Oh, darling, it was a marvelous afternoon. I am so thrilled, so happy. You just can't imagine."

"I, too," I said, apparently without enthusiasm, because she seemed perplexed.

"What's wrong?" she asked. "Didn't you enjoy yourself?"

"Oh, yes," I said, "very much. So very much. I can't tell you how much. It isn't that."

"Well, what is it, then?" she asked, almost with fear in her voice.

We had reached the student union then and I said we should eat first and talk about it later. The dinner hour seemed strained. We had little to talk about and couldn't carry on our usual easy conversation. Both of us were ready to leave as soon as dinner was over.

We walked to the quadrangle halfheartedly holding hands and stopped at James Duke's statue. He looked cold and uninterested there holding his cigar and cane.

Carolyn said, "Darling, what's wrong?"

"Nothing, really," I answered. "I'm just sort of mixed up in my thoughts right now."

"What's there to be mixed up about?" she asked.

"Well, I—don't misunderstand me. I enjoyed this afternoon more than anything that's ever happened to me. But somehow it just wasn't right." Uncomfortable silence followed, for what seemed forever.

"Oh, that's just peachy," she answered, annoyed. "I show you love the best way I know how and you say it wasn't right. How much more did you want?"

"I didn't mean that, that you and our love weren't the greatest and I never questioned your love for me. Understand, what you gave me was more than I could want or ever expected. It's just that what happened complicates our life so, when it was so simple before."

"Simple?" she questioned. "It was bound to happen when we loved each other this much. How does it complicate our life?"

"Well," I paused a long time. "You could get pregnant. That would complicate it." I hated to say that word, pregnant. It seemed as if by saying it, through magical thinking, it might come true.

"Oh, so that's it," she said, quieting some in her anger. "Let's not worry about that unless it happens."

"That's just the problem," I said. "Suppose it does happen. You'll be expelled from the nurses' program and not get your degree. And we'll have to get married. I'd be unable to support you as an intern."

"Suppose, suppose, suppose," she answered angrily. "You don't even know if I'm pregnant and already you're full of doubts. Let's worry about that when and if I am." I wondered why she didn't feel scared.

"But it's the responsibility that that possibility entails that upsets me," I spewed out like an erudite prig. "When are you due to have your period?"

"In two weeks," she answered.

Her answer shook me.

"You see, I'm right to worry. It's the worst possible time to have intercourse. You're probably ovulating right now."

"Well, then you should have asked me that before we even started or you should have brought something to keep me from getting pregnant." Now she was worried and angry. "After all, you're the doctor and you should be the one to know these things."

"Yeah, you're right. I'm just plain stupid. If you get pregnant it will be my fault and we'll have a real mess on our hands. My folks would never help me financially with a family in addition to med school, and I'm sure your family would be furious to think you got kicked out of the program because of me. That's a swell way to start our life together. And all because we got carried away."

She saw my frustration and self-disgust and tried to soothe it.

"Oh, honey, it's ridiculous to argue. We've never had an argument before. We love each other and I know we'll work out anything that happens."

"I know," I said, "but it's never happened to me before and I can't be criticized too sharply for worrying. After all, I only want everything to be right for you, and you stand to lose more than I do."

"I don't know about that," she said, "if I was pregnant, at least I'd be sure you'd be mine forever."

"I *am* yours," I said, again somewhat troubled by her possessiveness. I wondered then if she hadn't seemed more anxious to have intercourse than I, and consequently was less worried than I about the future. But then conjecture like that was all too ridiculous. She was probably worried like any other girl that now that I'd had her, I'd look for another girl to love and she'd lose me. Women are always more possessive than men it seems. Maybe she wanted to get pregnant to keep me. That thought unnerved me and I wished I hadn't thought it.

"I don't think you really were mine until this afternoon," she said.

"What do you mean by that?" I was really troubled and perplexed now.

"Oh, it's hard to explain," she answered, "but we've been dating for two years almost and never once have you made any real sexual advances to me. I was beginning to think I didn't appeal to you."

I roared with laughter. "Now, who's being ridiculous," I said, "you really thought I had no sexual drive? How could you want to marry a guy with no sexual drive?"

"It wasn't that way," she said. "I thought you looked at me as some sort of goddess to worship and adore but not someone to make real sexual love to. I'm glad to have you understand I'm a woman who wants a man in that way, and not a goddess to adore."

"You're right in a way," I said. "I'm guilty as charged. My mother always taught me a girl wasn't as interested in sex as a man and looked upon it as something disgusting. For me to make sexual advances would be to deface and defile your pristine self, I guess," I said laughingly. "I guess I thought women only agreed to such things out of duty and such duty starts only with the tying of the knot. Aren't you glad to find out I'm really a sexual being after all?" I laughed wryly.

"And a really good one, too," she said, snuggling.

"How do you know?" I kidded her, "without any comparison to use."

"A woman doesn't need comparison," she answered, "she just knows."

"The old superiority of the female bit, eh?" Somehow, I thought, if she does become pregnant, I'll have to feel she put one over on me and was indeed, in that way, superior. I wondered what it was about her that had made me have such a thought.

"It was such fun, though, and you were superior," she said.

"Yeah, that's the problem," I said, "we've found out how wonderful it can be and even if you're not pregnant, how much restraint are we going to be able to use to keep us from accidentally making the mistake. You know what Shakespeare said,

'Beggars mounted run their horse to death.'"

"Well," she said, "that's a rotten analogy."

"Yes," I apologized. "I meant only that I'm afraid once the nectar of your sexuality has been tasted I'll never be able to hold back my voracious appetite."

She seemed pleased at that. She uttered a "wow," anyhow.

"We'd better go," she said. "Curfew will be coming up soon."

I kissed her now, for all to see, in the quadrangle, right before James Duke's very eyes. As always, he seemed imperturbable, uninterested, immutable, inscrutable, and, not surprisingly, motionless. My effrontery to the rules hadn't rocked *his* foundation.

We walked back to the nursing home in better spirits than when we left it for dinner. As we walked to the door, I thought she looked troubled.

"Is something still wrong, honey?" I asked.

"No, I have just a slight headache," she said.

As I walked away, I remembered she had never complained of a headache before. But I certainly gave her one this evening. And maybe I gave myself one, too. Tomorrow would be another day and the next two weeks would be a bloody nightmare.

I awoke from my reveries. I hadn't even noticed that *A Hero's Life* was now on the center section with the needle going round and round in boring monotonous motion. I wondered how long ago the music had actually quit playing. "*A Hero's Life*" I thought, *that's funny. Some hero I turned out to be.*

I couldn't get Carolyn out of my mind. If only I'd been more intelligent and more positive she might never have died. I remembered again that wonderful day in the forest and how my conscience had bothered me later. It wasn't just worry about the future that had upset me. It was religious training and ideas about adultery. Funny, but I'd never had the courage to tell her that. It would have been like telling her that I was moral and she was amoral, though she probably had had the same doubts and ambivalence and was unwilling to voice them for the same reasons.

I arose, stretched, and then stopped the endless grinding of the phonograph. It was nine o'clock and I hadn't eaten. Today had been an unusual day and I couldn't help but wonder what the future would bring to Bennettsboro. I turned and looked out the window into the dark night. In the distance a dull light illuminated a cloud momentarily and I wondered if another storm was approaching. A storm probably would have fit my mood well. I looked in the direction of Sarah's house and wished I knew her thoughts. Across the street out of the shadows of the porch a man walked slowly away. He startled me. How stupid to be startled, I thought. A mood can make one imagine even a man on the street to be sinister. The embodiment of my conscience walking there across the street, I guess.

Morning came again as it always did and the next two weeks were very routine office work. Sarah and I worked as before, doctor and nurse, and for that I was grateful, curiously. She had thanked me that next day for the wonderful birthday party but her attitude obviously presumed nothing and expected nothing. She had apparently enjoyed the evening as much as I but had made no decisions or presumptions. Osler was right, "Live for today, the future is uncertain, and yesterday gone and unchangeable" or something like that. Such an attitude makes life easy: no demands, grateful for what we have, no regrets. As always, she was perfect, always reacting steadily in the proper way.

We enjoyed each other's company, or at least I thought we did. I know I enjoyed her. I wanted to ask her for a date but decided against it, since she was interested in someone else and not me. Why should I date her and maybe become hopelessly in love and then lose her in the end. I decided I'd wait and see what happened. Maybe she'd break up with her other boyfriend and maybe I'd have a chance later. What boyfriend? Another figment of my imagination?

Mrs. Jacobs returned to the office today to see me. Of course the narcotics I'd given her were helpful, yet temporary, and she now sought better relief. She didn't have a headache today, fortunately, and yet if she had had she might have been more anxious to pursue the cause of it.

Sarah showed her into the inner office for another conference. She looked much more composed than I had remembered her as being on the last visit. Her demeanor bore out the fact she was relieved of pain. She was pleasant, docile, even quiet in appearance, though not relaxed, since as she sat there I noticed that she pressed her lips tightly and squeezed her hands together showing white knuckles on occasion. She stared at me intently.

"How are you today?" I said.

"Fine," was her terse answer.

"Then you came back to see me in regard to your headaches?"

"Yes, I promised I would."

"Well, how have you been since I last saw you?"

She replied, "Really no better. Some days I'm fine, other days I do poorly."

"Would you mean by poorly you have headaches?"

"Yes, very bad ones. Sometimes I feel like I'll go blind when I have them."

"Do you go blind?" I asked. It annoyed her.

"I didn't say I went blind, I said I feel like I would."

"I know, but what I meant was, do you actually find yourself unable to see out of one eye, since migraine headaches sometimes cause loss of sight in one eye."

She was mollified temporarily.

"No, not that way, it's those kids, they make me blind-angry sometimes."

"Can you describe one of your headaches?" I asked.

"It just hurts," she said. "What else can I say?"

"Well, could you tell me where it hurts," I answered politely.

"In my head," she interrupted.

"I know, but I mean, in any particular part?"

"I don't know," she said, "I think all over." She moved her neck around and raised her shoulders as if stretching her neck, rubbing her neck in turn, sighing and closing her eyes.

"Do you have them every day?" I asked.

"Sometimes," was the inadequate answer.

"Do they last all day when you have them?"

"Sometimes three or four days," she replied. "Sometimes I wake up with them but more often than not they'll come after I get up and be there at night when I go to bed. They seem to get

131

steadily worse all day." There was a lot she could tell me if she wanted to.

"How long have you had them?" I asked.

"Well, ever since I had the kids, I guess worse after the last one was born."

"How old is your oldest?" I asked.

"Oh, she's fifteen now and sometimes I wish she was only three." She seemed more angry when she said that.

"Then you've been having headaches fifteen or more years?" I said, remembering that headaches which people have for so long are seldom due to organic disease, particularly frightening organic disease such as brain tumor. I was a little more relieved at that thought.

"Yes, I guess so," she said, "but lately they've been much worse and I even get sick to my stomach once in awhile."

Herein lay the problem of diagnosis. She could have had tension, emotional headaches, or headaches due to allergy or other causes all these years, and only recently have developed another more serious cause leading to the recent increase.

"Do you ever feel dizzy?" I asked

"Oh yes," she said, "when I have the headaches, I often do. Occasionally I think I see double. I don't know. They pound and pound so hard it's hard to tell and hard to remember." She rubbed her neck and then rested her chin on her hand. I thought her face looked drawn. I noticed a small burn mark on her hand when she raised it to rub her neck.

"You burned yourself?" I asked,

"Oh, it's nothing. I staggered a little the other day and burned it on the stove."

Staggering was an ominous sign, I thought. Surely she must have a brain tumor. It recalled another time in the past to me.

"But I've done that before," she added.

"Were you dizzy when it happened?" I asked.

"Well," she said, "I just seemed to lose my balance for an instant. It was only an instant, though, and I've done that before."

I got the feeling she thought she'd said something important and now was trying to minimize it. Maybe she'd seen the concern in my face when I reacted to her statement.

"Has your personality changed any in the last few months?" I asked, wondering about a frontal lobe tumor of the brain.

She tightened up on that question. It was obvious I'd hit on something unpleasant. She squeezed her forehead with one hand then ran her fingers down across her eyes ending at the bridge of the nose and then rubbed the back of her neck. "I'm getting another headache," she said.

"You didn't answer my question about your personality," I said.

"I don't know whether I have or haven't. I get accused of it by my husband a lot. He says I'm always angry lately." She smiled slightly and laughed in apology perhaps for being guilty as charged. I smiled back.

"Is it true?" I asked.

"Well, who wouldn't be angry," she said almost without hostility, "with four kids and not enough money to feed or clothe them well, and a daughter who's only fifteen and gettin' interested in boys. My husband works only part-time and sits around a lot and never helps one bit with the kids or home. I'm supposed to do all the chores. I can't even get my daughter to help me one bit. She just wants to lie around and moon about boys. She dresses up in a tight dress, the tightest you ever saw, and stands on the porch and makes eyes at anybody who'll look. A body gits mighty disgusted with that kind of behavior. Ain't like she was a grown woman or something."

She was getting angrier as she talked and from the amount she rubbed her neck and forehead I surmised her headache was getting much worse.

"Do you suppose your headaches could have something to do with your worries and tensions at home?" I said.

"No," she said emphatically, reinforcing my suspicion. "I've always been tense. I don't know why it should affect me now. I think something's seriously wrong with me and I want you to find a way to help me. I don't see how it could be my kids, though I guess they'll be the death of me yet, or these headaches will."

I thought it was interesting that she said either her kids or headaches would kill her, as though they were one and the

133

same. Still I didn't like the thought she had expressed about the headaches killing her. It made me anxious. I had to be sure that that particular ending would not be hers, even though, God knows, life itself, at best, was a disease with a poor prognosis.

Her manner changed suddenly from hostility to fear. "Doctor," she asked, very concerned, "do you think I might have something serious? It hurts so bad at times that I feel like I'm going to die. I've got so much to worry about I can't afford to die."

I hastened to reassure her, though I felt my anxiety rise as soon as I did. I wasn't able to answer such a question from a patient truthfully. I hated such questions. I always felt compelled to reassure the patient and, I guess, myself, that he or she had nothing serious. I often wondered if I wished to believe the lie only because I couldn't face the truth. Such a fault could result in a missed diagnosis one day. Even so, I felt so empathetic to most patients and particularly when they mentioned death that I had to reassure them even while terrified of missing the diagnosis and contributing to the demise.

Mrs. Jacobs was a woman with enormous responsibilities: four children, a husband out of a job much of the time; trying to manage a home; feed and clothe him, her, and the children; probably even grow some of that food; and wash and iron, sew, clean, cook, and, and, and—a million responsibilities.

I couldn't afford to take a chance on a diagnosis of tension headache even so. Certainly everything pointed to that particular diagnosis: fifteen years of headaches, increasing pain as the day progresses, arising suddenly, freedom from pain at times, occasionally severe enough pain to make her vomit, most prevalent in the forehead and back of the neck and hard to describe in a specific way. Her personality must be more than likely replete with hostility toward her husband, her daughter, and her responsibilities. No doubt her married life was certainly not what she had envisioned for herself when a young bride. The recent increase of pain could be due to a new cause such as a brain tumor; the vomiting might fit that, the dizziness, and the staggering as well. Staggering was an ominious sign. Perhaps the personality change suggested brain tumor, even some of the symptoms of the tension could be related, and she had said occasionally lately she "sees double—maybe." I began to feel more and more uneasy about her. She looked sick, tired, drawn, thin, sallow. Even this picture could be due to tension and lack of proper food, but it could be also associated with a tumor. And then my thorough examination revealed no positive sign suggesting brain tumor.

"Mrs. Jacobs," I said after returning her to my consultation room, "I really think your headaches are probably caused by tension and are not serious. You know, you've had them ever since your children were born, at which time your responsibility increased. Apparently you take your responsibilities too seriously. And apparently you get no help in relief of that from your husband."

She interjected, "That shiftless bum."

"Children can't be counted on for any help, but your daughter, at fifteen, certainly can and should."

"That's just it," she said, "she can't be counted on for anything. Spends all her time combing and brushing her long hair in front of the mirror. When I try to talk to her about her interest in boys she just doesn't seem to hear me at all. And if I push her to do somethin' she just gets angry and throws a fit. All she ever wants to do is stand around on the front porch in her tight dress showing off her body, for all those bums to look at. Sometimes I could thrash her."

"Does she have a boyfriend?" I asked.

"No," she said, but not with conviction as it took too long to answer my question. "I don't really think she does. But her ways sure are a headache to me."

She looked up, startled, in a way, and smiled—a smile of recognition that frustrations and tensions might be expressed physically as a specific sympton. The recognition needed no reinforcement. I decided she had understood the relationship sufficiently on her own. I hoped that that recognition might help alleviate some of her distress. She seemed ready to leave then, but I asked her if she needed some more tablets for her headache.

"No," she said, "I think I'll try it for awhile without anything." The insight she had gained seemed to offer enough encouragement that she felt medicines at present were not necessary. I encouraged her to see me soon again, partly for her and partly for my needs. She left looking a little better and less troubled, her face not as drawn. I felt much had been accomplished toward establishing the correct diagnosis and treating it properly. I heard footsteps descend the stairs. I fancied they had a lighter sound, one of more gaiety than the relentless beat of someone with a headache walking slowly and carefully to avoid any jarring of the body.

The day was still hot and oppressive, though. I walked to the front to speak to Sarah and she was in the waiting room talking to a patient. As she opened the door again to our inner office a slight breeze accompanied the swing of the door, one with mixed perspiration odor, verifying the heat. Sarah, however, seemed pristine in her white dress and was always perfumed and feminine. As she crossed in front of me, I had a strong desire to take her in my arms, hardly a professional attitude, but nevertheless almost overwhelming in its attraction. She smiled slightly as she led a patient that followed to the black side of the examining section. The brief perfumery that filled the air was destroyed by the sweaty odor that followed. The door closed behind her as she went by, deadening the monotonous drone of the electric fan in the waiting room oscillating back and forth in its prescribed arc. Sarah had disappeared into the room with the patient but emerged soon irresistibly attractive in every way. Very professionally, she indicated my next patient was in the opposite room, the black side of the hall and went back to her desk. In the enchantment of her femininity I forgot what I had set out to ask her about. I wondered as I entered the door if we shouldn't have painted these doors black and the others white on the opposite side. None of our patients then could wonder if we ever got confused. Often a white patient seemed to glance around as he entered the room as if to wonder if he was on the right side of the hall. Sarah never failed to keep things straight, though, and I was certain she cared as little as I did whether or not we maintained the segregation of rooms.

Amanda had returned to see me. "Good morning, Doctuh," she wheezed.

"Hi, Amanda," I answered. "How are you feeling?"

"Why, Ah's jist much finah than Ahse been fo' years. Ahse

never had such slim ankles since Ah was a girl."

"You look much better," I offered in corroboration. "You even sound better," I lied. She still wheezed almost every word.

"Oh, yessir," she said, "Ah can do much more of de chores since yu'all gave me dem pills for m'heart."

"We'll get you so well," I said, "that you will be able to go back to midwifery." I was kidding, of course. "And maybe you can help me on a delivery sometime."

"Lawsy me," she said, "Ah don't think Ah could e'er do that again. Though Ah sure seen a lot of young'uns into life in these parts."

"Did you enjoy it?" I asked.

"Oh yassuh, Ah certainly did," she replied.

I wondered how she could have enjoyed deliveries so much when they seemed to terrify me.

"It gave me much pleasure," she said, "and now Ah sees many of dem young'uns wanderin' round here and Ah feels mighty grateful de Lord gave me such a callin' and stood by my side to help me."

"Do you think He'd be willing to help me?" I asked, half kiddingly, half seriously.

"Oh yassuh, He helps everyone," she said, then paused and added, "most of the time, 'ceptin' for one time Ah recall. Ah remembers one time when Ah was assisting at the birth of Miz Bennett's grandnephew. You know Miz Bennett. She's de one whose granddaddy dis here town's named for."

I nodded assent. "Please tell me about that." I was overwhelmed with sudden curiosity.

"Well, Suh," she continued, "it was de worst night Ah ever seen in dese parts. A terrible storm. Ah hitched up my ol' mule and went down de road toward Miz Bennett's place. It was a dirt road in doz days, not dat nice paved road like today. My ol' wagon was catching in dem ruts and bouncin' somethin' fierce. And rain! Land sakes, it rained. Like a cloudburst, it was. De trees were a bendin' dis way an' adat way," she gestured. "Dere must have been all sorts of evil spirits lurkin' in dem woods."

I had expected her to say that sooner or later.

"The wind howled and blew, and my cape didn't keep me very dry. Ah turned into the lane where the Bennetts lived.

137

Y'all know, that's a spooky place." Her eyes widened and she looked around half expecting the devil to appear.

I remembered the time I was out to the Bennetts and the impression it had left on me, even in broad daylight.

"Well, Suh," she continued, "Ah almost turned back. It just weren't right out dere. Somethin' was mighty wrong. Ah knew it afore Ah ever got dere. Ah was certain a wet, cold hand touched mah face as Ah drove up the lane. De overseuh let me in the house and told me to hurry. Miz Abbey, dat was Bill's missus was havin' de baby and she was a carrying on somethin' the likes of which Ah never seed before. Possessed with the demons she was. Miz Abbey strained and strained and each time her mouth twisted and her eyes bulged right out at me. A witch was in her, Ah knows, Ah knows it sure as I knows Ah'm here. And den with a mighty screech she gave birth to dat young'un Master Ambrose. Dat child was possessed from de start. Dat scream of his was not human. Ah'll ne'er forgit dat scream. It rings in my ears today. Wicked, it was. And then the shutters banged and suddenly the window flew open and dere stood de devil—the devil himself—he had dat evil look in his face. And horns. Ah ran, Ah didn't e'en wait for the afterbirth. Ah just rand from dat wicked place. As Ah left the house, somethin' cold and wet touched my face again. Doctuh, do you think dat's when Ah got my heart trouble?"

"No, no," I reassured her. "I'll bet that wet hand was some spanish moss hanging low on a tree, wet with rain."

"No suh, it was a cold, clammy wet hand, Ah knows. Ah looked back and all around dat house was de miasma and in de upstairs window Ah saw de devil's face and heard dat wicked laugh again. Why, even my old mule felt the wickedness of dat place. He put his ears down and he ran like de wind, snorting all the way home. He liked to die from exhaustion and never was no good after dat night."

I couldn't help but make my own interpretation of that statement. She probably had whipped him all the way home in her terror and the poor thing was overtaxed. The whole evening had been too much for her: the awe of her mission, that morbid home, the stormy night, the responsibility, her superstition. I could hardly blame her.

"Well," I said, "I don't blame you for being scared. It sounds frightening."

"Ah's sure, Doctuh," she said, "dat ever since dat night some evil spirit follows me. De Bennetts never have mentioned dat night to me since." I smiled to myself, I should think not. Running off in terror from a patient in pain without even delivering the afterbirth must have merited little appreciation on their part.

"Well," I said, "maybe they have just forgotten the whole incident and that's why they've never mentioned it."

"Oh no," she answered, "Ah thinks dey was as scared as Ah was and dey must have see'd de devil too. Dey never wanted no one to learn he was dere dat night. Dey never told no one, and Ah didn't neither. Ya know, Doctuh, Ah nevveh could feel good about deliverin' young'uns after that. De Lord just wasn't with me dat night and maybe he meant dat Ah should quit. Ah don't know why, cause Ah's nevveh been a bad sinner, maybe once in a while a little sin, but—"

"Oh, Amanda," I said, "I'm sure the Lord is just and excuses the little sins that we commit and our mistakes. Except maybe the big ones," I added depressingly.

Suddenly a wave of morbid depressive recall crossed my mind and I was silent and pensive, and showed it, since Amanda asked, "Doctuh, are ya all right? Did Ah say somethin' to make ya sad?"

"No, no," I recovered, "I had an unpleasant memory. I'm sorry. Tell me, Amanda, did you see young Ambrose growing up?"

"Not too often—once in awhile they'd bring him to town. But he was a devil, screaming, hollering all the time and his momma slapped him and slapped him and he just screamed more. It was a diabolical scream, Doctuh, sort of the type you hears the witches yell. And when he wasn't screaming he was a-moanin, a low painful sort of moan, terrible to hear. But he grew up into a big man. Have you seen him, Doctuh?"

"No," I said. "He brought his great-aunt in to see me one time, but I didn't get to meet him. Why do you ask?"

"Oh, Ah just wondered. He didn't look right to me. Ah keeps wonderin' if the devil still possesses him."

139

I couldn't help but remember him on that horse vaulting hedgerows and pacing my auto when I paid my only visit to Miss Bennett's.

"Well, Amanda, I doubt he's possessed by the devil. I doubt anybody is, truly."

"Don't you know it's true?" She said. "Ah've seen many people like that."

"Yes, so have I," I replied remembering some of the schizophrenics I'd seen in training, but I could imagine the type she meant; people carried away during superstitious gatherings, shouting imprecations, exhorting the devil. From what I'd heard, it might even describe a Klan meeting, though I wouldn't dare express such sentiments in this area of the country. I found out long ago that in dealing with southerners one didn't cast aspersions on the Klan or its purpose. And it was not to be taken lightly, no matter how nauseating the idea was, no matter how ridiculous these horrid characters seemed in their hooded robes.

"Well, Amanda," I said, "I'd better let you go. You seem much improved to me. Keep taking your medicines as I suggested because your heart seems much stronger and it's obvious you are breathing easier. Thank you for telling me about the Bennetts. Sometime I'd like to have a long talk with you about it, when we have time."

"Oh yassuh, Doctuh," she said, "Ah'll be glad to." I think she was flattered that I'd want to ask for information and especially discuss her midwifery days with her.

She shuffled out of the door then, smiled and waved goodbye. A kindly old woman, I thought. One who's helped a lot of people and probably killed a lot, too, though not her fault. But I wished she'd get over that wheezing. It remained to remind me of the inadequacy of my treatment. Since there were no other patients in the waiting room to be seen, I retreated to my office and wrote my notes for the day in each patient's chart. It was still early, and apparently going to be a slow office day. Once the charts were completed I picked up my Osler medical text to read about headaches and their many causes. Still, as I read of the many diseases and their symptomatology, I couldn't help but become more and more frustrated. What could I do out here in the country to correctly diagnose esoteric diseases without all the tests and equipment good clinics enjoy? In addition, my personality did not allow mistakes and the threat of a mistake was frightening. Mrs. Jacobs must go to Duke, I decided, even though I felt certain her headaches were emotional—maybe migraine—probably one and the same. The perniciousness of brain tumor diagnosis reasserted itself as I read. And I felt a slight cold shudder even on this sultry day. I suddenly felt abnormally ignorant, helpless, and incapable as a physician and wondered what stupidity ever prompted me to decide to hide my inadequacies away in this small, miserable town. The more I dwelled on my inadequacy, the more abhorrently I viewed myself, to a point of hating everything about me—while all the time what was the most distasteful to me were my fears, doubts, and indecisiveness.

I had so lapsed into thought that I hadn't seen Sarah come in. She spoke my name and I, in my truculence, irascibly yelled, "Well, what is it?" with much too obvious bellicosity. Poor Sarah. She'd never seen me this way, and honestly I'd hoped never to let her see this side of my nature.

"Oh, Sarah," I apologized with my tone of voice. "Forgive me. Excuse my manner. I don't know what came over me," though I did know.

Dear Sarah wasn't ruffled, though, or at least not visibly so, as she was her usual calm and efficient self. She seemed un-annoyed at my anger.

"I wondered if you'd like some iced tea," she said. "We have some cubes frozen now."

"Yes, yes," I answered, "very much and bring some for yourself and let's talk."

Her presence once again stimulated desire for more than iced tea. I wished I could overcome my reticence and tell her. Why couldn't I? She'd worked for me several months now and we obviously enjoyed each other's company, yet I hadn't been able to broach the subject again after that first date.

She returned and I asked her to please sit down. She complied so easily I wished I'd said "over here next to me," but I was never that candid. My doubts about my attractiveness to her were far too deeply rooted to allow such effrontery.

"Well, Sarah," I said, "it's been a dull day."

That's not what I had meant and immediately demonstrated my thoughts by adding, "I meant slow day, never dull, with you here." There was a profound silence while neither of us spoke. After all, what could an employee say to her flirtatious employer making such an obvious remark. She certainly could not agree, nor disagree, nor take up my lead. Once again she was correct. She offered only silence and left me feeling embarrassed and idiotic. This was not the time nor the place for such advances. Next I found myself apologizing.

"It's not necessary to apologize," she said. "I liked it. I'm flattered that you hold me in such esteem."

I had an almost irrepressible urge to take her in my arms, but managed to exercise self-control. Without rejoinder to her remark another silence followed. She was the first to break the silence after several long, thirst-quenching, and delaying sips of cool tea.

"Doesn't Shakespeare have a line for this occasion?" she asked kiddingly and invitingly.

How marvelous she is, I thought. *If only I could tell her.*

"Let's see," I said. "Maybe he would have said, 'Why should a man whose blood is warm within sit like his grandsire cut in alabaster?'"

We laughed and laughed, and she said that probably my warm blood had been the reason she'd suggested iced tea. I certainly *needed* cooling off!

"Now it's my turn to quote Shakespeare," she said. "We cannot fight for love, as men may do. We should be wooed and were not made to woo." My heart raced with her suggestion.

"Sarah," I said admiringly, "are you a Shakespeare fan, too?"

"Well, not really," she admitted. "You see, I looked up a few in my dad's book of quotations so I could kid you when you quote them to me."

I admired her honesty.

"You know," I said, "I'd like to take you to a movie tonight; will you go?"

"Well," she said, and paused, "it depends on what's playing," laughed and added, "Of course I will, I'd love to."

Now my heart pounded and the iced tea took on an effervescent quality or was it just adrenaline surging through my arteries. I had to express my enthusiasm.

"What did you put in this," I said, "champagne?"

"Not a bad idea," she replied, "remembering the fun we had the last time we had champagne."

"The last time?" I confessed then, "the only time, and the first time, I hate to admit."

She said, "I sensed that, watching how expertly you handled the disappearing cork."

"What shall we do," I asked, "since the office hours are ended, shall we put on some dance music?"

"Why not?" she agreed.

Soon we were on our feet, I was behaving in gentlemanly fashion and asking for her arm in dance, she curtsying and fanning her face feverishly with the nonexistent fan in mock excitement. But the dance was no polka or gavotte. With the strains of Glenn Miller's theme "Moonlight Serenade" filling the room we glided around the office in absolute nirvana. She was meant for me, there was no doubt of it. Dancing had a very special effect, locked in each other's arms cheek-to-cheek perfection in unison, never faltering in our steps. The world was totally shut out. It belonged just to us.

Then, as if the Devil arrived in a burst of smoke I became aware of someone else standing in the room. My god, how my heart pounded and raced. I looked at Sarah, who was equally stunned. What does a physician say in explanation when caught with his nurse in his arms during office hours? Who in the hell was this intruder who invaded our privacy and enjoyment so unceremoniously, unannounced and unwelcome? All I could utter, while trembling in doubt about my tenuous position in the scheme of life was, "Well, where in hell did you come from?"

"I'm sorry to walk in this way, Doc, but I rang the bell and no one answered, several times, so I heard the music and wondered if you'd fallen asleep or something. I'm sorry to disturb you."

My anger and embarrassment lessened somewhat as I remembered I was a physician. I turned to speak to Sarah who

143

had, without my realizing it, disappeared back to her desk in front, obviously as embarrassed as I.

How would I explain what I was doing a minute ago? I made a mental note to have a lock put on that door so no one could ever walk in unannounced again.

"Well, what is it you want?" I finally managed to say politely, without anger or rancor.

"Doc, my missus, you're taking care of her, came home from your office today and suddenly got one of them blinding headaches again. This time it was also a sick headache. She's vomiting, can't stand up, dizzy as all get-out. I'm worried. Will ya come and see her?"

"Your missus is Mrs. Jacobs?" I asked. He nodded assent.

"Well," I hesitated, "I guess—of course—certainly. I'll just have to collect myself. Why don't you wait down at your car and I'll be down soon and follow you."

I still was ruffled and not sure of how I'd handle this. My heartbeat was still too fast. He left then without hesitancy. I sighed and walked sort of meaninglessly without direction trying to collect my thoughts. God, I wondered, suppose he blabs to this small town about what he saw. How that bit of gossip will speed and enlarge. The old doubts were back again. I got my professional symbol, the black bag, out of the corner, stuffed in the appropriate instruments for examination, and then found a vial of Demerol. Suddenly I realized Sarah would have been glad to help had I asked, so I called her. She emerged looking as sheepish and ill-at-ease as I felt.

"I've got to make a house call, Mrs. Jacobs"—she already knew that—"What do I need?"

She looked in the bag and said, "What you already have, I guess," still ruffled.

I wanted to offer some word of explanation, say something that would set it right. We looked at each other a long time, then she winked slyly and said, "I know what Shakespeare would have said about this."

"What?" I asked.

"For you and I are past our dancing days."

We laughed heartily.

"There was never anyone like you," I said in admiration.

"Close this stinking office and go home. I'll pick you up for dinner at seven and then the movie if we have time. Bye." I squeezed her hand goodbye and started out, and then remembered. "Oh," I said, "turn off the phonograph." It was still playing "Moonlight Serenade."

"Yes, Doctor," she answered politely and coquettishly.

Mr. Jacobs was waiting, somewhat impatiently, I felt, at the bottom of the stairs. He indicated if I'd follow him he'd show me the way. How often I had wished I'd known the locale of the homes of patients, but it was virtually impossible when I covered so many areas of this rural community. We passed Colonel Bennett on the way out the left fork of the **Y**. He hadn't changed; unmoved, and yet, somehow, as I passed the fieldpiece, I expected by his order a cannonball to demolish my car in the next instant, all because of my nonprofessional behavior.

The trip reminded me of the sad journey to Mary Belle Lincoln's home, though somehow I felt less anxious. This was probably because the present problem was certainly less of an emergency and fraught with fewer dangers of dire consequences resulting from deficient training and inadequate decisions. It called for no immediate heroic measures of life-saving character. I could even sit quietly observing symptoms and signs, and appear wise and sagacious. After all, what did they know about diseases. My word was gospel here. Somehow, though, this bravado was false, and I knew it. Whether the dire consequences were immediate or remote, the end was the same if improperly diagnosed and treated.

"Sick headache" he had said. "Headaches," I said aloud, "had differential diagnoses: brain tumor, migraine, tension, sinus problems, hypertension, a variety of acute illnesses, flu, cold, eyestrain, innumerable possibilities. Headache is probably the commonest complaint known to man." I'd been over it innumerable times since that terrible day I'd chanced it and lost when unable to diagnose the worst. I'd seen Mrs. Jacobs already today. I thought her headaches had been based on tension. Had I said anything to precipitate an attack? Let's see, what had she told me today? This is one time I wished I'd brought my chart or taken time to go over my notes of our two conversations for a possible clue.

Strangely, as I followed dutifully along behind my guide, I felt progressively less anxious. I wondered why, since it wasn't typical of my personality to lose anxiety before meeting the challenge and deciding whether or not I was capable of handling it. What had happened to change it? Sarah's last remark to me as I left came to mind, and I smiled in appreciation of her charm and warmth. Could it be, I wondered, that her affection had helped to give me back my self-confidence?

My thought was interrupted once again by Mr. Jacobs signaling me with a horn blast that we had arrived at our destination. One look at the house and I felt the doubts return. This house was in far better repair than the Lincoln place, I noted, and wondered how that could be, since hadn't Mrs. Jacobs called her husband a shiftless bum, out of work, who never helped with the chores, or was it someone else who said that? I wished I could remember the details better. There was a certain neatness about the house which I had noticed immediately upon walking up the straight walk. Why must walks always go straight to their destination, I wondered, the shortest, most utilitarian, and least delaying way? There was no doubt about it, I would soon arrive at the porch and enter into the problem. To each side of the stair I noticed a neat, trim and prim garden with flowers, many of which were losing their previous beauty by browning with age. But they had been cultivated with care in neat rows and the garden outlined with rounded stones which seemed curiously clean and not daubed with mud. I paused a moment to look around. I hadn't even noticed the walk had a neat lawn on each side, small, but definitely neat. The house was the usual two-story clapboard, sterile plan, typical of so many southern houses, a seemingly prefabricated job, stamped out by some machine in the hundreds of thousands and set down by another big machine, intact, already constructed. It didn't seem possible that carpenters had actually put these together piece-by-piece as a construction project. The sameness of design showed little originality. The porch roof had its usual posts holding it up, attached together by the usual railing, though as I thought about it, it actually was different. Many such houses had only posts and no railings. As I stepped up on to the porch, I noticed on my right a young girl moving around a post like a serpent would entwine a tree limb. She stared and said nothing. Her expression made me uneasy. It was flirtatious and provocative. Her mother's remark came back to me now. "Standing on the porch in a tight-fitting dress flirting with everyone that goes by."

"That's Mae," her father said, obviously noting my awareness of her.

I nodded assent and turned to the front door. Inside the house, the living room was also neat and well-kept. The usual amount of furniture, though used, looked in better condition than I expected. I was shown to the bedroom where Mrs. Jacobs lay in a double bed. The shades were drawn to cut down on light which obviously aggravated her headache. The bedroom was totally orderly, everything in its place. Only the bed alone was unorganized, out of necessity.

To see a home so orderly without real purpose other than individual need was probably significant as a sign of a compulsive personality. This was certainly consistent with a headache problem. Rigid control, ritualistic, compulsive orderliness. It fit. My diagnosis was made. She must have tremendously suppressed anger over her inability to control everything in the orderliness that she wished for or needed. My mind raced with psychiatric analyses. Her daughter was obviously one of the deepest thorns and harassments and the shiftless bum another. Without help, maintaining this orderliness on top of all of her other responsibilities including her need for perfection must have been a monumental and impossible task, leading her to express frustration and anger through symptoms. Too bad she couldn't explode, scream, and criticize like others might do. Such behavior would be foreign to the ladylike image she had chosen for herself, though. I had received a small bit of that anger when probing her about her symptomology on her office visits. I proceeded to my task. I said hello and received a grudging reply from her. I asked her how she felt and she said, with a trace of anger in her incisive manner, "Not well," thus fortifying my presumptive diagnosis.

"When did your headache start?" I asked.

She maintained her balled up position on her side in bed looking at the pillow and not at me and with reluctance answered, "When I got home," offering no additional information or help. She was defiant in her tone, challenging me to get any useful information out of her.

"Your husband said it was a sick headache," I persisted, as objectively as possible.

"What does he know," she said. "He's only mad I can't do all the work around here and have to be in bed."

I decided not to contradict her by reminding her that it was he who came to get me and who seemed very anxious about her condition. If I was to help her she must believe I would side with her and support her in any contest with him or her daughter.

"Were you vomiting?" I asked, leaving out that he had told me she was.

"Yes, I was," she admitted grudgingly. "But doesn't everyone when they get a bad enough headache?"

I decided to be her friend and agree.

"Yes," I said, "that's a common problem with bad headaches."

She had now turned her head to look at me when answering. She looked to be in pain. She squinted.

"Are you squinting," I asked, "because the light bothers your headache?"

"No," she said, "because I'm dizzy."

Dizziness didn't exactly fit with my provisional diagnosis, but I decided one symptom didn't have to fit.

I took my sphygmomanometer out of the bag and told her I was going to take her blood pressure, and then recalled the wonderful day in med school when they gave it to me along with my stethoscope, the first trappings to identify my glorious position in life. How proud I was. From that day forward a stethoscope hanging round my neck would dispel any doubts as to what my role in life was, should anyone wonder.

The cuff squeezed her arm as I shut off the circulation preparatory to listening at what point it opened up again as the pressure was reduced. Systolic pressure 144, diastolic 80. Well, that's a little high, I thought, but not enough to cause a headache of this magnitude. The slight hypertension could easily be associated with her suppressed anger, confirming my preconceived diagnosis. I produced my ophthalmoscope then and found an imaginary spot on the ceiling for her to focus on while I looked through her pupils at the retina. The optic nerves showed no edema, I was sure—the disc margins were distinct, not clouded and the discs did not protrude. The vessels were not reduced in size. In short, there were no signs of swelling of the nerve end. This signified no increased intracranial pressure transmitted through the optic nerve. That pretty much ruled out a brain tumor. I couldn't test her visual fields very accurately, though, and this dismayed me. I tested all her reflexes and they were normal and equal. She laughed a little when her leg jumped as I tested her knee jerks. I wondered again why patients so often laugh at this. In all honesty, there is little that is amusing about whether or not a leg moves, yet often a violent jerk would be met with open laughter. No other body functions, only reflexes, ever seemed to cause a similar reaction. As I examined her, I thought she seemed less in pain and more cooperative, as if my interest might have lessened her anger somewhat. I checked her cranial nerves and wondered if I could remember them. The olfactory nerve, number one, regulating her sense of smell, which she insisted was normal; no abnormal smells, no difficulty in detecting odors. The optic nerve, number two, I'd already checked. Her sight was good, she had said. The oculomotor nerve, number three, controlling so many eye functions, seemed normal. Her eyes moved normally, following my finger well as I moved it, and her pupil reacted appropriately to light by shrinking, and to distance by dilating. The eyelids also moved normally and equally. The eye exam also tested the fourth cranial nerve, the trochlear nerve. The fifth nerve, the trigeminal, is associated with feeling in the face and breaks into three branches, the frontal (forehead), maxillary (cheeks), and mandibular (jaw). I pricked these areas with a pin and she insisted that there seemed to be a diminution of the sensation in the maxillary portion on the left. I wondered if I had pricked that area as forcefully as the opposite sides. She insisted on re-exam that it was more numb than the right side. I went on. The sixth nerve, the abducens—let's see, what does that do—I thought awhile and then remembered it also was involved in eye movements and must be all right, since the eyes moved well in the same direction, its principal function of control. The seventh nerve, the facial, deals with movements of facial muscles. She could wrinkle her forehead, show me her teeth and she could smile without aberrations. The eighth nerve, the acoustic, deals with hearing, and though I couldn't test it here, she insisted there was nothing wrong with her hearing. In fact, she felt it was too good at times, as little noises bothered her terribly. I felt that that symptom was part of the anger associated with her compulsive problem. The ninth nerve, glossopharyngeal, I couldn't remember what it did, but as an afterthought, I had her swallow which she could do easily and decided that must be its principal function. The tenth, the vagus nerve, affects the heart rate, the acid output in the stomach and other functions, none of which I could test. The spinal accessory or eleventh nerve, deals with neck and shoulder movements and these functions all seemed intact. Lastly, the twelfth, hypoglossal nerve, deals mainly with tongue movement and this also was normal. She laughed when she was asked and complied by sticking her tongue out at me. I found no real evidence that intracranial pressure from a brain tumor was causing her headache, except maybe the facial numbness, if indeed it really existed. And even if it did it might have another relationship.

I felt the need to reassure her she had no brain tumor. She looked puzzled by my statement, since she had never brought it up as a worry before. I asked then if she had any other symptoms that were new since I'd last seen her. She said she had staggered badly with her headache this afternoon and she thought it was because of dizziness. She also "got sick to her stomach" once or twice. She declined to cooperate when I started to test all the cerebellar functions which might also be associated with these symptoms and left me in no better position of diagnosis. I couldn't fully rule out a brain tumor as a possibility. I tried to question her about problems at home but she turned her head aside again and said she was feeling too sick to talk about it. Her headache was much worse, she felt now. Suddenly she was nauseated and bolted from the room. I knew what was next to come and imagined it must have galled her to perform such an unladylike function. I waited. She came back holding her head in both hands, bent over, and looking very pained again. I had somehow, somewhere, lost her cooperation. Before I could ask another question she asked with pleading tone, "Please, Doctor, may I have something to relieve this headache. I can't answer any more questions. I just want to rest and sleep. Maybe tomorrow I can answer the rest of your questions and you can do the other tests. Please."

I couldn't resist her entreaty. It wasn't that urgent to find out information, though I was worried about her diagnosis and wanted to find out why she had headaches. I couldn't dispel the fear of serious illness, despite the exam and despite the favorable odds that no such problem existed.

I turned to my bag, picked out the Demerol vial and syringe. Drawing up to 100 milligrams I gave her an injection. She winced slightly as I put the needle in and again as the medication was injected. I felt nothing had been accomplished, though I had learned a lot about her personality. I stood up, looked at her pensively, still unsure I had done all I could. She was curled up on her side with one hand under her head. I told her the shot would help her soon and I'd leave her a few pain and sleeping pills for the next few days until I could see her again. I encouraged her to come and see me soon when she was better and then told her good-bye. As quietly as possible, I shut the door behind me, feeling much better than the last time I left a sickroom like this. Her husband was not in the living room as I returned so I automatically went to the porch. My eyes fell immediately on the serpent entwined on the pole.

"Hi, Doc," she said, in what I suspected was her sexiest voice. Somehow she annoyed rather than amused me. I didn't like her calling me Doc. Still I managed to return her greeting.

"Hello. Can you tell me where your father is?" I asked.

"He's in the barn," she answered. "Yuh sure I can't help yuh?"

"No, I don't think so unless you want to run and get him. I'd like to talk to him."

"Sure, Doc, anything you say, but do you mind if I walk instead of run?"

I didn't answer and she went off then towards the barn. Walk was hardly descriptive of her gait. Slink would be more fitting. I had to admit, though in quick appraisal, she had all of the feminine attributes to attract men, well demonstrated by her tight dress; moderately large, well-rounded breasts, thin figure, shapely legs, and her buttocks moved rhythmically as she slunk across the yard. Soon she was back with her father. His gait was rapid and concerned, and she had to give up her styled slink to keep up with him. I wondered what movie had taught her this sexy approach to me. Mr. Jacobs was very concerned about his wife. I reassured him that I thought she was not seriously ill and told him that I felt migraine was the most likely possibility, though that wasn't true. Somehow migraine is a diagnosis everyone knows and accepts easily. To say I thought the headaches were due to tension would require lengthy discussion of the background which I wasn't ready for now. To mention brain tumor would cause undue alarm. As I talked I noticed out of the corner of my eye that Mae was ogling me in her previous provocative way, head slightly lowered, mouthing a straw. How corny, I thought, too pat, too theatrical, yet this constant gaze and stare was somewhat unnerving. It was obvious her mind was on ideas other than concern for her mother's health.

I said good-bye to Mr. Jacobs then and started to my car. To my back I heard Mae say, "Bye, Doc." I wanted to turn and lecture her on her behavior, but that would have been presumptuous since all I knew about her was her mother's appraisal of that behavior and a few cursory ideas based on one slight encounter; mainly conjecture. I was glad to leave, however. She and the family problems bothered me. A disquieting afternoon. Sarah would be magnificent diversion tonight.

Chapter 8

Upon my return to town I went straight to the office. If I was to take Sarah out for a date tonight I must get a haircut. I rushed to the barber shop which was a hole in the wall next to the restaurant. Fortunately there was no one there but the barber, Bill Downey. Bill was Joe Downey's brother. One a butcher, the other a barber. Both must have had a thing about cutting instruments, and underneath, Joe probably was the more hostile, since his cutting instruments were more dangerous and damaging. But then thoughts of this nature should be stopped, I decided. Too much psychiatric baloney. I realized then that all the way back from the Jacobses' I had been deep in psychiatric analysis of the family constellation and had come to the conclusion that her headaches were without question a psychosomatic manifestation of hostile attitudes and conflicts; a compulsive personality. And now here I was analyzing the barber and the butcher, a rather worthless gesture.

Bill was certainly not hostile, despite his cutting instruments, nor was Joe—both had sublimated well. The thought amused me. Bill asked what I was smiling about. "A private thought," I said.

"Have many of those private thoughts, Doc?" he asked.

I felt an apprehensive moment as I wondered if Mr. Jacobs had said anything to anyone about my dancing with Sarah while he waited for me to meet him at the car. Had he said one word in this regard to anyone in this small town, I was certain all soon would know. It galled me to think others might be discussing my private life. But I dropped the subject of private thoughts and asked him to hurry.

"What's the hurry, Doc?" he asked. "Got a date?"

Innocuous question certainly, but the truth. Obviously, a question anyone might ask in reply to a request to hurry.

153

"No, a sick patient," I answered, and laughed. I hoped that would end it. But it didn't. Barbers like to talk, but then, I guess that seems normal. Otherwise they wouldn't be able to put up with the boredom. It was hard to imagine how any small business even could exist in a town this size. We discussed the weather and decided it might rain. It was cloudy and the air had a familiar muggy quality to it.

"Joe tells me y'all really fixed his finger up swell. Works like always, good as new. Neat scar, too. He says your sewing's as good as his cuttin'."

"Thanks, Bill, glad to hear it." I wanted to say it was nothing at all, easy to do, but honesty prevailed. So I passed it off with a concluding remark on the subject.

"Fortunately for him and me, he didn't cut it any worse than he did."

At this point our town's restaurateur, who obviously was not busy at this late afternoon hour, wandered in the door. Though I'd eaten in Hank's place many times I still couldn't find anything I particularly liked about this man. Usually the more one gets to know another, the more apt he is to find some quality in that person's personality with which he can identify. Yet, not this man. Everything about him repulsed me. He gave me his usual greeting, "Doc," with a nod, and then addressed Bill. They were soon in conversation about fishing or something. I somehow couldn't concentrate on the topic, only wished that Bill wouldn't pause so often from his clipping chores to put across a point. In the mirror opposite me I could see the scissors and comb poised in air while he ignored his job and me. I wondered why so many barbers were like this. I decided that it was merely that one personality has a need for communication with others at times, and even if that moment of need interferes with a most important activity at the time, it must be fulfilled. Not that cutting my hair was all that important, but I had said I was in a hurry. Why fight it.

I lapsed into my own thoughts as they jabbered. Every now and then I felt another snip, momentarily interrupting my thoughts. Dear Sarah, dear, dear Sarah. Tonight was to be very special. I knew it. Sarah had provided a lot for me. Her calm, accepting manner had done much to reassure me in my quest for self-confidence. She was always flattering, always gracious, always complimentary of my ability and, even more, was now accepting of me in the role of suitor. Or at least, I knew I was a suitor. She might not know, but I did. She must have sensed I was. I wondered if she was being coy and a lot more interested than I would allow myself to believe. Never! I knew that couldn't be. She was too open and honest. I really didn't feel that attractive, yet my attractiveness or lack of it was based solely on my degree of self-confidence at the time. Without self-confidence I doubted I could expect respect from her. And to hope to gain her for myself was too fantastic. But if only I could voice interest in her. Only doubt and fear prevented me from doing so. I knew instinctively I couldn't face her refusal nor a patronizing attitude. Certainly, though, I thought, this afternoon, without the assistance of champagne, she had seemed very agreeable and amenable to my approach, to my advances. She was so charming, so fabulously charming, so interested, even to the point of studying a few Shakespearean quotations in order to gain my favorable notice. My God, I thought, she obviously likes me. Hadn't this afternoon proved that? Of course, of course, how stupid I've been. What a fool not to recognize it, to have doubts. What a joy tonight held in store. I'd take her in my arms, I'd tell her I love her. "Sarah," I'd say, "darling, I love you."

"What'd you say, Doc?" someone far off asked. I looked up and saw in the mirror the reflection of two puzzled faces staring across the back of my head at my reflection.

My God, I thought, what did I say aloud in my reverie for these two to hear?

"I didn't say anything," I replied with annoyance. Denial or attack were the only two alternatives left to me. "What do you mean, what'd I say? I didn't say anything. When you two have quit fishing, I'd appreciate your finishing my haircut so I can leave."

"But," Bill stammered, "it's all done. You seemed to be lost someplace way off in your thoughts. Hated to disturb ya."

"Oh! Well!" I stammered. How dumb. "I'm sorry," I said. "Well, back to work." I got up from the barber chair, instinctively ran my forefinger around the inside of my collar and brushed my neck with it to get rid of the itchy clipped hairs, paid my fee, and waved a farewell. Hank also waved as well as Bill, and then said, "Have a good time tonight, Doc, wish I was young again."

Somehow, with all his vitriol, I couldn't believe he'd ever been young. I left without answering. I ignored the office steps as I passed by and went directly towards my house to change and shower. I'd call Sarah from there and set a time. This would really be a marvelous night. I wondered if maybe I was thinking too hastily that Sarah was ready for my declaration of love. After all, I really hadn't pursued her in a gradually increasing tempo that would demonstrate an increasing interest, one that had changed to love. To come out boldfaced and say, "I love you" would appear ridiculous. She might ask "Why? How?"— and with reason. But hell, how does anyone know how love originates? At what moment does casual interest, or affection, become love? What small event tells one it's love, and no longer just passion or infatuation? Common interests, ideals? Compassion for each other's faults and concern for each other's needs? I didn't want her to love me because she sensed my failures and weaknesses, my fears and doubts. I wanted to be loved as a man, not as a child to have his fears dispelled by a mother figure. But then don't older people also have doubts and fears? Isn't all love based on mutual needs? Is anyone without fears or doubts?

Once again I was nearly run down by a careless driver who didn't perceive my right to walk across the highway without looking. He honked and yelled a few vile words my way, something about being a stupid dolt. What effrontery, to almost run down the town doctor and then insult him in addition.

I entered my boarding house. Mrs. Apperson greeted me cheerily. She seemed genuinely interested in seeing me, very affable. Still, I couldn't help but wonder if part of this was her pride in having the town doctor as her star boarder. This gave her a certain prominence and God knows, people in a small town have little basis on which to feel important in the scheme of life. Such thoughts seemed unkind, though. Truly she was just a nice, kind, gentle human being with a love of humanity, nothing cluttered or dishonest, one of the few who met life daily for what it gave, and enjoyed people for what they were, good or bad.

"Well," I confided, "I have a date with a special person tonight. Believe it or not. Some bit of miracle wouldn't you say?"

"Heavens, no," she disagreed. "I think that's fine. You deserve a night off. Who's the lucky girl?"

She knew, I was sure, but I played the game.

"You mean you can't guess?"

"Must be that sweet girl Sarah, I assume," she said.

"Yep," I said smiling. She went on.

"She is such a sweet girl. Always has been, ever since she was a little girl, was always the town favorite. Her daddy was so proud of her, always said she'd grow up and be a nurse. He was so happy when she decided to go to nursing school up there in Baltimore. And just before he died he told me she was very much in love with a young doctor and hoped she would marry him soon."

My heart sank. My suspicions were confirmed, somehow I'd always known it. Well, that did it. Any declarations of love after such a short and uneventful courtship would be utterly absurd.

Mrs. Apperson sensed immediately my hurt and tried vainly to correct it.

"But I guess it didn't work out," she said. "She certainly hasn't seemed to be interested at all in returning to Baltimore since she went to work for you."

What was it Sarah said that night? "I've got to hurry home, I'm expecting a call from Baltimore." Yes, that was it. I knew it somehow. She was probably waiting for him to finish a residency and then he'd join some large clinic or university medical staff and marry her. Meanwhile, she worked for me and I presumed too much from our relationship. After all, why shouldn't she enjoy herself while waiting; nothing serious, nothing difficult to get over. She obviously couldn't imagine, on the basis of such a short and professional relationship, that I could be serious about her. Well, I'd just have to expect nothing and enjoy what little there was to be for as long as it lasted. In the past, it hadn't been characteristic of me to have too little confidence in my ability to woo and win a woman. Only since Carolyn died.

I excused myself from Mrs. Apperson, who now regretted her remarks. Before I could leave she again tried to make amends by telling me she hoped I'd forget what she'd said. It didn't help. My despair was too deeply implanted.

After my shower, while drying, there was a knock on the door. Mrs. Apperson said she was sorry to interrupt me but I was wanted on the phone. I hadn't heard the phone ring because of depressing thoughts, no doubt.

It was Charlotte, who answered my office phone and other phones at night. Dial phoning did not yet exist in this rural area, so the local operator really had considerable information as to the activities of the local citizens.

"What is it, Charlotte?" I asked, still dripping bath water slightly from beneath my robe.

"Mr. Ambrose Bennett," she drawled. "He says his aunt, Miz Bennett, is ill. Got some kind of bad grippe or something."

"Let me do the diagnosing, please," I remonstrated her. "That's what they pay *me* for. Put him on, please."

Ambrose sounded excited, too excited, I thought for the severity of the illness involved. I wondered why he was so overemotional about an old woman who was a distant relative, albeit, perhaps his only living relative, and especially since he must be her heir. Maybe I was too harsh in my interpretation, or perhaps calloused would be a better description. My own emotions were somewhat discombobulated anyhow, following Mrs. Apperson's remarks. I wondered, as I half-listened to Ambrose, if there was such a word as discombobulated, or if it was one of those colloquial words endemic to our area or era.

"Doc, are you listening to me?" he asked. The question reawakened me from stray thoughts to reality.

"Of course," I answered.

"Well then, what do you think, shouldn't you come and see her?" he demanded. At least the tone of his voice seemed demanding.

I hated to admit I probably hadn't heard a word he had said, so with his final demand and a vague recollection of his seeming alarm, I answered that I certainly agreed I'd better come to see her, and right away. I told him I'd be there just as soon as I could. After he hung up I wondered why I hadn't had the nerve to tell him I hadn't heard a word or at least asked some seemingly innocuous question to reopen discussion of her symptoms. Now I really had no idea what I was going out to treat. What was it dear Charlotte had said, "Got the grippe or something"? Thank God, I thought, she paid attention. I wondered why Miss Bennett hadn't called sooner and why her cold was lingering on, getting worse perhaps. Suddenly I felt cold all over. Had I missed a diagnosis of cancer—perhaps of the nose and throat, now metastatic to the lung and other places. I hastened to dress and hurried to the office for my bag, as if haste could ward off the impending death from the cancer my mind had now seized upon. The haste was I'm sure more to meet the problem as quickly as possible and reassure myself that no such calamity existed. I felt guilty and unsure already. A thought of sending her to Duke in the morning crossed my mind and then angered me. "Stupid insecurity," I said aloud in the car. I ran up the office steps and couldn't help but once again remember Mr. Lincoln's hurried steps up my stairs and the anxiety they created in me. Poor Mary Belle. I could never quite accept the defeat implied in death, though I knew it had to be a necessary end to all life. Maybe that's why I had chosen medicine, to play God, defeat death, give life, or maybe just ward off my own fears of death by superior knowledge of how to maintain life. Certainly, I'd failed miserably in Carolyn's case. Poor, sweet Carolyn, she relied on me so heavily and I let her down, and just because I had let my own emotions interfere with sound judgment. Just as I had done a minute ago by letting my concern over Mrs. Apperson's remark prevent me from hearing anything Ambrose had had to tell me. Damn it, damn it, I thought—why couldn't I put everything in its proper place. How many times I'd found myself listening to a chest with my stethoscope and realized later that other thoughts had kept me from hearing anything through that stethoscope, even though I'd gone through all the motions. I was glad patients didn't realize this. I wondered how many other doctors had had similar experiences.

The office seemed dark and gloomy. I didn't like to come

here at night. Every wall or floorboard or door creaked, it seemed, and I half-expected to meet somebody in the dark. After Carolyn died, a psychiatrist had told me what I expected to meet in the dark was the personification of my conscience, who would in my fantasy strike me dead for my sins, my guilt. Hell, I had thought—who doesn't expect to meet someone sinister in a dark place. Surely all people can't be guilty of some transgression. Transgression, indeed! A mild word for mistake. God knows I feel guilty, but personification of it, in the dark? That's too much to swallow.

As I filled my bag with the necessary medications and diagnostic instruments, I turned in my usual way to glance about to see if I'd forgotten anything, hoping again to see something that would instantly remind me of a necessary item. I turned off the lights. In the quiet of the room, I heard it, unmistakably, footsteps on the stairs outside, ascending the wooden steps with measured but not slow steps. A chill burst over me. Did I lock the door? I waited, frantically searching my mind for the ideal place to hide from the inevitable discovery I knew awaited me. It struck me as odd that in spite of this I didn't hide or run, even as my fear mounted, as if the punishment I was about to receive from this awaited and expected intruder had to be endured. Then I heard Sarah's voice.

"Dr. Jenson? Are you there?"

Dear, dear Sarah, why would she come here, I wondered, and then I remembered, I had made a date with her for tonight and it was now past the hour I was to have met her.

"I saw your car race by," she said, "and wondered what had happened. Do you have a house call to make?"

"Yes," I answered and wanted to say I had intended now to come and get her, though truthfully, I would have forgotten her. It didn't seem necessary to explain my absurd and erratic behavior to Sarah, though, so I totally avoided explanations and asked, "Will you mind going on the house call with me before our date?"

She sparkled at the request, I assumed. Or hoped, perhaps, since she was very agreeable.

"Are we going to have another baby?" she asked.

"No, not this time. Wish we were. That night was fun,

wasn't it? This time we are going to the Bennett mansion to treat Miss Bennett's grippe or ague." I laughed as I said it but felt no inner amusement. She didn't understand the joke.

"Well," she said, "at last I'm going to get a chance to see the inside of that house. I've always wondered what it was like." She seemed to want to discuss it more, but I wanted to leave so she agreed to tell me more on the way.

On the way, Sarah was almost gay with anticipation. She asked what it was like and I described it as best I could from the trip I'd made there. We approached the gates and I paused to get out and open them and then, once across the small bridge, again to close them. My shoes thumped as I crossed the bridge back and forth and the footstep noise died quickly in the vastness of the surrounding fields and woods. Once again, I had that uncomfortable feeling of being watched by a sinister being. I was glad to return to the car and the warmth of Sarah's presence and companionship. We drove up the tree lane, under the low-hanging moss to the circular drive and the porticoed house. The car lights flashed on the pillars as I made the final turn. When I turned off the car lights, the blackness of the heavily treed front lawn engulfed us. Only dim light showed through narrow and tall glass windows on each side of the front door. Sarah remarked to me she was glad to be going inside with me, her previous enthusiasm now somewhat dimmed by the aura that surrounded this house. She said, almost paradoxically, "I remember as a little girl how I envied the others who attended the festive parties here," while her tone of voice showed her obvious change of heart.

"Let's go in before we both faint from fear," I said, and she smiled, or at least, I assumed she did. It was very dark and she wasn't very visible.

I knocked on the door and the sound of the knock died instantly, muffled by the trees, moss and night; a chill night, I might add. After what seemed an interminable wait, the door slowly swung open, without the expected creaking. The overseer greeted me with his usual politeness. I said to him, almost apologetically, "I brought my nurse," and wondered if he wondered why I had since there was no logical explanation. And then quickly added, "She was with me."

161

He nodded and asked "us all" to come in. Once in the entry hall, the gloom of the house without bright lights confronted us. I asked him if there was somewhere my nurse could wait while I saw Miss Bennett and explained, again apologetically, that she hadn't wanted to wait in the car. Sarah telegraphed a look of annoyance to me at these seemingly inane apologies for her presence. Once again, though, with almost exquisite acceptance of our right to be there, this servant who was well schooled in matters concerning guest care, graciously nodded and said it would be fine for her to wait in the library. I walked in with Sarah as she smiled at the warmth of the library with its books, fire and dim light. My glance went back immediately to the painting of Lieutenant Bennett whose icy stare seemed to register disapproval of this intrusion. But Sarah exhibited none of the same feeling, smiling and looking visibly more relaxed. I told her I'd leave her now and be back as soon as possible. As I walked out, I glanced back at her, framed in a window behind her by those heavy old tied drapes of dark decaying velvet. I hated to leave her there alone. The overseer then showed me to the stairs. I couldn't remember his name and it annoyed me. Since he was so polite, it would have been gracious of me to remember.

He motioned to the stairs with his hand and said, "Y'all know the way, I'm sure, Doctuh."

How could I forget! As he walked off behind the stairs I ascended them. My footsteps were muffled and I wondered if the treads were solid thick slabs. The hall was unlighted as I passed the circular window on the stair landing, but a light from Miss Bennett's room shone sufficiently to guide me.

Though the door to the room was open, I knocked before entering and announced, "Hello! Dr. Jenson. May I come in?"

Miss Bennett replied, "Do come in."

When I entered, once again, she was in bed but looked ill, her complexion sallow, though she was propped up in bed and alert. Her housekeeper was also present and nodded hello to me. I tried to be cheery, without conviction, and it was obvious that nothing about the room, the patient, or the housekeeper called for such a demeanor. It is always difficult to start immediately asking about symptoms without some social amenities, yet the patient is, without question, more interested in his or her illness than trivial conversation. Still, it occasionally puts a patient at ease to find you have other qualities less machine-like. I went on with questioning, ignoring the housekeeper's presence, feeling that if Miss Bennett didn't desire her presence, she would ask her to leave. I always disliked questioning patients in front of any observers, perhaps feeling that someone would recognize my lack of skill and expertise by the limit of my questions. Yet, how could an untrained mind discern such limitations. It had to be my own vexatious guilt. Still, I remembered as a boy the visits of the local doctor to my home and his cheery bluff. I had often wondered if this facade didn't cover up his lack of ability and acumen. And yet, maybe his personality irritated me and I wanted to believe him to be a charlatan. Or maybe his God-like image annoyed me. It was always difficult to be objective with one's thoughts. As a boy, I possessed no such wisdom and now, since Carolyn died, my mind was a maze of contradictions, fears, ambivalences, and indecision. I was obviously lost in my thoughts, and noticeably so, since Miss Bennett asked me if "I was all right."

"Of course," I said. "Now will you tell me what is bothering you?"

"I don't know," she answered, which almost every patient answers as an opener.

"Are there any changes you've noticed?" I asked.

"Lately," she said. (That indefinite length of time! Yet patients rarely remember exactly when an illness began.) "I've been feeling poorly."

"Poorly?"

"Yes, I'm so weak and tired. It's an effort to do anything. My legs even feel wobbly when I stand or walk. It scares me a little."

"Of course it does," I reassured her. "Have you had any other symptoms?" Almost all people with an illness feel weak and wobbly.

"My head aches almost constantly and I'm dizzy." She looked at me with anticipation as though that would certainly be the symptom I desired to hear about and could use to secure my diagnosis.

Once again, so many illnesses are accompanied by headaches and dizziness, it was of little diagnostic help.

I asked, "Are you eating well?"

"No," she admitted, "but it's because my appetite is so poor and my mouth hurts so badly when I eat as if it were sore throughout. I'm embarrassed to say that when I eat, the saliva runs constantly." She lowered her eyes. I understood how distressing such a symptom must be to a lady of her breeding.

"It is so very distressing to me to have so much saliva," she reiterated. "Can you do something about that?"

I noticed how she tried to hold back the moisture as she talked, but little beads of saliva with bubbles appeared through her tightly drawn lips.

"I'm sure it is annoying," I said, "but maybe I can give you something to help that," I reassured her again. "Have you any other new symptoms?"

"No," she answered.

"Nothing?" I hoped for some other clues. Her Negro housekeeper offered a suggestion.

"Miz Bennett, don't y'all remember how your hair comes out when Ah combs it? That beautiful hair's almost getting thin," she said directly to me.

"Yes, I'd forgotten," Miss Bennett said and looked at me again. I felt a little embarrassed since I couldn't seem to phrase another question or comment thoughtfully on what had been said. I decided to toss the ball back to her with another request for symptoms. None of her symptoms so far were specific enough to diagnose a disease and even grouping them all together was of little additional help. They seemed vague and nonspecific and even unrelated, but the chances were that they were all related. A doctor must try to think of symptoms as belonging to one illness, since seldom is there more than one disease going on at the same time. Osler had said "common diseases are common" and we always sought the common and obvious solution. Stomatitis could be vitamin deficiency or trenchmouth. Ugh, trench mouth, a rotten disease. I remembered once I'd had it and how stringy and copious the saliva was. A filthy disease, spirochetal as a matter of fact. That fact always jarred me. And hair loss: thyroid deficiency, hormone deficiency, dandruff, seborrheic dermatitis, poisons, age. Weakness: poor diet, age, muscle disease, nervousness, fever, innumerable other diseases leading to generalized weakness. And the omnipresent headache and dizziness. I think the symptom headache was always henceforth to plague me, to arouse doubts and fears; and it was also always the common accompaniment of fever, malaise, nervousness, etc., etc.—name it and headache can be there.

"I had some tingling in my hands the other day," she offered after considerable thought, and then looked hopefully in my direction. Nothing registered in my provisional diagnoses. The next play was mine, obviously. I ignored her previous offering.

"When did you lose your appetite?" I blurted out almost as if by reflex. That's a question one asks all patients and I got the answer I would have expected.

"I don't remember," she said. (But why should she when probably it started slowly?) Then she added that she was slightly nauseated at times, also.

I asked if she vomited and she looked annoyed that I would suggest this fine lady vomited and said, "Of course not," with conviction and obvious pique. To change the subject slightly I asked, "Is there any time of day these symptoms are worse than other times?"

She seemed pleasantly surprised at my question as it did awaken more recall in her mind. Patients often are happy to have questions asked that cause them to remember heretofore forgotten symptoms. Instinctively, they want to help the doctor and are gratified to be able to.

"Oh yes," she said, almost cheerily while amazed she'd forgotten to tell me, "it is much worse, the nausea, that is, at night or in the morning. My morning milk always seems to help prevent it from occurring during the day."

"Do you drink milk only in the morning?" I asked. "Since it seems to help."

"Oh no," she said, "I drink it three times a day," with positive allusion to its beneficial quality. "And at bedtime," she added. "And I take my tonic elixir every day. That has vitamins and iron," she added further. And alcohol, also, I added silently. Why does everyone think tonics are the answer to aging and the general body dysfunction that attends aging.

"That's fine," I said with no honesty, and added, "Do you have any other symptoms?" She seemed to have no more thoughts, so I said, "Well, let's examine you now. Maybe you'll think of more."

The housekeeper arose quietly and slipped to the door. This apparently was her time to leave. I sat down on the edge of the bed. Miss Bennett adjusted her bedjacket to more completely hide her chest. Examining a patient in her own bed is unsatisfactory. It is awkward and sometimes difficult. But I went through all the motions. She held the thermometer very primly in her mouth as I simultaneously took her pulse. Surprisingly, her pulse was 110, even at rest. Is that nervousness, I wondered? Her temperature after the five-minute interval was 99.6. Using a Fahrenheit thermometer after a metric system training at Duke was a terrible desecration of my training but somehow, despite that fact, 99.6 meant more to me than 37.5. It seemed easier to understand. I had known in med school that almost all of the students converted the temperatures for easier understanding while using the metric figures only for school purposes. Her temperature and pulse were slightly elevated. I examined her eyes and ears with the ophthalmoscope and otoscope. They were seemingly normal. Her mouth looked inflamed, though the light from my flashlight was hardly bright enough. I made a mental note to get new batteries. There was definitely more saliva than usual and I wondered if her tongue was swollen. I could see no obvious reason for stomatitis and tongue changes—after all, she did take vitamins in her elixir. Old people often eat poorly but she denied this; though her appetite had been poor lately. Her skin seemed dry in areas. Yet, she said it had always been, though perhaps a bit worse lately. She also offered the help that eczema ran in her family. I didn't remember whether I had noted this in a previous examination or not. As I ran my hand down over the skin of her arm, feeling its texture, she suddenly said, "Ooh, that makes it tingle."

"Like pins and needles?" I asked.

"Yes."

Both arms tingled but not consistently.

So much for that. Her thyroid seemed to be of normal size and shape. No nodes were palpable in her neck or arms. Her heart tones were normal, regular with no murmurs. It was difficult to examine her heart since instinctively she held her bed clothes closed, hiding any glimpse of her breasts, a trait very common to female patients of her age group and era. I, too, was reluctant to ask to examine her breasts. This meant my exam wasn't thorough. Yet, the dereliction seemed propitious under the circumstances. She seemed relieved when I suggested we examine the abdomen next. I wanted to do a lung exam also, though it would require removing her bed jacket of which I was sure she wouldn't approve. She grumbled, but removed it. Her lungs were clear. Her liver seemed just a tad enlarged but she was very thin and I wondered if I wouldn't have felt it anyway. There were no abdominal masses. Pelvic exam and rectal were out of the question here, I decided, and once again had a twinge of conscience. My old professors would never have approved of the deletion of these parts of the anatomy.

Finished with the examination, I sat back on the bed wondering what to do next. My focus then suddenly drew to her neurologic complaints. I tested all of her reflexes—all normal. There were areas of questionable hypesthesia on her skin. The muscles of her legs were flaccid and emaciated. I wondered what it might mean, but she was thin from age, and probably atrophy of aging accounted for this fact. She said she was weak and walked unsteadily. Couldn't expect her to be strong. Her grip was weak but, after all, she was a frail lady. I flicked her finger to test neurologic sign and inadvertently broke her fingernail off. It startled me and I apologized profusely. I even picked it up and threw it into my bag as it seemed messy to leave it on the bed, and no waste receptacle was nearby. She seemed not at all surprised at the broken nail and said nothing.

With the exam completed I stood up and readied myself to give pronouncement of my intentions for her future treatment. I had in mind a poorly conceived plan for study and further testing, but had few words of encouragement to offer. It was at that very instant that I heard it. The first scream was muffled and only slightly distracted me, seeming unreal and far distant. The second scream, though unmistakably real, was inside the house and, determining direction, it came from the hall downstairs. A high terrified scream! Without question, Sarah's voice. And then another and another as I bounded out of the room and down the hall to the stairs. In the dim light, I stumbled at the landing of the stairs and fell against the wall. From that point, though, I could see Sarah standing alone in the main hall beneath the chandelier with her hands alongside her face, screaming in terror. A few seconds later, I was at her side. She fell against me and sobbed and sobbed.

"Sarah," I entreated, "it's all right, I'm here, I'm here," trying to soothe her. She continued to sob.

"Sarah," I said again, "what is it, what's wrong? Please! Tell me." The overseer had appeared now from nowhere and the housekeeper as well. They stood nearby observing the scene but offering no suggestions or solace.

Finally, Sarah through broken sobbing said, "That face, that face."

"What face?" I asked. "Where? Please tell me."

"In there," she said, motioning behind her by twisting her arm back, and pointing at the library, yet not looking herself. Of course, my next move should have been to go to the library immediately but a twinge of fear spread through me and kept me motionless. I noticed neither of the two observers made an effort to move either.

"What happened?" I asked, as I stalled from making the obvious move to investigate. "Please, Sarah." It wasn't like Sarah to be so hysterical and I knew whatever had upset her must have been very frightening. My first reaction was to remember the picture of the lieutenant, but it couldn't have upset her. "The window," she sobbed. Inwardly, I suspect everyone has that fear that he or she will look out a window at night and find someone looking back, someone with an evil, vicious face, and Sarah must have experienced such a confrontation just now. Perhaps it would be like looking in a mirror and seeing the real side of one's personality facing him, the side that he keeps covered and hidden, the one he tries not to face unless forced to. Another reason for my inertia must have been how desirable it felt to have Sarah clinging to me in desperate need of my supposed strength. The thought that she found me strong rather

168

than weak crossed my mind fleetingly. I liked being held by her for her protection. Her warm arms about me, her lithe body so close to mine was very exciting. Yet, I knew I must go in the library, look out that same window and face the prospect of seeing the same ghoulish face that had unnerved her, unless I wanted to risk the chance of seeming weak, particularly now, having just had strength imparted to me through her actions.

Tenderly, I extracted myself from her grasp, reassuring her that all would be set right. She should remain here with the overseer and housekeeper while I looked. It was an act of bravado on my part, not altogether accomplished with ease. Leaving her with these two people in a dimly lit hall wasn't altogether reassuring to her either, I suspected, since either of them might have been the face in the window. Yet, either could have walked in on her in the library without looking through the window. The face had to be an unknown interloper who couldn't chance being seen in the house itself, and out of necessity had to go about peering in windows to accomplish his purpose, whatever that purpose was.

As I was about to enter the library, I paused, my heart racing, my mind racing, too. What an unfair advantage the interloper had. The window looked like a mirror with the dark night beyond and the light from the fire within. In order to see out I must place my hands beside my head to screen out the inner light and my face directly against the window and even then with little chance of seeing him if he had stepped back into the shadows. As I bent to peer out, I felt as though I were looking into a dark abyss, a grave, cold and uninviting draped with heavy funereal velvet on either side. I looked out but a short time before retracting from the glass panes, considered briefly loosening the drapes from their ties and closing the interior from the outside view. I loosened the one tie and pulled the drape toward the center. It accomplished little since they were mainly decorative, not designed for closing light out or in, depending on one's point of view at the time. In addition, as I yanked it toward the center, a cloud of dust, some perhaps a hundred years old, spread out in the air and settled on me. I waved it aside in a futile gesture as it was heavy and thick. I coughed when it irritated my nostrils and throat and stepped back instinctively to avoid further contact. The dust seemed a malevolent sign. Just then, lightning flashed and for a brief, partially observed instant, I fancied I saw a form outside the window. A storm was approaching. A low, distant rumble of thunder followed. Still miles away, I thought. My instinct was to turn and run, but I walked quickly to the door, giving as little impression of haste as possible. I felt the piercing eyes of Lieutenant Bennett watching me as I moved toward the hall. The hall seemed like a sanctuary, centered as it was in the middle of the house not near any window or door through which one could be observed too easily.

"Didn't see anything there," I reassured Sarah.

"But it was there," she insisted sobbing slightly, "an evil-looking face, grinning at me. I wouldn't make it up." She seemed slightly annoyed.

"I know you wouldn't. I only said there is nothing there now. I didn't see anything." I lied a little when I said that and wondered if my face betrayed me.

I told the overseer that I was sorry I had loosened the drape. He seemed unannoyed yet concerned and went immediately to the library to refasten it in the position it had been in previously. I noticed he gave no impression of being scared. I told Sarah I had to go back up to Miss Bennett's room momentarily. She wouldn't remain by herself so I decided she should come with me. The lightning flashed again as we mounted the stairs and momentarily lit up the landing area through the round window. Sarah waited at the top of the stairs as I disappeared beyond into Miss Bennett's room.

I apologized for running out. Strangely, she seemed uninterested in who had screamed or why, asking only about herself and what I thought was wrong with her.

"I can't decide without further tests," I said. "Blood and urine tests. Would you mind coming to the office tomorrow so that I can draw blood? And will you bring a urine specimen?" I added.

"How will I do that?" she asked, obviously annoyed with the thought.

"In a bottle," was my simple answer. I was mildly annoyed now myself. I was truly more impatient than annoyed. Sarah was waiting by herself and I wanted to go back to her.

"Well, I suppose so," she said resignedly. I didn't feel assured she'd comply.

"Then, I'll see you tomorrow." I still couldn't understand why she didn't seem concerned or even interested in the commotion of but a few minutes ago.

Sarah was still at the top of the stairs and when I said we would leave now, she offered no argument. We swiftly descended the stairs to the hall and front door. No one was there to let us out. I disliked going out into the dark to the car but the car in a peculiar way seemed less malevolent than the house. I opened Sarah's car door in true gentlemanly fashion, resisting the terrible urge to just run and get in. I would seem too weak. She looked at me apprehensively just before the closing of the car door plunged her into total darkness. I walked around the back of the car which actually was a greater distance than around the front but for some strange reason, seemed safer. I got the door open, all the while expecting a sinister, cold hand to grab my shoulder and spin me around to face whatever that evil thing was I had to face. It seemed an age before I found the keyhole in the dashboard and was most grateful when the motor turned over and started the first time. I had never felt so eager to leave any place, even though I, myself, had seen no face nor had any terrible scare. I laughed to myself at how absurd it all seemed. Why had Sarah's fright unnerved me so much? Why couldn't the face in the window have been more frightened, more fearful, and weaker of character than us? Maybe he would even be afraid of us should we search around. Sarah shuddered. Her voice shattered my intellectual bravado as quickly as it had surged forth.

"It's cold," she said.

"Yes, it is," I answered. I didn't feel like making light conversation. The moss seemed to hang even lower as we started out the road, grasping fingers of a thousand damned people trying to include us in their misery. The lightning flashed again.

"Oh," Sarah screamed and looked at me with horror on her face. Her "oh" was a long drawn out "oh," one laced with terror. A chill ran down my spine, icy to the point of consolidation. I

171

would have been immobile, a solid icicle. I couldn't even ask what had frightened her so. My mouth opened but the voice refused to be commanded.

She explained herself. "A man! On horseback." Her voice was thin and weak and the words were choked out, as if someone was strangling her between each word.

Horseback! I, too, had seen someone on horseback. Prometheus, I remembered. Suddenly, I felt better. "Ambrose," I said aloud.

"What? Who? What did you say?" Sarah quizzed.

"Ambrose?" She didn't seem to comprehend.

"Ambrose. You know. Ambrose Bennett."

"Ambrose Bennett?" she parroted. She still didn't understand.

"Ambrose Bennett," I said again. "I saw him the last time I was out here. Not up close, but hurdling the bushes or hedges or whatever on his horse. He sort of hangs around the house, but never appears to be acknowledged. He followed me to the gate on his horse last time, but at a distance so I couldn't make out his features. I really don't know what he looks like. He's a spectre, an illusion, a face in the window." It just popped out, a thought from the subconscious. "That's it," I said, "the face in the window must have been Ambrose. Have you ever see him before?"

Sarah said she hadn't.

"How about the time he brought Miss Bennett to the office?"

She hesitated a minute before answering. "I don't think so. I don't believe he came in the office with her. I don't really remember."

"Well, little matter," I said, "he'll be bringing her in tomorrow for blood tests so you can get a look at him then and tell me if it's the face you saw."

"Oh, great! I'm not sure I want to see that face again," she answered.

Her manner though seemed more assured, as if her fear had been lessened. We came finally to the gate. I quickly opened it, drove through, and reclosed it, turning then to the road back to town. I went only a short distance, stopped, turned off the car motor and headlights.

"Listen," I said to Sarah. Somewhere in the night, to our side, in the fields were the sounds of horse's hooves. Their pounding paused, then started again and gradually faded into the distance.

"Let's go," Sarah said, "this place gives me the creeps."

All the way back to town we talked very little, deep in individual thought. What sort of man was Ambrose? Why the mystery? Why the reticence to be seen or met? Nothing made any sense. When we reached Sarah's home and had stopped, I turned to her. She was still quite upset and I felt a strong urge to assuage her fears and doubts. That's a laugh. Me, the leader of all doubters, the sole owner of all fears, the essence of indecision, comfort her in her need. The whole idea was ludicrous. The lightning flashed and thunder clapped sharply, a staccato slap echoing and resounding back and forth. That noise was the final straw in Sarah's evening. Her composure dissolved. She put her head over against my shoulder and cried, not wailing, but soft, quiet sobbing of a heartsick type. I slipped my arm around her and held her close and firm, enjoying immensely her need of my solace and comfort while feeling equally an intense attraction to her in her need. It all seemed so natural, so important, so real, so right, so dear and tender. She cried a considerable length of time. I lifted her head and looked into her eyes. I put my face close to hers to kiss her and tasted the salty flavor of those tears that had crossed her mouth. The moistness of her face was so inviting. I kissed her cheeks, her forehead, her chin, enjoying each warm caress and then her sensuous mouth lightly while she still cried softly, her lips quivering. After many tender moments, I sat back, feeling the time had come to be more realistic and lighthearted. It might help her.

"I really fouled up our date tonight, didn't I," I said apologetically.

She recovered her composure slightly and said, "It doesn't matter."

Rain had begun to gently fall on the car roof, first irregular tight little sounds, then finally a sonorous regular beat of sharp, staccato spats against the metal. Sarah raised her eyes toward the roof and I followed with mine.

"I don't think I can bear to be alone tonight," she said quietly. There was the invitation I'd longed to receive for so long, for all eternity it seemed. A direct indication of her feelings toward me. Nothing she could have said would have thrilled me more, yet I felt a sudden wave of doubts invade my entire fiber. My mind raced with feeble excuses for not accepting her invitation, none voiced. When faced with the need for a sudden decision, the mind is capable of incredibly fast thought, weighing and balancing conflicting ideas in a matter of seconds. I chose an evasive answer, no refusal, no acceptance, no decision.

"We'd better go in before it rains too hard."

By the time we'd started across the yard in a dead run, it had begun to hail, small pellets of ice that stung the skin when they struck. We stood on the porch and watched the barrage momentarily before entering. The icy missiles bounced in disarray to and fro as they struck the ground. The lawn took on the appearance of being alive with jumping creatures. Sarah shook slightly with the cold air and turned to enter. Once in the door, the sudden flooding of lights restored once again a warmth which had been lost in the darkness without. Yet Sarah, remembering, hastened to close all the shades, rolling each living room shade down to the sill for positive assurance of privacy from prying, sinister eyes.

I watched silently, then chose to further relieve her mind of fears.

"Sarah, isn't it amazing how different something appears when the truth is known. The face in the window must have been Ambrose's."

She didn't answer. I drew further on my psychiatric medical school training, meager as it was.

"And if (therein was the fallacy of my argument) it was Ambrose, he must be a weak character, running, hiding, peering through windows, never allowing himself to be seen or met."

She didn't look convinced. I tried flattery.

"Maybe his grin was not evil but more appreciation of your beauty."

She turned to look at me, but without the conviction that I had stumbled onto the truth.

"Would you like some brandy?" she asked in an exhausted tone of voice. "I would," she added.

"Of course, whatever you wish."

Immediately, I decided her invitation saying she couldn't stay alone was not an invitation for a romantic tryst, but a cry of helplessness, a need for strength she didn't have at this moment. To assume otherwise was prime idiocy, indulging myself in masculine vanity. She didn't want me to be in bed with her, just in the house. How could anyone be sexual when one had recently had a nerve-shattering fright? My fears had been lessened by my analysis of the situation, recognizing, at least assuming, it to be Ambrose, a weak frightened character, all truthfully a conjecture, but her fears were not gone—abated somewhat, perhaps, but still present. My attempts at reassurance had not lessened her fear. Furthermore, she was exhausted and literally incapable now of being placated by analysis of the situation. She needed rest, freedom from dissertation.

She returned with the brandy. We sat on the couch as we had before, next to each other, yet apart, and sipped quietly without speaking. I had never learned to drink brandy. As a matter of fact, I had never learned to drink, period. Liquor was not a part of my household as a child. The Devil's brew, my mother and dad had called it. Our religious beliefs had outlawed it totally. Yet my father seemed always to receive a gift of some bourbon at Christmas from grateful business associates. The bourbon was always kept deep in the rear of the bathroom linen closet and at times as a child I chanced to examine it closely, tipping the bottle, wondering why it was so fascinatingly attractive for people. I assumed it must taste very good since so many people drank it, and yet, at the same time I feared its magic for changing one's personality when used. So many times I longed to taste it but dared not break the seal which bound it. Year after year, new bottles appeared, to rest beside the previous years' cache, none apparently ever opened. I failed to understand why my father kept the Devil's brew within our household. If it was only "for medicinal purposes," as he had said, why had he never treated any illness with it? And how would the Lord accept the idea of a cache of Devil's brew kept in periodically augmented quantities within our house? Once I wondered if it was their way of being tempted and resisting sin, a prideful gesture. The bathroom thoughts reminded me also of other guilt feelings which I rarely thought of. I shuddered slightly before the punishing hand of the Lord.

Sarah asked, "Are you all right?"

How long, how long had I been distant, within my thought? I hated to feel stupid, and now I had done it again.

"Yes, of course," I said, "brandy has to be drunk in small sips, because it burns the throat so fiercely. I just choked on it a second ago."

"No, no," she said, "it should be drunk in small gulps, letting it pass quickly into the stomach or it will burn all the way down. The idea is to warm the stomach and later the body, not to burn the throat. It opens the nostrils with its aroma. Haven't you had brandy before?"

"Well, of course, I have," I said somewhat indignantly; but added to explain my lack of urbanity somewhat, "but not too often."

She smiled knowingly, but not disapprovingly. I thought for a minute she appreciated to some degree my naivete and found it charming rather than unmanly.

I wanted to rescue myself, to seem more sophisticated, so I lapsed into a dissertation of my previous dissolute encounters with the Devil's brew.

"Once when I was at Duke, a friend and I decided to buy corn likker at a country still. He was a country boy and talked their language, and, fortunately, he was older and appeared more mature. My face looked too young to allow any hope of buying illegal booze, even though I was of age. Anyhow, we went out into the country and backwoods until we found this dump of a filling station. We bought a couple of gallons of gas and my friend indulged in some country talk with the proprietor while I stayed in the car somewhat out of earshot so I don't know exactly what he said. But I did hear the proprietor say, 'Waaaal, now let's see,' his words drawn out, 'y'all go down that road about tew miles or more to Brown's farm and stop there and ask, he just might know where y'all could get some.'"

Sarah was amused at my attempts to be both country and southern in my dialect and smiled appreciatively. I went on, liking to tell a story anyhow, enjoying the audience, and glad I could lighten her gloom.

"Well, you know we drove to the Brown house and stopped. Farmer Brown wasn't there but someone, a hired hand, or someone else, disclaimed any knowledge of where we could buy it. Yet he also knew of someone down the road a mile or so to the right, to the left, et cetera. We went there. To get into that house, we had to step across a small creek or run, I guess they call them here."

She nodded assent.

"We circled the old house many times calling his name. I don't recall it now. Presently, he appeared as if from nowhere, an apparition suddenly becoming human in form, in a cloud of smoke." I was embellishing the story slightly now for effect.

"'Waaaal?' was his greeting. My friend stated our needs in his country talk. 'Waaaal' he said again, 'don't know as how I can help you. Don't know of a still in these parts. Make some fine peach brandy, myself, if that's interestin' to yu.' My friend knew how to handle the situation perfectly and said yes we'd try a little. We then were taken to his basement where the entire walls were lined with shelves and on the shelves sat jugs of peach dew. Mountain peach dew. He poured us each a small glass and re-corked the jug. Well, I was thirsty and proceeded to drink the nectar as I would an iced Coke, continuously swallowing. With the second swallow, I recognized I was truly on fire and would doubtless choke to death in a matter of seconds. I felt asthmatic, able to draw in breath but unable to exhale."

Sarah was laughing, a warm sound to me.

"My God, it burned." I shuddered slightly at my blasphemy. (In our home, the name of the Lord, God, was never taken in vain.) No punishing hand smote me on the spot, as I had often feared it would while blaspheming. Yet, I was sure another strike against me was being entered into the Book in Heaven where my record of iniquities was kept. I often had wondered how the ledger balanced now. I went on.

"Well, it was obvious what a greenhorn I was since my friend was smacking his lips appreciatively and complimenting the farmer on his rare aptitude for making brandy. Something in my friend's manner must have reassured him we were not revenooers since after we agreed to purchase two jugs of brandy at fifty cents apiece, he thought he just might be able to put his hands on a few jugs of corn likker, for a dollar a jug, he added quickly with a quizzical look, wondering if we were willing or able to pay that high a price. We were able, of course, since all medical students are rich."

Sarah laughed again, and I was spurred on with my tale by her raptured attention and apparent enjoyment.

"We then walked deep into the woods nearby to his still— yes, his, which my friend had instinctively known existed. A shed near the still was filled with gallon jugs of white lightning, clear glass, white clear liquid. My friend sampled it showing great appreciation for its fine quality, wiping his lips on his sleeve and taking a second drag on the bottle. I watched the bubbles burst into the bottle upwards to the bottom now tilted up towards the sky. He lowered the jug, smiled and offered the jug to me for my approval, also. I declined as my throat was already agonizingly painful and hot from the brandy. Anyhow, we took our find back to campus to a party. We were the center of attention and the envy of all because of our obvious urbanity and savoir-faire."

I quit at this point of the story as I learned long ago that stories dragged out too long can become boring and tedious and their flavor lost.

Sarah said, "That's a great story. I suspect that's where you learned to sip brandy, isn't it?"

"Yep, and this is my second try at it."

"You're supposed to take short gulps, enough to swallow quickly, a gulp at a time, with intervals in between. Both of your methods are wrong. Never continuous swallowing nor sipping tiny amounts to hurt your throat."

"Live and learn," I said. "I'll bet you could teach me many things."

We stared at each other appreciatively for a minute and suddenly my discomfiture at making the next move, the seem-ingly obvious one, led me to get up from the couch, glass in hand. I said, "I'll see if the rain stopped," as if it made any damn difference. I was avoiding my feelings for Sarah, avoiding disclosure of them by direct exposure, only able to express them in times of stress or gaiety, like kissing her so tenderly in the car but a short while ago. I paused a minute behind the couch, our eyes meeting, her expression longing for my love, and then crossed quickly to the nearby window. I leaned down and ran up the shade. An icy blast ran from the top of my head to my toes stiffening me, an altogether unexpected event. There I stared momentarily into the ghoulish, grinning, scarred and white face that must have been Sarah's undoing. It was there only momentarily and than a shadowy figure fled through the darkness across the lawn. Instinctively, I dropped my glass in surprise, raced to the door and out into the night. I paused on the lawn turning this way and that trying to recapture the image of a fleeing figure in any direction. There was none. Suddenly, I was overcome with a feeling of incredible fear. What incredible stupidity had brought me out here to grapple with the Devil or one of his disciples? What stupid bravado had led me to this senseless act? What insanity had led me to believe I could have been an even match in a contest with this demon? I found myself retreating to the locked sanctuary of the house as fast as I had left it. Closing the door behind me, I met Sarah's eyes. There was no doubt in her mind what I had seen. My face was an open book, telling all soundlessly. It was obvious her fear had returned.

"I'll stay," I said. "You go to bed and try to rest. I'll not sleep tonight."

Sarah went up the stairs to bed like a dutiful child and I to the living room to a lonely vigil.

Chapter 9

The hospital corridor was green; walls, floor, ceiling. I ran down it, looking for a door. There was but one set of doors at the end, doors through which I dare not pass. I clutched at the walls as if to create an opening. My hands became numb and then bled. The blood passed ever so slowly down the wall, my life's sustenance flowing away. The blood became green as it approached the floor. I grabbed at it as if to put it back whence it had come, but it escaped my grasp. I ran back and forth in the hall, now pulling, now shoving, now clutching. All the time, immovable, impenetrable bulwarks thwarted me. There was no escape except through those terrifying, swinging doors. I must go there, though my life's blood was flowing away. I must face the reality and fear behind those doors. Terrifying reality. Punishment for my guilt. Could I escape, would I never be seen or discovered?

I must hurry—there was so little time left. I can't. I must. I grabbed my finger. I held it tight, still the blood ran out and turned green. My finger was turning green, pale green. Soon my hand would be green and then my arm and when this creeping greenness reached my heart, I was doomed. No more life or love or beauty of happiness. Hurry, hurry, without my arm, without my heart, there was no chance. They would cut off my finger, my hand, my arm behind those doors. When a limb turned green, they cut it off. Those beasts, those beasts would cut off my most important appendage, deprive me of life, of love, of soul. They mustn't notice it was green when I passed by. I would hide it. Covering it with my other hand seemed to only make it more obvious. The time had come to pass through. I no longer could escape the inevitable. If only I could pass through without the beasts seeing my lifeless limb that hung so limp and green, so ineffectually in its place. I was at the door. I peered through the windows. No one in sight. Cautiously hiding my green, limp appendage, I slithered through the doors noiselessly. They swung shut behind me sounding the alarm. The gong rang loudly, bong, bong, bong, bong—would it never stop. O God, I'll never take your name in vain again. Stop the bong. Help me. I never meant any harm. Don't let them remove my ineffectual appendage. Save it. I know I can bring life back into it, if only I have the chance. I'm a doctor. I know the circulatory pattern. I know how to help it. God! Where are you? Have you forsaken me? Have I been too guilty of crimes? I know what to do. I'll go back through the doors. I'll stay in the hall forever. I'll not scratch for an opening anymore. Maybe then the flow will stop, the walls will be green no more. My limb will not be green. I'll not try to escape by using it again. My God. O pardon me, God. The doors are gone. I can't go back. What will I do? Where will I go? I'll run, run, run—there toward the light so far away. The circular light. It is so far away. My legs are leaden. O God, help me run. Don't let them catch me. Don't let them catch me. I hear them now, their footsteps running behind me. The stairs. I've reached it and I'll run up toward the light. I'm not too late. I hope. I must hurry. They will catch me and cut away my limb, my right arm, my hope for happiness. The light looms larger. I am almost there. I'm free. I'm free. I've escaped. O my God. That's not blasphemous. I beseech your help. They are here already. How did they get there ahead of me? The man with the cleaver is here. And a girl. She hates me. She loathes and despises me. My God, the top of her head is gone. She is green. The man with the cleaver is nearing me. His face, his hideous, ghoulish, grinning face. He takes up the cleaver in his hands and lifts it high. My green limb is so obvious. I can't cover it. Both hands can't cover it. My time has come. Bong, bong, bong, bong, bong, bong. Stop. Stop. Don't Don't. I don't want it cut off. Help me. O, God.

I awoke writhing and fighting, perspiring profusely. Where am I? What is this place? I stumbled to my feet. Nothing looked familiar. For a partial waking minute everything was confusion. Then I realized. Sarah's home. My lonely vigil. I must have fallen asleep. That dream. That awful dream. God, what was that dream I had! The grandfather clock read six o'clock. All was still. A slight light of approaching dawn glimmered beneath the drawn shade where I had seen that face. Suddenly, I wondered if being asleep had allowed the demon to bypass me to reach Sarah, my sweet Sarah. I considered going to see if she was all right but declined to wake her. It was stupid to even entertain the idea she had been hurt. Why would I think such a preposterous thought. Someone entering would surely have awakened me. I would have heard his footsteps. Footsteps, it seemed, were the bane of my existence. I would never have missed someone climbing the stairs.

But my doubts resurged at that point and I almost gave way to my need to reassure myself of her safety. The stairs somehow seemed forbidding and turned me away. I lifted the shade and looked out. There was no ghoulish face this time, nothing but approaching dawn. Small drops of dew or rain still present on the lawn sparkled in the horizontal light of the sun, tiny prisms, individual rainbows. Their effect was magical and held my attention. A lone automobile passed by, an early riser on some unknown mission. I watched it as it passed and saw the passenger glance in my direction. My God, I thought, I've got to get out of here. Someone will see my car parked out there and assume that Sarah and I have—my God, how idiotic can one be, in a small town like this. I wondered how many other passersby or neighbors had seen my car. I hated to run off without saying goodbye to Sarah, but I could explain later. She'd understand. She was safe now. Being already dressed, I went to the door, paused, looked up the stairs and then noiselessly went out the door. The screen door escaped my careful efforts and banged shut, like a single pistol shot, a loud burst of noise. My heart skipped several beats as I waited to be seen by everyone. Going directly to my auto, I was just about to enter when another car passed by. How incredibly guilty and trapped I felt. It was Sheriff Carstairs. He merely waved and though I couldn't hear his voice I could read his lips saying, "Mornin', Doc." Goddammit, I thought, of all times for him to drive by. What the hell was he doing up so early. Sooner or later, probably at breakfast at Hank's, I'd have to face them all and all their knowing looks and sniggering. And worse than that, none of their suspicions would be true. Yet, I couldn't tell them the truth as it would sound contrived and false, and would also reveal my own fright. To admit to any degree of cowardice, unmanliness, or whatever, was unthinkable.

I went to the office first, to freshen up. The dream still clung to a fringe of consciousness and occasionally pushed close to the surface causing feelings of uneasiness. I wasn't sure I wanted to remember its content. Dreams, though vivid in sleep, can be so frightening, and yet vanish on awakening without any memory of the content. All that is left is a general sense of marked uneasiness, a feeling that one has just passed through an episode of horrendous nature. To solve the conflict requires memory of the dream and ability to face the reality involved, and without expert assistance, this is not possible for most people. I remembered they taught me in medical school that Freud founded psychoanalysis by analyzing his own dreams, and I wondered how he had had the ability whereas others failed. Maybe his emotional conflicts were not as severe as mine.

The office was dank and smelled of wet wood and age, probably rot and moss and filth. Suddenly I hated this office, this town, these people, except for Sarah, of course. If only I could shed the whole mess, the bigotry, the snoopers, the gossipers, this snide, backward, inimical bunch of bastards. But in truth, I knew I was only angry at myself and, as they say in psychiatry, projecting my displeasure with myself into displeasure with all about me, except Sarah. Dear Sarah. I remembered how tender, how loving I felt last night kissing away her tears. How protective and strong. And then. Hell! I looked in the mirror at my bearded face and tousled hair. I didn't look like any Adonis. Nor any Norse god. "Jenson, you damned fool," I said aloud, "Sheriff Carstairs saw you looking the same." If only I'd combed my hair and straightened my tie, he might have thought I'd just gone there, and not just climbed out of bed. With a beard? He's no damn fool. Dammit, dammit. What the hell was he doing out at six A.M.? I decided I'd better get cleaned up and go eat breakfast. I hated to go in my present clothes, having slept in them, knowing how wrinkled they were, yet I hated to return to Mrs. Apperson's for fresh clothes and let yet another person or persons know I'd been out all night. I had a clean shirt to put on at the office, but my trousers had a million crisscrossing wrinkles in them due to the wet night air; they looked as if I slept in them. The thought crossed my mind; maybe they were evidence I hadn't taken them off last night at that and proof I wasn't in bed with Sarah. Such an optimistic thought was short-lived in any event. Anyone could get in bed with his pants on and fall asleep. What was the point of belaboring it in my mind.

The after-shave lotion stung my face but felt refreshing, somewhat like dunking my face in ice water. Hank's restaurant would be open and, perhaps, if I got there early and Hank had already been visited by the sheriff, I'd save myself the pain of their knowing looks. No such luck. There was the sheriff's car parked right in front. I entered. Only Hank and the sheriff were present and were talking at the counter. I definitely allowed the screen door to bang shut, to let them know I was aware of their conversation and knew damn well what was the topic.

"Mornin', Doc," Sheriff Carstairs drawled, "yur an early riser." There was his gibe. He couldn't resist his barb. I didn't answer, just nodded and seated myself at the counter a few stools away. Hank slid me a menu and added, "The po'k chops are good this mornin'."

Those greasy, lousy, crappy "po'k chops," I thought. Doesn't he ever run out of them. I cursed every goddamn pig that was ever born to load itself with lard and condemn man to an early grave from arteriosclerosis. I wanted to shout out that my religion dictated no one should eat pork, only animals that split the hoof or chew the cud, and those filthy rotten pigs did not. God, was I angry. A twinge of anxiety hit me. I must stop swearing or even thinking such words—one was as bad as the other in my religious training. I remembered my father had sworn all the time and mother had accepted it, though she constantly told us she didn't want us to be like him. He wouldn't even go to church, yet she was certain that though he worked on the Sabbath, and swore, and had smoked and drank—I wasn't sure of that—he'd be saved in the end. I never understood that logic.

Robbery? What had the sheriff said?

I turned my head toward them and said, "What?" Hank asked me what I'd have.

184

"Ah, po'k chops," I said in my stupor. Then, "No, no, not pork chops. Uh, bacon and eggs." Why, I wondered, could I eat bacon but not pork. "What did you say?" I asked the sheriff again.

"I've been tellin' Hank," he said, "about the robbery last night, over near the county seat." My heart lightened. Maybe he wasn't a blabbermouth. A good sheriff, like a good doctor, kept information he gained about people in strict confidence, using it only if necessary for the solution of a problem. Was he a good sheriff? I wondered. He went on.

"Another grocery store. Strange, eh?"

"Yeh," I said, "if you're gonna rob something, why not a bank?" Hank, who was busy burning my bacon, turned and grinned his half-toothless, halfwit grin. A thought crossed my mind. Could his be the face in the window? No! But it was bad enough to have been. Hank was too much of a rabbit to go around looking in windows.

"What did they steal?" I asked, wondering why I said they. I could have asked, "What was stolen?"

"The same thing, which puzzles me," he answered. "Three times now and it's always the same thing. Shotgun shells and rat poison. Someone sure as hell seems to want to do away with pests."

"Don't they take any money? Ever?"

"Nope," he answered, "never have. Don't quite understand it. So little missin', it's hardly worth investigating. Still it is a robbery. What would you do, Doc?"

"I don't know," I said, "it's perplexing."

"Per who?" Hank asked with his stupid grin, setting my unpalatable-looking plate in front of me. Maybe my mood had lightened, feeling the sheriff had not betrayed me, because the food tasted better than it looked, albeit greasy. There was a period of silence. I ate and the sheriff finished his coffee and arose to leave. Peculiarly, I felt the need to have someone else help with my mystery, so said as he was leaving, "Sheriff, there's something I'd like to talk to you about sometime when you get the chance."

"Anytime," he said, smiling, that knowing smile. *Not that*, I thought, *you stupid dolt. Something else.* My anger had rekin-

185

dled. He left before I could say more. I finished as fast as I could. Hank couldn't understand my passing up his coffee, or mud, depending on which side of the counter one stood, but I wasn't in the mood for explanations, and left.

Eight o'clock arrived. I waited. Five minutes after eight. Sarah was never late, usually early. Ten minutes after eight. I paced the floor. My anxiety mounted. Several times, I looked out my office window in the direction of her home, hoping to see her coming toward the office. No Sarah. An early patient had arrived, than another. I couldn't bring myself to see them without Sarah. I had an almost irresistible urge to go to her home but how would I explain to the two patients waiting. I wished over and over that I'd gone up those stairs before I left her home. Doubts, doubts, conflicting doubts; a desire to see if she was all right, while I was there a desire to leave and have no one see my car in front of her home, a desire not to wake her, and I had been unable to make any choice as to which was the most important. In the past, I hadn't been this way. Before Carolyn died.

Why don't I phone her? For God's sakes (Norse gods, that is) why didn't I think of that sooner? She wouldn't be annoyed. I called. The operator was interminably slow in ringing, other calls preceding mine. Then the line rang and rang, once, twice, three times, four, five. The operator told me it didn't answer.

"I know that," I snarled at her in anger born of anxiety, "ring again." Again and again it rang, my anxiety reaching a peak. I slammed the phone down, my heart racing. "There has to be an explanation," I said aloud, "a logical solution."

Then I heard footsteps running up the stairs, a woman's. My heart leaped in my chest. I ran to the inner office hall. Sarah appeared through the door, breathless from running, and the door slammed shut behind her. I embraced her holding her tight, and muttering, "Sarah, dear Sarah." She didn't seem surprised—in fact, seemed to enjoy it. When I had regained my composure and my anxiety had lessened, she offered a simple explanation. Considering the exhaustion of the previous evening and feeling protected with me in the house, she had simply overslept, having failed to set her alarm. But I had called. She obviously had been on the way here. Had I looked out the window once more, I would have seen her. There could no longer be any doubt in Sarah's mind how I felt toward her. Why didn't I say it, now, here, in the office? "I love you." Why couldn't I? Would she think I said it only out of weakness, not strength, out of need, not solid attraction? Goddamn, I was in such a turmoil.

"I left early," I said, "hope you didn't mind."

"You were sweet not to wake me," she said. "I'm sorry I'm late."

"Forget it. You don't know how happy I am to see you."

"I think I do," she said knowingly. I smiled. How warm and marvelous she was. Neither of us seemed anxious to talk about last night's events.

"We'd better get to the patients," she said.

It was hard to keep my mind on work. I wondered if the diagnoses and treatment of those first few patients were valid after they had left.

"Don't forget to watch for Ambrose," I reminded Sarah. She grimaced a little at the thought of staring into that face again should it be the one we'd seen and I could hardly blame her.

The moment arrived. Miss Bennett appeared in the waiting room, aided by a woman, not her housekeeper. A white woman. Sarah came to me, obviously frustrated.

"He didn't bring her. He didn't come with her."

"Dammit," I said and then felt guilty. I wondered if Sarah had ever heard me swear before. She was undismayed. It pleased me. I could imagine the disapproving face of my mother under similar circumstances.

"Well, bring her in," I said in frustration.

She was escorted in by a youngish, twenty-four or twenty-five-year-old woman who was quite attractive. I wondered who this was. The mystery was soon over as Miss Bennett said in her frail voice, "This is my grandnephew's wife, Melinda." Ambrose's wife, I thought. She's too attractive to have married a man with a ghoulish face. The name of the mystery face was now even more illusive. My thoughts, though, trained as they were by medical men, went immediately to Miss Bennett. She was so frail, so obviously weak. She had lowered her head when she spoke to hide the droplets of saliva that had spattered forth with each word. But I had seen one glint in the sun like the early morning dew despite her attempts to hide them. I was suddenly seized with the fearful and intuitive feeling that unless I did something quickly this woman was going to die. Her visage foreboded impending death. She had relied on me, placed her confidence in me, looked to me for a cure. And my feeble knowledge had not been sufficient, not helpful enough. I was seized with anxiety over her future. I liked her. I hated to see her die, right before my eyes. Some people do die. Natural causes. I, and all doctors, have to face it. Attempting to prolong their lives is unjust, unwarranted, and unquestionably cruel. Yet here was someone who was dying and I couldn't tell whether it was of natural or unnatural causes. Whatever it was, to cure it, I must diagnose it first.

I reviewed with her once more last night's discussion of symptoms, seeking a new clue, a new symptom, that would help in the diagnosis. There were none. I wished someone would write a book listing symptoms and diseases associated with them. It wouldn't narrow it completely to one disease but would help in limiting the number I'd have to read about and choose between. I drew some of her blood. She winced and her pupils contracted when I put the needle in the vein. Even in her weakened condition, she joked slightly about the fact "her blood was red, and she'd been told she was a blue blood." Green Blood! Where in the hell did the thought of green blood come from, I wondered. The thought was an uneasy one, I also noted. She had forgotten to bring the urine, though I suspected she really hadn't forgotten. A fine lady doesn't leave her waste products around for someone to handle or examine. I wanted to tell her that her fluid intake filtered out through her blood and kidneys to the final end product of urine. It was sterile at that point and one hell of a lot more sanitary than the water which was originally drunk, despite its dirty connotation and acrid odor. I could have understood her reluctance to bring in a stool specimen, as I had always shared her disgust with that and had disliked examining it in medical school, though it very often gave valuable information about disease processes, maybe more than urine. No, not true, I decided. Now that I had the blood I wondered what tests I would order done on it. I had drawn several tubes despite her protest that she would have none left when I was through. A 50-cc syringe full of blood does look like a lot to the patient, I'm sure. Less than two ounces in a total volume of some six quarts, but nevertheless, one hates to part with any part of his body, especially an important part. Another wave of uneasiness crossed my mind as she said, "My arm feels weak and limp like the blood draining out of it." I reassured her, feeling uneasy myself. It had been a rotten night. I was tired and my thoughts were in hellish turmoil.

"Would you consider letting me send you to Duke for diagnosis, Miss Bennett?" I asked.

"I don't think I could stand the trip," was her honest and realistic answer. "You'll have to be the one to help me." My wish to dump the case was thereby thwarted.

"I know," I said, "and I'll do my very best."

"I know you will," she said. "I put my trust in you." She was a gracious lady, worthy of her background and the Bennett name. When she left, I looked out the window and watched her being helped into the car. Ambrose was not with them. His wife had brought her by herself. I wondered why Ambrose had not come, being obviously stronger and more capable of helping her up the stairs. I looked out at the gray Fall day and felt depressed. Colonel Bennett's uniform was grayer than usual today, his expression sardonic. Because of my ineptitude I was certain his saber was meant for me. I half expected him to lift the saber and lop off my head, as ungentlemanly as that would be for a Confederate officer.

Sarah interrupted me. "Dr. Jenson." It seemed ludicrous for her to call me by my title now that I knew I was in love with her. At least, I thought so. She was probably observing office decorum. Yet, I really hadn't told her I loved her, had I? But she must know. Hadn't I told her by my actions last night and today? Last night, I was strong, today I was weak. Which side of me would tell her? I hope she didn't realize my weakness, my panic at the thought of losing her, my indecision.

"Yes," I answered deep in thought.

"Mrs. Jacobs is here."

"All right," I said, still not turning.

"Are you all right?" she asked, concerned.

"Oh sure," I lied. "Well, we didn't see Ambrose, did we?" I said, resignedly.

"No," she said, "and I'm really just as glad. I really didn't look forward to it. You must have been right, though. It all fits when you put the puzzle together. The horse, the elusive Ambrose. Who else could it have been? Wish I could remember what he looked like, if I ever have seen him. I'm not sure I have. It doesn't seem as frightening when you put it all together."

I didn't tell her of my doubts, of my wonderment about Ambrose's wife, her attractiveness. No need to frighten her again when she was obviously calmer.

"Bring Mrs. Jacobs in," I said. I looked out the window again. The colonel's face had an inscrutable smile. What did he know that I didn't?

Again, Sarah asked if I was alright.

"Yes," I sighed, turning away from the window. "I was just remembering what General Briggs said at Shiloh."

"At Shiloh?" she said, puzzled. "What's that?"

"Things look pretty bad right now."

"But the South *won* that battle, didn't they, despite his gloomy appraisal?" she asked.

"Yep, you did," I agreed. "Hope *we* win this battle."

Mrs. Jacobs walked in and sat down. Her hostility was readily apparent in her stature, her demeanor, her facial stiffness. She was defying me to help her, to find out what was wrong, even though she sought my help and needed it badly.

"Sit down, please," I said, wondering if that stiff straight ramrod would crack when she flexed her hips in the act of sitting. She sat erect, waiting, challenging.

"Are you any better?" I asked.

"No," she replied, curtly. Not "somewhat," not "a little so," not even "I don't know," any of which would have meant she was willing to work on it and would help in trying to come to a conclusion. In my tired state, I felt defeated, wished she'd go away. Or, perhaps, I could send her away. Headache cases were my downfall anyhow. I couldn't really dispel the fear of serious illness that I might overlook.

"Perhaps," I said, "since I've been so unsuccessful in helping you, you'd like to go to Duke Hospital and see a specialist."

"No, I can't afford it," she said. "You've got to help me." It was a demand. No more demands of this type, I said to myself. I won't accept a demand. I did that once before when in love with tragic results. Poor Carolyn. I didn't love this woman, though. I felt great empathy for her, though, for her plight, and wanted desparately to help her. I decided to confront her with her hostility. Maybe that would be a breakthrough.

"But your whole attitude toward me is one of defiance, almost daring me to try to find out what is wrong. Without your cooperation, I'm powerless to help."

"Oh, that's just not true," she said, "I wouldn't be here if I didn't want your help."

She had a point. The very fact she kept coming back was proof that she wanted my help, even though she found it hard to accept.

"Well, I guess you're right," I said. "Let's see. Have you any new symptoms?" I was terribly tired, feeling dejected and lonely.

She was more willing to cooperate since confronted with her hostility. I thought I saw her ramrod spine bend and droop a little. She wrung her hands.

"Not really," she said. "They are still driving, pounding headaches, bursting my temples, making me sick to my stomach, dizzy, blinding me."

"Really blinding ones?" I asked.

"Blinding?"

"I mean do they actually make you blind, is it impossible to see or is the vision blurred? Or double?" I added, angrily.

"No, not really," she said.

So much for ophthalmic migraine diagnosis—probably out the window.

"The worst thing is the pressure in my head, like it would explode."

Explode! I wondered if that was the key word to the solution of her problem.

"Mrs. Jacobs," I asked, "do you go to church?"

She was totally taken aback by this seemingly pointless question, and I wondered myself why I'd asked it. It must have come from my own unconscious somewhere.

"Why, yes," she said somewhat uncertainly, with a quizzical look on her face.

"What religion do you follow?" I asked.

"Baptist." I should have known.

"Are you strongly religious?" I asked. Yes, was her reply.

"Does your religion teach you to forgive your and others' sins?"

"Of course, doesn't everyone's?" What a spot I was in. Why had I started this. Oh yes, explode, that's what she said.

"Mrs. Jacobs," I said, "something's bothering you. Something you'd like to explode about, but instead are keeping in check for whatever reason. Am I right?" There was a long pause. Then she put her head down and began to cry. After allowing her a cry, one of contained grief further proving her inability to express herself, I asked her, "Please, Mrs. Jacobs, tell me what it is that's bothering you. You know your secret is totally safe with me. A doctor takes an oath never to reveal anything he's heard from a patient. Your information will be totally confidential. I won't tell anyone. I won't even write it in the chart for someone to read."

She continued crying, perhaps somewhat less. I then gave her another reason for telling me her deep secret, the one that must have been making her sick.

"Your secret, and the anger or frustration associated with it, could easily be causing your headaches."

She didn't answer. After a significant pause, I added, "Maybe, if you explode to me, you wouldn't have to take out your anger on yourself, and your headaches would disappear."

"You're right, Dr. Jenson," she said in conciliatory tones. The hostility toward me was gone.

"There is somethin' troubling me, and I should tell you. All my life, I've tried so hard to do everything right. I was a good child. I always helped my mother. I was the oldest of five. My poor mother died of old age at thirty-nine. At thirty-nine, mind you. She was just worn out. I took over the household chores, being the eldest, until I finally got married. I went to church every Sunday, saw to it that all the other children did and read the Bible to them every night just as Momma had done. But I was stepped on constantly. None of them, including my father, ever helped me in any way. The children never obeyed me well. Once I got so angry, I beat one of them, drawing blood. It scared me. I lied to my father about it. I read the Bible all night that night. I vowed if the Lord would forgive me, I'd never let my temper flare again like that. I never did."

"Nor have since," I added.

"No, never. I left home when I was twenty-two. Not until then. I did all the chores until that time."

"And hated it," I added.

"Well, sometimes. I got married. You know, I had vowed I'd never marry anybody like my dad, but I did. He's almost a dead ringer for my dad, a shiftless, no-good bum."

Strange, I thought, how people steeped in hate will develop deep guilt over their hate and repeat a pattern in life, almost as if to use this as punishment to atone for the sin of hate.

"And your daughter?" I added.

"That no-good child. Takes after her father. Shiftless, lazy harlot. That Jezebel." Here was where her anger originated. Mae was the main source.

Harlot? That was a strange choice of words. I remembered her in her role of serpentine temptress as she had exhibited herself the day I'd visited the farm, with the slithering walk to the barn, her buttocks spelling out her wishes. The thought excited me somewhat. Such reveries were dangerous and hard to dispel. What next? I decided harlot was too explosive a word to use in answer. It might cause her to clam up. I chose lazy.

"Lazy?"

"Yes, lazy, shiftless harlot." Harlot still held third position. I repeated.

"Lazy? Shiftless?"

"Yes, she never does anything but laze around or sit on the porch in those sexy, tight dresses revealing every bit of herself, tempting every decent or indecent man that comes by."

I remembered. She'd told me about this one other time. I didn't comment.

"And just as I predicted it got her in trouble."

This statement commanded my attention more.

"Trouble?" I asked, expectantly.

"I've been afraid of one of them social diseases," she said, "but she's got more trouble than that now, damn her hide." It was out of character for this religious woman to say damn, so it must have been a potent problem she faced with her daughter.

Mrs. Jacobs paused a minute, cried in her frustration and then as if hating every word she had to say, revealed the truth. "She's with child."

I understood how she must feel. A slut of a daughter, a shiftless, no-good husband, her need for perfection, her religious dedication, her aspirations drawn from a depressing, hostile childhood, everything crashing down on her head. Her anger and frustration must have been intolerable. I waited while she cried and recovered her composure. I tried to soothe the wound.

"Do you know who the father is?"

"Yes." No additional information.

"Anyone you would like her to marry?" I probed.

"Yes, but it won't work." Every admission by her had to be dragged out. She offered no additional information. Just a plain answer each time a question was posed.

"Why won't it work?" was the next question.

"He's already married."

I should have known. "Yes, that does pose a problem," I said.

"Can she have an abortion?" she asked.

"In North Carolina?" was my question answer. "You must be kidding." I was surprised that a religious woman would even entertain such an idea. Apparently, the problems posed in raising such an unwanted child and the stigma attached to the illegitimacy outweighed the religious background or moral feelings she might have had. A conflict between the two would certainly be sufficient cause for headaches.

"No, I'm afraid abortion is out of the question."

"Couldn't you do it without anyone knowing?" she asked.

I felt indignant. "Absolutely not," I said in a self-righteous tone, injured by her question. "I took an oath not to do illegal abortions."

She pushed on the back of her head with her hand. For a while I suspected the headache had disappeared as she aired her problem, but now the frustration of my denial of her solution was causing it to return. She was stymied, checkmated, with nowhere to move. I felt I'd erected the walls around her this time and must try to help her escape, lest her headaches recur.

"Isn't there any way you could get the father to support the child?"

"Hooboy," she crowed, "that's out. That's just not possible. Just revealing his name would cause a scandal in this town like it's never seen."

Who could it be? My curiosity was really titillated now. The lecherous old bastard from the furniture store, Mr. Robertson. I knew it must be him. The son-of-a-bitch had gone off to Atlanta to lay with daughters of joy and picked up the clap, or strain, and doubtless now his lust had led him to this Circe, this Lorelei, this irresistible child-temptress. I smiled inwardly. It would serve the ingrate right. Sanctimonious old fool. I felt like laughing aloud, but such action would never have been understood by Mrs. Jacobs.

"Well," I said, almost with gleeful anticipation and somewhat sanctimoniously, "maybe he should be exposed, despite the scandal it created." This revenge, though seemingly sweet, was out of character for a doctor; human, perhaps, but totally alien to a doctor's role. I had a pang of conscience after I had said it, realizing my tone of voice might have given away my true intent.

"No," she said plaintively and honestly. "The Bennetts would never accept it."

"The Bennetts?" I yelled, in total surprise, swiveling my chair and staring at her in total disbelief. I wished I hadn't reacted with such a loud voice.

"Yes," she said very calmly, "Ambrose. Hadn't you suspected?"

"Heavens no," I admitted. At my home I could say "Heavens, no" without fear, whereas "Hell, no" was swearing and punishable by another debit entry against me in the Book, plus a few sharp cuffs from my mother's hand. One phrase did sound better than the other, and perhaps different in a way, I had to admit.

"Well, you see my dilemma," she said. "He's been seeing

her night after night for months, practically every night."

Practically every night! But he couldn't be two places at once. His face in the window, trying to stare at Sarah, made sense though, in a way. Probably a lecherous Peeping Tom as well, not satisfied with one evening exploit, in need of repeated sexual gratification. The lousy Don Juan, licentious bum. The thought of him trying to peep at my Sarah incensed me. I'd kill him.

My facial expression betrayed my mental wanderings. Mrs. Jacobs said, "It seems to annoy you, too." How do I recover from this, I wondered briefly, but managed to do so by admitting it did annoy me, not an altogether unremarkable feeling.

"Yes, it does," I said with as much calm as I could muster, still plagued by the enigma of "practically every night." I wanted to ask her if he had been with her last night and until what hour, but these questions wouldn't have made any sense at all in relation to her problems. A doctor should never inject his own personal problems or needs into the care of a patient. Lousy medical practice. Lousy. My professors would disapprove seriously. I couldn't ask the question. I did, however, have the right to ask "Practically every night?" Since she had used those words and it wouldn't be prying to repeat her words hoping more information would be spontaneously forthcoming.

Her answer, "Oh, yes, Mae is over three months along."

"Well, she's too far along to be aborted," I said as if I had considered it. I blurted it out without thinking, as if my voice and brain were separate entities, one not controlling the other. Furthermore, the statement would close the subject of last night. What a dolt. Stop. Think. Look wise. Say naught until ready. A doctor's most powerful weapon is silence. A patient will accept an affirmative nod alone as wise, as sagacious thought and understanding, and then probably offer more herself. I, therefore, said nothing for the next minute. She, too. After much thought, I said, "Then, I guess we'll have to let her have the baby and, perhaps, I can arrange an adoption." If it can be adopted, I added soundlessly, remembering that grinning, ghoulish face and wondering if anybody could bring themselves to adopt a baby who looked like Ambrose.

"Oh, that should be no trouble," she said with motherly

pride. "My daughter, you know, is a beautiful girl, and Ambrose is a handsome man."

Once again, I betrayed my inner thoughts by parroting in a loud voice, "Handsome man?"

"Yes," she said, "quite. A fine, handsome young man."

Good God. All my conclusions destroyed in one fell swoop. My carefully constructed analytic framework blown to Hell. How could I ever tell Sarah that the face in the window was not Ambrose, was not the rider on the horse? But Miss Bennett had said it was Ambrose on the horse that day, hadn't she? But hadn't she also told me he was devoted to her? A handsome, fine young man. Makes sense. But why had he never shown himself? Why was he hiding? Well, in truth, maybe he wasn't. Maybe the opportunity had never arisen. Jesus Christ, what a confusing mess. Another debit in the wrong column in Heaven! Now I was getting a headache. And angry. Damned angry. Frustrated beyond words. Jesus, what next? Another strike against me.

Mrs. Jacobs asked me if I was all right. Too many people lately had asked me. Soon they'd wonder about my sanity. Smugly, I decided to attack her by not answering.

"Well, I suppose your headache is gone."

"No, not gone," she said resignedly, "just out in the open." Her tone of voice touched me.

"Don't worry," I said. "We'll manage to deliver the baby and I'm sure we can manage to get an adoption agency to take it, that is, if Mae will give it up."

"Oh, yes. She's too selfish to keep it. I just wish I didn't have to stand the shame and embarrassment it will bring to us, the knowing looks, the snickering, the sanctimonious church people. I don't think I'll go to church after she begins to show."

"That's silly," I said. "You haven't done anything wrong."

"I know, but you know what I mean," she said, rising to go.

Before she left, I explained that confiding her troubles to someone like myself relieved the pressure of trying to contain the anger which inevitably builds up and accompanies them, and how this anger and frustration can be expressed as headaches, like a feeling the head would explode. What was really on the verge of exploding was her wrath, rather than her head.

Her training and perfectionism, attempts to control her wrath were failing her under the tremendous pressure of unexpressed anger. I asked her to feel free to come and see me just to talk over her problems anytime, and encouraged her to express her anger more openly at home. "After all," I said, "you beat your sister when you were young and undisciplined. You're not likely to express anger in that manner again."

"All right, Doctor," she said wearily and turned to go.

I stood in the window, heard her footsteps descending the stairs and saw her wearily walk across to their truck where her shiftless husband had been waiting for her.

I looked at Colonel Bennett and watched another bird desecrate his image. "Serves you right, you bloody rebel," I said aloud, an unkind thought. What control could he have over the moral standards of this thrice-removed heir?

Chapter 10

When the office day was completed and the last patient seen, I was exhausted, emotionally and physically, monstrously confused, frightened at the aspect of Miss Bennett's impending death, warmed by the love I knew I felt for Sarah, undecided whether it was reciprocal, relieved and slightly proud that I'd probably found the cause of Mrs. Jacobs's headaches. At least, this was one headache case I'd solved and this one was of an emotional etiology. Not like Carolyn's. God, poor Carolyn. How I had betrayed her. I didn't deserve to be happy, God knew. He really knew. That use of God wasn't a strike in the Book against me. Happiness demands a certain freedom from constant stress. How could I be happy with all this confusion—wins, losses, unsolved problems? Such reward seemed unavailable to me. Sarah entered, as always at day's end, with receipts.

"Did we make any money today?" I asked wearily, not that it mattered any.

"A little," she said. She was weary, also.

I wanted to tell her about Ambrose, but medical ethics held me back, and it wouldn't have been fair anyhow to dash her security or composure to the ground by revealing my knowledge that Ambrose was not our man. *Who else*, I wondered, *who else?*

"Mrs. Jacobs looked somewhat better when she left," she said.

"Yeah," I said without enthusiasm, unwilling to further pursue the subject. I wished I could run and grasp her into my arms, embrace her, kiss her, pour out my love, as inconsistent as it would have been at this moment. I wondered why I couldn't. We'd been through hell together last night. I'd spent the night there. It was incongruous not to leave with her, not to spend from now on to eternity with her. But on what basis, a few nights or days of camaraderie? Does anyone fall in love that way, or was it more a case of team spirit engendered by facing similar problems and realizing success, such as in our instance? Were we drawn together only by a moment of peril, or need and not love? She has a boyfriend in Baltimore, Mrs. Apperson told me. When will she ask me to let her return there? When will she want to quit working here? I hope never. *If I don't tell her soon, I'll probably lose her. I know I will. Christ (there I go again), why can't I be decisive? What can I do to escape my imprisonment?* God, how the thoughts raced in my mind.

"Will you come to dinner?" she asked. How I wanted to accept.

"I wish I could," I said.

"Why can't you?" she asked.

"I'm not sure I'd have any appetite. Understand though, it's not that your cooking isn't great."

"I wish you would, there are things I would like to tell you."

Jesus, I wondered (another strike) would I want to hear what she has to say or not. Why not take a chance. I'm not sure I could endure another problem today. In the end, I couldn't accept. I had too many doubts, too many pressing problems. I decided I'd beg out on a medical excuse.

"Sarah," I said, "there is nothing that would be more appealing than having dinner with you right now, if only I didn't have so much on my mind. My appetite would probably be lousy, since I am so worried about Miss Bennett. She looked in bad shape today. Something is eluding me. I feel I'd better stay here tonight, get out the old books, and read up on it. I sure hope I can find the answer. It scares me, the thought of losing her."

I was amazed that I had admitted to someone it scared me. Sarah was undismayed by the revelation. She apparently thought it realistic.

"I would think so," she said. "It must be awful to have the responsibility of a life on your hands and have to worry about it. I understand. Please try to eat something, though. You didn't have lunch and maybe not breakfast."

"No, I ate breakfast. Sure. I'll try to get something. Don't worry about me. I've missed meals before. You go on home now. Want you to get there before dark. And lock your door," I yelled after her.

She left and I listened to her footsteps on the stairs. What was it about footsteps that I kept noticing them? I went to the window, as she knew I would. She turned after crossing the road and waved her little gesture as she had before. I felt lonely. Gloom settled on the room and stillness. God, it was quiet. And I could have accepted otherwise. *The door.* My heart raced slightly, as I hurried to the door. It was locked. Sarah had remembered. I returned slowly through the inner office door, past the dark waiting rooms so foreboding, finally to the lighted sanctuary at the end. This was to be a lonely, long, perhaps fruitless quest. I hoped not.

I took off my coat, threw it carelessly on the chair, loosened my tie and opened the top shirt button. Music might help, I decided, so I went to start the phonograph. It seemed a million years since last I'd played it. *Death and Transfiguration* lay on top of the record pile. Too lugubrious, I decided. Maybe some Tchaikovsky. Naw, had to be something inspirational. *A Hero's Life* had always been a favorite. Saint-Saëns's *Symphony No. 3*—that would be good. I know, *Thus Spake Zarathustra* filled the bill. The opening dynamic chords, the solidarity of fine orchestration and musicianship showed themselves. Stokowski and the Philadelphia, on the Victor label. I liked the Victors better than other companies. They had better clarity of tone, better orchestras. I wished that right now I was playing in that orchestra, rather than being here. If I'd stuck with music and never gone into medicine, I'd never have met Carolyn and never been here, either. I might be very comfortable and happy now. But then Sarah, dear Sarah, would never have been part of my life, either. It was worthless to reflect on what might have been. Osler told us in his *Way of Life* to live for today; yesterday is gone, irretrievable and unchangeable; and tomorrow unpredictable. Today is the most important day of my life. Tomorrow may be, but who knows until then. Wring every good moment out of each day and never regret yesterday's failings or tomorrow's unpredictability. If only I could have managed to do that. It was a good code of life, though not mine.

I selected Cecil's *Internal Medicine*, Third Edition, from the shelf, a thick tome, our text in school. I thumbed through the index in hopes some disease would loom large in my memory of symptoms. No such luck. Let's see, I mused. What are her symptoms and signs; stomatitis, glossitis, increased salivation. All of these were definite. No question about them. Muscle weakness, questionable. Muscle wasting—maybe hypesthesia, very questionable. Paresthesias—occasionally. Anorexia—definite. Skin eczema—slight. Skin dryness—questionable. Let's see—what was her original complaint—oh yes, she had a cold, Coryza. Headache too. God, headache again. What else? What else? Physical—eyes, nothing, except maybe conjunctivitis—didn't notice if they were jaundiced—my light was lousy. Wish I'd gone over her again today in better light. Ears—nothing. Nose and throat—inflamed. Neck—thyroid okay—no nodes. Heart and lungs—okay. Heart may be slightly enlarged—consistent with age. Breasts—not examined—breach of technique. God—suppose she had cancer there with metastases—well, nothing I could do anyhow, if that were the case. Abdomen—liver not enlarged—wish I'd felt that better, no masses. Spleen and Kidneys not felt. Pelvic and Rectal exams—not done—further breach. Neurologic—really forgot to do an adequate neurologic exam, but she did have questionable paresthesias and hypesthesia, and questionable muscle weakness and atrophy. No pain though, no twitching. So, there we are. Now to put them all together. Periarteritis nodosa. I laughed. Periarteritis nodosa is one of those rare diseases not understood. Questionably a hyperallergenic reaction that gives a bizarre symptom complex and eventually death. I remember clinical pathological conferences in med school when a patient who had died was presented in case form to the students—first the history, then the physical, then X-rays and lab work, then course in hospital. The students were supposed to make a diagnosis, write it down and hand it in. After all diagnoses were in, the pathologist presented the autopsy tissue findings and finally gave the diagnosis. Whenever we were stumped on a diagnosis, it was a standing joke among the students that we would diagnose periarteritis nodosa. Occasionally we were right. I remember once one student, when stumped, turned in a diagnosis of psychoneurosis, severe, and almost got expelled. Snide humor went unappreciated by our professors. Anyhow, this time I couldn't use the diagnosis periarteritis nodosa.

I looked up vitamin deficiency diseases. Not A deficiency surely. B complex?—mainly two—beriberi and pellagra. Both had some features she had, but she said she'd eaten well until lately and was taking a tonic elixir which was loaded with vitamins. Vitamin C?—scurvy—no. Vitamin D?—rickets—no! Vitamin E—little is known about its function and Vitamin PP— Vitamin K—no—no relationship. Let's see, muscle weakness; myasthenia gravis—no! Myotonias—no! Neurologic diseases— syringomyelia—no. Amyotrophic lateral sclerosis, Lou Gehrig's disease—no. God, there are a lot of neurologic diseases, some with symptoms similar to hers, but none fulfills all her complaints. How about tropical diseases? I arose and took down my textbook on that subject. I had liked this course in school, memory-type mainly. Spotted fever—tularemia—flukes— blood and liver. Hookworm, there was a lot of that in North Carolina. After I learned in medical school the hookworm larva invaded the body between bare toes where the skin was moist and soft, I never went romping through Duke Gardens barefooted with Carolyn again. Cancer?—of what organ?— didn't fit anyhow. Symptoms weren't right. Hours went by. I read so many disease courses over that my head was spinning. Tuberculosis—that can exhibit itself in many ways—but not this bizarre. How about undulant fever? That was a rare disease, hard to diagnose. Probably comes from contaminated milk. She drinks milk three times a day. I remembered she said that. I wondered where she got the milk, from their own cow or a dairy. My interest soared. But after reading about it, it didn't fit. God, maybe it was periarteritis nodosa after all. I was beginning to lose heart. What else could she get from milk? Nothing! Not nowadays.

I tipped back on my seat, swiveled around to look at the bookcase again. What other texts might help? The thunder crashed outside. It really scared me. Damn these lousy storms, I said, I wish they'd go away. I looked at my clock—9:35 P.M.—too late to go to Hank's. I wondered if there were cold cuts in the refrigerator, went and looked: a single piece of salami. I'd eat

203

it—beggars can't be choosers—my mother had said that so many times during the depression when I had balked at eating what I had been served. I somehow felt sad now that I hadn't recognized and understood my parents' problems then. I chewed the salami thoughtfully. It was aged, edges curled and darkened, not too palatable, but I ate it. The pepper stung my tongue. My mouth felt hot. I went to get a glass of water and spit out the pepper pod which had lodged on my tongue. I wondered if Miss Bennett had eaten something that made her mouth sore and swollen. "Jesus," I screamed aloud, that's it. Poison. Some kind of poison. Maybe lead from that old house's peeling paint. I raced for my toxicology book. Lead poisoning—it didn't fit; strychnine?—no, arsenic— *arsenic*!!!

> The most common symptoms of Arsenic poisoning are stomatitis and increased salivation. (A thrill passed through me.) Other early signs and symptoms of poisoning include mild upper respiratory symptoms such as coryza, inflammation of the nose, throat, mouth, tongue and conjunctiva. Skin afflictions include erythema, eczema, pigmentation, scaling and desquamation; brittle nails, loss of hair and nails, keratosis, signs of renal damage appear. Hepatomegaly with jaundice. Weakness is due to bone marrow suppression. Advanced symptoms of poisoning include neurologic symptoms—first loss of sensation, paresthesia, hypesthesia, pain—eventually paralysis and muscular atrophy—usually of the legs. (A cold chill crossed through my body and I shuddered a little. Was I too late?)
> Arsenic is excreted largely by the kidneys—feces, skin, hair, nails sometimes contain appreciable amounts.

And all I had was blood. No, I had a fingernail in my bag! And I'd get a urine tomorrow. I'd rush them to Duke laboratory by car and hope I could get back in time. I was excited beyond belief. I hooted my success. Sarah, I thought, I'll have to tell Sarah. I looked out the window toward her house to see if her lights were on. The lightning flashed and in a brief illuminated instant my eye recognized two things that made my blood run cold. Beneath me and across the street was a figure hidden in the shadows looking up at me, now there, now not, hidden by darkness of an overhanging porch in front of the store, except when the night was illuminated. The other was Sarah, walking briskly toward the office and very near the corner where the figure lurked. In my terror I cried out her name as loudly as I could shout, to no avail. I watched in horror as she came out of the shadows of the corner into the illumination of my office window and crossed the road. I expected the sinister monster to grab her at that precise moment, but he made no move toward her. I ran to the front door, threw it open, almost hitting Sarah who was hurrying because it had begun to rain. No one was following her. What an ideal opportunity it would have been for him to grab her if he had wanted to. I couldn't understand it, unless, unless it was me he wanted, not her. The thought chilled me, though I was relieved she was apparently safe from him.

"Sarah," I said, cradling her in my arms as though she had just escaped the jaws of death, squeezing her in disbelief that she was truly safe. Not having seen the figure lurking in the shadows, of course, she didn't understand my reaction. I hesitated to release her. Having her in my arms was most desirable and I had an irresistible wish to keep her there forever. She, however, had different ideas, pulling back, resisting my tight embrace.

"You'll break my ribs," she chided laughingly. I should have told her of the danger in explanation of my behavior, but was reluctant to worry her. Instead I lapsed into an explanation of my recently acquired diagnosis.

Arsenic poisoning! She couldn't believe it.

"It has to be that," I protested.

"But why? Who would want to poison her? And what would be gained by such nonsense?"

I couldn't answer that. It really didn't make sense. She was right. Maybe I'd been too ready to seize on this diagnosis in my fantastic need for some explanation. Damn it. Of course she was right. Had Sarah not come along at this precise time, I probably would have arrived at a similar conclusion.

"Ambrose," I offered in evidence.

"But why?" she said. "After all, Miss Bennett's old. He's her only heir. He would inherit whatever she has to leave soon anyway. No point in killing her."

"Yeah, that plantation and old house can't be that valuable nor productive. Maybe he's impatient."

"I can't believe that," she said.

"No, it doesn't sound plausible, does it? Maybe my diagnosis is wrong after all." Momentarily I felt plunged again into the dark abyss of indecision. I had nothing to support my diagnosis or symptoms, and no motive. "And Miss Bennett told me both Ambrose and his wife were devoted to her. It doesn't seem realistic to believe a devoted relative would try to do her in, especially a fine-looking young man." The words just blurted out, like thinking aloud sometimes leads one to say things they shouldn't.

"What did you say?" Sarah said in obvious dismay. God, I thought, the cat's out of the bag now. "A fine-looking young man? How do you know that?" Her voice was insistent, almost imperious, demanding an answer. Hurt too. As if I was withholding information from her. What a spot to be in! I would have to reveal what I knew. I dodged.

"I don't know why I said that."

"Don't kid me," she demanded, "you know something I don't, and I want to know." She obviously was frightened, remembering previous conversations, and I could almost feel in myself the fear that was engulfing her. Her face betrayed her anxiety.

"I can't tell you how I know, Sarah," I said. "I'm sorry. I just know he's supposed to be handsome." The turmoil in her mind must have been extreme, as she began to cry.

"Sarah," I entreated, "please Sarah, don't cry—we'll work it out. I'm sorry it's such a mess. I'll do the best I can.

"Listen, there's something else I haven't told you because it seemed to have no bearing on any of this, but Sheriff Carstairs told me there's been three robberies lately and all they steal is rat poison and shotgun shells. Rat poison contains arsenic. Whoever commits those burglaries could be using that to slowly poison Miss Bennett. Don't you see, it further confirms my diagnosis." In her frustration, she lashed out at me with anger.

"That's ridiculous, how do you know there's a connection? You can buy it in the store. You don't have to steal it."

"Of course," I said, "but whoever bought it would be suspect immediately."

"Ridiculous," she repeated. "There must be hundreds of people who've bought it." She was still angry, in a quandary, and anxious. And correct in her argument.

"But think how significant it would be if Ambrose or his wife had bought it. The finger of suspicion would point directly to them. They'd have to steal it so no one would know they had it."

"But possession of it, bought or stolen, doesn't prove they are poisoning her. Have you seen any of them force it down her throat or put it in the food. Have you? Maybe she's taking it herself. Maybe she's nuts and trying to kill herself. Your whole story's a myth." She was cruel now, so hurt and frightened that she couldn't be otherwise. I foresaw that further argument would only increase her anger. She had another problem on her mind. I decided to drop the subject.

"You're right. It is a myth. And I thought I'd solved it." I was dejected and she sensed it.

She apologized, wiped away a tear with her beautiful hand. Funny, I'd never noticed how delicate her hand was before this night.

"I'm really sorry," she said. "I know how worried you are and it isn't fair of me to take it out on you. You know what has upset me, I'm sure. I was so convinced the face in the window was Ambrose's. Your explanation was so plausible. Now I don't know who it is, and I have to face the prospect of seeing it again and again. He seems to be after me." She cried again.

"I don't think so," I said, but I couldn't explain to her why. I thought that she'd been through enough tonight. Suddenly I wondered what had brought her back here again at night. I asked.

"Why did you come back here anyhow?"

"Oh, I almost forgot," she said wearily. "I was worried you wouldn't eat so I brought you a sandwich. You didn't eat, did you!" It was a statement, not a question, almost accusatory, yet understanding.

"No, except a stale piece of salami in the refrigerator."

"That's been there for over a month," she said.

"Yes, I found that out," I said, remembering the peppery taste in the mouth. "That was sweet of you to bring me a sandwich," I said.

"I had an ulterior motive, also," she said. "I wanted to ask a favor."

"What?" I asked, somewhat apprehensive.

"I would like to have a few days off. I want to go to Baltimore."

"Baltimore?" I said, with obvious dismay, my heart sinking.

"I have some unfinished business." Yes, I knew she did and I knew what it was. Couldn't blame her for wanting to get away from here, from this mad, frenzied mess, this uninspiring office, dull town, bigoted people, from fear, and that crazy ghoul. It was difficult to let her go, but I had no alternative.

"Of course," I said. "I wish I could go with you. I have lots of memories there, some good, some lousy. Maybe it's best I never go back."

"Why?" she asked.

"Well, it's hard to explain." I wanted so very much to try, but couldn't. "Why are you going?"

"It's hard to explain also," she said. "I'd rather not at this time. After I get back." Her tone of voice entreated me not to ask more. I really didn't look forward to the day of her return somehow. How I longed to tell her I love her. How I hated to tell her, though, and be turned down, to hear the worst, how she loved another. Telling I loved her would sound insincere, contrived. If I had told her before the planned trip was announced, even last night, it might have sounded real. Now it would sound false, simply conjured up as a last-minute attempt. I wanted her to respect me as a man, not as a dependent child who was indecisive and needed solace and protection. I had little to offer, except love, and I wasn't certain it was the type she'd want. If only it could have been what I had to offer before Carolyn died. I can't be penitent forever. But before I offered love again I at least wanted no longer to have doubts about practicing medicine. I wanted to be able to choose, without indecision, a future, whether it be here or somewhere else, whether to remain a country doctor or go back for specialty training. I had to at least have solved that problem.

Sarah remarked, "I hope I haven't made you sad."

God, it showed on my face. I regretted that.

"No," I said and added quite honestly. "I'll miss you. You've become an important part of my life." She seemed pleased I'd said that.

"Yes," she said. "We've been through some unusual experiences together." There was little doubt of that. "Is there anything I can do for you while I'm in Baltimore?"

I smiled and said, "Yes, bring me back an application for residency training in neurosurgery."

"Are you serious?" she asked.

"Half. But you could look up my old chief, Gardiner Perry, and say hello for me. I really liked him. He was as close to being a prince as anyone I ever met."

"I remember him," she said. "I'll be glad to. I hate to ask, but could you take me over to the County Seat to catch the train in the morning?"

"Oh sure," I said, "be glad to. It's on my way."

"On your way?" she queried, puzzled.

"Yes, I've decided to go away for a day or two also. I want to take this blood sample of Miss Bennett's to Duke, can't wait for the mails. I've got to find out if it's full of arsenic, and soon. I'm afraid I'll lose her if I wait much longer. Wish I had a urine specimen also."

"We do have one," she said, "it's in the refrigerator. She gave it to me when she came in. I guess she was too embarrassed to tell you. I forgot to tell you, too."

"Great," I said heartened. "Maybe tomorrow will solve a lot of problems for me." Except those in Baltimore, I mused.

"I'd better go now," she said, "have to get ready to go tomorrow." A wave of fear invaded me. Was the figure in the shadows still there? I couldn't let her go home alone. Only a cowardly cad would allow that. It was too short a distance to drive, and I'd left my car in front of Hank's. I didn't relish walking down there to get it. It would necessitate walking past the store in front of which the figure lurked.

"I'll walk you home," I said.

"It's not necessary. I'll be all right." I wondered if that was true.

"No," I said, with false motive. "A gentleman never allows a beautiful young lady to walk home in the dark alone. My mother taught me that."

She accepted my courtliness with a curtsy. "Thank you, kind sir."

Offering my arm, I said, "Shall we go?"

She took my arm. I glanced quickly out the window. It was very dark out there. No chance to verify the presence of an intruder, and I wouldn't have expressed my concern to Sarah for all the tea in China. We descended the steps, and with each step my apprehension increased, sort of an inverse relationship. We stepped out across the road, with me trying not to glance in any direction, walking determinedly but seeming not to hurry. Only a couple of blocks, but such a long way. At the porch, I bid her good night. She was so lovely, so beautiful, so inviting. I kissed her briefly and tenderly on the corner of the mouth and said, "Good night, Sarah. Sleep well. See you tomorrow."

The walk to the Appersons' was a bit hastier and less courageous. Once in my bed, I wondered what tomorrow would bring. A final lightning flash illuminated the sky and projected the shadow of the window frame on the wall. My prison bars still existed.

Chapter 11

The Duke University campus seemed unchanged. The Gothic stone buildings were as before. No new ones had been built, a not unremarkable fact. To build one of those now would cost a bloody fortune, and, though the university was heavily endowed, none of the principal could be used—only the interest, and that was required for maintenance and administration. Tuitions hardly met the cost of educating students. Few could ever have afforded to pay the real cost of their education.

I left the blood and urine sample at the lab for analysis telling them of my special concern about arsenic. The lab technicians seemed puzzled at my request, somewhat mocking in their attitude and a bit haughty. Just another LMD as we used to say, local medical doctor. LMD was equated with stupidity, a country doctor. Some professors and all medical students regarded the LMD's with haughty disdain, as if the only place good medicine was practiced was in the teaching institutions, as these meccas of higher learning were euphemistically called. But it wasn't true only of Duke. The same attitude existed in all teaching institutions to a degree. Most of the medical research was done there, of course, and new discoveries did, to a degree, set them apart from the practitioners of the art. There was a lot to be said, however, for the plight of the lonely LMD who has to sit out the long, worrisome hours wondering whether the correct diagnosis has been made, whether his skills are sufficient to cope with the problem, and whether or not his patient will survive and not be crippled. These worries are shared by many in a large institution, where the loss of a patient is regarded more as the loss of a case than a human being. An LMD faces the family, the community, and eventually, himself. In many ways he is braver than these hangers-on who eventually become the imparters of the art to the lowly students. When one leaves school and graduate training and then goes into practice, he often reflects upon how meager his training and education really is, and how instructive the actual lonely practice of medicine by oneself can be. At that point, in truth, real learning begins, knowledge follows, then wisdom, everything prior being principally facts committed to memory.

But maybe I was overly harsh in my criticism. After all, I was depressed and I knew it. Sarah was gone, probably to the arms of another. I had a sick patient I was afraid might die before I managed to correctly diagnose her. And my own dislike for my indecisive personality topped it off. Dislike for oneself has to cause depression. To be happy, one has to like and respect himself, not only for his ability and accomplishments, but also for his integrity, honesty, and willingness to meet and carry responsibility with a reasonable degree of equanimity. Somehow, somewhere, I was failing to do all these and was unable to change it. It had never been that way before Carolyn died, yet before she died, I really hadn't met a lot of life, so who knows if whether she was alive or dead, I would have been the same.

Remembering Carolyn and being on campus awakened feelings of nostalgia. I had been enjoyably anxious to return, to see old friends, laugh about old experiences, say hello to professors I'd liked and admired. I'd waited a long time for this day. Even though the drive wasn't long, I'd never had or taken the time before. Now I was here. Happily I'd seen my old friends who stayed on in residency programs or as teachers, my old professors, some of whom half-remembered me. We swapped stories briefly and laughed about old times, but life had truly gone on without me, even though I'd only been gone a short time. Old stories hadn't the same flavor as they used to have. These men had work to do and I didn't. They shared current experiences, problems, successes, and losses in which I had no part. I was out of place. I felt it. I knew it. Everyone was gracious and kind, but there it stopped. One can't successfully return to the past because, as Osler said, the past is gone, the present is all that counts. You can't go home again. Wasn't it Thomas Wolfe that had written a book with that title—about here, as a matter of fact. He was so right. I was seized with an undeniable urge to run immediately back to Sarah. But, alas, she wasn't there either.

To utilize the time I had to wait, I automatically and somewhat uncontrollably retraced the steps that Carolyn and I had so often followed. Down the stairs from the Nurses' home, the step we kissed on. I could feel her warm, moist lips on mine, through the garden, that marvelous day when her heaving half-naked bosom had so excited me, to the woods where we first lay down. It hadn't been the only time, and she had never become pregnant that first time we had intercourse. Intercourse—coitus—a sterile word. Another crummy, animal word. Wasn't there some word that was more descriptive of the feeling, the excitement, the love, the lust, all of the emotions involved at the same time. I rubbed the back of my neck as I stood looking at the spot we had lain on. Somehow it had changed. My memory had either failed me or a new path had been trod. Somehow that seemingly hallowed spot was now unrecognizable. I went on to the log over the stream. It was still there, the stream lazily passing beneath. But as I stood there, I realized the wind was chill, the sky gray, and the leaves on the trees dead. I fled. I ran back to campus through the chill air until my lungs felt they would burst. I leaned against the pillar entering the campus, panting heavily. Once I'd been so excited to pass through these pillars to a new life, and now they were like gates to a cemetery. I went immediately back to the lab.

I *was* right! There were definite evidences of arsenic in the blood and urine, even in the fingernail I'd thrown in my bag and brought along. I whooped for joy. Exultation, misunderstood by the lab techs, filled me. How could anyone be happy at finding arsenic in blood and urine samples, they wondered. Their attitude didn't bother me. I contacted one of my internal medicine professors and explained quickly the case and made arrangements for her transfer to Duke to be treated with Bal, a new drug, capable of opening up the paralyzed kidneys and flushing the arsenic out of the body. They would be glad to take her as a patient. The professor complimented me on my astute diagnosis. Me! Of all people. I was transformed. King of the May—no, that's Queen of the May. King of the Mountain.

As I raced back to Bennettsboro, without concern for the

speed laws or my safety, I planned my course of action. Forests and trees and fields and farms, plantations, towns all flew by without recognition. Even though the day was gray, it seemed brighter somehow. I was convinced I'd win. Rather than return to the office first, I went immediately to the Bennett home. It was growing dark but I decided this was the time to see her, even unannounced. The sooner, the better. As I turned down the lane, I felt instinctively that this place was not as sinister as I'd known it. It probably had been a warm, lovely, and beautiful home, one to be proud of. When I turned into the circle beneath the trees and moss, however, it was like an evil spell had been cast over this small oasis, the water rancid, the trees dying. The feeling was undeniable. Exultation had changed as suddenly as that to despair. "My God," I said aloud, "I hope she isn't dead." Everything looked dead. There was even a malefic odor, seemingly contained within this small area, a stench of death. I shuddered. I raced to the door and tried to enter without knocking. The door was locked. I banged the knocker, over and over, listening to the echoes each time within the house. No one was aroused. I ran down off the porch, checked quickly in both directions for another possible entry and ran to the right, around the corner, past the windows through which Sarah had seen her ghoulish face, and made a mental note it was much less sinister from the outside. The black window reflecting the light outward now looked sinister within. I was at the back of the house, my anxiety mounting. I must hurry. Time was of the essence. I mustn't lose. I noted quickly the hedges of the garden over which Ambrose had vaulted his horse like an experienced equestrian that day so long ago. The back screen was ajar, the door unlocked. I was in the kitchen. It had a dank, musty odor. I raced into the hallway colliding with the overseer. He was puzzled with my erratic behavior. After a brief exchange in which he informed me that he had come to the door and that I should have waited, I realized my anxiety had overwhelmed me. Winning this one was of the utmost importance.

"Is she dead?" I asked, somewhat stupidly.

"Who dead?" he asked.

"Miss Bennett, of course," I said with trepidation and annoyance.

"Oh, no, Suh," he said, "she look bettuh today."

"Thank God, thank God," I said with all sincerity. This time my blasphemy wouldn't merit a strike or two in Heaven.

"I want to see her, immediately," I said with a positive tone.

"Yassuh," he replied, "Ah tinks y'all know da way."

I knew the way, all right. No question about that. Miss Bennett was sitting propped up in bed with her pretty lacy but antiquated bed costume on, and fairly cooed as I knocked and entered.

"How do you do," she said, but I recognized it was a weak frail voice, unchanged from a few days ago. And that trace of saliva pearled out of her mouth with each "do."

"Good afternoon," I said. "I came to see you because we must discuss your condition."

"Have you come to a conclusion?" she asked.

"Yes," I said and then wondered what I would say. How would I tell her? How could you broach the subject without causing undue emotional pain?

"What I've found out will sound absurd and ridiculous, I know. It will be almost unbelievable. Nevertheless, it is correct."

I paused a minute to allow her to digest those words. I hadn't even said I felt it was correct. My words were positive in nature. *It is correct. It was nice to be so certain for a change. My personality was stronger and I felt it.*

She waited for my next pronouncement, patiently, seriously. There were none of the traces of amusement in her face as had been there when I entered.

I told her slowly and succinctly so she would hear me correctly. "You are suffering from arsenic poisoning!"

She waited a long time before answering.

"That's absurd," she replied.

"It is not absurd. It is true. I have proof."

"You've made a mistake," she remonstrated, "I will not believe it."

"You must," I said. "You've come to me for care. I've observed your symptoms and signs. I've collected your blood and urine. I've taken them to Duke Hospital Laboratory and they have identified strong concentrations of arsenic in them. I've just returned now. The evidence is irrefutable. Someone is poisoning you."

She looked straight into my eyes without wavering for many minutes. I saw then the tears well up, and finally one tear burst over the lid and ran down the cheek. God, I felt sorry for her. What a blunt way to greet her. What an emotional shock it must be to realize someone dislikes you enough or wants what you own so insanely that he or she will resort to murder. More than that, whoever it is could be someone you trust. The silence following my statements was almost intolerable.

"But it can be corrected," I reassured. "You must go to Duke University Hospital in Durham and receive a new medicine that will make you well in a short time, probably no more than two weeks. I'll arrange for an ambulance to pick you up in the morning and deliver you there tomorrow. I've made all the arrangements there for your hospitalization. A fine doctor will be caring for you, someone I know you will like. Meanwhile, I don't want you to eat any more in this household."

"I've already eaten supper," she said, "but I don't think I'll go." She cried heavier now.

"You must," I said, "you may die if you don't." I hated to have to tell her that.

"I know," she said with tears, "but I'm old and useless now and whether I live or die really isn't important anymore." So many old people feel that way when faced with momentous decisions regarding life and death. I remembered patients during training who refused cancer therapy, desired to face the inevitable rather than undergo treatment, and all under the guise of age and lack of usefulness. In truth, it was hard to argue about usefulness with older people. To make them understand their worth involved understanding the meaning of life, the worth of a single life. I had to convince her.

"Miss Bennett," I said, "in truth, it's hard to give you a reason for choosing to live, as short as it may be even if cured of this, instead of certain death. The world could do without you, I suppose. We could get along without many things in life, without mountains perhaps, but they are beautiful and have some functions and it would be hard to part with them. We might get along without trees, though they do give us fruit and

216

wood for houses, and shade from the sun and oxygen and beauty. Each item has its meaning in the scheme of life, just as you and I have meaning in this town. Your name is a proud one. A heritage of which this town is proud. And I know you are proud of it too. You are a symbol, the granddaughter of their beloved colonel. More than that, you have meaning to your grandnephew, Ambrose, and his wife. They love you." I wondered if it were true. We still hadn't faced the issue of who was poisoning her. "Without you their lives would be less beautiful. Ambrose is devoted to you. Probably, basically the reason for living is love. Love is the only thing we get out of life, everything else is pain and work, worry, and misery. Love is the reason to live. The only reason! I've come to know you as a fine lady, of proud heritage, fine breeding and education. You have meaning to me now as well as the others." She looked touched. I went on. "In a small sense I've come to love you and I hope you will come to love me. Let's call it affection, if love seems too strong. Affection is but a degree of love. Even your overseer and housekeeper have affection for you. Without you, their lives would have little meaning. Please, consider it deeply, before you decide. I hope you choose life. I pray that you will."

What a speech. Didn't know I had it in me. Sarah would be proud. I knew it came from the heart, thoughts I'd had when in deep despair. After Carolyn's death, I, too, had to choose. It had been hard, but now that I'd met Sarah, I felt I had a chance and had made the right choice.

Miss Bennett seemed very impressed. "I'll do as you ask," she said, with conviction. "I'll go tomorrow."

Thank God, I said to myself, and went to leave.

"And thank you, Doctor," she said, extending her hand. Frail as it looked, it was warm and her grasp was firm. I kissed it and left.

The following morning, the ambulance from the County Seat met me at my office. I had arranged for it by phone the previous night. Doubtless, everyone in town knew its purpose since—more than likely—Charlotte listened in when I called. The ambulance followed me to the Bennetts. Miss Bennett was ready for the trip. She was dressed in her finery, just the same as I had seen her that first day in the office. I wondered how

Duke would receive this spectre of the past, who fit the description of an antique ghost completely. She protested mildly to being carried down the steps, somewhat an affront to her dignity, but demurred at my insistence.

They paused in the hallway long enough for me to bid her a pleasant trip. She insisted they not use the siren at any time and admonished the driver to proceed carefully. I reassured her again.

"Everything will be fine now." I wished I could be sure. "In two weeks or so you'll be back, nearly good as new, and you'll be treated very well there at Duke."

"I have no doubt of that," she said. "It is the first time I've left here in many, many years. And I'm not certain I'm coming back."

I told her I wouldn't allow her to talk that way.

"Nevertheless," she said, "it could be true. I want you to keep something for me. This packet of papers. Please keep them in a safe place. I want to be sure they don't get lost."

"But wouldn't it be better to leave them with Ambrose?" I asked.

"No," she said emphatically, "I want you to keep them."

It was silly to argue. I accepted. I could lock them in my desk. "Remember, I expect you to come back and show me the rest of the house as you promised," I said.

"Thank you," she said smiling. "I'll just do that. Now keep this place in order while I'm away," she said pointedly to her two servants. I wondered where Ambrose was. I was anxious to see him.

As the ambulance rounded the circle, she waved wanly from her bed and the three of us acknowledged her farewell. I saw a tear run down the cheek of the overseer and the housekeeper dabbed at her nose with her handkerchief, sniffing intermittently. Two devoted servants, a lifetime of servitude, and probably satisfaction, dedicated to her and their plantation.

"Doctuh," the overseer said, "will she really be back in two weeks' time?"

"Yes, I'm sure she will," I answered with conviction—not at all like me. I was glad to be relieved of the responsibility for her care, but realized that even if she was treated satisfactorily, before she could return, the mystery of who was poisoning her had to be solved!

"Bessie," I said to the housekeeper, "who cooks Miss Bennett's food?"

"Land sakes," she said in her squeaky voice, "y'all don't think my cookin' made her sick?" I knew then that they didn't know the diagnosis.

"No, no, but she has a condition which might be related to her eating," I said evasively, "and I need to know something about her."

"She ain't de least bit finicky, she eats anything I prepares."

"Do you always cook it? Does anyone else help you?"

"No, Suh," she said with pride. "Ah does all cookin'."

"And the serving?"

"And the servin', every bit, 'cepting maybe her nightly milk. Master Ambrose's wife comes o'er here most every night and takes her warm milk."

Aha, my mind clicked—warm milk. Rot! Too Hollywood-ish—too pat. And why would Ambrose's wife want to poison her? To inherit this old mansion? Hardly seemed possible.

The housekeeper then added, "Ah gets her de pan to heat it and Ambrose's missus merely takes it to her."

Could drop something in it on the way, I thought. But why? And these two devoted servants wouldn't poison her. Suddenly I wondered if the packet contained a will. I wondered if they were beneficiaries, and knew it. Might make sense. What non-sense! She'd never tell them they were beneficiaries, even if true. Suddenly I realized I was playing detective as well as doctor, two divergently different professions. I'd better discuss it with the sheriff.

I took my leave, telling them I'd let them know if anything happened. They were very grateful "thanking me kindly" over and over.

Turning down the lane, I was torn between the wish to go immediately to the sheriff and the responsibility to open the office for work. I'd call him, I decided. Maybe he could come over. Leaving the house, I proceeded down the lane. Damnation. There in the distance, by God, was that damned somebody on horseback following me on a parallel. Much too distant to

219

see his face! I rolled the window down. "Damn you, Ambrose," I said, "come out and show your lecherous face, you lousy coward." But he didn't.

The office had a veil of gloom over it. It was because Sarah wasn't there, I guess. "A few days," she'd said. This was only the third day. In a short time I heard the door close and muffled sounds of some woman admonishing her son for some transgression, he crying in turn. Despite their presence, I called the sheriff. They could wait. He wasn't in, naturally. A good sheriff should be out of the office most of the time. I told his office, "Get him on the radio, and have him call me." They accepted my order. "Yes, Sir!"

Johnny Buell had another earache. (Not another!) He fought the exam all the way, but more successfully this time without the expert help of Sarah to pin him down. I was in no mood for clever repartee with him, remaining purely clinical in my approach, which he didn't like at all. The damned imp kicked me after he got up from the table. His mother didn't see it, though. I prescribed the usual medicine and told her someday she'd have to take him to a hospital for a tonsillectomy and adenoidectomy to put an end to all this. She wasn't as yet ready for that. God knows he wasn't ready. As he left, I hoped his 'gator would eat him. The day passed slowly. Every phone call was the wrong one. The sheriff never called, nor Sarah either. She was to let me know when she was getting back so I could pick her up at the station.

Toothache, earache, cold, pain in the abdomen, sore back, too heavy a period, infected toe, sore throat—a not too interesting or challenging day. Almost all of them would get well without my help. I remembered my dean saying to us the first day of med school that 90 percent of our patients in practice would get well without our help, so if we didn't cure better than 90 percent, we could consider ourselves a flop. Somewhat harsh, but true.

Mrs. Jacobs did bring Mae in and have her pregnancy confirmed. She was four months along. I couldn't blame Ambrose too much for taking up with her. She certainly was attractive physically. Mentally and emotionally, though, a complete zero, goose egg, double zero. I wondered how, when pregnant by another man, she could flirt with me and cast her wily, seductive charms in my direction. She was totally selfish also, glad to give up the baby, didn't want it anyhow. I wondered if Ambrose knew of the pregnancy. For one brief moment I wondered if, having no children of his own, he wanted to have this one, give it the family name, and maybe even murder his great-aunt to—what rot—I was really reaching for a motive. Mae agreed to come for prenatal care, which I strongly doubted she would do. Trying to tell her how to take care of herself prenatally was like talking to a brick wall, a zero, as I said. As I talked, she cooed, and smiled, and winked, and squirmed, and wiggled, and primped. Once her mother slapped her face, openly, in front of me, and received in return a hateful sneer. But what a change for Mrs. Jacobs—open and honest expression of hostility. God, I thought, deliver me from Mae, or better yet, deliver her. I didn't like the thought of that future date I must face. She would be uncontrollable in labor. Her sins would come home to roost that particular day through pain, especially with a home delivery and few medications to help. I had asked her who the father was while examining her, and she had answered, "Can't tell yu that. It's a deeeeep dark seeeeecret." I wondered if she'd ever seen a Mae West or Garbo movie. Her drawl wouldn't have fit either star, though.

Anyhow, the day was a bust. At day's end, I was glad to sit down and relax. Evening came sooner now. Most of the trees had shed their leaves. The fall beauty was mostly gone. I remembered I'd forgotten to eat and went to Hank's. Mrs. Apperson would think I'd moved out. Fortunately for me, some Klan people were in the restaurant planning some diabolic evening in low tones, and I therefore needn't make small talk. Hank was engulfed in their business and seemed annoyed even at having to wait on me. I ate my greasy food in silence. A squeal of glee was emitted by Hank intermittently as he wiggled with enthusiasm over their plans. *When would the cross burn, tonight or tomorrow?* I wondered. I at least knew where the torch was burning. Here in my chest. I really missed Sarah. All I could envision was her in the arms of some dynamic physician in Baltimore, a new Kelley or Osler or Williams—loving, admiring, adoring him, promising to soon join him in holy matri-

221

mony. I knew how to kill myself with doubts and unhappiness when I desired. If only I'd told her I loved her before she left. But she'd be proud of me when she returned, though. She'd be glad to find out I'd made the correct diagnosis of Miss Bennett's problem. You'll notice I didn't say case. We LMD's regard our patients as people, friends, not cases. No need to dig the university, though. The disdain for LMD's was truly not the professors' doing, but, rather, the arrogant, supercilious idiocy of young, immature physicians still green behind the ears, and drawing on the image of the university for their haughtiness. God, there's a lot to learn in medical school, humility being of first magnitude in importance. These Klansmen could use some of that knowledge.

I went back to the office. I really had nothing to do. I called the sheriff's office again. His operator there said the office was closed, but she was certain he had received the message. No, he wasn't at home and his wife didn't know where he'd gone. It was dark now. I played a record, didn't even look when I put it on—*Till Eulenspiegel's Merry Pranks*. When it finished and I got up to change it, I was desperately depressed, yet elated—so unfulfilled. I remembered Shakespeare's line, "I never knew anyone with so old a head, and yet so young a body." At least I thought it was Shakespeare. Next I chose the Rachmaninoff *Concerto Number Three*. I listened a few minutes while standing and then turned back to the swivel chair. A distant glow in the sky caught my eye. I looked again. Far away, glowing, leaping fingers of fire stabbed toward the sky. The portrait seemed obvious enough. Something on fire. A burning cross perhaps? Someone on trial tonight? Thank God it isn't me, I said to myself. I watched it glow for a long time and then slowly die once more, plunging the horizon into blackness. I wished for company, any company. This was a lonely spot, had never seemed as lonely or as foreboding before. With Sarah gone, I felt as if the only friend I'd known or had in this town was absent. Should I need help now, this very minute, whom could I turn to? Sitting with my feet up, I drowsed off for quite awhile, maybe a couple of hours. The phone rang, startling me. I answered, my heart still pounding from the adrenaline surge. It was Sheriff Carstairs. I really was glad to hear from him.

"Sheriff," I addressed him with enthusiasm and relief, "I'm glad to hear from you. I need your help."

"Sorry I didn't call sooner, Doc," he said. "It's been a hard night. Had lots to do."

"Could I see you now?" I asked.

"How about tomorrow, Doc. Still got lots to do. Unless, of course, it's urgent."

"Well, sort of. I kind of hate to let it wait, but if you're too busy or tired I'll understand."

"Couldn't be until late, lessen maybe—" He paused, then continued, "Lessen maybe you'd considuh ridin' along with me whilst I finished this other problem. Might need you, whadda ya say?"

"No trouble at all," I hastened to agree.

"Might be a long time."

"Doesn't matter. I've plenty of that available."

"Ah'll pick yu up in ten minutes," he said.

His honk startled me, but I grabbed my coat and ran down to meet him. We made a circle of the Y and headed out the highway towards the Bennetts. For quite a while we drove without conversation. The sheriff seemed deep in thought.

"What's the matter?" I asked, "you've been out all day."

"Oh," he said, with a long pause, "some trouble over near Cade Jackson's place."

"Cade Jackson?" I said. "Don't know him."

"Oh, he's a nigger lives over behind the Bennett place."

"Oh, I think I know who you mean. Handsome, big, strapping man," I said, identifying him in my mind.

"Yeh, that's the one. Troublemaker. Lives by himself out there. Shiftless. Does odd jobs here and there. Works over at the Jacobs place most of the time."

We drove to Cade's place. He wasn't home. We went back to the highway and south again. Eventually the sheriff turned down a side road, badly rutted and narrow. The car lurched and heaved as we slowly wound for seemingly miles into a wooded area at a snail's pace. The car came to a halt and he switched off the lights. He waited and listened. Only night sounds were present—frogs, crickets, wind rustling through the trees. An owl hooted in the distance. Presently, he turned the lights on,

223

for which I was grateful, and we proceeded slowly. I was certain we were going up a hill gradually, though almost imperceptibly. Again we stopped and he turned off the road, waited, and listened. I wondered how he knew of this side road so camouflaged by the trees and underbrush.

"Sheriff," I said.

"Ssh," he cautioned, "not now."

We waited there an interminable length of time. Then I heard what he must have expected, muffled voices in the distance, growing gradually louder, behind the car. Men! Walking down the road. I craned my head to see out the back window. Only shadows in the night passed, seen only through their movement. One stopped, lit a match and cigarette. The sudden glow in the night was almost a shock. Why we weren't seen by the match lighter I'll never understand, but many things go unseen when the observer is not expecting to see anything unusual. In medical school we were trained to look, to see, to observe constantly, so that no small item escaped our attention. One small clue, if observed, might give us the key to a diagnosis. I remembered Miss Bennett and all of the signs she had. They had been observed by me but had no meaning for too long a time.

The glow of the match, though, illuminated the two men lighting cigarettes. They were dressed in long white robes and hoods, though the hoods had been thrown back so their faces were visible.

"Hank," I said, in complete surprise.

"Ssh," remonstrated the sheriff.

The match was extinguished almost as fast as it had illuminated, though as he fanned it out by shaking it, it made crazy little orange tracings against the dark background. Once again, we were plunged into the blackness of forest and night. Other muffled voices passed, then a movement of shadows, and then a sadistic laugh or giggle. The voices were voices unattached to physical beings—like ghosts talking without substantive form.

After a long while, when no more voices were audible, no more rustling heard or shadows seen, Sheriff Carstairs said to me, "C'mon, Doc, we're going on up the hill on foot." He got out of the car. I had mixed emotions, ambivalence they call it in psychiatry, on the matter of going along. What I might face up there on the hill was none too attractive to contemplate, yet remaining alone here in the car in this black hole was no more attractive. Safety in numbers, they say. So I went. We walked without talking up the road, also without the benefit of light. I felt then I knew somewhat, for the first time, what it was like to be blind, groping inch by inch along this rutted road using tactile sensations in my feet to assure my passage. It was not enjoyable. Coupled with that was the tension, let's say fear, of what we'd find at the top. Suddenly, the sheriff extended his arm in front of me, stopping me soundlessly. A cold chill went up and down my spine.

"Get in the woods," he said, in almost an unaudible whisper. "Someone's coming."

I went to the right, he to the left. It was incredible how soundlessly that big man entered the woods. I crashed in. Crouching there, I wished I'd gone to his side of the road and had the almost irresistible compulsion to run across. But it was too late. Even I could hear the voices now of two men coming toward us in the night. I hadn't heard anything before. The sheriff was like a well-trained hound-dog, no offense meant, one who senses the slightest rustle before the hunter is even aware. My heart pounded as I crouched there awaiting what seemed like almost certain discovery. If they hadn't heard me dive into those woods in my fearful haste, certainly they would hear my heart pounding. Momentarily I expected to die of a heart attack. It had happened to people in sudden moments of terror. Worse than that, I wondered how close to me in this underbrush might lurk a copperhead snake that I had disturbed in the night. *God*, I said to myself, *suppose one bites me.* In my mind's eye I could see him there, fangs bared, coiled and ready to strike. I remembered that first copperhead victim I'd seen soon after I arrived here to practice. Leg swollen and blue, gasping his last breaths while the poison shut off his life.

The voices were directly in front of me now.

"That'll teach that damn black bastard a lesson."

The other just said, "Yeah." They passed by. One of the voices, I fancied, was Mr. Robertson, the furniture store owner, but in the night with no face to confirm it I couldn't be sure. My own bias was showing now. Once before recently I'd believed him to be a lecherous old man, father of an illegitimate child, and been totally wrong.

Presently the sheriff whispered, "Doc, Doc, c'mon, let's go." I was ready to depart my hideout. We inched our way on up the road. Soon the smell of charred wood and acrid smoke reached my nostrils. Its odor became stronger and stronger. We reached a clearing in the woods, a knoll, the small amount of night light silhouetting a partially destroyed cross against the sky. The cross was suddenly bathed, or seemed bathed, in light from the sheriff's flashlight. Actually the light was only a thin beam, but the contrast from dark to some light was immense. Smoking embers of wood glowed slightly when the sheriff turned his light away. I stood quietly looking at the remains of this fiery cross, all that was left of the glow I'd seen earlier this evening in the distance.

Suddenly the sheriff yelled loudly, "Doc, Doc, c'mere, quick."

I ran over to him.

"Help me," he said. He played the light on the face of Cade Jackson hanging from a limb by a knotted rope. His tongue swollen and protruding from the corner of his mouth, his eyes wide open staring in horror. I held the nude body by the feet, trying to lift it and ease the tension on the neck. It surprised me how heavy it was to lift. The sheriff, with great effort, cut the rope, then helped me lower it to the ground. Something liquid made my hands sticky. The sheriff played his light again on the face and neck. I listened to the heart through his nude chest. He was dead. His neck had a large ugly bruise where the rope knot had broken his larynx and crushed his trachea. I stood up. We ran the flashlight down across his large muscular chest and shoulders, on down the body. My God in Heaven, they had emasculated him, blood matted in the hair of the groin where once his symbol of manhood had been. I wanted to vomit. I nearly did. Convulsively, I wiped the sticky blood off my hand. Throughout my medical school training and internship, I'd seen many grisly, gruesome sights; stabbings, beatings, infected wounds and infected cancers that smelled malodorously, but nothing previously had ever affected me like this. The sheriff spoke out.

"Jesus Christ, those lousy sons-of-bitches!" It was the first time I'd ever seen him express emotion. His reaction had been like mine. Hanging is one thing, but this sadistic, bestial act, desecration of the body. He spoke again.

"I've seen a lot of lynchings, but this, I—" His words ended. There was nothing reasonable to say further. Presently, he said, "Well, we'd better get back, Doc. No more good we can do here."

I agreed, anxious to leave. "We'll get the body in the morning," he said. I hated to leave it lying there, but guessed it was best from the standpoint of clues.

The trip out of the area was even more gloomy than the one in, but a different type of gloom, one of despair, depression, frustration, helplessness. My anger mounted.

"Sheriff," I said, "what are you gonna do about this?"

"Nothing, probably," he said. He angered me.

"What do you mean, nothing?" I said.

"What can I do?" he said. "Who am I going to accuse?"

"I recognized Hank," I fairly shouted at him. "When he lit that match."

"Yeah, so did I," he answered, "and the other one too. But we didn't see them do it, did we?"

"I'll be your witness that I was here. I'll verify it."

"Won't do no good," he said, almost authoritatively.

"God," I said, "you must have had an idea what was going on. Why didn't you stop them on the road, identify them?"

"What were they doing wrong at that time, walking on the road, burning a cross? No law against that."

"Then why did we hide? Jesus, you had a shotgun. They had nothing."

"Didn't they?" he said. A statement. "Listen, Doc, maybe they didn't have guns, and maybe we could have arrested them, or some of them, but there would always be another day when you or I didn't have a gun. Don't fancy finding myself hanging up there or someplace else. I've even heard whisperings about you being a nigger lover, Doc."

That sent a chill through me. I saw his point.

"But aren't you going to do anything?" I asked.

"Oh sure, I'm pledged to uphold the law. I'll arrest Hank and Sam, but it won't do no good. No white jury will convict

227

them for killing a nigger who raped a white girl and made her pregnant."

I saw his Southern logic clearly, but the rape surprised me.

"I haven't heard of any rapings," I said. "Who'd he rape?"

"The Jacobs girl," he said, "don't you know?"

"That's a lie, a damn lie," I said shouting. "He was not the father of her child."

"Who was then?" he asked.

"Ambrose Bennett," I said with authority, violating my oath of confidentiality.

"Ambrose?" he drawled in utter disbelief. "You gotta be kiddin'. How do you know that?"

"Mrs. Jacobs told me," I said, again with authority. "I'll testify to it."

He laughed. "Doc, what makes you think she told the truth? Your evidence ain't worth a tinker's dam. It's hearsay. Do you really think she'd be willing to tell you her grandchild-to-be was sired by a nigger. Her, so prim and proper?"

"Well, what evidence do you have?" I challenged.

"The girl says so," he offered.

"Rubbish! An immature, well-known nymphomanical, hysterical girl claims a colored man raped her in order to save her shame at being pregnant, making her some kind of befouled saint, I suppose. That's evidence? Sounds like the Salem witch trials."

"Better'n yours," he said, "and it's recognized in court. Gal gits up there on the stand, says, 'Cade raped me, and I'm carrying his child.' Can you imagine anyone hanging Hank or Sam or the others for doing away with the depraved, black, nasty dog who did it?"

He stared at me. He was right. There was no chance, not even a glimmer of a chance. Killers, more than just Hank and Sam, whoever Sam was, would go free, free of punishment for a foul, despicable crime, a man murdered on the word of an immature hysterical girl, a harlot, her mother had said. A mother would never testify against her daughter, particularly this one. Maybe the sheriff was right, maybe she had lied to me, unable to tell me her daughter carried a negro child in her. That would give her a headache. Maybe she'd like to believe Ambrose was the father. It would give her prominence in this town. Maybe she'd heard I was a "nigger lover" also and wouldn't tell me for that reason. Maybe, maybe. Where was the truth, the real truth? How does one tell when another is lying? What can one believe in? I hated this place, I wanted to leave, now, forever.

The sheriff spoke again.

"Doc, what was it you wanted to speak to me about when you called?"

I'd forgotten all about Miss Bennett. Yet I didn't feel capable of trying to solve that mystery tonight. This evening had already been more than I'd bargained for.

"It'll have to wait," I said. "How about tomorrow?"

"Well, I might be busy," he said, and I could accept that, but then he added, "but maybe late in the day, say after supper."

"That would be fine," I said. "I'll meet you at my office."

He dropped me at the Appersons'. How I longed for Sarah. She had said, "a few days" and she had been gone three now. Her absence affirmed more deeply my love for her. As I went to bed, exhausted, I dreaded tomorrow's loneliness.

Chapter 12

October thirtieth. I'd hardly realized we were that close to winter. The weather had been rainy, but this morning there was a light frost. Mrs. Apperson was pleasant at breakfast, but a little bit prying in her questions about my comings and goings. I didn't want to explain my reasons. I knew I'd never eat at Hank's again. How would I explain to Mrs. Apperson that from now on I'd eat here every morning—that is, until Sarah and I were married. Married! Curiously I'd thought of love, but never actually entertained the thought of marriage. It sounded right, the obvious course of action. I wondered what sort of husband I'd be, if I'd ever overcome the guilt of Carolyn's death and really be free. Suddenly, a feeling of deep uneasiness, of despair, grasped me. *Sarah, in Baltimore, making decisions with another man, a man capable of making decisions.* Again, I was filled with doubts, weighing possibilities of her love, analyzing things she had said, wondering if they could be interpreted as love. She must be in love with me, she must. All of her actions seem to indicate that. She couldn't love anyone else. The idea was unthinkable. I love her, she loves me. She does, I know she does.

Mrs. Apperson said, "What did you say, Doctor?" She startled me. I hoped I hadn't been talking out loud. The children tittered. I smiled at them. They were cute. Too bad children have to become adults, I thought; complicated, ignorant, biased adults. Children seem to have little of those problems, acquiring them as they grow, due to teaching of the so-called mature people. But this morning's despair was left over from last night, and in truth, Mrs. Apperson seemed to be an exception to the bigots as did her husband, and Sarah, and the sheriff. There were exceptions, thank God.

The office was cold, clammy, and bleak. No sparkle, just as

yesterday. I wished it were Sunday so I could avoid meeting people today. It was a light workday, thank God. At noon, rather than go to Hank's restaurant, which I abhorred, I went to the grocery for a few items. I hadn't done that in a long time. My landlord was very convivial. So was the butcher, showed me his finger, told me it was "good as new."

"Haven't seen Miss Sarah lately," the landlord said, "not since the other morning, when was it, Tuesday?"

They really kept tabs on us, these townspeople. I wondered if Brownley had been in the car that passed that morning. No, I just was feeling guilty all of a sudden, I decided. He was only being nice.

"You're right, Tuesday. She went to Baltimore on business."

"Bet you miss her. Fine lady, that Miss Sarah."

"I second the motion," I said in jest. What did I care if they knew I liked her. "She runs the office. I work for her."

They laughed. They seemed like good people. But I couldn't help but wonder if last night they had been hooded monsters, out there on the hill. Sheep in wolves' clothing, now transformed once again to sheep. Goddamn hypocrites. Lawless bastards. I left.

The afternoon was dull. The usual snotty noses and trivial junk. Most of the medical practice was dull, uninteresting maladies, challenging in no way. The only part of such a day, or most such days that allowed it to be endurable, was communication between myself and the patient. Personality interchange is what makes the average practice enjoyable. Few doctors conquer serious illnesses or do life-saving surgeries daily. Meeting people is the enjoyable part. I wasn't in the mood to enjoy myself another such day. Therefore they, the patients, were relegated to the case level, snotty noses, etc. I smiled at the thought that I actually longed for a challenging case to brighten the dull routine. Quite a change.

The afternoon wore on and evening came. No phone call from Sarah, nor from the sheriff. How I wished Sarah would call. It was unlikely she'd return today. The train would be about due to arrive at the Country Seat and I was certain she would have called earlier. The phone rang. My heart leaped. It was the sheriff. He would be over about seven he said. I went home to the Appersons' for dinner. Mrs. Apperson was surprised again to see me. I apologized for giving her such little advance notice. Eating quickly, I returned to the office.

The sheriff arrived and honked. I ran down to meet him. I had expected him to come up. "Doc," he said, "how about going for another ride with me?"

"Not if it's going to be like last night," I said.

"No, no, nuthin' like that. We can talk in the car."

"Okay," I said. "I'll run up and tell Charlotte I'll be gone awhile. How long, an hour?" He nodded assent.

I ran back up the stairs, switched on the light, grabbed Sarah's front phone and called. Then back to the car. Hated to keep him waiting. I really didn't have to worry. Once on our way, I asked him how today had gone.

"Usual," he drawled. "I got the judge to swear out warrants for the arrest of Hank and Sam. Picked up Sam. Hank seems to have disappeared. Going over to his brother's place now to see if he knows anything. Word travels fast, I guess. Someone must have known about them warrants and warned him."

"Have any new clues?" I asked.

"No, not really. Few tire tracks, but they could've been there a long time. 'Fraid we ain't got much else other than seeing 'em."

"Yeah, leaves little hope of conviction," I said dejectedly.

"What's on your mind?" he asked.

"Well, I hate to dump another problem in your lap," I said "but there's another sticky mess to clean up." I remembered suddenly my hand from last night and the dirtied clothes.

"Oh, yeah?" he queried. "What?"

"An attempted poisoning."

"Poisoning?" He seemed surprised, for a change. "Who?"

"Miss Bennett," I said.

"Miss Bennett?" he repeated incredulously. "Who'd want to poison her?"

"That's what I want to know."

I then told him about her history, the physical findings, the discovery of the poison in her blood and urine and even fingernail, somewhat superciliously. I even proposed the possibility that the store burglar and the poisoner were one and the same.

"You've done a lot of sleuthing," he said. "You know, I almost caught the burglar one night but he lost me back in the woods behind Miss Bennett's house. I stopped at Ambrose's, but he'd been home all night. His wife verified it. He lives back there, you know," pointing. "They hadn't seen anybody. Whoever it was, was white though, 'cause I saw him running away from the store. I'm not sure, but he, I think, had a horse stashed away in the woods, somewhere. I'd swear I heard horse's hooves." My interest heightened. I told him about my encounters with horses, Miss Bennett's statement about Ambrose, and the face in the window.

"Ambrose is a good-looking boy," he said. "Can't be him."

"What do you know about Ambrose and the Bennetts?" I asked. "Ambrose sure is a mystery character. Never have seen him."

"Well, he keeps to himself," he said, "has a horse, I know. See his missus more. Hear he's devoted to his great-aunt. Let's see, his father was named Bill. The old Colonel had one son, or was it two, and a daughter, Miss Bennett."

"Two," I confirmed.

"Horses have been a prominent part of that family," he said. "I hear tell the father was killed by his own son, Bill, about a horse."

"About a horse?" I said in disbelief.

"Yeah. Seems the father was a great hunter, took after the colonel that way. Fox, coon, rabbits, bear, you know. Had two sons, Ambrose and Bill. Ambrose was the apple of his eye, namesake and all, fearless child. But Bill was a weak sort, didn't like huntin' and killin'. Ambrose died when not too old—smallpox, I think, or something. Heard Bill was very upset too, probably hated his brother, seeing as how the colonel favored Ambrose. Anyhow, the colonel tried to make Bill into the man he wanted in Ambrose. Bill hated hunting and horses though. Also his father probably. Anyhow, Bill's father forced him to go on a hunt one day with him and when Bill came back he was sobbing and sobbing, said his father was dead, he had accidentally shot him. Well, he was so upset that Miss Bennett sent him to an asylum. Years later he got out, got married, and had Ambrose, kind of late in life. Ambrose's mother died in childbirth, I think." I remembered then Amanda James abandoning her patient with the placenta still undelivered. Ambrose's mother had probably bled to death.

"Well," he went on, "Bill finally committed suicide. With a shotgun. Blew his head off. Left a suicide note explaining as how he had killed his father. What had really happened was that Bill accidentally, shootin' toward a fox, had killed his father's horse—named Prom—Prom—something."

"Prometheus," I said.

"Yeah, that's it. How'd you know?"

"Miss Bennett told me about the horse once," I answered.

"Oh," he said and went on. "Well, Bill's father was so angered at the loss of his horse that he began to whip Bill like all git-out, and Bill, in pain and hysterical, I guess, shot him. Poor boy. What misery he must have had in his lifetime."

"Well, that makes more sense than a lot of killings," I said, remembering last night. "Still none of that explains who's poisoning Miss Bennett unless it's Ambrose, and that face in the window—"

"I guess I'd better go out there tomorrow," the sheriff said, "and talk to Ben and Bessie. Maybe they can give me some idea what's going on.

"Here we are," he said, turning in at a farm. Hank's brother knew nothing of Hank's whereabouts, of course. The sheriff told him to be sure to call if he saw him. We returned to town talking little. At the office, I got out and went upstairs, deep in thought. I turned on the waiting room light. That damned dark hall and examining rooms really bothered me as I walked by. I hurried by and into my consultation room, flooding it with light immediately. I went to the window and looked out, half expecting to see someone lurking in the shadows. But there was no one. I pulled the curtain, though. This time I wanted to not be observed. I wondered if I'd locked the door. I was sure I had. I remembered turning the lock. In any event, I wouldn't have walked back past those examining rooms for anything, or anyone, except Sarah. I sat down in my swivel chair, leaning back pondering, wondering. Suddenly I remembered the packet, the one Miss Bennett gave me. I unlocked the drawer and lifted it out. No, I said to myself, no matter how much you need a clue, you can't open that. It was left with me in trust. I looked down at my desk and the packet. It lay on top of a carelessly opened patient's medical chart which had been carelessly placed, as well. In fact it was upside down. I didn't recall leaving a chart there. I turned it around. It was Miss Bennett's. I arose and went immediately to the file cabinet. One of the upper drawers was still open. I was filled with apprehension. Someone had been in my office. I went immediately to the phone and picked it up to call the sheriff. A slight rustling noise occurred behind my back. Icy chills crept up my spine. I turned slowly with that hideous terrifying awareness that some unwanted intruder was in the room with me. The hair on my arms stood erect and my arms and legs felt weak. There he stood. That grisly, ghoulish, grinning, scarred face, attached now to a large hulking man with a shotgun hanging under one arm. His nose and one ear were missing and the skin was horribly scarred and disfigured. There were no eyebrows and the left corner of the mouth sagged, showing surprisingly white teeth. He must have been in one of the examining rooms when I came in. I surprised him in the act of looking for information. He was demented. It was obvious. Mad!

"Caught yu, didn't I? Yu'all—know—somethin—I—don't," he singsonged.

"What," I said.

"Yu'all knows what Ah's talking about."

"No I don't," I said haltingly. "Who are you?" I asked terrified. "Ambrose?"

He laughed wildly. "That sissy bastard? Hell, no, I'm his brother. C'mon now, you'd better tell me. Bettttter hurry," he threatened.

"I don't know what you're talking about," I hedged. I really didn't know.

"De hell yu'all don't. Yu'd better tell me. Ah killed my great-aunt 'cause she'all wouldn't. Ah wouldn't think twice 'bout killin' yu'all too."

"You didn't kill her," I said, "she's alive."

"Yu'all's a damn liar," he said. "Ah poisoned her with rat poison." He laughed with excitement at the thought.

235

"How?" I challenged.

With a gleeful giggle, he said, "Ah put it in her tonic elixir. She took dat stuff evree day." He looked at me as if expecting approval of his ingenious method. He was very sick, very mentally ill, schizophrenic, probably hebephrenic.

"That's clever," I said, remembering some of my psychiatric training in handling homicidal maniacs.

"Ain't it though?" he agreed. Somewhere out of my medical training background, I remembered that when facing a pathologic killer in confrontation, to avoid being murdered, one must make him feel one is on his side. My palms perspired badly. I could feel the sweat pouring down my back. If I hadn't been leaning on the desk, I might have collapsed.

"What's your name?" I asked.

"Daniel," he said.

"Daniel," I asked, "was there something special that you wanted to kill your great-aunt for?"

"None of your business," he said, snarling again.

"Maybe I could help you," I said.

"How?" he asked.

"Whatever it is you want, maybe I can tell you how to find it."

"Did she'all tell yu?" he said.

"Could have." I was playing a dangerous game and I knew it.

"Before she'all died?" he asked. He still didn't believe she was alive.

"Yes, possibly," I said, hedging.

"Well, tell me then, right now," he commanded. How would I get out of this impasse.

"Would you share it with me?" I said, a stab in the dark.

"The treasure?" he said perplexed. "No!" He was almost childlike. "It's mine. Nobody else's."

"That's true," I said, "it's yours. But first we've got to find it."

"What'd she tell y'all when y'all came to see her?"

"Well, really nothing, but she gave me this," I said lifting the packet, "maybe it tells in here." I sure hoped to hell it did.

It did. Opening the packet, only one item was contained

therein, a map. A map, dog-eared and old, a treasure map. Jesus, I thought, how corny. His eyes lit up with obvious glee, he was ecstatic, a child opening a package with a bright bow.

"Ah got it now," he said. "Ah got it. She'd ne'er giv' it to me before. Ah asked and asked, but she'd ne'er giv' it to me. Ah had to poison her to git it. Yu'all know what Ah mean. Ah had to. Ah just had to."

"Of course," I said, "you had no choice. Now you better go and get the treasure before someone else gets there first." He looked alarmed.

"Yu'all wouldn't try to git it, would yu?" His glare was menacingly frightening.

"I'm your friend. I'd help you, if you wanted me to," I reassured him.

"No," he said, "Ah don't need your help. But Ah don't think Ah'll take a chance," he said, and raised the gun.

"You've got no time to lose," I said, my heart pounding, "someone else may have that map also."

"Yu'all's right," he said, lowering the gun. "I'd better hurry." He turned toward the door, then around again.

"Don't try tuh leave, yuh hear?"

"No," I assured him. Absolutely not. "Better hurry."

He left. God, was I shaking and perspiring. I stayed glued to my desk until I heard his footsteps run down the stairs. Running footsteps! This time they were welcome noise. I then ran to the door and made certain it was locked. I went back to the phone, immediately. By accident, I'd left it off the hook when he confronted me. "Charlotte," I said.

"Are you all right, Doctuh?" she asked.

"Yes, thank God," I said. "Did you hear that conversation?"

"Yes," she said, "sorry, but do you want me to find the sheriff?"

"If you can," I said. "I'll wait here."

I could use a drink now, I thought. Wish I had some of that champagne.

Very shortly the sheriff called. He hadn't realized I was looking for him.

"Doc," he said, "I was out to the Bennetts'—Ambrose's place. Been talking to them. They said there's another brother—

name of Daniel. I never knew it and neither did anyone else. He's crazy, Doc, has a terrible face, got it burned in a fire—the overseer told me it was a fire created by the devil. Wow, these people are sure superstitious. Amanda Jones delivered it."

"She told me she delivered Ambrose," I said.

"Made a mistake. She brought Daniel into the world. They got mad at her for running off and didn't call her when Ambrose was born. Daniel was always strange. Since they've always hid Daniel, I guess Amanda naturally thought she delivered the only child seen around, Ambrose. Anyhow, being crazy, they've kept Daniel here in Miss Bennett's house ever since. She pledged everyone to secrecy. So no one ever knew about it."

"Now I know why Miss Bennett wasn't upset when Sarah screamed."

"What? What was that, Doc?" he asked.

"Oh, nothing. Listen, I have something to tell you. Daniel was here. Yes, here at the office. He was after something of hers. A map. A map of some treasure location. She gave it to me when she left for Duke. I gave it to him. It was the only way of stopping him from killing me. He's on his way there. He has a shotgun. I'd suggest you don't try to stop him. Let him dig his treasure and when he has it don't try to take it away from him. He'll probably discard the shotgun for the treasure. Tomorrow we can make arrangements for commitment. He admitted trying to kill Miss Bennett, put rat poison in her tonic elixir that she takes each night."

"Well, I'll be damned," he said. "Okay, Doc, thanks. I'll let you know if anything else happens."

"Pick up that bottle of elixir for evidence," I said.

"Trying to tell me my job?" he chided. "Sure will, though, don't worry. So long, Doc."

I hung up the phone. I sat back and heaved a sigh of relief.

The office was much less sinister appearing. All in the mind, that sinister stuff. When one is afraid, every shadow, every corner, every unusual occurrence seems diabolical. But when the fear is gone, everything seems familiar, and, in a way, warm and friendly, natural I guess. Right now I felt relaxed, relieved, untroubled, feelings I hadn't experienced in a long time. Better than champagne. If only Sarah could be here to enjoy it with me. Sarah! God, I thought, why hasn't she called me? What is taking her so long? Doubts and fears crept slowly back into awareness. I felt uneasy again, troubled. I couldn't sit here any longer. I got up, pulled the drapes and looked out the window. Once again the night was black and slightly frightening. Why didn't she call? I sat down again, tried to concentrate on writing notes in charts. I threw the pen across the room in anger. Work was pointless. I couldn't concentrate. Why hadn't I told her I loved her? This would be another uneasy night, another night locked in the prison I had created for myself. My own prison of doubts and fears without physical bars, but no less confining. I went home with a heavy heart, yet noticed as I passed by the colonel that I no longer feared the shadows and walked home slowly with no need for haste.

Morning came and I watched the early light flood through my window, waking me. I showered and dressed early, not trying to continue sleeping. Once awake and troubled, there was no point in trying to sleep further. Lying there tossing and turning seemed absurd. I heard the phone ring, Miss Apperson was soon at my door.

"Phone, Doctor," she said. My heart skipped a beat. Sarah.

It wasn't Sarah. It was Mrs. Jacobs. Her daughter was bleeding and cramping. Aborting, no doubt. I told her to bring her to the office in an hour, I'd see what I could do. I wondered what they had done. Had they tried to abort her, or had she herself done it?

When Mae arrived at the office, she was obviously very ill. She had bled a good deal and was probably infected. Had a high fever. She writhed in pain, with her rhythmic contractions, twisting and contorting her body and face with each contraction. Though it might slow the contractions, I gave her morphine, which eased her for a short time. Her mother told me someone, of course she knew not who, had put slippery elm into her uterus, a common abortifacient. While I was waiting for the abortion, the phone rang. It *was* Sarah. She was excited to talk to me, at least she said she was, asked how I was, and told me she was anxious to return. I managed to tell her I missed her very much and was anxious for her return also.

"Will you be able to pick me up at seven tonight?" she asked.

"Of course I will, darling," I said, my verbal affection surprising me not at all. "Sarah, I have so much to tell you."

"Me too," she said.

Mae cried out in pain. It must be nearing the time, I thought.

"I've got to go, Sarah," I said. "Mae Jacobs is aborting."

"Aborting?" she asked, surprised.

"Yeah, tell you about it later," I said, "and, Sarah, I wish I'd told you this before. I love you." There was silence on the other end.

"I'm *so* glad you do. Oh, I'm so happy," she said and so warmly, I imagined. "You'd better go. See you tonight."

"Bye-bye," I said, and hung up the phone.

Mae let out a shriek. I ran back into the examining room to find the fetus extruded from the vagina on the table, still attached through its lifeline, the umbilical cord to the placenta. It wiggled a few worthless movements toward survival. Pressure with my hand on the fundus of the uterus to deliver the placenta was accompanied by loud screaming of the patient. Such action wasn't necessarily that painful, but she was frightened, immature, and just plain dumb. Fortunately for her and me, the placenta delivered easily and looked intact. She'd probably be all right. I warned her mother and her of the dangers of infection, instructed them to keep her in bed two days, gave her some pain pills and ergotrate and then sent her home. After they had left, I looked at the fetus and placenta. A fetus of this age was red, due to lack of subcutaneous fat. No one would ever be able to tell by this cursory exam whether or not it was black or white in origin. As I held it in my hand, I thought what a pity it was that Cade's life had been sacrificed for something he hadn't done, or if he had done it, was now ending in this way. Maybe legalized abortion made sense sometimes.

I phoned the State Hospital and made arrangements for the commitment of Daniel. To commit him required either a court order, which could easily have been obtained in view of the attempted murder, or by signature of a close relative. I chose to ask Ambrose for that permission. I drove to his place. It was not in good condition. Obviously, the income from the plantation, which he managed, was insufficient to improve either his home or the old plantation house. He was cordial, though, and handsome, to which Mrs. Jacobs and others had attested. I presented him with the alternatives. He, of course, already knew about the attempted poisoning through the sheriff, and had been informed that Daniel would have to be tried or committed. Obtaining a court order would have revealed the presence of Daniel and his felonious crime. Commitment by a relative would not. The desire for secrecy and lack of scandal was of paramount importance to him. He signed the commitment papers readily. I called the sheriff, who came over to pick up Daniel for transportation to the hospital. We went to the Bennett plantation. I told him of Mae's abortion. He shook his head resignedly and dejectedly. "Damn bastards. Stupid waste," he said. I knew what he meant.

Daniel was in his room, a room directly across from Miss Bennett's room. I felt relieved I had not accidentally run into him in a dark hall on previous trips to the Bennetts. He was docile and cooperative. We told him we were taking him to a place where he would be very safe from people. He appeared willing to go knowing that.

"Can Ah take my treasure?" he asked.

I looked at the sheriff, since I didn't know what it was. The sheriff nodded yes, and from his expression I knew it couldn't be something valuable. I agreed also. Daniel, in true childish fashion, said that he liked me.

As we put him in the car, I wondered if he'd ever ridden in one before. He appeared excited, like a kid on a merry-go-round. The sheriff came around the car.

"Great job, Doc," he said, extending his hand.

"Thanks," I answered. "By the way, what was the treasure after all?"

"An old iron box, full of Confederate money and a few pieces of family silver. They probably hid it years ago to keep the Yankees from getting it. He didn't want the silver, it's in the house. Counted his money many times, though, like that king, what was his name?"

"Midas," I answered.

"Yeah, that's the one. God, Doc, the whole family's crazy. Can you imagine hoarding a map all these years without digging it up?"

"Nope, I can't," I said. "But Miss Bennett's harmless anyhow. I guess Ambrose was willing to wait his turn."

"So long, Doc, see you around. Oh by the way, in that treasure box there was an Army surgeon's report that showed the colonel really died of smallpox and not even at Antietam. Beats all, eh?" He drove off. The second Bennett had left the plantation in three days. I wondered how the colonel looked today.

Though the train was on time, I was certain it would be late. As Sarah stepped off the train, she looked more radiant than I'd ever seen her, more beautiful than I could ask for. I kissed her, openly, for all to see. I took her bag to the car and excitedly and happily we started back to Bennettsboro. I spent the first hour telling her about Miss Bennett, about Daniel, and Ambrose, Mae and poor Cade. She was aghast that he was killed. After regaling her with all the news, I became anxious. By talking so long I had avoided the inevitable, her trip. We stopped at her house and went in.

"Did you have a good time in Baltimore?" I asked.

"Yes and no," she said. I was heartened.

"I had unfinished business there," she added.

I waited, uneasy. She avoided talking about her trip for a while longer.

"I was very happy to hear what you had to tell me on the phone," she said calmly. I knew what she meant.

"I meant it, sincerely, deeply," I assured her.

"I know. I've known for a long time," she said quietly, "and that's why I had to go to Baltimore."

"I don't understand," I said.

"I've suspected for a long time that you loved me, but couldn't say so. At least I hoped you did. I wondered if it was my previous friend in Baltimore that stopped you from telling me. I had to know also how I felt about him, so I had to go up there and find out. I did find out. I don't love him. I love you."

I smiled broadly. A thrill pervaded my being. And peace. Peace such as I hadn't known in years. She laughed. "Say it again," I entreated. "I love you," she repeated. I drew her gently to me and we kissed. Her lips were warm and inviting. My heart sang.

"Sarah, how long I've waited for this moment. I've wanted to tell you I loved you for so long, but doubts and fears always prevented it. I want to marry you. Every fiber in my body knows it is right for us, that we will always be happy. I wanted to ask you before, but had to wait until I felt more secure, more secure about the practice, more secure about my emotions and my abilities. I wanted to have something to offer you."

"You do," she said, determined, "just yourself. Don't you know I love you, despite your doubts and fears, that these are normal for all people?"

"Not like mine," I argued, "I'm like a frightened child at times. I'm indecisive. I might even have lost you being afraid to tell you I love you."

"You nearly did," she said. "Telling me you loved me on the phone convinced me I'd made the right decision. When I left I was thinking of leaving you, going back to Baltimore, even though I never could have married my other friend. He didn't need me. And I need to be needed. I wanted to be part of his life, but he lives and breathes medicine. I realized I never could marry him. He has none of your attributes of tenderness, kindness, and gentleness, and a few others I won't mention now. His whole life would be medicine and I only an appendage to that, to be dragged out on occasions when protocol or furtherment of his career were involved. He'll be famous someday and his wife will be Mrs. Burns, wife of the famous surgeon who is adored by his patients for his skill and manly attractiveness, but she'll be miserable and unhappy and lonely, I'll bet. I want to be needed and loved and appreciated, most of all needed, particularly at times when my husband has doubts and fears from the responsibility he carries. If I can, in even a little way, ease his pain and reassure him, it will give me some purpose for living. When I think of it, it's amazing how much you've taught me since I met you, without even knowing you did."

"I do need you, Sarah, but I wanted to be sure I needed you out of strength, also, not out of weakness."

"We're all weak to some degree," she said.

"I know, but mine has been overwhelming until recently. I doubted everything I did, every decision I made. I was never that way before Carolyn died." There, I had said it, out loud, to

Sarah. She looked puzzled. I went on.

"I was always friendly and sensitive, just as I hope I am now, and confident and I did want a wife with whom I could share living. Someone like you. But after Carolyn died, I went all to pieces, lost all confidence in myself."

"Can you tell me about it?" she asked.

"Yes, I'd like to tell you. I couldn't before now. I know you'll understand. I met Carolyn in medical school. She was in nurses' training. We thought we were madly in love. She was beautiful, and we had lots of fun. Something about her, though, always bothered me and I couldn't quite put my finger on it exactly. Sort of an overpossessiveness, though I thought probably it was just that I was resisting being tied down. Well, anyhow, when I moved to Baltimore to intern, she came along to nurse in the area and be near me. She worked at a nearby hospital. She had started having headaches while we were at Duke. At first, I ignored them, thinking maybe she was tense. About that time, I became a neurosurgical resident. I was so proud, so self-assured, and doing so well, Carolyn always asked me to find out what her headaches were due to, since I was supposed to know all about it. She was also proud of me and wanted to marry me so badly. The headaches got worse and worse. I tried many times to have her see my chief, but she always said 'No, I have faith in you, you're my doctor.' Finally, it was obvious, even to me, that something serious, something organic was going on. She saw my chief at my insistence and he operated on her immediately. God, I'll never forget that awful day. I couldn't watch the surgery. My chief told me to go about my business and not worry. I heard my name paged, 'Dr. Jenson, to Neurosurgery, stat.' I panicked. The elevator wasn't fast enough so I ran up the stairs. My feet were leaden. I'll never forget how my steps echoed in the stairwell as I ran up several flights. On the surgical floor, I ran down those lousy green halls to the surgical suite. The swinging doors came open and Dr. Perry, my chief came out. I knew something was wrong from his face. 'She's dead,' he said, 'I'm sorry.' I called him a butcher. I screamed at him, 'Butcher, butcher.' God, I was upset. He said 'if only we had been able to operate sooner.' All of a sudden I was flooded with guilt feelings. God, oh God, I thought, I really

244

killed her, it was my fault. He had just said so. 'If only we had been able to operate sooner.' I turned and fled. I resigned my job that very day and decided to come to some town like Bennettsboro to hide. I killed her. I killed her because I loved her too much. I was so flattered by her insistence that I take care of her that I didn't insist she see someone else. In truth, I didn't want to believe she had anything serious. I missed the diagnosis until it was too late. She might be alive today if it weren't for my stupidity and vanity. Here I am, hiding from reality, fearful of killing someone else with my stupidity, fearful of killing someone because of liking or loving them, and even fearful of loving or trying to love with all the guilt I feel."

"When did Carolyn die?" she asked. Her question surprised me.

"Why, it was May tenth."

"Well, when did she first have headaches?" Sarah asked.

"Oh, at least two years before that, I guess, but they weren't bad until the last six months."

"You were in Baltimore about, let's see, seventeen months or so before she died, is that right?"

"Yes, that's right," I answered. "How did you know?"

"Did you know that she saw Dr. Perry for her headaches a year before she died?" she asked.

"No," I corrected her, "she never saw him until just before surgery."

"No, you're wrong," she insisted. "You remember that you asked me to see Dr. Perry while I was in Baltimore. Well, I did. We talked about you. He feels very bad about your leaving. He understood how in your grief you wanted to. He told me he had been seeing her for a year for her headaches, did all the studies that proved she had a brain tumor, and advised surgery long before she actually had it, but she wouldn't let him operate. He pleaded with her. She said she had decided to go back to Duke for surgery. He thought she had. He never saw her again until you brought her in just before surgery, and never realized you loved her until that day of surgery."

"My God," I said, "I don't understand. I don't understand. It's almost as if she wanted to die. It can't be true. It doesn't make sense."

"It does to me," Sarah said. "Dr. Perry told her she had a fifty-fifty chance of survival when he first saw her. I think she knew she was going to die and wanted to keep you as hers alone forever."

I felt as though someone had just flooded the house with light and warmth. The weight of the world had just been lifted from my shoulders.

"You're right, you're right, Sarah," I fairly shouted. "My God, it all makes sense. Her overpossessiveness killed her. She wanted to hold onto me even after death. The last thing she said to me before she went to surgery was 'Promise me we'll be together forever.' At that point I would have promised her anything. Knowing she would die, she had planned it all to make me think my ineptitude had killed her. She must have hoped I would commit suicide and we could be together forever. My God, she almost got her wish. My whole life since has been sort of suicide."

I turned to Sarah in disbelief. She was smiling, understanding, happy. I shouted, "I'm free, I'm free. At last I'm free. No more doubts or fears to hold me back. I can be my old self again. We can be married." I jumped in wild enthusiasm, hugging Sarah.

She said, "I'd like that but you've never asked me."

"Then I do," I said.

"Tell me," she asked, "didn't your Shakespeare say, 'Love casteth out fear?' "

"He did, he did. Yes, he did. He also said, 'Our doubts are traitors, and oft would make us lose what we might gain, by fearing to attempt.' Thank God I didn't give up."

She smiled, an approving smile, and kissed me lovingly.